BATTLE OF THE LABYRINTH

Books by Rick Riordan

PERCY JACKSON AND THE LIGHTNING THIEF
PERCY JACKSON AND THE SEA OF MONSTERS
PERCY JACKSON AND THE TITAN'S CURSE
PERCY JACKSON AND THE BATTLE OF THE
LABYRINTH

percyjackson.co.uk

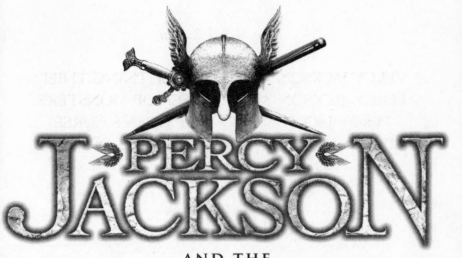

PERCY JACKSON

AND THE
BATTLE OF
THE LABYRINTH

RICK RIORDAN

PUFFIN

To Becky, who always guides me through the maze

PUFFIN BOOKS

Published by the Penguin Group
Penguin Books Ltd, 80 Strand, London WC2R 0RL, England
Penguin Group (USA) Inc., 375 Hudson Street, New York, New York 10014, USA
Penguin Group (Canada), 90 Eglinton Avenue East, Suite 700, Toronto, Ontario, Canada M4P 2Y3
(a division of Pearson Penguin Canada Inc.)
Penguin Ireland, 25 St Stephen's Green, Dublin 2, Ireland (a division of Penguin Books Ltd)
Penguin Group (Australia), 250 Camberwell Road, Camberwell, Victoria 3124, Australia
(a division of Pearson Australia Group Pty Ltd)
Penguin Books India Pvt Ltd, 11 Community Centre, Panchsheel Park, New Delhi – 110 017, India
Penguin Group (NZ), 67 Apollo Drive, Rosedale, North Shore 0632, New Zealand
(a division of Pearson New Zealand Ltd)
Penguin Books (South Africa) (Pty) Ltd, 24 Sturdee Avenue, Rosebank, Johannesburg 2196, South Africa

Penguin Books Ltd, Registered Offices: 80 Strand, London WC2R 0RL, England

puffinbooks.com

First published in the USA by Hyperion Books for Children 2008
First published in Great Britain in Puffin Books 2008

1

Copyright © Rick Riordan, 2008

The moral right of the author has been asserted

Set in Centaur MT
Typeset by Palimpsest Book Production Limited, Grangemouth, Stirlingshire
Made and printed in England by Clays Ltd, St Ives plc

British Library Cataloguing in Publication Data
A CIP catalogue record for this book is available from the British Library

HARDBACK
ISBN: 978-0-141-38291-3

TRADE PAPERBACK
ISBN: 978-0-141-38292-0

www.greenpenguin.co.uk

CONTENTS

1 • I Battle the Cheerleading Squad *1*

2 • The Underworld Sends Me a Prank Call *17*

3 • We Play Tag with Scorpions *41*

4 • Annabeth Breaks the Rules *60*

5 • Nico Buys Happy Meals for the Dead *78*

6 • We Meet the God with Two Faces *90*

7 • Tyson Leads a Jailbreak *103*

8 • We Visit the Demon Dude Ranch *116*

9 • I Scoop Poop *141*

10 • We Play the Game Show of Death *154*

11 • I Set Myself on Fire *177*

12 • I Take a Permanent Vacation *196*

13 • We Hire a New Guide *214*

14 • My Brother Duels Me to the Death *237*

15 • We Steal Some Slightly Used Wings *255*

16 • I Open a Coffin *274*

17 • The Lost God Speaks *290*

18 • Grover Causes a Stampede *301*

19 • The Council Gets Cloven *319*

20 • My Birthday Party Takes a Dark Turn *329*

I BATTLE THE CHEERLEADING SQUAD

The last thing I wanted to do on my summer break was blow up another school. But there I was Monday morning, the first week of June, sitting in my mom's car in front of Goode High School on East 81st.

Goode was this big brownstone building overlooking the East River. A bunch of BMWs and Lincoln Town Cars were parked out front. Staring up at the fancy stone archway, I wondered how long it would take me to get kicked out of this place.

'Just relax.' My mom didn't sound relaxed. 'It's only an orientation tour. And remember, dear, this is Paul's school. So try not to . . . you know.'

'Destroy it?'

'Yes.'

Paul Blofis, my mom's boyfriend, was standing out front, greeting future ninth graders as they came up the steps. With his salt-and-pepper hair, denim clothes and leather jacket, he reminded me of a TV actor, but he was just an English teacher. He'd managed to convince Goode High School to accept me for ninth grade, despite the fact that I'd been kicked out of every school I'd ever attended. I'd tried to warn him it wasn't a good idea, but he wouldn't listen.

I looked at my mom. 'You haven't told him the truth about me, have you?'

She tapped her fingers nervously on the wheel. She was dressed up for a job interview – her best blue dress and high-heeled shoes.

'I thought we should wait,' she admitted.

'So we don't scare him away.'

'I'm sure orientation will be fine, Percy. It's only one morning.'

'Great,' I mumbled. 'I can get expelled before I even start the school year.'

'Think positive. Tomorrow you're off to camp! After orientation, you've got your date –'

'It's not a date!' I protested. 'It's just Annabeth, Mom. Jeez!'

'She's coming all the way from camp to meet you.'

'Well, yeah.'

'You're going to the movies.'

'Yeah.'

'Just the two of you.'

'Mom!'

She held up her hands in surrender, but I could tell she was trying hard not to smile. 'You'd better get inside, dear. I'll see you tonight.'

I was about to get out of the car when I looked over at the steps of the school. Paul Blofis was greeting a girl with frizzy red hair. She wore a maroon T-shirt and ratty jeans decorated with marker drawings. When she turned, I caught a glimpse of her face, and the hairs on my arms stood straight up.

'Percy?' my mom asked. 'What's wrong?'

'N-nothing,' I stammered. 'Does the school have a side entrance?'

'Down the block on the right. Why?'

'I'll see you later.'

My mom started to say something, but I got out of the car and ran, hoping the redheaded girl wouldn't see me.

What was *she* doing here? Not even *my* luck could be this bad.

Yeah, right. I was about to find out my luck could get a whole lot worse.

Sneaking into orientation didn't work out too well. Two cheerleaders in purple-and-white uniforms were standing at the side entrance, waiting to ambush freshmen.

'Hi!' They smiled, which I figured was the first and last time any cheerleaders would be that friendly to me. One was blonde with icy blue eyes. The other was African American with dark curly hair like Medusa's (and, believe me, I know what I'm talking about). Both girls had their names stitched in cursive on their uniforms, but with my dyslexia, the words looked like meaningless spaghetti.

'Welcome to Goode,' the blonde girl said. 'You are *so* going to love it.'

But as she looked me up and down, her expression said something more like, *Eww, who is this loser?*

The other girl stepped uncomfortably close to me. I studied the stitching on her uniform and made out: *Kelli.* She smelled like roses and something else I recognized from riding lessons at camp – the scent of freshly washed horses. It was a weird smell for a cheerleader. Maybe she owned a horse or something. Anyway, she stood so close I got the feeling she was going to try to push me down the steps. 'What's your name, fish?'

'Fish?'

'Freshman.'

'Uh, Percy.'

The girls exchanged looks.

'Oh, Percy Jackson,' the blonde one said. 'We've been waiting for you.'

That sent a major *Uh-oh* chill down my back. They were blocking the entrance, smiling in a not-very-friendly way. My hand crept instinctively towards my pocket, where I kept my lethal ballpoint pen, Riptide.

Then another voice came from inside the building: 'Percy?' It was Paul Blofis, somewhere down the hallway. I'd never been so glad to hear his voice.

The cheerleaders backed off. I was so anxious to get past them I accidentally kneed Kelli in the thigh.

Clang.

Her leg made a hollow, metallic sound, like I'd just hit a flagpole.

'Ow,' she muttered. 'Watch it, *fish*.'

I glanced down, but her leg looked like a regular old leg. I was too freaked out to ask questions. I dashed into the hall, the cheerleaders laughing behind me.

'There you are!' Paul told me. 'Welcome to Goode!'

'Hey, Paul – uh, Mr Blofis.' I glanced back, but the weird cheerleaders had disappeared.

'Percy, you look like you've seen a ghost.'

'Yeah, uh –'

Paul clapped me on the back. 'Listen, I know you're nervous, but don't worry. We get a lot of kids here with ADHD and dyslexia. The teachers know how to help.'

I almost wanted to laugh. If only ADHD and dyslexia

were my biggest worries. I mean, I knew Paul was trying to help, but if I told him the truth about me, he'd either think I were crazy or he'd run away screaming. Those cheerleaders, for instance. I had a bad feeling about them . . .

Then I looked down the hall, and I remembered I had another problem. The redheaded girl I'd seen on the front steps was just coming in the main entrance.

Don't notice me, I prayed.

She noticed me. Her eyes widened.

'Where's the orientation?' I asked Paul.

'The gym. That way. But –'

'Bye.'

'Percy?' he called, but I was already running.

I thought I'd lost her.

A bunch of kids were heading for the gym, and soon I was just one of three hundred fourteen-year-olds all crammed into the stands. A marching band played an out-of-tune fight song that sounded like somebody hitting a bag of cats with a metal baseball bat. Older kids, probably student-council members, stood up in front modelling the Goode school uniform and looking all, *Hey, we're cool.* Teachers milled around, smiling and shaking hands with students. The walls of the gym were plastered with big purple-and-white banners that said WELCOME, FUTURE FRESHMEN, GOODE IS GOOD, WE'RE ALL FAMILY, and a bunch of other happy slogans that pretty much made me want to throw up.

None of the other freshmen looked thrilled to be here, either. I mean, coming to orientation in June is not cool when school doesn't even start until September, but at

Goode, 'We prepare to excel early!' At least that's what the brochure said.

The marching band stopped playing. A guy in a pinstripe suit came to the microphone and started talking, but the sound echoed around the gym so I had no idea what he was saying. He might've been gargling.

Someone grabbed my shoulder. 'What are you doing here?'

It was her: my redheaded nightmare.

'Rachel Elizabeth Dare,' I said.

Her jaw dropped like she couldn't believe I had the nerve to remember her name. 'And you're Percy somebody. I didn't get your full name last December when you tried to *kill* me.'

'Look, I wasn't – I didn't – What are *you* doing here?'

'Same as you, I guess. Orientation.'

'You live in New York?'

'What, you thought I lived at Hoover Dam?'

It had never occurred to me. Whenever I thought about her (and I'm *not* saying I *thought* about her; she just, like, crossed my mind from time to time, okay?), I always figured she lived in the Hoover Dam area, since that's where I'd met her. We'd spent maybe ten minutes together, during which time I'd accidentally swung a sword at her, she'd saved my life and I'd run away, chased by a band of supernatural killing machines. You know, your typical chance meeting.

Some guy behind us whispered, 'Hey, shut up. The cheerleaders are talking!'

'Hi, guys!' a girl bubbled into the microphone. It was

the blonde I'd seen at the entrance. 'My name is Tammi, and this is, like, Kelli.' Kelli did a cartwheel.

Next to me, Rachel yelped like someone had stuck her with a pin. A few kids looked over and snickered, but Rachel just stared at the cheerleaders in horror. Tammi didn't seem to notice the outburst. She started talking about all the great ways we could get involved during our freshman year.

'Run,' Rachel told me. 'Now.'

'Why?'

Rachel didn't explain. She pushed her way to the edge of the stands, ignoring the frowning teachers and grumbling kids she was stepping on.

I hesitated. Tammi was explaining how we were about to break into small groups and tour the school. Kelli caught my eye and gave me an amused smile, like she was waiting to see what I'd do. It would look bad if I left right now. Paul Blofis was down there with the rest of the teachers. He'd wonder what was wrong.

Then I thought about Rachel Elizabeth Dare, and the special ability she'd shown last winter at Hoover Dam. She'd been able to see a group of security guards who weren't guards at all, who weren't even human. My heart pounding, I got up and followed her out of the gym.

I found Rachel in the band room. She was hiding behind a bass drum in the percussion section.

'Get over here!' she said. 'Keep your head down!'

I felt pretty silly, hiding behind a bunch of bongos, but I crouched beside her.

'Did they follow you?' Rachel asked.

'You mean the cheerleaders?'

She nodded nervously.

'I don't think so,' I said. 'What are they? What did you see?'

Her green eyes were bright with fear. She had a sprinkle of freckles on her face that reminded me of constellations. Her maroon T-shirt read HARVARD ART DEPT. 'You . . . you wouldn't believe me.'

'Oh yeah, I would,' I promised. 'I know you can see through the Mist.'

'The what?'

'The Mist. It's . . . well, it's like this veil that hides the way things really are. Some mortals are born with the ability to see through it. Like you.'

She studied me carefully. 'You did that at Hoover Dam. You called me a mortal. Like you're not.'

I felt like punching a bongo. What was I thinking? I could never explain. I shouldn't even try.

'Tell me,' she begged. 'You know what it means. All these horrible things I see?'

'Look, this is going to sound weird. Do you know anything about Greek myths?'

'Like . . . the Minotaur and the Hydra?'

'Yeah, just try not to say those names when I'm around, okay?'

'And the Furies,' she said, warming up. 'And the Sirens, and –'

'Okay!' I looked around the band room, sure that Rachel was going to make a bunch of bloodthirsty nasties pop out of the walls, but we were still alone. Down the hallway, I heard a mob of kids coming out of the gymnasium. They were starting the group tours. We didn't have long to talk.

'All those monsters,' I said, 'all the Greek gods — they're real.'

'I knew it!'

I would've been more comfortable if she'd called me a liar, but Rachel looked like I'd just confirmed her worst suspicion.

'You don't know how hard it's been,' she said. 'For years I thought I was going crazy. I couldn't tell anybody. I couldn't —' Her eyes narrowed. 'Wait. Who are you? I mean *really?*'

'I'm not a monster.'

'Well, I know that. I could *see* if you were. You look like . . . you. But you're not human, are you?'

I swallowed. Even though I'd had three years to get used to who I was, I'd never talked about it with a regular mortal before — I mean, except for my mom, but she already knew. I don't know why, but I took the plunge.

'I'm a half-blood,' I said. 'I'm half human.'

'And half what?'

Just then Tammi and Kelli stepped into the band room. The doors slammed shut behind them.

'There you are, Percy Jackson,' Tammi said. 'It's time for your orientation.'

'They're horrible!' Rachel gasped.

Tammi and Kelli were still wearing their purple-and-white cheerleader costumes, holding pom-poms from the rally.

'What do they really look like?' I asked, but Rachel seemed too stunned to answer.

'Oh, forget her.' Tammi gave me a brilliant smile and started walking towards us. Kelli stayed by the doors, blocking our exit.

They'd trapped us. I knew we'd have to fight our way out, but Tammi's smile was so dazzling it distracted me. Her blue eyes were beautiful, and the way her hair swept over her shoulders . . .

'Percy,' Rachel warned.

I said something really intelligent like, 'Uhhh?'

Tammi was getting closer. She held out her pom-poms.

'Percy!' Rachel's voice seemed to be coming from a long way away. 'Snap out of it!'

It took all my willpower, but I got my pen out of my pocket and uncapped it. Riptide grew into a metre-long bronze sword, its blade glowing with a faint golden light. Tammi's smile turned to a sneer.

'Oh, come on,' she protested. 'You don't need that. How about a kiss instead?'

She smelled like roses and clean animal fur – a weird but somehow intoxicating smell.

Rachel pinched my arm, hard. 'Percy, she wants to bite you! Look at her!'

'She's just jealous.' Tammi looked back at Kelli. 'May I, mistress?'

Kelli was still blocking the door, licking her lips hungrily. 'Go ahead, Tammi. You're doing fine.'

Tammi took another step forward, but I levelled the tip of my sword at her chest. 'Get back.'

She snarled. 'Freshmen,' she said with disgust. 'This is *our* school, half-blood. We feed on whom we choose!'

Then she began to change. The colour drained out of her face and arms. Her skin turned as white as chalk, her eyes completely red. Her teeth grew into fangs.

'A vampire!' I stammered. Then I noticed her legs. Below the cheerleader skirt, her left leg was brown and shaggy, with a donkey's hoof. Her right leg was shaped like a human leg, but it was made of bronze. 'Uhh, a vampire with –'

'Don't mention the legs!' Tammi snapped. 'It's rude to make fun!'

She advanced on her weird, mismatched legs. She looked totally bizarre, especially with the pom-poms, but I couldn't laugh – not facing those red eyes and sharp fangs.

'A vampire, you say?' Kelli laughed. 'That silly legend was based on *us*, you fool. We are *empousai*, servants of Hecate.'

'Mmmm.' Tammi edged closer to me. 'Dark magic formed us from animal, bronze and ghost! We exist to feed on the blood of young men. Now come, give me that kiss!'

She bared her fangs. I was so paralysed I couldn't move, but Rachel threw a snare drum at the *empousa's* head.

The demon hissed and batted the drum away. It went rolling along the aisles between music stands, its springs rattling against the drum head. Rachel threw a xylophone, but the demon just swatted that away, too.

'I don't usually kill girls,' Tammi growled. 'But for you, mortal, I'll make an exception. Your eyesight is a little *too* good!'

She lunged at Rachel.

'No!' I slashed with Riptide. Tammi tried to dodge my blade, but I sliced straight through her cheerleader uniform, and with a horrible wail she exploded into dust all over Rachel.

Rachel coughed. She looked like she'd just had a sack of flour dumped on her head. 'Gross!'

'Monsters do that,' I said. 'Sorry.'

'You killed my trainee!' Kelli yelled. 'You need a lesson in school spirit, half-blood!'

Then she, too, began to change. Her wiry hair turned to flickering flames. Her eyes turned red. She grew fangs. She loped towards us, her brass foot and hoof clopping unevenly on the band-room floor.

'I am senior *empousa*,' she growled. 'No hero has bested me in a thousand years.'

'Yeah?' I said. 'Then you're overdue!'

Kelli was a lot faster than Tammi. She dodged my first strike and rolled into the brass section, knocking over a row of trombones with a mighty crash. Rachel scrambled out of the way. I put myself between her and the *empousa*. Kelli circled us, her eyes going from me to the sword.

'Such a pretty little blade,' she said. 'What a shame it stands between us.'

Her form shimmered – sometimes a demon, sometimes a pretty cheerleader. I tried to keep my mind focused, but it was really distracting.

'Poor dear.' Kelli chuckled. 'You don't even know what's happening, do you? Soon, your pretty little camp in flames, your friends made slaves to the Lord of Time, and there's nothing you can do to stop it. It would be merciful to end your life now, before you have to see that.'

From down the hall, I heard voices. A tour group was approaching. A man was saying something about locker combinations.

The *empousa's* eyes lit up. 'Excellent! We're about to have company!'

She picked up a tuba and threw it at me. Rachel and I ducked. The tuba sailed over our heads and crashed through the window.

The voices in the hall died down.

'Percy!' Kelli shouted, pretending to be scared. 'Why did you throw that?'

I was too surprised to answer. Kelli picked up a music stand and swiped a row of clarinets and flutes. Chairs and musical instruments crashed to the floor.

'Stop it!' I said.

People were tromping down the hall now, coming in our direction.

'Time to greet our visitors!' Kelli bared her fangs and ran for the doors. I charged after her with Riptide. I had to stop her from hurting the mortals.

'Percy, don't!' Rachel shouted. But I hadn't realized what Kelli was up to until it was too late.

Kelli flung open the doors. Paul Blofis and a bunch of freshmen stepped back in shock. I raised my sword.

At the last second, the *empousa* turned towards me like a cowering victim. 'Oh no, please!' she cried. I couldn't stop my blade. It was already in motion.

Just before the celestial bronze hit her, Kelli exploded into flames like a Molotov cocktail. Waves of fire splashed over everything. I'd never seen a monster do that before, but I didn't have time to wonder about it. I backed into the band room as flames engulfed the doorway.

'Percy?' Paul Blofis looked completely stunned, staring at me from across the fire. 'What have you done?'

Kids screamed and ran down the hall. The fire alarm wailed. Ceiling sprinklers hissed into life.

In the chaos, Rachel tugged on my sleeve. 'You have to get out of here!'

She was right. The school was in flames and I'd be held responsible. Mortals couldn't see through the Mist properly. To them it would look like I'd just attacked a helpless cheerleader in front of a group of witnesses. There was no way I could explain it. I turned from Paul and sprinted for the broken band-room window.

I burst out of the alley onto East 81st and ran straight into Annabeth.

'Hey, you're out early!' She laughed, grabbing my shoulders to keep me from tumbling into the street. 'Watch where you're going, Seaweed Brain.'

For a split second she was in a good mood and everything was fine. She was wearing jeans and an orange camp T-shirt and her clay bead necklace. Her blonde hair was pulled back in a ponytail. Her grey eyes sparkled. She looked like she was ready to catch a movie, have a cool afternoon hanging out together.

Then Rachel Elizabeth Dare, still covered in monster dust, came charging out of the alley, yelling, 'Percy, wait up!'

Annabeth's smile melted. She stared at Rachel, then at the school. For the first time, she seemed to notice the black smoke and the ringing fire alarms.

She frowned at me. 'What did you do this time? And who is this?'

'Oh, Rachel – Annabeth. Annabeth – Rachel. Um, she's a friend. I guess.'

I wasn't sure what else to call Rachel. I mean, I barely knew her, but after being in two life-or-death situations together, I couldn't just call her nobody.

'Hi,' Rachel said. Then she turned to me. 'You are in *so* much trouble. And you still owe me an explanation!'

Police sirens wailed on FDR Drive.

'Percy,' Annabeth said coldly, 'we should go.'

'I want to know more about half-bloods,' Rachel insisted. 'And monsters. And this stuff about the gods.' She grabbed my arm, whipped out a permanent marker and wrote a phone number on my hand. 'You're going to call me and explain, okay? You owe me that. Now get going.'

'But –'

'I'll make up some story,' Rachel said. 'I'll tell them it wasn't your fault. Just go!'

She ran back towards the school, leaving Annabeth and me in the street.

Annabeth stared at me for a second. Then she turned and took off.

'Hey!' I jogged after her. 'There were these two *empousai*,' I tried to explain. 'They were cheerleaders, see, and they said camp was going to burn, and –'

'You told a mortal girl about half-bloods?'

'She can see through the Mist. She saw the monsters before I did.'

'So you told her the truth.'

'She recognized me from Hoover Dam, so –'

'You've met her *before*?'

'Um, last winter. But, seriously, I barely know her.'

'She's kind of cute.'

'I – I never thought about it.'

Annabeth kept walking towards York Avenue.

'I'll deal with the school,' I promised, anxious to change the subject. 'Honest, it'll be fine.'

Annabeth wouldn't even look at me. 'I guess our afternoon is off. We should get you out of here, now that the police will be searching for you.'

Behind us, smoke billowed up from Goode High School. In the dark column of ashes, I thought I could almost see a face – a she-demon with red eyes, laughing at me.

Your pretty little camp in flames, Kelli had said. *Your friends made slaves to the Lord of Time.*

'You're right,' I told Annabeth, my heart sinking. 'We have to get to Camp Half-Blood. *Now.*'

2 THE UNDERWORLD SENDS ME A PRANK CALL

Nothing caps off the perfect morning like a long taxi ride with an angry girl.

I tried to talk to Annabeth, but she was acting like I'd just punched her grandmother. All I managed to get out of her was that she'd had a monster-infested spring in San Francisco, she'd come back to camp twice since Christmas but wouldn't tell me why (which kind of ticked me off, because she hadn't even told me she was in New York) and she'd learned nothing about the whereabouts of Nico di Angelo (long story).

'Any word on Luke?' I asked.

She shook her head. I knew this was a touchy subject for her. Annabeth had always admired Luke, the former head counsellor for Hermes who had betrayed us and joined the evil Titan Lord Kronos. She wouldn't admit it, but I knew she still liked him. When we'd fought Luke on Mount Tamalpais last winter, he'd somehow survived a fifteen-metre fall off a cliff. Now, as far as I knew, he was still sailing around on his demon-infested cruise ship while his chopped-up Lord Kronos re-formed, bit by bit, in a golden sarcophagus, biding his time until he had enough power to challenge the Olympian gods. In demigod-speak, we call this a 'problem'.

'Mount Tam is still overrun with monsters,' Annabeth

said. 'I didn't dare go close, but I don't think Luke is up there. I think I would know if he was.'

That didn't make me feel much better. 'What about Grover?'

'He's at camp,' she said. 'We'll see him today.'

'Did he have any luck? I mean, with the search for Pan?'

Annabeth fingered her bead necklace, the way she does when she's worried.

'You'll see,' she said. But she didn't explain.

As we headed through Brooklyn, I used Annabeth's phone to call my mom. Half-bloods try not to use cell phones if we can avoid it, because broadcasting our voices is like sending up a flare to the monsters: *Here I am! Please eat me now!* But I figured this call was important. I left a message on our home voice mail, trying to explain what had happened at Goode. I probably didn't do a very good job. I told my mom I was fine, she shouldn't worry, but I was going to stay at camp until things cooled down. I asked her to tell Paul Blofis I was sorry.

We rode in silence after that. The city melted away until we were off the expressway and rolling through the countryside of northern Long Island, past orchards and wineries and fresh produce stands.

I stared at the phone number Rachel Elizabeth Dare had scrawled on my hand. I knew it was crazy, but I was tempted to call her. Maybe she could help me understand what the *empousa* had been talking about – the camp burning, my friends imprisoned. And why had Kelli exploded into flames?

I knew monsters never truly died. Eventually – maybe weeks, months or years from now – Kelli would re-form out of the primordial nastiness seething in the Underworld. But, still, monsters didn't usually let themselves get destroyed so easily. If she really *was* destroyed.

The taxi exited on Route 25A. We headed through the woods along the North Shore until a low ridge of hills appeared on our left. Annabeth told the driver to pull over on Farm Road 3.141, at the base of Half-Blood Hill.

The driver frowned. 'There ain't nothing here, miss. You sure you want out?'

'Yes, please.' Annabeth handed him a roll of mortal cash, and the driver decided not to argue.

Annabeth and I hiked to the crest of the hill. The young guardian dragon was dozing, coiled around the pine tree, but he lifted his coppery head as we approached and let Annabeth scratch under his chin. Steam hissed out of his nostrils like a kettle and he went cross-eyed with pleasure.

'Hey, Peleus,' Annabeth said. 'Keeping everything safe?'

The last time I'd seen the dragon he'd been two metres long. Now he was at least twice that, and as thick around as the tree itself. Above his head, on the lowest branch of the pine tree, the Golden Fleece shimmered, its magic protecting the camp's borders from invasion. The dragon seemed relaxed, like everything was okay. Below us, Camp Half-Blood looked peaceful – green fields, forest, shiny white Greek buildings. The four-storey farmhouse we called the Big House sat proudly in the midst of the strawberry fields. To the north, past the beach, the Long Island Sound glittered in the sunlight.

Still . . . something felt wrong. There was tension in the air, as if the hill itself were holding its breath, waiting for something bad to happen.

We walked down into the valley and found the summer session in full swing. Most of the campers had arrived last Friday, so I already felt out of it. The satyrs were playing their pipes in the strawberry fields, making the plants grow with woodland magic. Campers were having flying horseback lessons, swooping over the woods on their pegasi. Smoke rose from the forges and hammers rang as kids made their own weapons for arts & crafts. The Athena and Demeter teams were having a chariot race around the track, and over at the canoe lake some kids in a Greek trireme were fighting a large orange sea serpent. A typical day at camp.

'I need to talk to Clarisse,' Annabeth said.

I stared at her as if she'd just said *I need to eat a large smelly boot.* 'What for?'

Clarisse from the Ares cabin was one of my least favourite people. She was a mean, ungrateful bully. Her dad, the war god, wanted to kill me. She tried to beat me to a pulp on a regular basis. Other than that, she was just great.

'We've been working on something,' Annabeth said. 'I'll see you later.'

'Working on what?'

Annabeth glanced towards the forest.

'I'll tell Chiron you're here,' she said. 'He'll want to talk to you before the hearing.'

'What hearing?'

But she jogged down the path towards the archery field without looking back.

'Yeah,' I muttered. 'Great talking with you, too.'

As I made my way through camp, I said hi to some of my friends. In the Big House's driveway, Connor and Travis

Stoll from the Hermes cabin were hot-wiring the camp's van. Silena Beauregard, the head counsellor for Aphrodite, waved at me from her pegasus as she flew past. I looked for Grover, but I didn't see him. Finally I wandered into the sword arena, where I usually go when I'm in a bad mood. Practising always calms me down. Maybe that's because swordplay is one thing I actually understand.

I walked into the amphitheatre and my heart almost stopped. In the middle of the arena floor, with its back to me, was the biggest hellhound I'd ever seen.

I mean, I've seen some pretty big hellhounds. One the size of a rhino tried to kill me when I was twelve. But *this* hellhound was bigger than a tank. I had no idea how it had got past the camp's magic boundaries. It looked right at home, lying on its belly, growling contentedly as it chewed the head off a combat dummy. It hadn't noticed me yet, but if I made a sound, I knew it would sense me. There was no time to go for help. I pulled out Riptide and uncapped it.

'Yaaaaah!' I charged. I brought down the blade on the monster's enormous backside, when out of nowhere another sword blocked my strike.

CLANG!

The hellhound pricked up its ears. 'WOOF!'

I jumped back and instinctively struck at the swordsman – a grey-haired man in Greek armour. He parried my attack with no problem.

'Whoa there!' he said. 'Truce!'

'WOOF!' The hellhound's bark shook the arena.

'That's a hellhound!' I shouted.

'She's harmless,' the man said. 'That's Mrs O'Leary.'

I blinked. 'Mrs O'Leary?'

At the sound of her name, the hellhound barked again. I realized she wasn't angry. She was excited. She nudged the soggy, badly chewed target dummy towards the swordsman.

'Good girl,' the man said. With his free hand he grabbed the armoured manikin by the neck and heaved it towards the stands. 'Get the Greek! Get the Greek!'

Mrs O'Leary bounded after her prey and pounced on the dummy, flattening its armour. She began chewing on its helmet.

The swordsman smiled dryly. He was in his fifties, I guess, with short grey hair and a clipped grey beard. He was in good shape for an older guy. He wore black mountain-climbing trousers and a bronze breastplate strapped over an orange camp T-shirt. At the base of his neck was a strange mark, a purplish blotch like a birthmark or a tattoo, but before I could make out what it was, he shifted his armour straps and the mark disappeared under his collar.

'Mrs O'Leary is my pet,' he explained. 'I couldn't let you stick a sword in her rump, now, could I? That might have scared her.'

'Who are you?'

'Promise not to kill me if I put my sword away?'

'I guess.'

He sheathed his sword and held out his hand. 'Quintus.'

I shook his hand. It was as rough as sandpaper.

'Percy Jackson,' I said. 'Sorry about – How did you, um –'

'Get a hellhound for a pet? Long story, involving many close calls with death and quite a few giant chew toys. I'm the new sword instructor, by the way. Helping Chiron out while Mr D is away.'

'Oh.' I tried not to stare as Mrs O'Leary ripped off the target dummy's shield with the arm still attached and shook it like a frisbee. 'Wait, Mr D is away?'

'Yes, well . . . busy times. Even old Dionysus must help out. He's gone to visit some old friends. Make sure they're on the right side. I probably shouldn't say more than that.'

If Dionysus was gone, that was the best news I'd had all day. He was only our camp director because Zeus had sent him here as a punishment for chasing some off-limits wood nymph. He hated the campers and tried to make our lives miserable. With him away, this summer might actually be cool. On the other hand, if Dionysus had got off his butt and actually started helping the gods recruit against the Titan threat, things must be looking pretty bad.

Off to my left, there was a loud BUMP. Six wooden crates the size of picnic tables were stacked nearby, and they were rattling. Mrs O'Leary cocked her head and bounded towards them.

'Whoa, girl!' Quintus said. 'Those aren't for you.' He distracted her with the bronze shield frisbee.

The crates thumped and shook. There were words printed on the sides, but with my dyslexia they took me a few minutes to decipher:

TRIPLE G RANCH
FRAGILE
THIS WAY UP

Along the bottom, in smaller letters:

OPEN WITH CARE.

TRIPLE G RANCH IS NOT RESPONSIBLE FOR PROPERTY
DAMAGE, MAIMING OR EXCRUCIATINGLY PAINFUL
DEATHS.

'What's in the boxes?' I asked.

'A little surprise,' Quintus said. 'Training activity for
tomorrow night. You'll love it.'

'Uh, okay,' I said, though I wasn't sure about the
'excruciatingly painful deaths' part.

Quintus threw the bronze shield, and Mrs O'Leary
lumbered after it. 'You young ones need more challenges.
They didn't have camps like this when I was a boy.'

'You — you're a half-blood?' I didn't mean to sound so
surprised, but I'd never seen an old demigod before.

Quintus chuckled. 'Some of us *do* survive into adulthood,
you know. Not all of us are the subject of terrible
prophecies.'

'You know about my prophecy?'

'I've heard a few things.'

I wanted to ask *what* few things, but just then Chiron
clip-clopped into the arena. 'Percy, there you are!'

He must've just come from teaching archery. He had a
quiver and bow slung over his 'NO. 1 CENTAUR' T-shirt.
He'd trimmed his curly brown hair and beard for the
summer, and his lower half, which was a white stallion, was
flecked with mud and grass.

'I see you've met our new instructor.' Chiron's tone was
light, but there was an uneasy look in his eyes. 'Quintus,
do you mind if I borrow Percy?'

'Not at all, Master Chiron.'

'No need to call me "master",' Chiron said, though he sounded sort of pleased. 'Come, Percy. We have much to discuss.'

I took one more glance at Mrs O'Leary, who was now chewing off the target dummy's legs.

'Well, see you,' I told Quintus.

As we were walking away, I whispered to Chiron, 'Quintus seems kind of —'

'Mysterious?' Chiron suggested. 'Hard to read?'

'Yeah.'

Chiron nodded. 'A very qualified half-blood. Excellent swordsman. I just wish I understood . . .'

Whatever he was going to say, he apparently changed his mind. 'First things first, Percy. Annabeth told me you met some *empousai.*'

'Yeah.' I told him about the fight at Goode, and how Kelli had exploded into flames.

'Mm,' Chiron said. 'The more powerful ones can do that. She did not die, Percy. She simply escaped. It is not good that the she-demons are stirring.'

'What were they doing there?' I asked. 'Waiting for me?'

'Possibly.' Chiron frowned. 'It is amazing you survived. Their powers of deception . . . almost any male hero would've fallen under their spell and been devoured.'

'I would've been,' I admitted. 'Except for Rachel.'

Chiron nodded. 'Ironic to be saved by a mortal, yet we owe her a debt. What the *empousa* said about an attack on camp — we must speak of this further. But for now, come, we should get to the woods. Grover will want you there.'

'Where?'

'At his formal hearing,' Chiron said grimly. 'The Council of Cloven Elders is meeting now to decide his fate.'

Chiron said we needed to hurry, so I let him give me a ride on his back. As we galloped past the cabins, I glanced at the dining hall — an open-air Greek pavilion on a hill overlooking the sea. It was the first time I'd seen the place since last summer, and it brought back bad memories.

Chiron plunged into the woods. Nymphs peeked out of the trees to watch us pass. Large shapes rustled in the shadows — monsters that were kept in here as a challenge to the campers.

I thought I knew the forest pretty well after playing capture the flag here for two summers, but Chiron took me a way I didn't recognize, through a tunnel of old willow trees, past a little waterfall and into a glade blanketed with wildflowers.

A bunch of satyrs was sitting in a circle on the grass. Grover stood in the middle, facing three really old, really fat satyrs who sat on topiary thrones shaped out of rose bushes. I'd never seen the three old satyrs before, but I guessed they must be the Council of Cloven Elders.

Grover seemed to be telling them a story. He twisted the bottom of his T-shirt, shifting nervously on his goat hooves. He hadn't changed much since last winter, maybe because satyrs age half as fast as humans. His acne had flared up. His horns had got a little bigger, so they just stuck out over his curly hair. I realized with a start that I was taller than him now.

Standing off to one side of the circle were Annabeth, another girl I'd never seen before, and Clarisse. Chiron dropped me next to them.

Clarisse's stringy brown hair was tied back with a camouflage bandanna. If possible, she looked even buffer, like she'd been working out. She glared at me and muttered, 'Punk,' which must've meant she was in a good mood. Usually she says hello by trying to kill me.

Annabeth had her arm around the other girl, who looked like she'd been crying. She was small – petite, I guess you'd call it – with wispy hair the colour of amber and a pretty, elfish face. She wore a green *chiton* and laced sandals, and she was dabbing her eyes with a handkerchief. 'It's going terribly,' she sniffled.

'No, no.' Annabeth patted her shoulder. 'He'll be fine, Juniper.'

Annabeth looked at me and mouthed the words *Grover's girlfriend.*

At least I thought that's what she said, but that made no sense. Grover with a girlfriend? Then I looked at Juniper more closely, and I realized her ears were slightly pointed. Her eyes, instead of being red from crying, were tinged green, the colour of chlorophyll. She was a tree nymph – a dryad.

'Master Underwood!' the council member on the right shouted, cutting off whatever Grover was trying to say. 'Do you seriously expect us to believe this?'

'B-but, Silenus,' Grover stammered. 'It's the truth!'

The council guy, Silenus, turned to his colleagues and muttered something. Chiron cantered up to the front and stood next to them. I remembered he was an honorary member of the council, but I'd never thought about it much. The elders didn't look very impressive. They reminded me of the goats in a petting zoo – huge bellies, sleepy expressions, and glazed eyes that couldn't see past the next handful of goat chow. I wasn't sure why Grover looked so nervous.

Silenus tugged his yellow polo shirt over his belly and adjusted himself on his rosebush throne. 'Master Underwood, for six months – *six months* – we have been hearing these scandalous claims that you heard the wild god Pan speak.'

'But I did!'

'Impudence!' said the elder on the left.

'Now, Maron,' Chiron said. 'Patience.'

'Patience, indeed!' Maron said. 'I've had it up to my horns with this nonsense. As if the wild god would speak to . . . to *him*.'

Juniper looked like she wanted to charge the old satyr and beat him up, but Annabeth and Clarisse held her back. 'Wrong fight, girlie,' Clarisse muttered. 'Wait.'

I don't know what surprised me more: Clarisse holding somebody back from a fight, or the fact that she and Annabeth, who despised each other, almost seemed like they were working together.

'For six months,' Silenus continued, 'we have indulged you, Master Underwood. We let you travel. We allowed you to keep your searcher's licence. We waited for you to bring proof of your preposterous claim. And what have you found in six months of travel?'

'I just need more time,' Grover pleaded.

'Nothing!' the elder in the middle chimed in. 'You have found nothing.'

'But, Leneus –'

Silenus raised his hand. Chiron leaned in and said something to the satyrs. The satyrs didn't look happy. They muttered and argued among themselves, but Chiron said something else, and Silenus sighed. He nodded reluctantly.

'Master Underwood,' Silenus announced, 'we will give you one more chance.'

Grover brightened. 'Thank you!'

'One more week.'

'What? But, sir! That's impossible!'

'One more week, Master Underwood. And then, if you cannot prove your claims, it will be time for you to pursue another career. Something to suit your dramatic talents. Puppet theatre, perhaps. Or tap dancing.'

'But, sir, I — I can't lose my searcher's licence. My whole life —'

'This meeting of the council is adjourned,' Silenus said. 'And now let us enjoy our noonday meal!'

The old satyr clapped his hands and a bunch of nymphs melted out of the trees with platters of vegetables, fruits, tin cans and other goat delicacies. The circle of satyrs broke and charged the food. Grover walked dejectedly towards us. His faded blue T-shirt had a picture of a satyr on it. It read: *Got Hooves?*

'Hi, Percy,' he said, so depressed he didn't even offer to shake my hand. 'That went well, huh?'

'Those old goats!' Juniper said. 'Oh, Grover, they don't know how hard you've tried!'

'There is another option,' Clarisse said darkly.

'No. No.' Juniper shook her head. 'Grover, I won't let you.'

His face was ashen. 'I — I'll have to think about it. But we don't even know where to look.'

'What are you talking about?' I asked.

In the distance, a conch horn sounded.

Annabeth pursed her lips. 'I'll fill you in later, Percy. We'd better get back to our cabins. Inspection is starting.'

It didn't seem fair that I'd have to do cabin inspection when I just got to camp, but that's the way it worked. Every afternoon, one of the senior counsellors came around with a papyrus-scroll checklist. Best cabin got first shower hour, which meant hot water guaranteed. Worst cabin got kitchen patrol after dinner.

The problem for me: I was usually the only one in the Poseidon cabin, and I'm not exactly what you would call neat. The cleaning harpies only came through on the last day of summer, so my cabin was probably just the way I'd left it on winter break: my chocolate wrappers and crisp bags still on my bunk, my armour for capture the flag lying in pieces all around the cabin.

I raced towards the commons area, where the twelve cabins – one for each Olympian god – made a U around the central green. The Demeter kids were sweeping out theirs and making fresh flowers grow in their window boxes. Just by snapping their fingers they could make honeysuckle vines bloom over their doorway and daisies cover their roof, which was totally unfair. I don't think they ever got last place in inspection. The guys in the Hermes cabin were scrambling around in a panic, stashing dirty laundry under their beds and accusing each other of taking stuff. They were slobs, but they still had a head start on me.

Over at the Aphrodite cabin, Silena Beauregard was just coming out, checking items off the inspection scroll. I cursed under my breath. Silena was nice, but she was an absolute neat freak, the worst inspector. She liked things to be pretty. I didn't do 'pretty'. I could almost feel my arms getting heavy from all the dishes I would have to scrub tonight.

The Poseidon cabin was at the end of the row of 'male god' cabins on the right side of the green. It was made of grey shell-encrusted sea rock, long and low like a bunker, but it had windows that faced the sea and it always had a good breeze blowing through it.

I dashed inside, wondering if maybe I could do a quick under-the-bed cleaning job like the Hermes guys, and I found my half-brother Tyson sweeping the floor.

'Percy!' he bellowed. He dropped his broom and ran at me. If you've never been charged by an enthusiastic Cyclops wearing a flowered apron and rubber cleaning gloves, I'm telling you, it'll wake you up quick.

'Hey, big guy!' I said. 'Ow, watch the ribs. The ribs.'

I managed to survive his bear hug. He put me down, grinning like crazy, his single calf-brown eye full of excitement. His teeth were as yellow and crooked as ever, and his hair was a rat's nest. He wore ragged XXXL jeans and a tattered flannel shirt under his flowered apron, but he was still a sight for sore eyes. I hadn't seen him in almost a year, since he'd gone under the sea to work at the Cyclopes' forges.

'You are okay?' he asked. 'Not eaten by monsters?'

'Not even a little bit.' I showed him that I still had both arms and both legs, and Tyson clapped happily.

'Yay!' he said. 'Now we can eat peanut butter sandwiches and ride fish ponies! We can fight monsters and see Annabeth and make things go BOOM!'

I hoped he didn't mean all at the same time, but I told

him absolutely, we'd have a lot of fun this summer. I couldn't help smiling; he was so enthusiastic about everything.

'But first,' I said, 'we've gotta worry about inspection. We should . . .'

Then I looked around and realized Tyson had been busy. The floor was swept. The bunk beds were made. The saltwater fountain in the corner had been freshly scrubbed so the coral gleamed. On the windowsills, Tyson had set out water-filled vases with sea anemones and strange glowing plants from the bottom of the ocean, more beautiful than any flower bouquets the Demeter kids could whip up.

'Tyson, the cabin looks . . . amazing!'

He beamed. 'See the fish ponies? I put them on the ceiling!'

A herd of miniature bronze hippocampi hung on wires from the ceiling, so it looked like they were swimming through the air. I couldn't believe Tyson, with his huge hands, could make things so delicate. Then I looked over at my bunk, and I saw my old shield hanging on the wall.

'You fixed it!'

The shield had been badly damaged in a manticore attack last winter, but now it was perfect again — not a scratch. All the bronze pictures of my adventures with Tyson and Annabeth in the Sea of Monsters were polished and gleaming.

I looked at Tyson. I didn't know how to thank him.

Then somebody behind me said, 'Oh, my.'

Silena Beauregard was standing in the doorway with her inspection scroll. She stepped into the cabin, did a quick twirl, then raised her eyebrows at me. 'Well, I had my doubts. But you clean up nicely, Percy. I'll remember that.'

She winked at me and left the room.

Tyson and I spent the afternoon catching up and just hanging out, which was nice after a morning of getting attacked by demon cheerleaders.

We went down to the forge and helped Beckendorf from the Hephaestus cabin with his metalworking. Tyson showed us how he'd learned to craft magic weapons. He fashioned a flaming double-bladed war axe so fast even Beckendorf was impressed.

While he worked, Tyson told us about his year under the sea. His eye lit up when he described the Cyclopes' forges and the palace of Poseidon, but he also told us how tense things were. The old gods of the sea, who'd ruled during Titan times, were starting to make war on our father. When Tyson had left, battles were raging all over the Atlantic. Hearing that made me feel anxious, like I should be helping out, but Tyson assured me that Dad wanted us both at camp.

'Lots of bad people above the sea, too,' Tyson said. 'We can make them go boom.'

After the forges, we spent some time at the canoe lake with Annabeth. She was really glad to see Tyson, but I could tell she was distracted. She kept looking over at the forest, like she was thinking about Grover's problem with the council. I couldn't blame her. Grover was nowhere to be seen, and I felt really bad for him. Finding the lost god Pan had been his lifelong goal. His father and his uncle had both disappeared, following the same dream. Last winter,

Grover had heard a voice in his head: *I await you* – a voice he was sure belonged to Pan – but apparently his search had led nowhere. If the council took away his searcher's licence now, it would crush him.

'What's this "other way"?' I asked Annabeth. 'The thing Clarisse mentioned?'

She picked up a stone and skipped it across the lake. 'Something Clarisse scouted out. I helped her a little this spring. But it would be dangerous. Especially for Grover.'

'Goat boy scares me,' Tyson murmured.

I stared at him. Tyson had faced down fire-breathing bulls and sea monsters and cannibal giants. 'Why would you be scared of Grover?'

'Hooves and horns,' Tyson muttered nervously. 'And goat fur makes my nose itchy.'

And that pretty much ended our Grover conversation.

Before dinner, Tyson and I went down to the sword arena. Quintus was glad to have company. He still wouldn't tell me what was in the wooden crates, but he did teach me a few sword moves. The guy was good. He fought the way some people play chess – like he was putting all the moves together and you couldn't see the pattern until he made the last stroke and won with a sword at your throat.

'Good try,' he told me. 'But your guard is too low.'

He lunged and I blocked.

'Have you always been a swordsman?' I asked.

He parried my overhead cut. 'I've been many things.'

He jabbed and I sidestepped. His shoulder strap slipped down, and I saw that mark on his shoulder – the purple blotch. But it wasn't a random mark. It had a definite shape – a bird with folded wings, like a quail or something.

'What's that on your neck?' I asked, which was probably a rude question, but you can blame my ADHD. I tend to just blurt things out.

Quintus lost his rhythm. I hit his sword hilt and knocked the blade out of his hand.

He rubbed his fingers. Then he shifted his armour to hide the mark. It wasn't a tattoo, I realized. It was an old burn . . . like he'd been branded.

'A reminder.' He picked up his sword and forced a smile. 'Now, shall we go again?'

He pressed me hard, not giving me time for any more questions.

While he and I fought, Tyson played with Mrs O'Leary, whom he called the 'little doggie'. They had a great time wrestling for the bronze shield and playing Get the Greek. By sunset, Quintus hadn't even broken a sweat, which seemed kind of strange, but Tyson and I were hot and sticky, so we hit the showers and got ready for dinner.

I was feeling good. It was almost like a normal day at camp. Then dinner came, and all the campers lined up by their cabins and marched into the dining pavilion. Most of them ignored the sealed fissure in the marble floor at the entrance – a three-metre-long jagged scar that hadn't been there last summer – but I was careful to step over it.

'Big crack,' Tyson said when we were at our table. 'Earthquake, maybe?'

'No,' I said. 'Not an earthquake.'

I wasn't sure I should tell him. It was a secret only Annabeth and Grover and I knew. But looking in Tyson's big eye, I knew I couldn't hide anything from him.

'Nico di Angelo,' I said, lowering my voice. 'He's this half-blood kid we brought to camp last winter. He, uh . . . he asked me to guard his sister on a quest, and I failed. She died. Now he blames me.'

Tyson frowned. 'So he put a crack in the floor?'

'These skeletons attacked us,' I said. 'Nico told them to go away, and the ground just opened up and swallowed them. Nico . . .' I looked around to make sure no one was listening. 'Nico is a son of Hades.'

Tyson nodded thoughtfully. 'The god of dead people.'

'Yeah.'

'So the Nico boy is gone now?'

'I – I guess. I tried to search for him this spring. So did Annabeth. But we didn't have any luck. This is secret, Tyson. Okay? If anyone found out he is a son of Hades, he would be in danger. You can't even tell Chiron.'

'The bad prophecy,' Tyson said. 'Titans might use him if they knew.'

I stared at him. Sometimes it was easy to forget that, as big and childlike as he was, Tyson was pretty smart. He knew that the next child of the Big Three gods – Zeus, Poseidon or Hades – who turned sixteen was prophesied to either save or destroy Mount Olympus. Most people assumed that meant me, but if I died before I turned sixteen, the prophecy could just as easily apply to Nico.

'Exactly,' I said. 'So –'

'Mouth sealed,' Tyson promised. 'Like the crack in the ground.'

*   *   *

I had trouble falling asleep that night. I lay in bed listening to the waves on the beach, and the owls and monsters in the woods. I was afraid once I drifted off I'd have nightmares.

See, for half-bloods, dreams are hardly ever just dreams. We get messages. We see things that are happening to our friends or enemies. Sometimes we even glimpse the past or the future. And at camp, my dreams were always more frequent and vivid.

So I was still awake around midnight, staring at the bunk-bed mattress above me, when I realized there was a strange light in the room. The saltwater fountain was glowing.

I threw off the covers and walked cautiously towards it. Steam rose from the hot salt water. Rainbow colours shimmered through it, though there was no light in the room except for the moon outside. Then a pleasant female voice spoke from the steam: *Please deposit one drachma.*

I looked over at Tyson, but he was still snoring. He sleeps about as heavily as a tranquillized elephant.

I didn't know what to think. I'd never had a collect Iris-message before. One golden *drachma* gleamed at the bottom of the fountain. I scooped it up and tossed it through the Mist. The coin vanished.

'O, Iris, Goddess of the Rainbow,' I whispered. 'Show me . . . uh, whatever you need to show me.'

The Mist shimmered. I saw the dark shore of a river. Wisps of fog drifted across black water. The beach was strewn with jagged volcanic rock. A young boy squatted at the riverbank, tending a campfire. The flames burned an unnatural blue colour. Then I saw the boy's face. It was Nico di Angelo. He was throwing pieces of paper into the fire – Mythomagic trading cards, part of the game he'd been obsessed with last winter.

Nico was only ten, or maybe eleven by now, but he looked older. His hair had grown longer. It was shaggy and almost touched his shoulders. His eyes were dark. His olive skin had turned paler. He wore ripped black jeans and a battered aviator's jacket that was several sizes too big, unzipped over a black shirt. His face was grimy, his eyes a little wild. He looked like a kid who'd been living on the streets.

I waited for him to look at me. No doubt he'd get crazy angry, start accusing me of letting his sister die. But he didn't seem to notice me.

I stayed quiet, not daring to move. If he hadn't sent this Iris-message, who had?

Nico tossed another trading card into the blue flames. 'Useless,' he muttered. 'I can't believe I ever liked this stuff.'

'A childish game, master,' another voice agreed. It seemed to come from near the fire, but I couldn't see who was talking.

Nico stared across the river. On the far shore was a black beach shrouded in haze. I recognized it: the Underworld. Nico was camping at the edge of the River Styx.

'I've failed,' he muttered. 'There's no way to get her back.'

The other voice kept silent.

Nico turned towards it doubtfully. 'Is there? Speak.'

Something shimmered. I thought it was just firelight. Then I realized it was the form of a man – a wisp of blue smoke, a shadow. If you looked at him head-on, he wasn't there. But if you looked out of the corner of your eye, you could make out his shape. A ghost.

'It has never been done,' the ghost said. 'But there may be a way.'

'Tell me,' Nico commanded. His eyes shone with a fierce light.

'An exchange,' the ghost said. 'A soul for a soul.'

'I've offered!'

'Not yours,' the ghost said. 'You cannot offer your father a soul he will eventually collect anyway. Nor will he be anxious for the death of his son. I mean a soul that should have died already. Someone who has cheated death.'

Nico's face darkened. 'Not that again. You're talking about murder.'

'I'm talking about justice,' the ghost said. 'Vengeance.'

'Those are not the same thing.'

The ghost laughed dryly. 'You will learn differently as you get older.'

Nico stared at the flames. 'Why can't I at least summon her? I want to talk to her. She would . . . she would help me.'

'*I* will help you,' the ghost promised. 'Have I not saved you many times? Did I not lead you through the maze and teach you to use your powers? Do you want revenge for your sister or not?'

I didn't like the ghost's tone of voice. He reminded me of a kid at my old school, a bully who used to convince other kids to do stupid things like steal lab equipment and vandalize the teachers' cars. The bully never got into trouble himself, but he got tons of other kids suspended.

Nico turned from the fire so the ghost couldn't see him, but I could. A tear traced its way down his face. 'Very well. You have a plan?'

'Oh, yes,' the ghost said, sounding quite pleased. 'We have many dark roads to travel. We must start –'

The image shimmered. Nico vanished. The woman's voice from the Mist said, *Please deposit one drachma for another five minutes.*

There were no other coins in the fountain. I grabbed for my pockets, but I was wearing pyjamas. I lunged for the nightstand to check for spare change, but the Iris-message had already blinked out, and the room went dark again. The connection was broken.

I stood in the middle of the cabin, listening to the gurgle of the saltwater fountain and the ocean waves outside.

Nico was alive. He was trying to bring his sister back from the dead. And I had a feeling I knew whose soul he wanted to exchange – someone who had cheated death. Vengeance.

Nico di Angelo would come looking for me.

3 WE PLAY TAG WITH SCORPIONS

The next morning there was a lot of excitement at breakfast.

Apparently around three in the morning an Aethiopian drakon had been spotted at the borders of camp. I was so exhausted I slept right through the noise. The magical boundaries had kept the monster out, but it prowled the hills, looking for weak spots in our defences, and it didn't seem anxious to go away until Lee Fletcher from Apollo's cabin led a couple of his siblings in pursuit. After a few dozen arrows lodged in the chinks of the drakon's armour, it got the message and withdrew.

'It's still out there,' Lee warned us during announcements. 'Twenty arrows in its hide, and we just made it mad. The thing was ten metres long and bright green. Its eyes –' He shuddered.

'You did well, Lee.' Chiron patted him on the shoulder. 'Everyone stay alert, but stay calm. This has happened before.'

'Aye,' Quintus said from the head table. 'And it will happen again. More and more frequently.'

The campers murmured among themselves.

Everyone knew the rumours: Luke and his army of monsters were planning an invasion of the camp. Most of us expected it to happen this summer, but no one knew how or when. It didn't help that our attendance was down. We only had about eighty campers. Three years ago, when I'd started, there had been more than a hundred. Some had died. Some had joined Luke. Some had just disappeared.

'This is a good reason for new war games,' Quintus continued, a glint in his eyes. 'We'll see how you all do with that tonight.'

'Yes . . .' Chiron said. 'Well, enough announcements. Let us bless this meal and eat.' He raised his goblet. 'To the gods!'

We all raised our glasses and repeated the blessing.

Tyson and I took our plates to the bronze brazier and scraped a portion of our food into the flames. I hoped the gods liked raisin toast and Cheerios.

'Poseidon,' I said. Then I whispered, 'Help me with Nico, and Luke, and Grover's problem . . .'

There was so much to worry about I could've stood there all morning, but I headed back to my table.

Once everyone was eating, Chiron and Grover came over to visit. Grover was bleary-eyed. His shirt was inside out. He slid his plate onto the table and slumped next to me.

Tyson shifted uncomfortably. 'I will go . . . um . . . polish my fish ponies.'

He lumbered off, leaving his breakfast half eaten.

Chiron tried for a smile. He probably wanted to look reassuring, but in centaur form he towered over me, casting a shadow across the table. 'Well, Percy, how did you sleep?'

'Uh, fine.' I wondered why he asked that. Was it possible

he knew something about the weird Iris-message I'd got?

'I brought Grover over,' Chiron said, 'because I thought you two might want to, ah, discuss matters. Now, if you'll excuse me, I have some Iris-messages to send. I'll see you later in the day.' He gave Grover a meaningful look, then trotted out of the pavilion.

'What's he talking about?' I asked Grover.

Grover chewed his eggs. I could tell he was distracted, because he bit off the tines of his fork and chewed those down, too. 'He wants you to convince me,' he mumbled.

Somebody else slid next to me on the bench: Annabeth.

'I'll tell you what it's about,' she said. 'The Labyrinth.'

It was hard to concentrate on what she was saying, because everybody in the dining pavilion was stealing glances at us and whispering. And Annabeth was right next to me. I mean *right* next to me.

'You're not supposed to be here,' I said.

'We need to talk,' she insisted.

'But the rules . . .'

She knew as well as I did that campers weren't allowed to switch tables. Satyrs were different. They weren't really demigods. But the half-bloods had to sit with their cabins. I wasn't even sure what the punishment was for switching tables. I'd never seen it happen. If Mr D had been here, he probably would've strangled Annabeth with magical grapevines or something, but Mr D wasn't here. Chiron had already left the pavilion. Quintus looked over and raised an eyebrow, but he didn't say anything.

'Look,' Annabeth said. 'Grover is in trouble. There's

only one way we can figure out to help him. It's the Labyrinth. That's what Clarisse and I have been investigating.'

I shifted my weight, trying to think clearly. 'You mean the maze where they kept the Minotaur, back in the old days?'

'Exactly,' Annabeth said.

'So . . . it's not under the king's palace in Crete any more,' I guessed. 'The Labyrinth is under some building in America.'

See? It only took me a few years to work things out. I knew that important places moved around with Western Civilization, like Mount Olympus being over the Empire State Building, and the Underworld entrance being in Los Angeles. I was feeling pretty proud of myself.

Annabeth rolled her eyes. 'Under a building? Please, Percy. The Labyrinth is *huge*. It wouldn't fit under a single city, much less a single building.'

I thought about my dream of Nico at the River Styx. 'So . . . is the Labyrinth part of the Underworld?'

'No.' Annabeth frowned. 'Well, there may be passages from the Labyrinth down *into* the Underworld. I'm not sure. But the Underworld is way, way down. The Labyrinth is right under the surface of the mortal world, kind of like a second skin. It's been growing for thousands of years, lacing its way under Western cities, connecting everything together underground. You can get anywhere through the Labyrinth.'

'If you don't get lost,' Grover muttered. 'And die a horrible death.'

'Grover, there has to be a way,' Annabeth said. I got

the feeling they'd had this conversation before. 'Clarisse lived.'

'Barely!' Grover said. 'And the other guy —'

'He was driven insane. He didn't die.'

'Oh, joy.' Grover's lower lip quivered. 'That makes me feel much better.'

'Whoa,' I said. 'Back up. What's this about Clarisse and a crazy guy?'

Annabeth glanced over towards the Ares table. Clarisse was watching us like she knew what we were talking about, but then she fixed her eyes on her breakfast plate.

'Last year,' Annabeth said, lowering her voice, 'Clarisse went on a mission for Chiron.'

'I remember,' I said. 'It was secret.'

Annabeth nodded. Despite how serious she was acting, I was happy she wasn't mad at me any more. And I kind of liked the fact that she'd broken the rules to come sit next to me.

'It was secret,' Annabeth agreed, 'because she found Chris Rodriguez.'

'The guy from the Hermes cabin?' I remembered him from two years ago. We'd eavesdropped on Chris Rodriguez aboard Luke's ship, the *Princess Andromeda*. Chris was one of the half-bloods who'd abandoned camp and joined the Titan army.

'Yeah,' Annabeth said. 'Last summer he just appeared in Phoenix, Arizona, near Clarisse's mom's house.'

'What do you mean, he just appeared?'

'He was wandering around the desert, in fifty degrees, in full Greek armour, babbling about string.'

'String,' I said.

'He'd been driven completely insane. Clarisse brought him back to her mom's house so the mortals wouldn't institutionalize him. She tried to nurse him back to health. Chiron came out and interviewed him, but it wasn't much good. The only thing they got out of him: Luke's men have been exploring the Labyrinth.'

I shivered, though I wasn't sure exactly why. Poor Chris . . . He hadn't been that bad a guy. What could've driven him mad? I looked at Grover, who was chewing up the rest of his fork.

'Okay,' I asked. 'Why were they exploring the Labyrinth?'

'We weren't sure,' Annabeth said. 'That's why Clarisse went on a scouting expedition. Chiron kept things hushed up because he didn't want anyone panicking. He got me involved because . . . well, the Labyrinth has always been one of my favourite subjects. The architecture involved –' Her expression turned a little dreamy. 'The builder, Daedalus, was a genius. But the point is, the Labyrinth has entrances everywhere. If Luke could figure out how to navigate it, he could move his army around with incredible speed.'

'Except it's a maze, right?'

'Full of horrible traps,' Grover agreed. 'Dead ends. Illusions. Psychotic goat-killing monsters.'

'But not if you had Ariadne's string,' Annabeth said. 'In the old days, Ariadne's string guided Theseus out of the maze. It was a navigation instrument of some kind, invented by Daedalus. And Chris Rodriguez was mumbling about string.'

'So Luke is trying to find Ariadne's string,' I said. 'Why? What's he planning?'

Annabeth shook her head. 'I don't know. I thought maybe he wanted to invade camp through the maze, but that doesn't make any sense. The closest entrances Clarisse found were in Manhattan, which wouldn't help Luke get past our borders. Clarisse explored a little way into the tunnels, but . . . it was very dangerous. She had some close calls. I researched everything I could find out about Daedalus. I'm afraid it didn't help much. I don't understand exactly what Luke's planning, but I do know this: the Labyrinth might be the key to Grover's problem.'

I blinked. 'You think Pan is underground?'

'It would explain why he's been impossible to find.'

Grover shuddered. 'Satyrs hate going underground. No searcher would ever try going in *that* place. No flowers. No sunshine. No coffee shops!'

'But,' Annabeth said, 'the Labyrinth can lead you almost anywhere. It reads your thoughts. It was designed to fool you, to trick you and kill you; but if you can make the Labyrinth work *for* you –'

'It could lead you to the wild god,' I said.

'I can't do it.' Grover hugged his stomach. 'Just thinking about it makes me want to throw up my silverware.'

'Grover, it may be your last chance,' Annabeth said. 'The council is serious. *One* week or you learn to tap dance!'

Over at the head table, Quintus cleared his throat. I got the feeling he didn't want to make a scene, but Annabeth was really pushing it, sitting at my table so long.

'We'll talk later.' Annabeth squeezed my arm a little too hard. 'Convince him, will you?'

She returned to the Athena table, ignoring all the people who were staring at her.

Grover buried his head in his hands. 'I can't do it, Percy. My searcher's licence. Pan. I'm going to lose it all. I'll have to start a puppet theatre.'

'Don't say that! We'll figure something out.'

He looked at me, teary-eyed. 'Percy, you're my best friend. You've seen me underground. In that Cyclops's cave. Do you really think I could . . .'

His voice faltered. I remembered the Sea of Monsters, when he'd been stuck in a Cyclops's cave. He'd never liked underground places to begin with, but now Grover really hated them. Cyclopes gave him the creeps, too. Even Tyson . . . Grover tried to hide it, but Grover and I could sort of read each other's emotions because of this empathy link Grover had made between us. I knew how he felt. Grover was terrified of the big guy.

'I have to leave,' Grover said miserably. 'Juniper's waiting for me. It's a good thing she finds cowards attractive.'

After he was gone, I looked over at Quintus. He nodded gravely, like we were sharing some dark secret. Then he went back to cutting his sausage with a dagger.

In the afternoon I went down to the pegasus stables to visit my friend Blackjack.

Yo, boss! He capered around in his stall, his black wings buffeting the air. *Ya bring me some sugar cubes?*

'You know those aren't good for you, Blackjack.'

Yeah, so you brought me some, huh?

I smiled and fed him a handful. Blackjack and I went back a long way. I sort of helped rescue him from Luke's demon cruise ship a few years ago, and ever since he insisted on repaying me with favours.

So we got any quests coming up? Blackjack asked. *I'm ready to fly, boss!*

I patted his nose. 'Not sure, man. Everybody keeps talking about underground mazes.'

Blackjack whinnied nervously. *Nuh-uh. Not for this horse! You ain't gonna be crazy enough to go in no maze, boss. Are ya? You'll end up in the glue factory!*

'You may be right, Blackjack. We'll see.'

Blackjack crunched down his sugar cubes. He shook his mane like he was having a sugar seizure. *Whoa! Good stuff! Well, boss, you come to your senses and want to fly somewhere, just give a whistle. Ole Blackjack and his buddies, we'll stampede anybody for ya!*

I told him I'd keep it in mind. Then a group of younger campers came into the stables to start their riding lessons, and I decided it was time to leave. I had a bad feeling I wasn't going to see Blackjack for a long time.

That night after dinner, Quintus had us suit up in combat armour like we were getting ready for capture the flag, but the mood among the campers was a lot more serious. Sometime during the day, the crates in the arena had disappeared, and I had a feeling whatever was in them had been emptied into the woods.

'Right,' Quintus said, standing on the head dining table. 'Gather round.'

He was dressed in black leather and bronze. In the torchlight, his grey hair made him look like a ghost. Mrs O'Leary bounded happily around him, foraging for dinner scraps.

'You will be in teams of two,' Quintus announced.

When everybody started talking and trying to grab their friends, he yelled: 'Which have already been chosen!'

'AWWWWW!' everybody complained.

'Your goal is simple: collect the gold laurels without dying. The wreath is wrapped in a silk package, tied to the back of one of the monsters. There are six monsters. Each has a silk package. Only one holds the laurels. You must find the wreath before the other teams. And of course . . . You will have to slay the monster to get it, and stay alive.'

The crowd started murmuring excitedly. The task sounded pretty straightforward. Hey, we'd all slain monsters before. That's what we trained for.

'I will now announce your partners,' Quintus said. 'There will be no trading. No switching. No complaining.'

'Aroooof!' Mrs O'Leary buried her face in a plate of pizza.

Quintus produced a big scroll and started reading off names. Beckendorf would be with Silena Beauregard, which Beckendorf looked pretty happy about. The Stoll brothers, Travis and Connor, would be together. No surprise. They did everything together. Clarisse was with Lee Fletcher from the Apollo cabin – melee and ranged combat combined, they would be a tough combo to beat. Quintus kept rattling off the names until he said, 'Percy Jackson with Annabeth Chase.'

'Nice.' I grinned at Annabeth.

'Your armour is crooked,' was her only comment, and she redid my straps for me.

'Grover Underwood,' Quintus said, 'with Tyson.'

Grover just about jumped out of his goat fur. 'What? B-but —'

'No, no,' Tyson whimpered. 'Must be a mistake. Goat boy —'

'No complaining!' Quintus ordered. 'Get with your partner. You have two minutes to prepare!'

Tyson and Grover both looked at me pleadingly. I tried to give them an encouraging nod, and gestured that they should move together. Tyson sneezed. Grover started chewing nervously on his wooden club.

'They'll be fine,' Annabeth said. 'Come on. Let's worry about how we're going to stay alive.'

It was still light when we got into the woods, but the shadows from the trees made it feel like midnight. It was cold, too, even in summer. Annabeth and I found tracks almost immediately — scuttling marks made by something with a lot of legs. We began to follow the trail.

We jumped a creek and heard some twigs snapping nearby. We crouched behind a boulder, but it was only the Stoll brothers tripping through the woods and cursing. Their dad was the god of thieves, but they were about as stealthy as water buffaloes.

Once the Stolls had passed, we forged deeper into the west woods, where the monsters were wilder. We were standing on a ledge overlooking a marshy pond when Annabeth tensed. 'This is where we stopped looking.'

It took me a second to realize what she meant. Last winter, when we'd been searching for Nico di Angelo, this was where we'd given up hope of finding him. Grover, Annabeth and I had stood on this rock, and I'd convinced them not to tell Chiron the truth: that Nico was a son of Hades. At the time it seemed the right thing to do. I wanted to protect his identity. I wanted to be the one to find him and make things right for what had happened to his sister. Now, six months later, I hadn't even come close to finding him. It left a bitter taste in my mouth.

'I saw him last night,' I said.

Annabeth knitted her eyebrows. 'What do you mean?'

I told her about the Iris-message. When I was done, she stared into the shadows of the woods. 'He's summoning the dead? That's not good.'

'The ghost was giving him bad advice,' I said. 'Telling him to take revenge.'

'Yeah . . . spirits are never good advisers. They've got their own agendas. Old grudges. And they resent the living.'

'He's going to come after me,' I said. 'The spirit mentioned a maze.'

She nodded. 'That settles it. We *have* to figure out the Labyrinth.'

'Maybe,' I said uncomfortably. 'But who sent the Iris-message? If Nico didn't know I was there –'

A branch snapped in the woods. Dry leaves rustled. Something large was moving in the trees, just beyond the ridge.

'That's not the Stoll brothers,' Annabeth whispered.

Together we drew our swords.

We got to Zeus's Fist, a huge pile of boulders in the middle of the west woods. It was a natural landmark where campers often rendezvoused on hunting expeditions, but now there was nobody around.

'Over there,' Annabeth whispered.

'No, wait,' I said. 'Behind us.'

It was weird. Scuttling noises seemed to be coming from several different directions. We were circling the boulders, our swords drawn, when someone right behind us said, 'Hi.'

We whirled around, and the tree nymph Juniper yelped.

'Put those down!' she protested. 'Dryads don't like sharp blades, okay?'

'Juniper,' Annabeth exhaled. 'What are you doing here?'

'I live here.'

I lowered my sword. 'In the boulders?'

She pointed towards the edge of the clearing. 'In the juniper. Duh.'

It made sense, and I felt kind of stupid. I'd been hanging around dryads for years, but I never really talked to them much. I knew they couldn't go very far from their tree, which was their source of life. But I didn't know much else.

'Are you guys busy?' Juniper asked.

'Well,' I said, 'we're in the middle of this game against a bunch of monsters and we're trying not to die.'

'We're not busy,' Annabeth said. 'What's wrong, Juniper?'

Juniper sniffled. She wiped her silky sleeve under her eyes. 'It's Grover. He seems so distraught. All year he's been out looking for Pan. And every time he comes back, it's worse. I thought maybe, at first, he was seeing another tree.'

'No,' Annabeth said, as Juniper started crying. 'I'm sure that's not it.'

'He had a crush on a blueberry bush once,' Juniper said miserably.

'Juniper,' Annabeth said, 'Grover would never even *look* at another tree. He's just stressed out about his searcher's licence.'

'He can't go underground!' she protested. 'You can't let him.'

Annabeth looked uncomfortable. 'It might be the only way to help him; if we just knew where to start.'

'Ah.' Juniper wiped a green tear off her cheek. 'About that . . .'

Another rustle in the woods, and Juniper yelled, 'Hide!'

Before I could ask why, she went *poof* into green mist.

Annabeth and I turned. Coming out of the woods was a glistening amber insect, three metres long, with jagged pincers, an armoured tail and a sting as long as my sword. A scorpion. Tied to its back was a red silk package.

'One of us gets behind it,' Annabeth said, as the thing clattered towards us. 'Cut off its tail while the other distracts it in front.'

'I'll take point,' I said. 'You've got the invisibility hat.'

She nodded. We'd fought together so many times we knew each other's moves. We could do this, easy. But it all went wrong when the other two scorpions appeared from the woods.

'*Three?*' Annabeth said. 'That's not possible! The whole woods, and half the monsters come at us?'

I swallowed. One, we could take. Two, with a little luck. Three? Doubtful.

The scorpions scurried towards us, whipping their barbed tails like they'd come here just to kill us. Annabeth and I put our backs against the nearest boulder.

'Climb?' I said.

'No time,' she said.

She was right. The scorpions were already surrounding us. They were so close I could see their hideous mouths foaming, anticipating a nice juicy meal of demigods.

'Look out!' Annabeth parried away a sting with the flat of her blade. I stabbed with Riptide, but the scorpion backed out of range. We clambered sideways along the boulders, but the scorpions followed us. I slashed at another one, but going on the offensive was too dangerous. If I went for the body, the tail stabbed downward. If I went for the tail, the thing's pincers came from either side and tried to grab me. All we could do was defend, and we wouldn't be able to keep that up for very long.

I took another step sideways, and suddenly there was nothing behind me. It was a crack between two of the largest boulders, something I'd probably passed by a million times, but . . .

'In here,' I said.

Annabeth sliced at a scorpion then looked at me like I was crazy. '*In there?* It's too narrow.'

'I'll cover you. Go!'

She ducked behind me and started squeezing between the two boulders. Then she yelped and grabbed my armour straps, and suddenly I was tumbling into a pit that hadn't been there a moment before. I could see the scorpions above us, the purple evening sky and the trees, and then the hole shut like the lens of a camera, and we were in complete darkness.

Our breathing echoed against stone. It was wet and cold. I was sitting on a bumpy floor that seemed to be made of bricks.

I lifted Riptide. The faint glow of the blade was just enough to illuminate Annabeth's frightened face and the mossy stone walls on either side of us.

'Wh-where are we?' Annabeth said.

'Safe from scorpions, anyway.' I tried to sound calm, but I was freaking out. The crack between the boulders couldn't have led into a cave. I would've known if there was a cave here; I was sure of it. It was like the ground had opened up and swallowed us. All I could think of was the fissure in the dining room pavilion, where those skeletons had been consumed last summer. I wondered if the same thing had happened to us.

I lifted my sword again for light.

'It's a long room,' I muttered.

Annabeth gripped my arm. 'It's not a room. It's a corridor.'

She was right. The darkness felt . . . emptier in front of us. There was a warm breeze, like in subway tunnels, only it felt older, more dangerous somehow.

I started forward, but Annabeth stopped me. 'Don't take another step,' she warned. 'We need to find the exit.'

She sounded really scared now.

'It's okay,' I promised. 'It's right –'

I looked up and realized I couldn't see where we'd fallen in. The ceiling was solid stone. The corridor seemed to stretch endlessly in both directions.

Annabeth's hand slipped into mine. Under different

circumstances I would've been embarrassed, but here in the dark I was glad to know where she was. It was about the only thing I was sure of.

'Two steps back,' she advised.

We stepped backwards together like we were in a minefield.

'Okay,' she said. 'Help me examine the walls.'

'What for?'

'The mark of Daedalus,' she said, as if that were supposed to make sense.

'Uh, okay. What kind of –'

'Got it!' she said with relief. She set her hand on the wall and pressed against a tiny fissure, which began to glow blue. A Greek symbol appeared: Δ, the Ancient Greek Delta.

The roof slid open and we saw night sky, stars blazing. It was a lot darker than it should've been. Metal ladder rungs appeared in the side of the wall, leading up, and I could hear people yelling our names.

'Percy! Annabeth!' Tyson's voice bellowed the loudest, but others were calling out, too.

I looked nervously at Annabeth. Then we began to climb.

We made our way around the rocks and ran into Clarisse and a bunch of other campers carrying torches.

'Where have you two been?' Clarisse demanded. 'We've been looking forever.'

'But we were only gone a few minutes,' I said.

Chiron trotted up, followed by Tyson and Grover.

'Percy!' Tyson said. 'You are okay?'

'We're fine,' I said. 'We fell in a hole.'

The others looked at me sceptically, then at Annabeth.

'Honest!' I said. 'There were three scorpions after us, so we ran and hid in the rocks. But we were only gone a minute.'

'You've been missing for almost an hour,' Chiron said. 'The game is over.'

'Yeah,' Grover muttered. 'We would've won, but a Cyclops sat on me.'

'Was an accident!' Tyson protested, and then he sneezed.

Clarisse was wearing the gold laurels, but she didn't even brag about winning them, which wasn't like her. 'A hole?' she said suspiciously.

Annabeth took a deep breath. She looked around at the other campers. 'Chiron . . . maybe we should talk about this at the Big House.'

Clarisse gasped. 'You found it, didn't you?'

Annabeth bit her lip. 'I – Yeah. Yeah, we did.'

A bunch of campers started asking questions, looking about as confused as I was, but Chiron raised his hand for silence. 'Tonight is not the right time, and this is not the right place.' He stared at the boulders as if he'd just noticed how dangerous they were. 'All of you, back to your cabins. Get some sleep. A game well played, but curfew is past!'

There was a lot of mumbling and complaints, but the campers drifted off, talking amongst themselves and giving me suspicious looks.

'This explains a lot,' Clarisse said. 'It explains what Luke is after.'

'Wait a second,' I said. 'What do you mean? What did we find?'

Annabeth turned towards me, her eyes dark with worry. 'An entrance to the Labyrinth. An invasion route straight into the heart of the camp.'

4 ANNABETH BREAKS THE RULES

Chiron had insisted we talk about it in the morning, which was kind of like, *Hey, your life's in mortal danger. Sleep tight!* It was hard to fall asleep, but when I finally did, I dreamed of a prison.

I saw a boy in a Greek tunic and sandals crouching alone in a massive stone room. The ceiling was open to the night sky, but the walls were seven metres high and polished marble, completely smooth. Scattered around the room were wooden crates. Some were cracked and tipped over, as if they'd been flung in there. Bronze tools spilled out of one —a compass, a saw and a bunch of other things I didn't recognize.

The boy huddled in the corner, shivering from cold, or maybe fear. He was spattered in mud. His legs, arms and face were scraped up as if he'd been dragged here along with the boxes.

Then the double oak doors moaned open. Two guards in bronze armour marched in, holding an old man between them. They flung him to the floor in a battered heap.

'Father!' The boy ran to him. The man's robes were in tatters. His hair was streaked with grey, and his beard was long and curly. His nose had been broken. His lips were bloody.

The boy took the old man's head in his arms. 'What

did they do to you?' Then he yelled at the guards, 'I'll kill you!'

'There will be no killing today,' a voice said.

The guards moved aside. Behind them stood a tall man in white robes. He wore a thin circlet of gold on his head. His beard was pointed like a spear blade. His eyes glittered cruelly. 'You helped the Athenian kill my Minotaur, Daedalus. You turned my own daughter against me.'

'You did that yourself, Your Majesty,' the old man croaked.

A guard planted a kick in the old man's ribs. He groaned in agony. The young boy cried, 'Stop it!'

'You love your maze so much,' the king said, 'I have decided to let you stay here. This will be your workshop. Make me new wonders. Amuse me. Every maze needs a monster. You shall be mine!'

'I don't fear you,' the old man groaned.

The king smiled coldly. He locked his eyes on the boy. 'But a man cares about his son, eh? Displease me, old man, and the next time my guards inflict a punishment, it will be on him!'

The king swept out of the room with his guards, and the doors slammed shut, leaving the boy and his father alone in the darkness.

'What will we do?' the boy moaned. 'Father, they will kill you!'

The old man swallowed with difficulty. He tried to smile, but it was a gruesome sight with his bloody mouth.

'Take heart, my son.' He gazed up at the stars. 'I – I will find a way.'

A bar lowered across the doors with a fatal BOOM, and I woke in a cold sweat.

I was still feeling shaky the next morning when Chiron called a war council. We met in the sword arena, which I thought was pretty strange – trying to discuss the fate of the camp while Mrs O'Leary chewed on a life-size squeaky pink rubber yak.

Chiron and Quintus stood at the front by the weapon racks. Clarisse and Annabeth sat next to each other and led the briefing. Tyson and Grover sat as far away from each other as possible. Also present around the table: Juniper the tree nymph, Silena Beauregard, Travis and Connor Stoll, Beckendorf, Lee Fletcher, even Argus, our hundred-eyed security chief. That's how I knew it was serious. Argus hardly ever shows up unless something really major is going on. The whole time Annabeth spoke, he kept his hundred blue eyes trained on her so hard, his whole body turned bloodshot.

'Luke must have known about the Labyrinth entrance,' Annabeth said. 'He knew everything about camp.'

I thought I heard a little pride in her voice, like she still respected the guy, as evil as he was.

Juniper cleared her throat. 'That's what I was trying to tell you last night. The cave entrance has been there a long time. Luke used to use it.'

Silena Beauregard frowned. 'You knew about the Labyrinth entrance, and you didn't say anything?'

Juniper's face turned green. 'I didn't know it was important. Just a cave. I don't like yucky old caves.'

'She has good taste,' Grover said.

'I wouldn't have paid any attention except . . . well, it was Luke.' She blushed a little greener.

Grover huffed. 'Forget what I said about good taste.'

'Interesting.' Quintus polished his sword as he spoke. 'And you believe this young man, Luke, would dare use the Labyrinth as an invasion route?'

'Definitely,' Clarisse said. 'If he could get an army of monsters inside Camp Half-Blood, just pop up in the middle of the woods without having to worry about our magical boundaries, we wouldn't stand a chance. He could wipe us out easy. He must've been planning this for months.'

'He's been sending scouts into the maze,' Annabeth said. 'We know because . . . because we found one.'

'Chris Rodriguez,' Chiron said. He gave Quintus a meaningful look.

'Ah,' Quintus said. 'The one in the . . . Yes. I understand.'

'The one in the what?' I asked.

Clarisse glared at me. 'The point is, Luke has been looking for a way to navigate the maze. He's searching for Daedalus's workshop.'

I remembered my dream the night before — the bloody old man in tattered robes. 'The guy who created the maze.'

'Yes,' Annabeth said. 'The greatest architect, the greatest inventor of all time. If the legends are true, his workshop is in the centre of the Labyrinth. He's the only one who knew how to navigate the maze perfectly. If Luke managed to find the workshop and convince Daedalus to help him, Luke wouldn't have to fumble around searching for paths, or risk losing his army in the maze's traps. He could navigate anywhere he wanted – quickly and safely. First to Camp Half-Blood to wipe us out. Then . . . to Olympus.'

The arena was silent except for Mrs O'Leary's toy yak getting disembowelled: *SQUEAK! SQUEAK!*

Finally Beckendorf put his huge hands on the table. 'Back up a sec. Annabeth, you said "convince Daedalus". Isn't Daedalus dead?'

Quintus grunted. 'I would hope so. He lived, what, three thousand years ago? And, even if he were alive, don't the old stories say he fled from the Labyrinth?'

Chiron clopped restlessly on his hooves. 'That's the problem, my dear Quintus. No one knows. There are rumours . . . well, there are *many* disturbing rumours about Daedalus, but one is that he disappeared back into the Labyrinth towards the end of his life. He might still be down there.'

I thought about the old man I'd seen in my dream. He'd looked so frail it was hard to believe he'd last another week, much less three thousand years.

'We need to go in,' Annabeth announced. 'We have to find the workshop before Luke does. If Daedalus is alive, we convince him to help us, not Luke. If Ariadne's string still exists, we make sure it never falls into Luke's hands.'

'Wait a second,' I said. 'If we're worried about an attack, why not just blow up the entrance? Seal the tunnel?'

'Great idea!' Grover said. 'I'll get the dynamite!'

'It's not so easy, stupid,' Clarisse growled. 'We tried that at the entrance we found in Phoenix. It didn't go well.'

Annabeth nodded. 'The Labyrinth is magical architecture,

Percy. It would take huge power to seal even one of its entrances. In Phoenix, Clarisse demolished a whole building with a wrecking ball, and the maze entrance just shifted a few metres. The best we can do is prevent Luke from learning to navigate the Labyrinth.'

'We could fight,' Lee Fletcher said. 'We know where the entrance is now. We can set up a defensive line and wait for them. If an army tries to come through, they'll find us waiting with our bows.'

'We will certainly set up defences,' Chiron agreed. 'But I fear Clarisse is right. The magical borders have kept this camp safe for hundreds of years. If Luke manages to get a large army of monsters into the centre of camp, bypassing our boundaries . . . we may not have the strength to defeat them.'

Nobody looked very happy about that news. Chiron usually tried to be upbeat and optimistic. If he was predicting we couldn't hold off an attack, that wasn't good.

'We have to get to Daedalus's workshop first,' Annabeth insisted. 'Find Ariadne's string and prevent Luke from using it.'

'But if nobody can navigate in there,' I said, 'what chance do we have?'

'I've been studying architecture for years,' she said. 'I know Daedalus's Labyrinth better than anybody.'

'From reading about it.'

'Well, yes.'

'That's not enough.'

'It has to be!'

'It isn't!'

'Are you going to help me or not?'

I realized everyone was watching Annabeth and me like a tennis match. Mrs O'Leary's squeaky yak went *EEK!* as she ripped off its pink rubber head.

Chiron cleared his throat. 'First things first. We need a quest. Someone must enter the Labyrinth, find the workshop of Daedalus and prevent Luke from using the maze to invade this camp.'

'We all know who should lead this,' Clarisse said. 'Annabeth.'

There was a murmur of agreement. I knew Annabeth had been waiting for her own quest since she was a little kid, but she looked uncomfortable.

'You've done as much as I have, Clarisse,' she said. 'You should go, too.'

Clarisse shook her head. 'I'm not going back in there.'

Travis Stoll laughed. 'Don't tell me you're scared. Clarisse, chicken?'

Clarisse got to her feet. I thought she was going to pulverize Travis, but she said in a shaky voice: 'You don't understand anything, punk. I'm never going in there again. Never!'

She stormed out of the arena.

Travis looked around sheepishly. 'I didn't mean to —'

Chiron raised his hand. 'The poor girl has had a difficult year. Now, do we have agreement that Annabeth should lead the quest?'

We all nodded except Quintus. He folded his arms and stared at the table, but I wasn't sure anyone else noticed.

'Very well.' Chiron turned to Annabeth. 'My dear, it's

your time to visit the Oracle. Assuming you return to us in one piece, we shall discuss what to do next.'

Waiting for Annabeth was harder than visiting the Oracle myself.

I'd heard it speak prophecies twice before. The first time had been in the dusty attic of the Big House, where the spirit of Delphi slept inside the body of a mummified hippie lady. The second time, the Oracle had come out for a little stroll in the woods. I still had nightmares about that.

I'd never felt threatened by the Oracle's presence, but I'd heard stories: campers who'd gone insane, or who'd seen visions so real they died of fear.

I paced the arena, waiting. Mrs O'Leary ate her lunch, which consisted of fifty kilograms of ground beef and several dog biscuits the size of trashcan lids. I wondered where Quintus got dog biscuits that size. I didn't think you could just walk into Pet Zone and put those in your shopping cart.

Chiron was deep in conversation with Quintus and Argus. It looked to me like they were disagreeing about something. Quintus kept shaking his head.

On the other side of the arena, Tyson and the Stoll brothers were racing miniature bronze chariots that Tyson had made out of armour scraps.

I gave up on pacing and left the arena. I stared across the fields at the Big House's attic window, dark and motionless. What was taking Annabeth so long? I was pretty sure it hadn't taken me this long to get my quest.

'Percy,' a girl whispered.

Juniper was standing in the bushes. It was weird how she almost turned invisible when she was surrounded by plants.

She gestured me over urgently. 'You need to know: Luke wasn't the only one I saw around that cave.'

'What do you mean?'

She glanced back at the arena. 'I was trying to say something, but he was right there.'

'Who?'

'The sword master,' she said. 'He was poking around the rocks.'

My stomach clenched. 'Quintus? When?'

'I don't know. I don't pay attention to time. Maybe a week ago, when he first showed up.'

'What was he doing? Did he go in?'

'I – I'm not sure. He's creepy, Percy. I didn't even see him come into the glade. Suddenly he was just *there*. You have to tell Grover it's too dangerous –'

'Juniper?' Grover called from inside the arena. 'Where'd you go?'

Juniper sighed. 'I'd better go in. Just remember what I said. Don't trust that man!'

She ran into the arena.

I stared at the Big House, feeling more uneasy than ever. If Quintus was up to something . . . I needed Annabeth's advice. She might know what to make of Juniper's news. But where the heck was she? Whatever was happening with the Oracle, it shouldn't be taking this long.

Finally I couldn't stand it any more.

It was against the rules, but then again nobody was

watching. I ran down the hill and headed across the fields.

The front parlour of the Big House was strangely quiet. I was used to seeing Dionysus by the fireplace, playing cards and eating grapes and griping at satyrs, but Mr D was still away.

I walked down the hallway, floorboards creaking under my feet. When I got to the base of the stairs, I hesitated. Four floors above would be a little trapdoor leading to the attic. Annabeth would be up there somewhere. I stood quietly and listened. But what I heard wasn't what I had expected.

Sobbing. And it was coming from below me.

I crept around the back of the stairs. The basement door was open. I didn't even know the Big House *had* a basement. I peered inside and saw two figures in the far corner, sitting amid a bunch of stockpiled cases of ambrosia and strawberry preserves. One was Clarisse. The other was a teenage Hispanic guy in tattered camouflage combats and a dirty black T-shirt. His hair was greasy and matted. He was hugging his shoulders and sobbing. It was Chris Rodriguez, the half-blood who'd gone to work for Luke.

'It's okay,' Clarisse was telling him. 'Try a little more nectar.'

'You're an illusion, Mary!' Chris backed further into the corner. 'G-get away.'

'My name's not Mary.' Clarisse's voice was gentle but really sad. I never knew Clarisse could sound that way. 'My name is Clarisse. Remember. Please.'

'It's dark!' Chris yelled. 'So dark!'

'Come outside,' Clarisse coaxed. 'The sunlight will help you.'

'A . . . a thousand skulls. The earth keeps healing him.'

'Chris,' Clarisse pleaded. It sounded like she was close to tears. 'You have to get better. Please. Mr D will be back soon. He's an expert in madness. Just hang on.'

Chris's eyes were like a cornered rat's – wild and desperate. 'There's no way out, Mary. No way out.'

Then he caught a glimpse of me and made a strangled, terrified sound. 'The son of Poseidon! He's horrible!'

I backed away, hoping Clarisse hadn't seen me. I listened for her to come charging out and yell at me, but instead she just kept talking to Chris in a sad pleading voice, trying to get him to drink the nectar. Maybe she thought it was part of Chris's hallucination, but . . . *son of Poseidon?* Chris had been looking at me, and yet why did I get the feeling he hadn't been talking about me at all?

And Clarisse's tenderness – it had never even occurred to me that she might like someone, but the way she said Chris's name . . . She'd known him before he changed sides. She'd known him a lot better than I realized. And now he was shivering in a dark basement, afraid to come out, and mumbling about someone named Mary. No wonder Clarisse didn't want anything to do with the Labyrinth. What had happened to Chris in there?

I heard a creak from above – like the trapdoor opening – and I ran for the front door. I needed to get out of that house.

✵   ✵   ✵

'My dear,' Chiron said. 'You made it.'

Annabeth walked into the arena. She sat on a stone bench and stared at the floor.

'Well?' Quintus asked.

Annabeth looked at me first. I couldn't tell if she was trying to warn me, or if the look in her eyes was just plain fear. Then she focused on Quintus. 'I got the prophecy. I will lead the quest to find Daedalus's workshop.'

Nobody cheered. I mean, we all liked Annabeth, and we wanted her to have a quest, but this one seemed insanely dangerous. After what I'd seen of Chris Rodriguez, I didn't even want to think about Annabeth descending into that weird maze again.

Chiron scraped a hoof on the dirt floor. 'What did the prophecy say exactly, my dear? The wording is important.'

Annabeth took a deep breath. 'I, ah . . . well, it said, *You shall delve in the darkness of the endless maze . . .*'

We waited.

'*The dead, the traitor and the lost one raise.*'

Grover perked up. 'The lost one! That must mean Pan! That's great!'

'With the dead and the traitor,' I added. 'Not so great.'

'And?' Chiron asked. 'What is the rest?'

'*You shall rise or fall by the ghost king's hand,*' Annabeth said, '*the child of Athena's final stand.*'

Everyone looked around uncomfortably. Annabeth was a daughter of Athena, and a final stand didn't sound good.

'Hey . . . we shouldn't jump to conclusions,' Silena said. 'Annabeth isn't the only child of Athena, right?'

'But who's this ghost king?' Beckendorf asked.

No one answered. I thought about the Iris-message I'd seen of Nico summoning spirits. I had a bad feeling the prophecy was connected to that.

'Are there more lines?' Chiron asked. 'The prophecy does not sound complete.'

Annabeth hesitated. 'I don't remember exactly.'

Chiron raised an eyebrow. Annabeth was known for her memory. She never forgot something she had heard.

Annabeth shifted on her bench. 'Something about . . . *Destroy with a hero's final breath.*'

'And?' Chiron asked.

She stood. 'Look, the point is, I have to go in. I'll find the workshop and stop Luke. And . . . I need help.' She turned to me. 'Will you come?'

I didn't even hesitate. 'I'm in.'

She smiled for the first time in days, and that made it all worthwhile. 'Grover, you too? The wild god is waiting.'

Grover seemed to forget how much he hated the underground. The line about the 'lost one' had completely energized him. 'I'll pack extra recyclables for snacks!'

'And Tyson,' Annabeth said. 'I'll need you, too.'

'Yay! Blow-things-up time!' Tyson clapped so hard he woke up Mrs O'Leary, who was dozing in the corner.

'Wait, Annabeth,' Chiron said. 'This goes against the ancient laws. A hero is allowed only two companions.'

'I need them all,' she insisted. 'Chiron, it's important.'

I didn't know why she was so certain, but I was happy she'd included Tyson. I couldn't imagine leaving him behind. He was huge and strong and great at figuring out mechanical things. Unlike satyrs, Cyclopes had no problem underground.

'Annabeth.' Chiron flicked his tail nervously. 'Consider well. You would be breaking the ancient laws, and there are always consequences. Last winter, five went on a quest to save Artemis. Only three came back. Think on that. Three is a sacred number. There are three Fates, three Furies, three Olympian sons of Kronos. It is a good strong number that stands against many dangers. Four . . . this is risky.'

Annabeth took a deep breath. 'I know. But we have to. Please.'

I could tell Chiron didn't like it. Quintus was studying us, like he was trying to decide which of us would come back alive.

Chiron sighed. 'Very well. Let us adjourn. The members of the quest must prepare themselves. Tomorrow at dawn, we send you into the Labyrinth.'

Quintus pulled me aside as the council was breaking up.

'I have a bad feeling about this,' he told me.

Mrs O'Leary came over, wagging her tail happily. She dropped her shield at my feet, and I threw it for her. Quintus watched her romp after it. I remembered what Juniper had said about him scouting out the maze. I didn't trust him, but when he looked at me, I saw real concern in his eyes.

'I don't like the idea of you going down there,' he said. 'Any of you. But if you must, I want you to remember something. The Labyrinth exists to fool you. It will distract you. That's dangerous for half-bloods. We are easily distracted.'

'You've been in there?'

'Long ago.' His voice was ragged. 'I barely escaped with my life. Most who enter aren't that lucky.'

He gripped my shoulder. 'Percy, keep your mind on what matters most. If you can do that, you might find the way. And, here, I wanted to give you something.'

He handed me a little silver tube. It was so cold I almost dropped it.

'A whistle?' I asked.

'A dog whistle,' Quintus said. 'For Mrs O'Leary.'

'Um, thanks, but —'

'How will it work in the maze? I'm not a hundred percent certain it will. But Mrs O'Leary is a hellhound. She can appear when called, no matter how far away she is. I'd feel better knowing you had this. If you really need help, use it, but be careful: the whistle is made of Stygian ice.'

'*What* ice?'

'From the River Styx. Very hard to craft. Very delicate. It cannot melt, but it will shatter when you blow it, so you can only use it once.'

I thought about Luke, my old enemy. Right before I'd gone on my first quest, Luke had given me a gift, too — magic shoes that had been designed to drag me to my death. Quintus seemed so nice. So concerned. And Mrs O'Leary liked him, which had to count for something. She dropped the slimy shield at my feet and barked excitedly.

I felt ashamed that I could even think about mistrusting Quintus. But, then again, I'd trusted Luke once.

'Thanks,' I told Quintus. I slipped the freezing whistle into my pocket, promising myself that I would never use it, and I dashed off to find Annabeth.

As long as I'd been at camp, I'd never been inside the Athena cabin.

It was a silvery building, nothing fancy, with plain white curtains and a carved stone owl over the doorway. The owl's onyx eyes seemed to follow me as I walked closer.

'Hello?' I called inside.

Nobody answered. I stepped in and caught my breath. The place was a workshop for brainiac kids. The bunks were all pushed against one wall as if sleeping didn't matter very much. Most of the room was filled with workbenches and tables and sets of tools and weapons. The back of the room was a huge library, crammed with old scrolls and leather-bound books and paperbacks. There was an architect's draughting table with a bunch of rulers and protractors, and some 3-D models of buildings. Huge old war maps were plastered to the ceiling. Sets of armour hung under the windows, their bronze plates glinting in the sun.

Annabeth stood in the back of the room, rifling through old scrolls.

'Knock, knock?' I said.

She turned with a start. 'Oh . . . hi. Didn't hear you.'

'You okay?'

She frowned at the scroll in her hands. 'Just trying to do some research. Daedalus's Labyrinth is so huge. None of the stories agree about anything. The maps just lead from nowhere to nowhere.'

I thought about what Quintus had said, how the maze tries to distract you. I wondered if Annabeth knew that already.

'We'll figure it out,' I promised.

Her hair had come loose and was hanging in a tangled blonde curtain all around her face. Her grey eyes looked almost black.

'I've wanted to lead a quest since I was seven,' she said.

'You're going to be awesome.'

She looked at me gratefully, but then stared down at all the books and scrolls she'd pulled from the shelves. 'I'm worried, Percy. Maybe I shouldn't have asked you to do this. Or Tyson and Grover.'

'Hey, we're your friends. We wouldn't miss it.'

'But . . .' She stopped herself.

'What is it?' I asked. 'The prophecy?'

'I'm sure it's fine,' she said in a small voice.

'What was the last line?'

Then she did something that really surprised me. She blinked back tears and put out her arms.

I stepped forward and hugged her. Butterflies started turning my stomach into a mosh pit.

'Hey, it's . . . it's okay.' I patted her back.

I was aware of everything in the room. I felt like I could read the tiniest print on any book on the shelves. Annabeth's hair smelled like lemon soap. She was shivering.

'Chiron might be right,' she muttered. 'I'm breaking the rules. But I don't know what else to do. I need you three. It just feels right.'

'Then don't worry about it,' I managed. 'We've had plenty of problems before, and we solved them.'

'This is different. I don't want anything happening to . . . any of you.'

Behind me, somebody cleared his throat.

It was one of Annabeth's half-brothers, Malcolm. His face was bright red. 'Um, sorry,' he said. 'Archery practice is starting, Annabeth. Chiron said to come find you.'

I stepped away from Annabeth. 'We were just looking at maps,' I said stupidly.

Malcolm stared at me. 'Okay.'

'Tell Chiron I'll be right there,' Annabeth said, and Malcolm left in a hurry.

Annabeth rubbed her eyes. 'You go ahead, Percy. I'd better get ready for archery.'

I nodded, feeling more confused than I ever had in my life. I wanted to run from the cabin . . . but then again I didn't.

'Annabeth?' I said. 'About your prophecy. The line about a hero's last breath –'

'You're wondering which hero? I don't know.'

'No. Something else. I was thinking the last line usually rhymes with the one before it. Was it something about – did it end in the word *death?*'

Annabeth stared down at her scrolls. 'You'd better go, Percy. Get ready for the quest. I'll – I'll see you in the morning.'

I left her there, staring at maps that led from nowhere to nowhere, but I couldn't shake the feeling that one of us wasn't going to come back from this quest alive.

5 NICO BUYS HAPPY MEALS
     FOR THE DEAD

At least I got a good night's sleep before the quest, right?
Wrong.

That night in my dreams, I was in the stateroom of
the *Princess Andromeda*. The windows were open on a moonlit
sea. Cold wind rustled the velvet drapes.

Luke knelt on a Persian rug in front of the golden
sarcophagus of Kronos. In the moonlight, Luke's blond
hair looked pure white. He wore an Ancient Greek *chiton*
and a white *himation*, a kind of cape that flowed down his
shoulders. The white clothes made him look timeless and
a little unreal, like one of the minor gods on Mount
Olympus. The last time I'd seen him, he'd been broken and
unconscious after a nasty fall from Mount Tam. Now he
looked perfectly fine. Almost *too* healthy.

'Our spies report success, my lord,' he said. 'Camp
Half-Blood is sending a quest, as you predicted. Our side
of the bargain is almost complete.'

Excellent. The voice of Kronos didn't so much speak as
pierce my mind like a dagger. It was freezing with cruelty.
*Once we have the means to navigate, I will lead the vanguard through
myself.*

Luke closed his eyes as if collecting his thoughts. 'My
lord, perhaps it is too soon. Perhaps Krios or Hyperion
should lead –'

No. The voice was quiet but absolutely firm. *I will lead. One more heart shall join our cause, and that will be sufficient. At last, I shall rise fully from Tartarus.*

'But the form, my lord . . .' Luke's voice started shaking.

Show me your sword, Luke Castellan.

A jolt went through me. I realized I'd never heard Luke's last name before. It had never even occurred to me.

Luke drew his sword. Backbiter's double edge glowed wickedly – half steel, half celestial bronze. I'd almost been killed several times by that sword. It was an evil weapon, able to kill both mortals and monsters. It was the only blade I really feared.

You pledged yourself to me, Kronos reminded him. *You took this sword as proof of your oath.*

'Yes, my lord. It's just –'

You wanted power. I gave you that. You are now beyond harm. Soon you will rule the world of gods and mortals. Do you not wish to avenge yourself? To see Olympus destroyed?

A shiver ran through Luke's body. 'Yes.'

The coffin glowed, golden light filling the room. *Then make ready the strike force. As soon as the bargain is done, we shall move forward. First, Camp Half-Blood will be reduced to ashes. Once those bothersome heroes are eliminated, we will march on Olympus.*

There was a knock on the stateroom doors. The light of the coffin faded. Luke rose. He sheathed his sword, adjusted his white clothes, and took a deep breath.

'Come in.'

The doors opened. Two *dracaenae* slithered in – snake women with double serpent trunks instead of legs. Between them walked Kelli, the *empousa* cheerleader from my freshman orientation.

'Hello, Luke.' Kelli smiled. She was wearing a red dress and she looked awesome, but I'd seen her real form. I knew what she was hiding: mismatched legs, red eyes, fangs and flaming hair.

'What is it, demon?' Luke's voice was cold. 'I told you not to disturb me.'

Kelli pouted. 'That's not very nice. You look tense. How about a nice shoulder massage?'

Luke stepped back. 'If you have something to report, say it. Otherwise leave!'

'I don't know why you're so huffy these days. You *used* to be fun to hang out with.'

'That was before I saw what you did to that boy in Seattle.'

'Oh, he meant nothing to me,' Kelli said. 'Just a snack, really. You know my heart belongs to you, Luke.'

'Thanks, but no thanks. Now report or get out.'

Kelli shrugged. 'Fine. The advance team is ready, as you requested. We can leave –' She frowned.

'What is it?' Luke asked.

'A presence,' Kelli said. 'Your senses are getting dull, Luke. We're being watched.'

She scanned the stateroom. Her eyes focused right on me. Her face withered into a hag's. She bared her fangs and lunged.

I woke with a start, my heart pounding. I could've sworn the *empousa's* fangs were an inch from my throat.

Tyson was snoring in the next bunk. The sound calmed me down a little.

I didn't know how Kelli could sense me in a dream, but I'd heard more than I wanted to know. An army was ready. Kronos would lead it personally. All they needed was a way to navigate the Labyrinth so they could invade and destroy Camp Half-Blood, and Luke apparently thought that was going to happen very soon.

I was tempted to go and wake up Annabeth and tell her, middle of the night or not. Then I realized the room was lighter than it should have been. A blue-and-green glow was coming from the saltwater fountain, brighter and more urgent than the night before. It was almost like the water was humming.

I got out of bed and approached.

No voice spoke out of the water asking for a deposit this time. I got the feeling the fountain was waiting for me to make the first move.

I probably should've gone back to bed. Instead I thought about what I'd seen last night – the weird image of Nico at the banks of the River Styx.

'You're trying to tell me something,' I said.

No response from the fountain.

'All right,' I said. 'Show me Nico di Angelo.'

I didn't even throw a coin in, but this time it didn't matter. It was like some other force had control of the water besides Iris the messenger goddess. The water shimmered. Nico appeared, but he was no longer in the Underworld. He was standing in a graveyard under a starry sky. Giant willow trees loomed all around him.

He was watching some gravediggers at work. I heard shovels and saw dirt flying out of a hole. Nico was dressed in a black cloak. The night was foggy. It was warm and humid and frogs were croaking. A large Wal-Mart bag sat next to Nico's feet.

'Is it deep enough yet?' Nico asked. He sounded irritated.

'Nearly, my lord.' It was the same ghost I'd seen Nico with before, the faint shimmering image of a man. 'But, my lord, I tell you, this is unnecessary. You already have me for advice.'

'I want a second opinion!' Nico snapped his fingers, and the digging stopped. Two figures climbed out of the hole. They weren't people. They were skeletons in ragged clothes.

'You are dismissed,' Nico said. 'Thank you.'

The skeletons collapsed into piles of bones.

'You might as well thank the shovels,' the ghost complained. 'They have as much sense.'

Nico ignored him. He reached into his Wal-Mart bag and pulled out a twelve-pack of Coke. He popped open a can. Instead of drinking it, he poured it into the grave.

'Let the dead taste again,' he murmured. 'Let them rise and take this offering. Let them remember.'

He dropped the rest of the Cokes into the grave and pulled out a white paper bag decorated with cartoons. I hadn't seen one in years, but I recognized it – a McDonald's Happy Meal.

He turned it upside down and shook the fries and hamburger into the grave.

'In my day, we used animal blood,' the ghost mumbled. 'It's perfectly good enough. They can't taste the difference.'

'I will treat them with respect,' Nico said.

'At least let me keep the toy,' the ghost said.

'Be quiet!' Nico ordered. He emptied another twelve-pack of soda and three more Happy Meals into the grave, then began chanting in Ancient Greek. I only caught some of the words — a lot about the dead and memories and returning from the grave. Real happy stuff.

The grave started to bubble. Frothy brown liquid rose to the top like the whole thing was filling with soda. The fog thickened. The frogs stopped croaking. Dozens of figures began to appear among the gravestones: bluish, vaguely human shapes. Nico had summoned the dead with Coke and cheeseburgers.

'There are too many,' the ghost said nervously. 'You don't know your own powers.'

'I've got it under control,' Nico said, though his voice sounded fragile. He drew his sword — a short blade made of solid black metal. I'd never seen anything like it. It wasn't celestial bronze or steel. Iron, maybe? The crowd of shades retreated at the sight of it.

'One at a time,' Nico commanded.

A single figure floated forward and knelt at the pool. It made slurping sounds as it drank. Its ghostly hands scooped french fries out of the pool. When it stood again, I could see it much more clearly — a teenage guy in Greek armour. He had curly hair and green eyes, a clasp shaped like a seashell on his cloak.

'Who are you?' Nico said. 'Speak.'

The young man frowned as if trying to remember. Then he spoke in a voice like dry, crumpling paper: 'I am Theseus.'

No way, I thought. This couldn't be *the* Theseus. He was just a kid. I'd grown up hearing stories about him fighting the Minotaur and stuff, but I'd always pictured him as this huge, buff guy. The ghost I was looking at wasn't strong or tall. And he wasn't any older than I was.

'How can I retrieve my sister?' Nico asked.

Theseus's eyes were lifeless as glass. 'Do not try. It is madness.'

'Just tell me!'

'My stepfather died,' Theseus remembered. 'He threw himself into the sea because he thought I was dead in the Labyrinth. I wanted to bring him back, but I could not.'

Nico's ghost hissed, 'My lord, the soul exchange! Ask him about that!'

Theseus scowled. 'That voice. I know that voice.'

'No you don't, fool!' the ghost said. 'Answer the lord's questions and nothing more!'

'I know you,' Theseus insisted, as if struggling to recall.

'I want to hear about my sister,' Nico said. 'Will this quest into the Labyrinth help me win her back?'

Theseus was looking for the ghost, but apparently couldn't see him. Slowly he turned his eyes back on Nico. 'The Labyrinth is treacherous. There is only one thing that saw me through: the love of a mortal girl. The string was only part of the answer. It was the princess who guided me.'

'We don't need any of that,' the ghost said. 'I will guide you, my lord. Ask him if it is true about an exchange of souls. He will tell you.'

'A soul for a soul,' Nico asked. 'Is it true?'

'I – I must say yes. But the spectre –'

'Just answer the questions, knave!' the ghost said.

Suddenly, around the edges of the pool, the other ghosts became restless. They stirred, whispering in nervous tones.

'I want to see my sister!' Nico demanded. 'Where is she?'

'He is coming,' Theseus said fearfully. 'He has sensed your summons. He comes.'

'Who?' Nico demanded.

'He comes to find the source of this power,' Theseus said. 'You must release us!'

The water in my fountain began to tremble, humming with power. I realized the whole cabin was shaking. The noise grew louder. The image of Nico in the graveyard started to glow until it was painful to watch.

'Stop,' I said out loud. 'Stop it!'

The fountain began to crack. Tyson muttered in his sleep and turned over. Purple light threw horrible, ghostly shadows on the cabin walls, as if the spectres were escaping right out of the fountain.

In desperation I uncapped Riptide and slashed at the fountain, cleaving it in two. Salt water spilled everywhere, and the great stone font crashed to the floor in pieces. Tyson snorted and muttered, but he kept sleeping.

I sank to the ground, shivering from what I'd seen. Tyson found me there in the morning, still staring at the shattered remains of the saltwater fountain.

Just after dawn, the quest group met at Zeus's Fist. I'd packed my backpack – Thermos with nectar, bag of ambrosia, bedroll, rope, clothes, flashlights and lots of extra batteries. I had Riptide in my pocket. The magic shield/ wristwatch Tyson had made for me was on my wrist.

It was a clear morning. The fog had burned off and the sky was blue. Campers would be having their lessons today, flying pegasi and practising archery and scaling the lava wall. Meanwhile, we would be heading underground.

Juniper and Grover stood apart from the group. Juniper had been crying again, but she was trying to keep it together for Grover's sake. She kept fussing with his clothes, straightening his Rasta cap and brushing goat fur off his shirt. Since we had no idea what we would encounter, he was dressed as a human, with the cap to hide his horns, and jeans, fake feet and trainers to hide his goat legs.

Chiron, Quintus and Mrs O'Leary stood with the other campers who'd come to wish us well, but there was too much activity for it to feel like a happy send-off. A couple of tents had been set up by the rocks for guard duty. Beckendorf and his siblings were working on a line of defensive spikes and trenches. Chiron had decided we needed to guard the Labyrinth exit at all times, just in case.

Annabeth was doing one last check on her supply pack. When Tyson and I came over, she frowned. 'Percy, you look terrible.'

'He killed the water fountain last night,' Tyson confided.

'What?' she asked.

Before I could explain, Chiron trotted over. 'Well, it appears you are ready!'

He tried to sound upbeat, but I could tell he was anxious. I didn't want to freak him out any more, but I thought about last night's dream, and before I could change my mind, I said, 'Hey, uh, Chiron, can I ask you a favour while I'm gone?'

'Of course, my boy.'

'Be right back, guys.' I nodded towards the woods. Chiron raised an eyebrow, but he followed me out of earshot.

'Last night,' I said, 'I dreamed about Luke and Kronos.' I told him the details. The news seemed to weigh on his shoulders.

'I feared this,' Chiron said. 'Against my father, Kronos, we would stand no chance in a fight.'

Chiron rarely called Kronos his father. I mean, we all knew it was true. Everybody in the Greek world – god, monster or Titan – was related to one other somehow. But it wasn't exactly something Chiron liked to brag about. *Oh, my dad is the all-powerful evil Titan lord who wants to destroy Western Civilization. I want to be just like him when I grow up!*

'Do you know what he meant about a bargain?' I asked.

'I am not sure, but I fear they seek to make a deal with Daedalus. If the old inventor is truly alive, if he has not been driven insane by millennia in the Labyrinth . . . well, Kronos can find ways to twist anyone to his will.'

'Not anyone,' I promised.

Chiron managed a smile. 'No. Perhaps not anyone. But, Percy, you must beware. I have worried for some time that Kronos may be looking for Daedalus for a different reason, not just passage through the maze.'

'What else would he want?'

'Something Annabeth and I were discussing. Do you remember what you told me about your first trip to the

Princess Andromeda, the first time you saw the golden coffin?'

I nodded. 'Luke was talking about raising Kronos, little pieces of him appearing in the coffin every time someone new joined his cause.'

'And what did Luke say they would do when Kronos had risen completely?'

A chill went down my spine. 'He said they would make Kronos a new body, worthy of the forges of Hephaestus.'

'Indeed,' Chiron said. 'Daedalus was the world's greatest inventor. He created the Labyrinth, but much more. Automatons, thinking machines . . . What if Kronos wishes Daedalus to make him a new form?'

That was a really pleasant thought.

'We've got to get to Daedalus first,' I said, 'and convince him not to.'

Chiron stared off into the trees. 'One other thing I do not understand . . . this talk of a last soul joining their cause. That does not bode well.'

I kept my mouth shut, but I felt guilty. I'd made the decision not to tell Chiron about Nico being a son of Hades. The mention of souls, though – What if Kronos knew about Nico? What if he managed to turn him evil? It was almost enough to make me want to tell Chiron, but I didn't. For one thing, I wasn't sure Chiron could do anything about it. I had to find Nico myself. I had to explain things to him, make him listen.

'I don't know,' I said at last. 'But, uh, something Juniper said, maybe you should hear.' I told him how the tree nymph had seen Quintus poking around the rocks.

Chiron's jaw tightened. 'That does not surprise me.'

'It doesn't sur— you mean you knew?'

'Percy, when Quintus showed up at camp, offering his services . . . well, I would have to be a fool not to be suspicious.'

'Then why did you let him in?'

'Because sometimes it is better to have someone you mistrust close to you, so that you can keep an eye on him. He may be just what he says: a half-blood in search of a home. Certainly he has done nothing openly that would make me question his loyalty. But, believe me, I will keep an eye —'

Annabeth trudged over, probably curious about why we were taking so long.

'Percy, you ready?'

I nodded. My hand slipped into my pocket, where I kept the ice whistle Quintus had given me. I looked over and saw Quintus watching me carefully. He raised his hand in farewell.

Our spies report success, Luke had said. The same day we decided to send a quest, Luke had known about it.

'Take care,' Chiron told us. 'And good hunting.'

'You, too,' I said.

We walked over to the rocks, where Tyson and Grover were waiting. I stared at the crack between the boulders — the entrance that was about to swallow us.

'Well,' Grover said nervously, 'goodbye, sunshine.'

'Hello, rocks,' Tyson agreed.

And, together, the four of us descended into darkness.

6 WE MEET THE GOD WITH TWO FACES

We made it thirty metres before we were hopelessly lost.

The tunnel looked nothing like the one Annabeth and I had stumbled into before. Now it was round like a sewer, constructed of red brick with iron-barred portholes every three metres. I shone a light through one of the portholes out of curiosity, but I couldn't see anything. It opened into infinite darkness. I thought I heard voices on the other side, but it may have been just the cold wind.

Annabeth tried her best to guide us. She had this idea that we should stick to the left wall.

'If we keep one hand on the left wall and follow it,' she said, 'we should be able to find our way out again by reversing course.'

Unfortunately, as soon as she said that, the left wall disappeared. We found ourselves in the middle of a circular chamber with eight tunnels leading out, and no idea how we'd got there.

'Um, which way did we come in?' Grover said nervously.

'Just turn around,' Annabeth said.

We each turned towards a different tunnel. It was ridiculous. None of us could decide which way led back to camp.

'Left walls are mean,' Tyson said. 'Which way now?'

Annabeth swept her flashlight beam over the archways of the eight tunnels. As far as I could tell, they were identical. 'That way,' she said.

'How do you know?' I asked.

'Deductive reasoning.'

'So . . . you're guessing.'

'Just come on,' she said.

The tunnel she'd chosen narrowed quickly. The walls turned to grey cement, and the ceiling got so low that pretty soon we were hunching over. Tyson was forced to crawl.

Grover's hyperventilating was the loudest noise in the maze. 'I can't stand it any more,' he whispered. 'Are we there yet?'

'We've been down here maybe five minutes,' Annabeth told him.

'It's been longer than that,' Grover insisted. 'And why would Pan be down here? This is the opposite of the wild!'

We kept shuffling forward. Just when I was sure the tunnel would get so narrow it would squish us, it opened into a huge room. I shone my light around the walls and said, 'Whoa.'

The whole room was covered in mosaic tiles. The pictures were grimy and faded, but I could still make out the colours – red, blue, green, gold. The frieze showed the Olympian gods at a feast. There was my dad, Poseidon, with his trident, holding out grapes for Dionysus to turn into wine. Zeus was partying with satyrs, and Hermes was flying through the air on his winged sandals. The pictures were beautiful, but they weren't very accurate. I'd seen the gods. Dionysus was not that handsome, and Hermes's nose wasn't that big.

In the middle of the room was a three-tiered fountain. It looked like it hadn't held water in a long time.

'What is this place?' I muttered. 'It looks —'

'Roman,' Annabeth said. 'Those mosaics are about two thousand years old.'

'But how can they be Roman?' I wasn't that great on ancient history, but I was pretty sure the Roman Empire never made it as far as Long Island.

'The Labyrinth is a patchwork,' Annabeth said. 'I told you, it's always expanding, adding pieces. It's the only work of architecture that grows by itself.'

'You make it sound like it's alive.'

A groaning noise echoed from the tunnel in front of us.

'Let's not talk about it being alive,' Grover whimpered. 'Please?'

'All right,' Annabeth said. 'Forward.'

'Down the hall with the bad sounds?' Tyson said. Even he looked nervous.

'Yeah,' Annabeth said. 'The architecture is getting older. That's a good sign. Daedalus's workshop would be in the oldest part.'

That made sense. But soon the maze was toying with us — we went fifteen metres and the tunnel turned back to cement, with brass pipes running down the sides. The walls were spray-painted with graffiti. A neon tag sign read: MOZ RULZ.

'I'm thinking this is not Roman,' I said helpfully.

Annabeth took a deep breath, then forged ahead.

Every few metres the tunnels twisted and turned and branched off. The floor beneath us changed from cement to mud to bricks and back again. There was no sense to any of it. We stumbled into a wine cellar – a bunch of dusty bottles in wooden racks – like we were walking through somebody's basement, only there was no exit ahead of us, just more tunnels leading on.

Later the ceiling turned to wooden planks, and I could hear voices above us and the creaking of footsteps, as if we were walking under some kind of bar. It was reassuring to hear people, but then again we couldn't get to them. We were stuck down here with no way out. Then we found our first skeleton.

He was dressed in white clothes, like some kind of uniform. A wooden crate of glass bottles sat next to him.

'A milkman,' Annabeth said.

'What?' I asked.

'They used to deliver milk.'

'Yeah, I know what they are, but . . . that was when my mom was little, like a million years ago. What's he doing here?'

'Some people wander in by mistake,' Annabeth said. 'Some come exploring on purpose and never make it back. A long time ago, the Cretans even sent people in here as human sacrifices.'

Grover gulped. 'He's been down here a long time.' He pointed to the skeleton's bottles, which were coated with white dust. The skeleton's fingers were clawing at the brick wall, like he had died trying to get out.

'Only bones,' Tyson said. 'Don't worry, goat boy. The milkman is dead.'

'The milkman doesn't bother me,' Grover said. 'It's the smell. Monsters. Can't you smell it?'

Tyson nodded. 'Lots of monsters. But underground smells like that. Monsters and dead milk people.'

'Oh, good,' Grover whimpered. 'I thought maybe I was wrong.'

'We have to get deeper into the maze,' Annabeth said. 'There has to be a way to the centre.'

She led us to the right, then the left, through a corridor of stainless steel like some kind of air shaft, and we arrived back in the Roman tile room with the fountain.

This time, we weren't alone.

What I noticed first were his faces. Both of them. They jutted out from either side of his head, staring over his shoulders, so his head was much wider than it should've been, kind of like a hammerhead shark's. Looking straight at him, all I saw were two overlapping ears and mirror-image sideburns.

He was dressed like a New York City doorman: a long black overcoat, shiny shoes and a black top hat that somehow managed to stay on his double-wide head.

'Well, Annabeth?' said his left face. 'Hurry up!'

'Don't mind him,' said the right face. 'He's terribly rude. Right this way, miss.'

Annabeth's jaw dropped. 'Uh . . . I don't . . .'

Tyson frowned. 'That funny man has two faces.'

'The funny man has ears, you know!' the left face scolded. 'Now come along, miss.'

'No, no,' the right face said. 'This way, miss. Talk to *me*, please.'

The two-faced man regarded Annabeth as best he could out of the corners of his eyes. It was impossible to look at him straight on without focusing on one side or the other. And suddenly I realized that's what he was asking – he wanted Annabeth to choose.

Behind him were two exits, blocked by wooden doors with huge iron locks. They hadn't been there our first time through the room. The two-faced doorman held a silver key, which he kept passing from his left hand to his right hand. I wondered if this were a different room completely, but the frieze of the gods looked exactly the same.

Behind us, the doorway we'd come through had disappeared, replaced by more mosaics. We wouldn't be going back the way we'd come.

'The exits are closed,' Annabeth said.

'Duh!' the man's left face said.

'Where do they lead?' she asked.

'One probably leads the way you wish to go,' the right face said encouragingly. 'The other leads to certain death.'

'I – I know who you are,' Annabeth said.

'Oh, you're a smart one!' the left face sneered. 'But do you know which way to choose? I don't have all day.'

'Why are you trying to confuse me?' Annabeth asked.

The right face smiled. 'You're in charge now, my dear. All the decisions are on your shoulders. That's what you wanted, isn't it?'

'I –'

'We know you, Annabeth,' the left face said. 'We know what you wrestle with every day. We know your indecision. You will have to make your choice sooner or later. And the choice may kill you.'

I didn't know what they were talking about, but it sounded

like it was about more than a choice between doors.

The colour drained out of Annabeth's face. 'No . . . I don't –'

'Leave her alone,' I said. 'Who are you, anyway?'

'I'm your best friend,' the right face said.

'I'm your worst enemy,' the left face said.

'I'm Janus,' both faces said in harmony. 'God of Doorways. Beginnings. Endings. Choices.'

'I'll see you soon enough, Perseus Jackson,' said the right face. 'But for now it's Annabeth's turn.' He laughed giddily. 'Such fun!'

'Shut up!' his left face said. 'This is serious. One bad choice can ruin your whole life. It can kill you and all your friends. But no pressure, Annabeth. Choose!'

With a sudden chill, I remembered the words of the prophecy: *the child of Athena's final stand.*

'Don't do it,' I said.

'I'm afraid she has to,' the right face said cheerfully.

Annabeth moistened her lips. 'I – I choose –'

Before she could point to a door, a brilliant light flooded the room.

Janus raised his hands to either side of his head to cover his eyes. When the light died, a woman was standing at the fountain.

She was tall and graceful, with long hair the colour of chocolate, braided in plaits with gold ribbons. She wore a simple white dress, but when she moved, the fabric shimmered with colours like oil on water.

'Janus,' she said. 'Are we causing trouble again?'

'N-no, milady!' Janus's right face stammered.

'Yes!' the left face said.

'Shut up!' the right face said.

'Excuse me?' the woman asked.

'Not you, milady! I was talking to myself.'

'I see,' the lady said. 'You know very well your visit is premature. The girl's time has not yet come. So I give *you* a choice: leave these heroes to me, or I shall turn *you* into a door and break you down.'

'What kind of door?' the left face asked.

'Shut up!' the right face said.

'Because French doors are nice,' the left face mused. 'Lots of natural light.'

'Shut up!' the right face wailed. 'Not you, milady! Of course I'll leave. I was just having a bit of fun. Doing my job. Offering choices.'

'Causing indecision,' the woman corrected. 'Now begone!'

The left face muttered, 'Party pooper,' then he raised his silver key, inserted it into the air and disappeared.

The woman turned towards us, and fear closed around my heart. Her eyes shone with power. *Leave these heroes to me.* That didn't sound good. For a second, I almost wished we could've taken our chances with Janus. But then the woman smiled.

'You must be hungry,' she said. 'Sit with me and talk.'

She waved her hand, and the old Roman fountain began to flow. Jets of clear water sprayed into the air. A marble table appeared, laden with platters of sandwiches and pitchers of lemonade.

'Who . . . who are you?' I asked.

'I am Hera.' The woman smiled. 'Queen of Heaven.'

* * *

I'd seen Hera once before, at a council of the gods, but I hadn't paid much attention to her. At the time I'd been surrounded by a bunch of other gods who were debating whether or not to kill me.

I didn't remember her looking so normal. Of course, gods are usually seven metres tall when they're on Olympus, so that makes them look a lot less normal. But, now, Hera looked like a regular mom.

She served us sandwiches and poured lemonade.

'Grover, dear,' she said. 'Use your napkin. Don't eat it.'

'Yes, ma'am,' Grover said.

'Tyson, you're wasting away. Would you like another peanut-butter sandwich?'

Tyson stifled a belch. 'Yes, nice lady.'

'Queen Hera,' Annabeth said. 'I can't believe it. What are you doing in the Labyrinth?'

Hera smiled. She flicked one finger and Annabeth's hair combed itself. All the dirt and grime disappeared from her face.

'I came to see you, naturally,' the goddess said.

Grover and I exchanged nervous looks. Usually when gods come looking for you, it's not out of the goodness of their hearts. It's because they want something.

Still, that didn't keep me from chowing down on turkey-and-Swiss-cheese sandwiches and crisps and lemonade. I hadn't realized how hungry I was. Tyson was inhaling one peanut-butter sandwich after another, and Grover was loving the lemonade, crunching the Styrofoam cup like an ice-cream cone.

'I didn't think –' Annabeth faltered. 'Well, I didn't think you liked heroes.'

Hera smiled indulgently. 'Because of that little spat I had with Hercules? Honestly, I got so much bad press because of one disagreement.'

'Didn't you try to kill him, like, a lot of times?' Annabeth asked.

Hera waved her hand dismissively. 'Water under the bridge, my dear. Besides, he was one of my loving husband's children by *another* woman. My patience wore thin, I'll admit it. But Zeus and I have had some excellent marriage counselling sessions since then. We've aired our feelings and come to an understanding — especially after that last little incident.'

'You mean when he sired Thalia?' I guessed, but immediately wished I hadn't. As soon as I said the name of our friend, the half-blood daughter of Zeus, Hera's eyes turned towards me frostily.

'Percy Jackson, isn't it? One of Poseidon's . . . children.' I got the feeling she was thinking of another word besides 'children'. 'As I recall, I voted to let you live at the winter solstice. I hope I voted correctly.'

She turned back to Annabeth with a sunny smile. 'At any rate, I certainly bear you no ill will, my girl. I appreciate the difficulty of your quest. Especially when you have troublemakers like Janus to deal with.'

Annabeth lowered her gaze. 'Why was he here? He was driving me crazy.'

'Trying to,' Hera agreed. 'You must understand, the minor gods like Janus have always been frustrated by their small parts to play in the universe. Some, I fear, have little love for Olympus, and could easily be swayed to support the rise of my father.'

'Your father?' I said. 'Oh. Right.'

I'd forgotten that Kronos was Hera's dad, too, along with Zeus, Poseidon and all the eldest Olympians. I guess that made Kronos my grandfather, but that thought was so weird I put it out of my mind.

'We must watch the minor gods,' Hera said. 'Janus. Hecate. Morpheus. They give lip service to Olympus, and yet –'

'That's where Dionysus went,' I remembered. 'He was checking on the minor gods.'

'Indeed.' Hera stared at the fading mosaics of the Olympians. 'You see, in times of trouble, even gods can lose faith. They start putting their trust in the wrong things, petty things. They stop looking at the big picture and start being selfish. But I'm the goddess of marriage, you see. I'm used to perseverance. You have to rise above the squabbling and chaos and keep believing. You have to always keep your goals in mind.'

'What are your goals?' Annabeth asked.

She smiled. 'To keep my family, the Olympians, together, of course. At the moment, the best way I can do that is by helping you. Zeus does not allow me to interfere much, I am afraid. But once every century or so, for a quest I care deeply about, he allows me to grant a wish.'

'A wish?'

'Before you ask it, let me give you some advice, which I can do for free. I know you seek Daedalus. His Labyrinth is as much a mystery to me as it is to you. But if you want to know his fate, I would visit my son Hephaestus at his forge. Daedalus was a great inventor, a mortal after Hephaestus's heart. There has never been a mortal

Hephaestus admired more. If anyone would have kept up with Daedalus and could tell you his fate, it is Hephaestus.'

'But how do we get there?' Annabeth asked. 'That's my wish. I want a way to navigate the Labyrinth.'

Hera looked disappointed. 'So be it. You wish for something, however, that you have already been given.'

'I don't understand.'

'The means is already within your grasp.' She looked at me. 'Percy knows the answer.'

'I do?'

'But that's not fair,' Annabeth said. 'You're not telling us what it is!'

Hera shook her head. 'Getting something and having the wits to use it . . . those are two different things. I'm sure your mother, Athena, would agree.'

The room rumbled like distant thunder. Hera stood. 'That would be my cue. Zeus grows impatient. Think on what I have said, Annabeth. Seek out Hephaestus. You will have to pass through the ranch, I imagine. But keep going. And use all the means at your disposal, however common they may seem.'

She pointed towards the two doors and they melted away, revealing twin corridors, open and dark. 'One last thing, Annabeth. I have postponed your day of choice. I have not prevented it. Soon, as Janus said, you *will* have to make a decision. Farewell!'

She waved a hand and turned into white smoke. So did the food, just as Tyson chomped down on a sandwich that turned to mist in his mouth. The fountain trickled to a stop. The mosaic walls dimmed and turned grungy and faded again. The room was no longer any place you'd want to have a picnic.

Annabeth stamped her foot. 'What sort of help was that? "Here, have a sandwich. Make a wish. Oops, I can't help you!" Poof!'

'Poof,' Tyson agreed sadly, looking at his empty plate.

'Well,' Grover sighed, 'she said Percy knows the answer. That's something.'

They all looked at me.

'But I don't,' I said. 'I don't know what she was talking about.'

Annabeth sighed. 'All right. Then we'll just keep going.'

'Which way?' I asked. I really wanted to ask what Hera had meant – about the choice Annabeth needed to make. But then Grover and Tyson both tensed. They stood up together, like they'd rehearsed it. 'Left,' they both said.

Annabeth frowned. 'How can you be sure?'

'Because something is coming from the right,' Grover said.

'Something big,' Tyson agreed. 'In a hurry.'

'Left is sounding pretty good,' I decided. Together we plunged into the dark corridor.

7 TYSON LEADS A JAILBREAK

The good news: the left tunnel was straight with no side exits, twists or turns. The bad news: it was a dead end. After sprinting a hundred metres, we ran into an enormous boulder that completely blocked our path. Behind us, the sounds of dragging footsteps and heavy breathing echoed down the corridor. Something – definitely not human – was on our trail.

'Tyson,' I said, 'can you –'

'Yes!' He slammed his shoulder against the rock so hard the whole tunnel shook. Dust trickled from the stone ceiling.

'Hurry!' Grover said. 'Don't bring the roof down, but hurry!'

The boulder finally gave way with a horrible grinding noise. Tyson pushed it into a small room, and we dashed through behind it.

'Close the entrance!' Annabeth said.

We all got on the other side of the boulder and pushed. Whatever was chasing us wailed in frustration as we heaved the rock back into place and sealed the corridor.

'We trapped it,' I said.

'Or trapped ourselves,' Grover said.

I turned. We were in a six-metre-square cement room,

and the opposite wall was covered with metal bars. We'd tunnelled straight into a cell.

'What in Hades?' Annabeth tugged on the bars. They didn't budge. Through the bars we could see rows of cells in a ring around a dark courtyard – at least three stories of metal doors and metal catwalks.

'A prison,' I said. 'Maybe Tyson can break –'

'Shh,' said Grover. 'Listen.'

Somewhere above us, deep sobbing echoed through the building. There was another sound, too – a raspy voice muttering something that I couldn't make out. The words were strange, like rocks in a tumbler.

'What's that language?' I whispered.

Tyson's eye widened. 'Can't be.'

'What?' I asked.

He grabbed two bars on our cell door and bent them wide enough for even a Cyclops to slip through.

'Wait!' Grover called.

But Tyson wasn't about to wait. We ran after him. The prison was dark, only a few dim fluorescent lights flickering above.

'I know this place,' Annabeth told me. 'This is Alcatraz.'

'You mean that island near San Francisco?'

She nodded. 'My school took a field trip here. It's like a museum.'

It didn't seem possible that we could've popped out of the Labyrinth on the other side of the country, but Annabeth had been living in San Francisco all year, keeping an eye on Mount Tamalpais, just across the bay. She probably knew what she was talking about.

'Freeze,' Grover warned.

But Tyson kept going. Grover grabbed his arm and pulled him back with all his strength. 'Stop, Tyson!' he whispered. 'Can't you see it?'

I looked where he was pointing, and my stomach did a somersault. On the second-floor balcony, across the courtyard, was a monster more horrible than anything I'd ever seen before.

It was sort of like a centaur, with a woman's body from the waist up. But instead of a horse's lower body, it had the body of a dragon — at least seven metres long, black and scaly with enormous claws and a barbed tail. Her legs looked like they were tangled in vines, but then I realized they were sprouting snakes, hundreds of vipers darting around, constantly looking for something to bite. The woman's hair was also made of snakes, like Medusa's. Weirdest of all, around her waist, where the woman part met the dragon part, her skin bubbled and morphed, occasionally producing the heads of animals — a vicious wolf, a bear, a lion, as if she were wearing a belt of ever-changing creatures. I got the feeling I was looking at something half formed, a monster so old it was from the beginning of time, before shapes had been fully defined.

'It's her,' Tyson whimpered.

'Get down!' Grover said.

We crouched in the shadows, but the monster wasn't paying us any attention. It seemed to be talking to someone inside a cell on the second floor. That's where the sobbing was coming from. The dragon woman said something in her weird rumbling language.

'What's she saying?' I muttered. 'What's that language?'

'The tongue of the old times.' Tyson shivered. 'What Mother Earth spoke to Titans and . . . her other children. Before the gods.'

'You understand it?' I asked. 'Can you translate?'

Tyson closed his eyes and began to speak in a horrible, raspy woman's voice. 'You will work for the master or suffer.'

Annabeth shuddered. 'I hate it when he does that.'

Like all Cyclopes, Tyson had superhuman hearing and an uncanny ability to mimic voices. It was almost like he entered a trance when he spoke in other voices.

'I will not serve,' Tyson said in a deep, wounded voice.

He switched to the monster's voice: 'Then I shall enjoy your pain, Briares.' Tyson faltered when he said that name. I'd never heard him break character when he was mimicking somebody, but he let out a strangled gulp. Then he continued in the monster's voice. 'If you thought your first imprisonment was unbearable, you have yet to feel true torment. Think on this until I return.'

The dragon lady tromped towards the stairwell, vipers hissing around her legs like grass skirts. She spread wings that I hadn't noticed before – huge bat wings she kept folded against her dragon back. She leaped off the catwalk and soared across the courtyard. We crouched lower in the shadows. A hot sulphurous wind blasted my face as the monster flew over. Then she disappeared around the corner.

'H-h-horrible,' Grover said. 'I've never smelled any monster that strong.'

'Cyclopes' worst nightmare,' Tyson murmured. 'Kampê.'

'Who?' I asked.

Tyson swallowed. 'Every Cyclops knows about her.

Stories about her scare us when we're babies. She was our jailer in the bad years.'

Annabeth nodded. 'I remember now. When the Titans ruled, they imprisoned Gaea and Ouranos's earlier children – the Cyclopes and the Hekatonkheires.'

'The Heka-what?' I asked.

'The Hundred-handed Ones,' she said. 'They called them that because . . . well, they had a hundred hands. They were elder brothers of the Cyclopes.'

'Very powerful,' Tyson said. 'Wonderful! As tall as the sky. So strong they could break mountains!'

'Cool,' I said. 'Unless you're a mountain.'

'Kampê was the jailer,' he said. 'She worked for Kronos. She kept our brothers locked up in Tartarus, tortured them always, until Zeus came. He killed Kampê and freed Cyclopes and Hundred-handed Ones to help fight against the Titans in the big war.'

'And now Kampê is back,' I said.

'Bad,' Tyson summed up.

'So who's in that cell?' I asked. 'You said a name –'

'Briares!' Tyson perked up. 'He is a Hundred-handed One. They are as tall as the sky and –'

'Yeah,' I said. 'They break mountains.'

I looked up at the cells above us, wondering how something as tall as the sky could fit in a tiny cell, and why he was crying.

'I guess we should check it out,' Annabeth said, 'before Kampê comes back.'

As we approached the cell, the weeping got louder. When I first saw the creature inside, I wasn't sure what I was looking at. He was human-size and his skin was very pale, the colour of milk. He wore a loincloth like a big diaper. His feet seemed too big for his body, with cracked dirty toenails, eight toes on each foot. But the top half of his body was the weird part. He made Janus look downright normal. His chest sprouted more arms than I could count, in rows, all around his body. The arms looked like normal arms, but there were so many of them, all tangled together, that his chest looked kind of like a forkful of spaghetti somebody had twirled together. Several of his hands were covering his face as he sobbed.

'Either the sky isn't as tall as it used to be,' I muttered, 'or he's short.'

Tyson didn't pay any attention. He fell to his knees.

'Briares!' he called.

The sobbing stopped.

'Great Hundred-handed One!' Tyson said. 'Help us!'

Briares looked up. His face was long and sad, with a crooked nose and bad teeth. He had deep brown eyes – I mean completely brown with no whites or black pupils, like eyes formed out of clay.

'Run while you can, Cyclops,' Briares said miserably. 'I cannot even help myself.'

'You are a Hundred-handed One!' Tyson insisted. 'You can do anything!'

Briares wiped his nose with five or six hands. Several others were fidgeting with little pieces of metal and wood from a broken bed, the way Tyson always played with spare parts. It was amazing to watch. The hands seemed to have a mind of their own. They built a toy boat out of wood, then disassembled it just as fast. Other hands were scratching at the cement floor for no apparent reason. Others were playing rock, paper, scissors. A few others were making ducky and doggie shadow puppets against the wall.

'I cannot,' Briares moaned. 'Kampê is back! The Titans will rise and throw us back into Tartarus.'

'Put on your brave face!' Tyson said.

Immediately Briares's face morphed into something else. Same brown eyes, but otherwise totally different features. He had an upturned nose, arched eyebrows and a weird smile, like he was trying to act brave. But then his face turned back to what it had been before.

'No good,' he said. 'My scared face keeps coming back.'

'How did you do that?' I asked.

Annabeth elbowed me. 'Don't be rude. The Hundred-handed Ones have fifty different faces.'

'Must make it hard to get a yearbook picture,' I said.

Tyson was still entranced. 'It will be okay, Briares! We will help you! Can I have your autograph?'

Briares sniffled. 'Do you have one hundred pens?'

'Guys,' Grover interrupted. 'We have to get out of here. Kampê will be back. She'll sense us sooner or later.'

'Break the bars,' Annabeth said.

'Yes!' Tyson said, smiling proudly. 'Briares can do it. He is very strong. Stronger than Cyclopes, even! Watch!'

Briares whimpered. A dozen of his hands started playing pat-a-cake, but none of them made any attempt to break the bars.

'If he's so strong,' I said, 'why is he stuck in jail?'

Annabeth elbowed me again. 'He's terrified,' she whispered.

'Kampê imprisoned him in Tartarus for thousands of years. How would you feel?'

The Hundred-handed One covered his face again.

'Briares?' Tyson asked. 'What . . . what is wrong? Show us your great strength!'

'Tyson,' Annabeth said, 'I think you'd better break the bars.'

Tyson's smile melted slowly.

'I will break the bars,' he repeated. He grabbed the cell door and ripped it off its hinges like it was made of wet clay.

'Come on, Briares,' Annabeth said. 'Let's get you out of here.'

She held out her hand. For a second, Briares's face morphed to a hopeful expression. Several of his arms reached out, but twice as many slapped them away.

'I cannot,' he said. 'She will punish me.'

'It's all right,' Annabeth promised. 'You fought the Titans before, and you won, remember?'

'I remember the war.' Briares's face morphed again – furrowed brow and a pouting mouth. His brooding face, I guess. 'Lightning shook the world. We threw many rocks. The Titans and the monsters almost won. Now they are getting strong again. Kampê said so.'

'Don't listen to her,' I said. 'Come on!'

He didn't move. I knew Grover was right. We didn't have much time before Kampê returned. But I couldn't just leave him here. Tyson would cry for weeks.

'One game of rock, paper, scissors,' I blurted out. 'If I win, you come with us. If I lose, we'll leave you in jail.'

Annabeth looked at me like I was crazy.

Briares's face morphed to doubtful. 'I always win rock, paper, scissors.'

'Then let's do it!' I pounded my fist in my palm three times.

Briares did the same with all one hundred hands, which sounded like an army marching three steps forward. He came up with a whole avalanche of rocks, a classroom set of scissors and enough paper to make a fleet of aeroplanes.

'I told you,' he said sadly. 'I always —' His face morphed to confusion. 'What is that you made?'

'A gun,' I told him, showing him my finger gun. It was a trick Paul Blofis had pulled on me, but I wasn't going to tell him that. 'A gun beats anything.'

'That's not fair.'

'I didn't say anything about fair. Kampê's not going to be fair if we hang around. She's going to blame you for ripping off the bars. Now come on!'

Briares sniffled. 'Demigods are cheaters.' But he slowly rose to his feet and followed us out of the cell.

I started to feel hopeful. All we had to do was get downstairs and find the Labyrinth entrance. But then Tyson froze.

On the ground floor right below, Kampê was snarling at us.

'The other way,' I said.

We bolted down the catwalk. This time Briares was happy to follow us. In fact he sprinted out front, a hundred arms waving in panic.

Behind us, I heard the sound of giant wings as Kampê took to the air. She hissed and growled in her ancient language, but I didn't need a translation to know she was planning to kill us.

We scrambled down the stairs, through a corridor and past a guard's station – out into another block of prison cells.

'Left,' Annabeth said. 'I remember this from the tour.'

We burst outside and found ourselves in the prison yard, ringed by security towers and barbed wire. After being inside so long, the daylight almost blinded me. Tourists were milling around, taking pictures. The wind whipped cold off the bay. In the south, San Francisco gleamed all white and beautiful, but in the north, over Mount Tamalpais, huge storm clouds swirled. The whole sky seemed like a black top spinning from the mountain where Atlas was imprisoned, and where the Titan palace of Mount Othrys was rising anew. It was hard to believe the tourists couldn't see the supernatural storm brewing, but they didn't give any hint that anything was wrong.

'It's even worse,' Annabeth said, gazing to the north. 'The storms have been bad all year, but that –'

'Keep moving,' Briares wailed. 'She is behind us!'

We ran to the far end of the yard, as far from the cell block as possible.

'Kampê's too big to get through the doors,' I said hopefully.

Then the wall exploded.

Tourists screamed as Kampê appeared from the dust and rubble, her wings spread out as wide as the yard. She was holding two swords – long bronze scimitars that glowed with a weird greenish aura, boiling wisps of vapour that smelled sour and hot even across the yard.

'Poison!' Grover yelped. 'Don't let those things touch you or . . .'

'Or we'll die?' I guessed.

'Well . . . after you shrivel slowly to dust, yes.'

'Let's avoid the swords,' I decided.

'Briares, fight!' Tyson urged. 'Grow to full size!'

Instead, Briares looked like he was trying to shrink even smaller. He appeared to be wearing his 'absolutely terrified' face.

Kampê thundered towards us on her dragon legs, hundreds of snakes slithering around her body.

For a second I thought about drawing Riptide and facing her, but my heart crawled into my throat. Then Annabeth said what I was thinking: 'Run.'

That was the end of the debate. There was no fighting this thing. We ran through the jail yard and out the gates of the prison, the monster right behind us. Mortals screamed and ran. Emergency sirens began to blare.

We hit the wharf just as a tour boat was unloading. The new group of visitors froze as they saw us charging towards them, followed by a mob of frightened tourists, followed by . . . I don't know what they saw through the Mist, but it could not have been good.

'The boat?' Grover asked.

'Too slow,' Tyson said. 'Back into the maze. Only chance.'

'We need a diversion,' Annabeth said.

Tyson ripped a metal lamppost out of the ground. 'I will distract Kampê. You run around, back to the prison.'

'I'll help you,' I said.

'No,' Tyson said. 'You go. Poison will hurt Cyclopes. A lot of pain. But it won't kill.'

'Are you sure?'

'Go, brother. I will meet you inside.'

I hated the idea. I'd almost lost Tyson once before, and I didn't want to ever risk that again. But there was no time to argue, and I had no better idea. Annabeth, Grover and I each took one of Briares's hands and dragged him towards the concession stands while Tyson bellowed, lowered his pole and charged Kampê like a jousting knight.

She'd been glaring at Briares, but Tyson got her attention as soon as he nailed her in the chest with the pole, pushing her back into the wall. She shrieked and slashed with her swords, slicing the pole to shreds. Poison dripped in pools all around her, sizzling into the cement.

Tyson jumped back as Kampê's hair lashed and hissed, and the vipers around her legs darted their tongues in every direction. A lion popped out of the weird half-formed faces around her waist and roared.

As we sprinted for the cell blocks, the last thing I saw was Tyson picking up an ice-cream stand and throwing it at Kampê. Ice cream and poison exploded everywhere, all the little snakes in Kampê's hair dotted with chocolate sauce. We dashed back into the jail yard.

'Can't make it,' Briares huffed.

'Tyson is risking his life to help you!' I yelled at him. 'You *will* make it.'

As we reached the door of the cell block, I heard an angry roar. I glanced back and saw Tyson running towards us at full speed, Kampê right behind him. She was plastered in ice cream and T-shirts. One of the bear heads on her waist was now wearing a pair of crooked plastic Alcatraz sunglasses.

'Hurry!' Annabeth said, like I needed to be told that.

We finally found the cell where we'd come in, but the back wall was completely smooth – no sign of a boulder or anything.

'Look for the mark!' Annabeth said.

'There!' Grover touched a tiny scratch, and it became a Greek Δ. The mark of Daedalus glowed blue, and the stone wall ground open.

Too slowly. Tyson was coming through the cell block, Kampê's swords lashing out behind him, slicing indiscriminately through cell bars and stone walls.

I pushed Briares inside the maze, then Annabeth and Grover.

'You can do it!' I told Tyson. But immediately I knew he couldn't. Kampê was gaining. She raised her swords. I needed a distraction – something big. I slapped my wristwatch and it spiralled into a bronze shield. Desperately, I threw it at the monster's face.

SMACK! The shield hit her in the face and she faltered just long enough for Tyson to dive past me into the maze. I was right behind him.

Kampê charged, but she was too late. The stone door closed and its magic sealed us in. I could feel the whole tunnel shake as Kampê pounded against it, roaring furiously. We didn't stick around to play knock, knock with her, though. We raced into the darkness, and for the first time (and the last) I was glad to be back in the Labyrinth.

We finally stopped in a room full of waterfalls. The floor was one big pit, ringed by a slippery stone walkway. Around us on all four walls, water tumbled from huge pipes. The water spilled down into the pit, and even when I shone a light, I couldn't see the bottom.

Briares slumped against the wall. He scooped up water in a dozen hands and washed his face. 'This pit goes straight to Tartarus,' he murmured. 'I should jump in and save you trouble.'

'Don't talk that way,' Annabeth told him. 'You can come back to camp with us. You can help us prepare. You know more about fighting Titans than anybody.'

'I have nothing to offer,' Briares said. 'I have lost everything.'

'What about your brothers?' Tyson asked. 'The other two must still stand tall as mountains! We can take you to them.'

Briares's expression morphed to something even sadder: his grieving face. 'They are no more. They faded.'

The waterfalls thundered. Tyson stared into the pit and blinked tears out of his eye.

'What exactly do you mean, *they faded?*' I asked. 'I thought monsters were immortal, like the gods.'

'Percy,' Grover said weakly. 'Even immortality has limits.

Sometimes . . . sometimes monsters get forgotten and they lose their will to stay immortal.'

Looking at Grover's face, I wondered if he were thinking of Pan. I remembered something Medusa had told us once: how her sisters, the other two gorgons, had passed on and left her alone. Then last year Apollo said something about the old god Helios disappearing and leaving him with the duties of the sun god. I'd never thought about it too much, but now, looking at Briares, I realized how terrible it would be to be so old – thousands and thousands of years old – and totally alone.

'I must go,' Briares said.

'Kronos's army will invade camp,' Tyson said. 'We need help.'

Briares hung his head. 'I cannot, Cyclops.'

'You are strong.'

'Not any more.' Briares rose.

'Hey.' I grabbed one of his arms and pulled him aside, where the roar of the water would hide our words. 'Briares, we need you. In case you haven't noticed, Tyson believes in you. He risked his life for you.'

I told him about everything – Luke's invasion plan, the Labyrinth entrance at camp, Daedalus's workshop, Kronos's golden coffin.

Briares just shook his head. 'I cannot, demigod. I do not have a finger gun to win this game.' To prove his point, he made one hundred finger guns.

'Maybe that's why monsters fade,' I said. 'Maybe it's not about what the mortals believe. Maybe it's because *you* give up on yourself.'

His pure brown eyes regarded me. His face morphed

into an expression I recognized – shame. Then he turned and trudged off down the corridor until he was lost in the shadows.

Tyson sobbed.

'It's okay.' Grover hesitantly patted his shoulder, which must've taken all his courage.

Tyson sneezed. 'It is not okay, goat boy. He was my hero.'

I wanted to make him feel better, but I wasn't sure what to say.

Finally, Annabeth stood and shouldered her backpack. 'Come on, guys. This pit is making me nervous. Let's find a better place to camp for the night.'

We settled in a corridor made of huge marble blocks. It looked like it could've been part of a Greek tomb, with bronze torch holders fastened to the walls. It had to be an older part of the maze, and Annabeth decided this was a good sign.

'We must be close to Daedalus's workshop,' she said. 'Get some rest, everybody. We'll keep going in the morning.'

'How do we know when it's morning?' Grover asked.

'Just rest,' she insisted.

Grover didn't need to be told twice. He pulled a heap of straw out of his pack, ate some of it, made a pillow out of the rest and was snoring in no time. Tyson took longer getting to sleep. He tinkered with some metal scraps from his building kit for a while, but whatever he was making, he wasn't happy with it. He kept disassembling the pieces.

'I'm sorry I lost the shield,' I told him. 'You worked so hard to repair it.'

Tyson looked up. His eye was bloodshot from crying. 'Do not worry, brother. You saved me. You wouldn't have had to if Briares had helped.'

'He was just scared,' I said. 'I'm sure he'll get over it.'

'He is not strong,' Tyson said. 'He is not important any more.'

He heaved a big sad sigh, then closed his eye. The metal pieces fell out of his hand, still unassembled, and Tyson began to snore.

I tried to fall asleep myself, but I couldn't. Something about getting chased by a large dragon lady with poison swords made it really hard to relax. I picked up my bedroll and dragged it over to where Annabeth was sitting, keeping watch.

I sat down next to her.

'You should sleep,' she said.

'Can't. You doing all right?'

'Sure. First day leading the quest. Just great.'

'We'll get there,' I said. 'We'll find the workshop before Luke does.'

She brushed her hair out of her face. She had a smudge of dirt on her chin, and I imagined what she must've looked like when she was little, wandering around the country with Thalia and Luke. Once she'd saved them from the mansion of the evil Cyclops when she was only seven. Even when she looked scared, like now, I knew she had a lot of guts.

'I just wish the quest was *logical*,' she complained. 'I mean, we're travelling but we have no idea where we'll end up. How can you walk from New York to California in a day?'

'Space isn't the same in the maze.'

'I know, I know. It's just . . .' She looked at me hesitantly. 'Percy, I was kidding myself. All that planning and reading – I don't have a clue where we're going.'

'You're doing great. Besides, we *never* know what we're doing. It always works out. Remember Circe's island?'

She snorted. 'You made a cute guinea pig.'

'And Waterland, how you got us thrown off that ride?'

'*I* got us thrown off? That was totally your fault!'

'See? It'll be fine.'

She smiled, which I was glad to see, but the smile faded quickly.

'Percy, what did Hera mean when she said you knew the way to get through the maze?'

'I don't know,' I admitted. 'Honestly.'

'You'd tell me if you did?'

'Sure. Maybe . . .'

'Maybe what?'

'Maybe if you told me the last line of the prophecy, it would help.'

Annabeth shivered. 'Not here. Not in the dark.'

'What about the choice Janus mentioned? Hera said –'

'Stop,' Annabeth snapped. Then she took a shaky breath. 'I'm sorry, Percy. I'm just stressed. But I don't . . . I've got to think about it.'

We sat in silence, listening to strange creaks and groans in the maze, the echo of stones grinding together as tunnels changed, grew and expanded. The dark made me think about the visions I'd seen of Nico di Angelo, and suddenly I realized something.

'Nico is down here somewhere,' I said. 'That's how he

disappeared from camp. He found the Labyrinth. Then he found a path that led down even further — to the Underworld. But now he's back in the maze. He's coming after me.'

Annabeth was quiet for a long time. 'Percy, I hope you're wrong. But if you're right . . .' She stared at the flashlight beam casting a dim circle on the stone wall. I had a feeling she was thinking about her prophecy. I'd never seen her look more tired.

'How about I take first watch?' I said. 'I'll wake you if anything happens.'

Annabeth looked like she wanted to protest, but she just nodded, slumped onto her bedroll and closed her eyes.

When it was my turn to sleep, I dreamed I was back in the old man's Labyrinth prison.

It looked more like a workshop now. Tables were littered with measuring instruments. A forge burned red hot in the corner. The boy I'd seen in the last dream was stoking the bellows, except he was taller now, almost my age. A weird funnel device was attached to the forge's chimney, trapping the smoke and heat and channelling it through a pipe into the floor, next to a big bronze manhole cover.

It was daytime. The sky above was blue, but the walls of the maze cast deep shadows across the workshop. After being in tunnels so long, I found it weird that part of the Labyrinth could be open to the sky. Somehow that made the maze seem like an even crueller place.

The old man looked sickly. He was terribly thin, his hands raw and red from working. White hair covered his eyes, and his tunic was smudged with grease. He was bent over a table, working on some kind of long metal patchwork – like a swathe of chain mail. He picked up a delicate curl of bronze and fitted it into place.

'Done,' he announced. 'It's done.'

He picked up his project. It was so beautiful my heart leaped – metal wings constructed from thousands of interlocking bronze feathers. There were two sets. One still lay on the table. Daedalus stretched the frame, and the wings expanded to seven and a half metres. Part of me knew it could never fly. It was too heavy, and there'd be no way to get off the ground. But the craftsmanship was amazing. Metal feathers caught the light and flashed thirty different shades of gold.

The boy left the bellows and ran over to see. He grinned, despite the fact that he was grimy and sweaty. 'Father, you're a genius!'

The old man smiled. 'Tell me something I don't know, Icarus. Now hurry. It will take at least an hour to attach them. Come.'

'You first,' Icarus said.

The old man protested, but Icarus insisted. 'You made them, Father. You should get the honour of wearing them first.'

The boy attached a leather harness to his father's chest, like climbing gear, with straps that ran from his shoulders to his wrists. Then he began fastening on the wings, using a metal canister that looked like an enormous hot-glue gun.

'The wax compound should hold for several hours,' Daedalus said nervously as his son worked. 'But we must let it set first. And we would do well to avoid flying too high or too low. The sea would wet the wax seals –'

'And the sun's heat would loosen them,' the boy finished. 'Yes, Father. We've been through this a million times!'

'One cannot be too careful.'

'I have complete faith in your inventions, Father! No one has ever been as smart as you.'

The old man's eyes shone. It was obvious he loved his son more than anything in the world. 'Now I will do your wings, and give mine a chance to set properly. Come!'

It was slow going. The old man's hands fumbled with the straps. He had a hard time keeping the wings in position while he sealed them. His own metal wings seemed to weigh him down, getting in his way while he tried to work.

'Too slow,' the old man muttered. 'I am too slow.'

'Take your time, Father,' the boy said. 'The guards aren't due until –'

BOOM!

The workshop doors shuddered. Daedalus had barred them from the inside with a wooden brace, but still they shook on their hinges.

'Hurry!' Icarus said.

BOOM! BOOM!

Something heavy was slamming into the doors. The brace held, but a crack appeared in the left door.

Daedalus worked furiously. A drop of hot wax spilled onto Icarus's shoulder. The boy winced but did not cry out. When his left wing was sealed to the straps, Daedalus began working on the right.

'We must have more time,' Daedalus murmured. 'They are too early! We need more time for the seal to hold.'

'It'll be fine,' Icarus said as his father finished the right wing. 'Help me with the manhole –'

CRASH! The doors splintered and the head of a bronze battering ram emerged through the breach. Axes cleared the debris, and two armed guards entered the room, followed by the king with the golden crown and the spear-shaped beard.

'Well, well,' the king said with a cruel smile. 'Going somewhere?'

Daedalus and his son froze, their metal wings glimmering on their backs.

'We're leaving, Minos,' the old man said.

King Minos chuckled. 'I was curious to see how far you'd get on this little project before I dashed your hopes. I must say I'm impressed.'

The king admired their wings.

'You look like metal chickens,' he decided. 'Perhaps we should pluck you and make a soup.'

The guards laughed stupidly.

'Metal chickens,' one repeated. 'Soup.'

'Shut up,' the king said. Then he turned again to Daedalus. 'You let my daughter escape, old man. You drove my wife to madness. You killed my monster and made me the laughing stock of the Mediterranean. You will never escape me!'

Icarus grabbed the wax gun and sprayed it at the king, who stepped back in surprise. The guards rushed forward, but each got a stream of hot wax in his face.

'The vent!' Icarus yelled to his father.

'Get them!' King Minos raged.

Together, the old man and his son prised open the manhole cover, and a column of hot air blasted out of the ground. The king watched, incredulous, as the inventor and his son shot into the sky on their bronze wings, carried by the updraught.

'Shoot them!' the king yelled, but his guards had brought no bows. One threw his sword in desperation, but Daedalus and Icarus were already out of reach. They wheeled above the maze and the king's palace, then zoomed across the city of Knossos and out past the rocky shores of Crete.

Icarus laughed. 'Free, Father! You did it.'

The boy spread his wings to their full limit and soared away on the wind.

'Wait!' Daedalus called. 'Be careful!'

But Icarus was already out over the open sea, heading north and laughing for their good luck. He soared up and scared an eagle out of its flight path, then plummeted towards the sea like he was born to fly, pulling out of a nosedive at the last second. His sandals skimmed the waves.

'Stop that!' Daedalus called. But the wind carried his voice away. His son was drunk on his own freedom.

The old man struggled to catch up, gliding clumsily after his son.

They were miles from Crete, over deep sea, when Icarus looked back and saw his father's worried expression.

Icarus smiled. 'Don't worry, Father! You're a genius! I trust your handiwork –'

The first metal feather shook loose from his wings and fluttered away. Then another. Icarus wobbled in midair. Suddenly he was shedding bronze feathers, which twirled away from him like a flock of frightened birds.

'Icarus!' his father cried. 'Glide! Extend the wings. Stay as still as possible!'

But Icarus flapped his arms, desperately trying to reassert control.

The left wing went first — ripping away from the straps.

'Father!' Icarus cried. And then he fell, the wings stripped away until he was just a boy in a climbing harness and a white tunic, his arms extended in a useless attempt to glide.

I woke with a start, feeling like I was falling. The corridor was dark. In the constant moaning of the Labyrinth, I thought I could hear the anguished cry of Daedalus calling his son's name, as Icarus, his only joy, plummeted towards the sea, a hundred metres below.

There was no morning in the maze, but once everyone woke up and had a fabulous breakfast of granola bars and juice boxes, we kept travelling. I didn't mention my dream. Something about it had really freaked me out, and I didn't think the others needed to know that.

The old stone tunnels changed to earth with cedar beams, like a gold mine or something. Annabeth started getting agitated.

'This isn't right,' she said. 'It should still be stone.'

We came to a cave where stalactites hung low from the ceiling. In the centre of the dirt floor was a rectangular pit, like a grave.

Grover shivered. 'It smells like the Underworld in here.'

Then I saw something glinting at the edge of the pit — a foil wrapper. I shone my flashlight into the hole and saw a half-chewed cheeseburger floating in brown carbonated muck.

'Nico,' I said. 'He was summoning the dead again.'

Tyson whimpered. 'Ghosts were here. I don't like ghosts.'

'We've got to find him.' I don't know why, but standing at the edge of that pit gave me a sense of urgency. Nico was close. I could feel it. I couldn't let him wander around down here, alone except for the dead. I started to run.

'Percy!' Annabeth called.

I ducked into a tunnel and saw light up ahead. By the time Annabeth, Tyson and Grover caught up with me, I was staring at daylight streaming through a set of bars above my head. We were under a steel grate made out of metal pipes. I could see trees and blue sky.

'Where are we?' I wondered.

Then a shadow fell across the grate and a cow stared down at me. It looked like a normal cow except it was a weird colour – bright red, 'like a cherry. I didn't know cows came in that shade.

The cow mooed, put one hoof tentatively on the bars, then backed away.

'It's a cattle grid,' Grover said.

'A what?' I asked.

'They put them at the gates of ranches so cows can't get out. They can't walk on them.'

'How do you know that?'

Grover huffed indignantly. 'Believe me, if *you* had hooves, you'd know about cattle grids. They're annoying!'

I turned to Annabeth. 'Didn't Hera say something about a ranch? We need to check it out. Nico might be up there.'

She hesitated. 'All right. But how do we get out?'

Tyson solved that problem by hitting the cattle grid

with both hands. It popped off and went flying out of sight. We heard a *CLANG!* and a startled '*Moo!*' Tyson blushed.

'Sorry, cow!' he called.

Then he gave us a boost out of the tunnel.

We were on a ranch, all right. Rolling hills stretched to the horizon, dotted with oak trees and cacti and boulders. A barbed-wire fence ran from the gate in either direction. Cherry-coloured cows roamed around, grazing on clumps of grass.

'Red cattle,' Annabeth said. 'The cattle of the sun.'

'What?' I asked.

'They're sacred to Apollo.'

'Holy cows?'

'Exactly. But what are they doing –'

'Wait,' Grover said. 'Listen.'

At first everything seemed quiet . . . but then I heard it: the distant baying of dogs. The sound got louder. Then the underbrush rustled, and two dogs broke through. Except it wasn't two dogs. It was *one* dog with two heads. It looked like a greyhound, long and snaky and sleek brown, but its neck V'ed into two heads, both of them snapping and snarling and generally not very glad to see us.

'Bad Janus dog!' Tyson cried.

'Arf!' Grover told it, and raised a hand in greeting.

The two-headed dog bared its teeth. I guess it wasn't impressed that Grover could speak animal. Then its master lumbered out of the woods, and I realized the dog was the least of our problems.

He was a huge guy with stark white hair, a straw cowboy hat and a braided white beard – kind of like Father Time, if Father Time went redneck and worked out. He was wearing jeans, a *Don't Mess with Texas* T-shirt, and a denim jacket with the sleeves ripped off so you could see his muscles. On his right bicep was a crossed-swords tattoo. He held a wooden club about the size of a nuclear warhead, with twenty-centimetre spikes bristling at the business end.

'Heel, Orthus,' he told the dog.

The dog growled at us once more, just to make his feelings clear, then circled back to his master's feet. The man looked us up and down, keeping his club ready.

'What've we got here?' he asked. 'Cattle rustlers?'

'Just travellers,' Annabeth said. 'We're on a quest.'

The man's eye twitched. 'Half-bloods, eh?'

I started to say, 'How did you know –'

Annabeth put her hand on my arm. 'I'm Annabeth, daughter of Athena. This is Percy, son of Poseidon. Grover the satyr. Tyson the –'

'Cyclops,' the man finished. 'Yes, I can see that.' He glowered at me. 'And I know half-bloods because I *am* one, sonny. I'm Eurytion, the cowherd for this here ranch. Son of Ares. You came through the Labyrinth like the other one, I reckon.'

'The other one?' I asked. 'You mean Nico di Angelo?'

'We get a load of visitors from the Labyrinth,' Eurytion said darkly. 'Not many ever leave.'

'Wow,' I said. 'I feel welcome.'

The cowherd glanced behind him like someone was watching. Then he lowered his voice. 'I'm only going to say this once, demigods. Get back in the maze now. Before it's too late.'

'We're not leaving,' Annabeth insisted. 'Not until we see this other demigod. Please.'

Eurytion grunted. 'Then you leave me no choice, missy. I've got to take you to see the boss.'

I didn't feel like we were hostages or anything. Eurytion walked alongside us with his club across his shoulder. Orthus the two-headed dog growled a lot and sniffed at Grover's legs and shot into the bushes once in a while to chase animals, but Eurytion kept him more or less under control.

We walked down a dirt path that seemed to go on forever. It must've been close to forty degrees, which was a shock after San Francisco. Heat shimmered off the ground. Insects buzzed in the trees. Before we'd gone very far, I was sweating like crazy. Flies swarmed us. Every so often we'd see a pen full of red cows or even stranger animals. Once we passed a corral where the fence was coated in asbestos. Inside, a herd of fire-breathing horses milled around. The hay in their feeding trough was on fire. The ground smoked around their feet, but the horses seemed tame enough. One big stallion looked at me and whinnied, columns of red flame billowing out of his nostrils. I wondered if it hurt his sinuses.

'What are *they* for?' I asked.

Eurytion scowled. 'We raise animals for lots of clients. Apollo, Diomedes, and . . . others.'

'Like who?'

'No more questions.'

Finally we came out of the woods. Perched on a hill above us was a big ranch house – all white stone and wood and big windows.

'It looks like a Frank Lloyd Wright!' Annabeth said.

I guess she was talking about some architectural thing. To me it just looked like the kind of place where a few demigods could get into serious trouble. We hiked up the hill.

'Don't break the rules,' Eurytion warned as we walked up the steps to the front porch. 'No fighting. No drawing weapons. And don't make any comments about the boss's appearance.'

'Why?' I asked. 'What does he look like?'

Before Eurytion could reply, a new voice said, 'Welcome to the Triple G Ranch.'

The man on the porch had a normal head, which was a relief. His face was weathered and brown from years in the sun. He had slick black hair and a black pencil moustache like villains have in old movies. He smiled at us, but the smile wasn't friendly; more amused, like *Oh boy, more people to torture!*

I didn't ponder that very long, though, because then I noticed his body . . . or bodies. He had three of them. Now, you'd think I would've got used to weird anatomy after Janus and Briares, but this guy was three complete people. His neck connected to the middle chest like normal, but he had two more chests, one to either side, connected at the shoulders, with a few centimetres in between. His left arm grew out of his left chest, and the same on the right, so he had two arms, but four armpits, if that makes any sense. The chests all connected into one enormous torso, with two regular but very beefy legs, and he wore the most oversized pair of Levis I'd ever seen. His chests each wore a different colour Western shirt – green, yellow, red, like a stoplight. I wondered how he dressed the middle chest, since it had no arms.

The cowherd Eurytion nudged me. 'Say hello to Mr Geryon.'

'Hi,' I said. 'Nice chests – uh, ranch! Nice ranch you have.'

Before the three-bodied man could respond, Nico di Angelo came out of the glass doors onto the porch. 'Geryon, I won't wait for –'

He froze when he saw us. Then he drew his sword. The blade was just like I'd seen in my dream: short, sharp and dark as midnight.

Geryon snarled when he saw it. 'Put that away, Mr di Angelo. I ain't gonna have my guests killin' each other.'

'But that's –'

'Percy Jackson,' Geryon supplied. 'Annabeth Chase. And a couple of their monster friends. Yes, I know.'

'Monster friends?' Grover said indignantly.

'That man is wearing three shirts,' Tyson said, like he was just realizing this.

'They let my sister die!' Nico's voice trembled with rage. 'They're here to kill me!'

'Nico, we're not here to kill you.' I raised my hands. 'What happened to Bianca was –'

'Don't speak her name! You're not worthy to even talk about her!'

'Wait a minute.' Annabeth pointed at Geryon. 'How do you know our names?'

The three-bodied man winked. 'I make it my business to keep informed, darlin'. Everybody pops into the ranch from time to time. Everyone needs something from ole

Geryon. Now, Mr di Angelo, put that ugly sword away before I have Eurytion take it from you.'

Eurytion sighed, but he hefted his spiked club. At his feet, Orthus growled.

Nico hesitated. He looked thinner and paler than he had in the Iris-messages. I wondered if he'd eaten in the last week. His black clothes were dusty from travelling in the Labyrinth, and his dark eyes were full of hate. He was too young to look so angry. I still remembered him as the cheerful little kid who played with Mythomagic cards.

Reluctantly, he sheathed his sword. 'If you come near me, Percy, I'll summon help. You don't want to meet my helpers, I promise.'

'I believe you,' I said.

Geryon patted Nico's shoulder. 'There, we've all made nice. Now come along, folks. I want to give you a tour of the ranch.'

Geryon had a trolley thing – like one of those kiddie trains that take you around zoos. It was painted black and white in a cowhide pattern. The driver's car had a set of longhorns stuck to the hood, and the horn sounded like a cowbell. I figured maybe this was how he tortured people. He embarrassed them to death, riding around in the moo-mobile.

Nico sat in the very back, probably so he could keep an eye on us. Eurytion crawled in next to him with his spiked club and pulled his cowboy hat over his eyes like he was going to take a nap. Orthus jumped in the front seat next to Geryon and began barking happily in two-part harmony.

Annabeth, Tyson, Grover and I took the middle two cars.

'We have a huge operation!' Geryon boasted as the moo-mobile lurched forward. 'Horses and cattle mostly, but all sorts of exotic varieties, too.'

We came over a hill, and Annabeth gasped. 'Hippalektryons? I thought they were extinct!'

At the bottom of the hill was a fenced-in pasture with a dozen of the weirdest animals I'd ever seen. Each had the front half of a horse and the back half of a rooster. Their rear feet were huge yellow claws. They had feathery tails and red wings. As I watched, two of them got in a fight over a pile of seed. They reared up on their back legs and whinnied and flapped their wings at each other until the smaller one galloped away, its rear bird-legs putting a little hop in its step.

'Rooster ponies,' Tyson said in amazement. 'Do they lay eggs?'

'Once a year!' Geryon grinned in the rearview mirror. 'Very much in demand for omelettes!'

'That's horrible!' Annabeth said. 'They must be an endangered species!'

Geryon waved his hand. 'Gold is gold, darling. And you haven't tasted the omelettes.'

'That's not right,' Grover murmured, but Geryon just kept narrating the tour.

'Now, over here,' he said, 'we have our fire-breathing horses, which you may have seen on your way in. They're bred for war, naturally.'

'What war?' I asked.

Geryon grinned slyly. 'Oh, whichever one comes along.

And over yonder, of course, are our prize red cows.'

Sure enough, hundreds of the cherry-coloured cattle were grazing the side of a hill.

'So many,' Grover said.

'Yes, well, Apollo is too busy to see to them,' Geryon explained, 'so he subcontracts to us. We breed them vigorously because there's such a demand.'

'For what?' I asked.

Geryon raised an eyebrow. 'Meat, of course! Armies have to eat.'

'You kill the sacred cows of the sun god for hamburger meat?' Grover said. 'That's against the ancient laws!'

'Oh, don't get so worked up, satyr. They're just animals.'

'Just animals!'

'Yes, and if Apollo cared, I'm sure he would tell us.'

'If he knew,' I muttered.

Nico sat forward. 'I don't care about any of this, Geryon. We had business to discuss, and this wasn't it!'

'All in good time, Mr di Angelo. Look over here: some of my exotic game.'

The next field was ringed in barbed wire. The whole area was crawling with giant scorpions.

'Triple G Ranch,' I said, suddenly remembering. 'Your mark was on the crates at camp. Quintus got his scorpions from you.'

'Quintus . . .' Geryon mused. 'Short grey hair, muscular, swordsman?'

'Yeah.'

'Never heard of him,' Geryon said. 'Now, over here are my prize stables! You must see them.'

I didn't need to see them, because as soon as we got within three hundred metres I started to smell them. Near the banks of a green river was a horse corral the size of a football field. Stables lined one side of it. About a hundred horses were milling around in the muck – and when I say muck, I mean horse poop. It was the most disgusting thing I'd ever seen, like a poop blizzard had come through and dumped a metre-deep pile of the stuff overnight. The horses were really gross from wading through it, and the stables were just as bad. It reeked like you would not believe – worse than the garbage boats on the East River.

Even Nico gagged. 'What *is* that?'

'My stables!' Geryon said. 'Well, actually they belong to Aegeas, but we watch over them for a small monthly fee. Aren't they lovely?'

'They're disgusting!' Annabeth said.

'Lots of poop,' Tyson observed.

'How can you keep animals like that?' Grover cried.

'Y'all gettin' on my nerves,' Geryon said. 'These are flesh-eating horses, see? They like these conditions.'

'Plus, you're too cheap to have them cleaned,' Eurytion mumbled from under his hat.

'Quiet!' Geryon snapped. 'All right, perhaps the stables are a bit challenging to clean. Perhaps they do make me nauseous when the wind blows the wrong way. But so what? My clients still pay me well.'

'What clients?' I demanded.

'Oh, you'd be surprised how many people will pay for a flesh-eating horse. They make great garbage disposals. Wonderful way to terrify your enemies. Great at birthday parties! We rent them out all the time.'

'You're a monster,' Annabeth decided.

Geryon stopped the moo-mobile and turned to look at her. 'What gave it away? Was it the three bodies?'

'You have to let these animals go,' Grover said. 'It's not right!'

'And the clients you keep talking about,' Annabeth said. 'You work for Kronos, don't you? You're supplying his army with horses, food, whatever they need.'

Geryon shrugged, which was very weird since he had three sets of shoulders. It looked like he was doing the wave all by himself. 'I work for anyone with gold, young lady. I'm a businessman. And I sell them anything I have to offer.'

He climbed out of the moo-mobile and strolled towards the stables as if enjoying the fresh air. It would've been a nice view, with the river and the trees and hills and all, except for the quagmire of horse muck.

Nico got out of the back car and stormed over to Geryon. The cowherd Eurytion wasn't as sleepy as he looked. He hefted his club and walked after Nico.

'I came here for business, Geryon,' Nico said. 'And you haven't answered me.'

'Mmm.' Geryon examined a cactus. His left arm reached over and scratched his middle chest. 'Yes, you'll get a deal, all right.'

'My ghost told me you could help. He said you could guide us to the soul we need.'

'Wait a second,' I said. 'I thought *I* was the soul you wanted.'

Nico looked at me like I was crazy. 'You? Why would I want *you*? Bianca's soul is worth a thousand of yours! Now, can you help me, Geryon, or not?'

'Oh, I imagine I could,' the rancher said. 'Your ghost friend, by the way, where is he?'

Nico looked uneasy. 'He can't form in broad daylight. It's hard for him. But he's around somewhere.'

Geryon smiled. 'I'm sure. Minos likes to disappear when things get . . . difficult.'

'*Minos?*' I remembered the man I'd seen in my dreams, with the golden crown, the pointed beard, and the cruel eyes. 'You mean that evil king? *That's* the ghost who's been giving you advice?'

'It's none of your business, Percy!' Nico turned back to Geryon. 'And what do you mean about things getting difficult?'

The three-bodied man sighed. 'Well, you see, Nico – can I call you Nico?'

'No.'

'You see, Nico, Luke Castellan is offering very good money for half-bloods. Especially powerful half-bloods. And I'm sure when he learns your little secret, who you really are, he'll pay very, very well indeed.'

Nico drew his sword, but Eurytion knocked it out of his hand. Before I could get up, Orthus pounced on my chest and growled, his faces barely centimetres away from mine.

'I would stay in the car, all of you,' Geryon warned. 'Or Orthus will tear Mr Jackson's throat out. Now, Eurytion, if you would be so kind, secure Nico.'

The cowherd spat into the grass. 'Do I have to?'

'Yes, you fool!'

Eurytion looked bored, but he wrapped one huge arm around Nico and lifted him up like a wrestler.

'Pick up the sword, too,' Geryon said with distaste. 'There's nothing I hate worse than Stygian iron.'

Eurytion picked up the sword, careful not to touch the blade.

'Now,' Geryon said cheerfully, 'we've had the tour. Let's go back to the lodge, have some lunch, and send an Iris-message to our friends in the Titan army.'

'You fiend!' Annabeth cried.

Geryon smiled at her. 'Don't worry, my dear. Once I've delivered Mr di Angelo, you and your party can go. I don't interfere with quests. Besides, I've been paid well to give you safe passage, which does not, I'm afraid, include Mr di Angelo.'

'Paid by whom?' Annabeth said. 'What do you mean?'

'Never you mind, darlin'. Let's be off, shall we?'

'Wait!' I said, and Orthus growled. I stayed perfectly still so he wouldn't tear my throat out. 'Geryon, you said you're a businessman. Make me a deal.'

Geryon narrowed his eyes. 'What sort of deal? Do you have gold?'

'I've got something better. Barter.'

'But, Mr Jackson, you've got nothing.'

'You could have him clean the stables,' Eurytion suggested innocently.

'I'll do it!' I said. 'If I fail, you get all of us. You can trade us all to Luke for gold.'

'Assuming the horses don't eat you,' Geryon observed.

'Either way, you get my friends,' I said. 'But, if I succeed, you've got to let all of us go, including Nico.'

'No!' Nico screamed. 'Don't do me any favours, Percy. I don't want your help!'

Geryon chuckled. 'Percy Jackson, those stables haven't been cleaned in a thousand years . . . though it's true I might be able to sell more stable space if all that poop was cleared away.'

'So what have you got to lose?'

The rancher hesitated. 'All right, I'll accept your offer, but you have to get it done by sunset. If you fail, your friends get sold, and I get rich.'

'Deal.'

He nodded. 'I'm going to take your friends with me, back to the lodge. We'll wait for you there.'

Eurytion gave me a funny look. It might have been sympathy. He whistled, and the dog jumped off me and onto Annabeth's lap. She yelped. I knew Tyson and Grover would never try anything as long as Annabeth was a hostage.

I got out of the car and locked eyes with her.

'I hope you know what you're doing,' she said quietly.

'I hope so, too.'

Geryon got behind the driver's wheel. Eurytion hauled Nico into the back seat.

'Sunset,' Geryon reminded me. 'No later.'

He laughed at me once more, sounded his cowbell horn, and the moo-mobile rumbled off down the trail.

9 I SCOOP POOP

I lost hope when I saw the horses' teeth.

As I got closer to the fence I held my shirt over my nose to block the smell. One stallion waded through the muck and whinnied angrily at me. He bared his teeth, which were pointed like a bear's.

I tried to talk to him in my mind. I can do that with most horses.

Hi, I told him. *I'm going to clean your stables. Won't that be great?*

Yes! The horse said. *Come inside! Eat you! Tasty half-blood!*

But I'm Poseidon's son, I protested. *He created horses.*

Usually this gets me VIP treatment in the equestrian world, but not this time.

Yes! The horse agreed enthusiastically. *Poseidon can come in, too! We will eat you both! Seafood!*

Seafood! The other horses chimed in as they waded through the field. Flies were buzzing everywhere, and the heat of the day didn't make the smell any better. I'd had some idea that I could do this challenge, because I remembered how Hercules had done it. He'd channelled a river into the stables and cleaned them out that way. I figured I could maybe control the water. But if I couldn't get close to the horses without getting eaten, that was a problem. And the river was downhill from the stables, a lot further away than I'd realized, almost a kilometre. The problem of the poop looked a lot bigger up close. I picked up a rusted shovel and experimentally scooped some away from the fence line. Great. Only four billion shovelfuls to go.

The sun was already sinking. I had a few hours at best. I decided the river was my only hope. At least it would be easier to think at the riverside than it was here. I set off downhill.

When I got to the river, I found a girl waiting for me. She was wearing jeans and a green T-shirt and her long brown hair was braided with river grass. She had a stern look on her face. Her arms were crossed.

'Oh no you don't,' she said.

I stared at her. 'Are you a naiad?'

She rolled her eyes. 'Of course!'

'But you speak English. And you're out of the water.'

'What, you don't think we can act human if we want to?'

I'd never thought about it. I felt kind of stupid, though, because I'd seen plenty of naiads at camp, and they'd never done much more than giggle and wave at me from the bottom of the canoe lake.

'Look,' I said, 'I just came to ask –'

'I know who you are,' she said. 'And I know what you want. And the answer is no! I'm not going to have my river used again to clean that filthy stable.'

'But –'

'Oh, save it, sea boy. You ocean-god types always think you're soooo much more important than some little river, don't you? Well let me tell you, *this* naiad is not going to be pushed around just because your daddy is Poseidon. This is freshwater territory, mister. The last guy who asked me this favour – oh, he was way better-looking than you, by the way – he convinced me, and that was the worst mistake I've ever made! Do you have any idea what all that horse manure does to my ecosystem? Do I look like a sewage-treatment plant to you? My fish will die. I'll *never* get the muck out of my plants. I'll be sick for years. NO THANK YOU!'

The way she talked reminded me of my mortal friend, Rachel Elizabeth Dare – kind of like she was punching me with words. I couldn't blame the naiad. Now that I thought about it, I'd be pretty mad if somebody dumped two thousand tons of manure in my home. But still . . .

'My friends are in danger,' I told her.

'Well, that's too bad! But it's not my problem. And you're not going to ruin my river.'

She looked like she was ready for a fight. Her fists were balled, but I thought I heard a little quaver in her voice. Suddenly I realized that, despite her angry attitude, she was afraid of me. She probably thought I was going to fight her for control of the river, and she was worried she would lose.

The thought made me sad. I felt like a bully, a son of Poseidon throwing his weight around.

I sat down on a tree stump. 'Okay, you win.'

The naiad looked surprised. 'Really?'

'I'm not going to fight you. It's your river.'

She relaxed her shoulders. 'Oh. Oh, good. I mean – good thing for you!'

'But my friends and I are going to get sold to the Titans

if I don't clean those stables by sunset. And I don't know how.'

The river gurgled along cheerfully. A snake slid through the water and ducked its head under. Finally the naiad sighed.

'I'll tell you a secret, son of the sea god. Scoop up some dirt.'

'What?'

'You heard me.'

I crouched down and scooped up a handful of Texas dirt. It was dry and black and spotted with tiny clumps of white rock . . . No, something besides rock.

'Those are shells,' the naiad said. 'Petrified seashells. Millions of years ago, even before the time of the gods, when only Gaea and Ouranos reigned, this land was under water. It was part of the sea.'

Suddenly I saw what she meant. There were little pieces of ancient sea urchins in my hand, mollusc shells. Even the limestone rocks had impressions of seashells embedded in them.

'Okay,' I said. 'What good does that do me?'

'You're not so different from me, demigod. Even when I'm out of the water, the water is within me. It is my life source.' She stepped back, put her feet in the river, and smiled. 'I hope you find a way to rescue your friends.'

And with that she turned to liquid and melted into the river.

The sun was touching the hills when I got back to the stables. Somebody must've come by and fed the horses, because they were tearing into huge animal carcasses. I couldn't tell what kind of animal, and I really didn't want to know. If it was possible for the stables to get more disgusting, fifty horses tearing into raw meat did it.

Seafood! one thought when he saw me. *Come in! We're still hungry.*

What was I supposed to do? I couldn't use the river. And the fact that this place had been underwater a million years ago didn't exactly help me now. I looked at the little calcified seashell in my palm, then at the huge mountain of dung.

Frustrated, I threw the shell into the poop. I was about to turn my back on the horses when I heard a sound.

PFFFFFFT! Like a balloon with a leak.

I looked down where I had thrown the shell. A tiny spout of water was shooting out of the muck.

'No way,' I muttered.

Hesitantly, I stepped towards the fence. 'Get bigger,' I told the waterspout.

SPOOOOOOOSH!

Water shot a metre into the air and kept bubbling. It was impossible, but there it was. A couple of horses came over to check it out. One put his mouth to the spring and recoiled.

Yuck! he said. *Salty!*

It was seawater in the middle of a Texas ranch. I scooped up another handful of dirt and picked out the shell fossils. I didn't really know what I was doing, but I ran around the length of the stable, throwing shells into the dung piles. Everywhere a shell hit, a saltwater spring erupted.

Stop! The horses cried. *Meat is good! Baths are bad!*

Then I noticed the water wasn't running out of the

stables or flowing downhill like water normally would. It simply bubbled around each spring and sank into the ground, taking the dung with it. The horse poop dissolved in the saltwater, leaving regular old wet earth.

'More!' I yelled.

There was a tugging sensation in my gut, and the waterspouts exploded like the world's largest carwash. Salt water shot six metres into the air. The horses went crazy, running back and forth as the geysers sprayed them from all directions. Mountains of poop began to melt like ice.

The tugging sensation became more intense, painful even, but there was something exhilarating about seeing all that salt water. I had made this. I had brought the ocean to this hillside.

Stop, lord! a horse cried. *Stop, please!*

Water was sloshing everywhere now. The horses were drenched, and some were panicking and slipping in the mud. The poop was completely gone, tons of it just dissolved into the earth, and the water was now starting to pool, trickling out of the stable, making a hundred little streams down towards the river.

'Stop,' I told the water.

Nothing happened. The pain in my gut was building. If I didn't shut off the geysers soon, the salt water would run into the river and poison the fish and plants.

'Stop!' I concentrated all my might on shutting off the force of the sea.

Suddenly the geysers shut down. I collapsed to my knees, exhausted. In front of me was a shiny, clean horse stable, a field of wet, salty mud and fifty horses that had been scoured so thoroughly, their coats gleamed. Even the meat scraps between their teeth had been washed out.

We won't eat you! The horses wailed. *Please, lord! No more salty baths!*

'On one condition,' I said. 'You only eat the food your handlers give you from now on. Not people. Or I'll be back with more seashells!'

The horses whinnied and made me a whole lot of promises that they would be good flesh-eating horses from now on, but I didn't stick around to chat. The sun was going down. I turned and ran full speed towards the ranch house.

I smelled barbecue before I reached the house, and that made me madder than ever, because I really love barbecue.

The deck was set up for a party. Streamers and balloons decorated the railing. Geryon was flipping burgers on a huge barbecue cooker made from an oil drum. Eurytion lounged at a picnic table, picking his fingernails with a knife. The two-headed dog sniffed the ribs and burgers that were frying on the grill. And then I saw my friends: Tyson, Grover, Annabeth and Nico all tossed in a corner, tied up like rodeo animals, with their ankles and wrists roped together and their mouths gagged.

'Let them go!' I yelled, still out of breath from running up the steps. 'I cleaned the stables!'

Geryon turned. He wore an apron on each chest, with one word on each, so together they spelled out: KISS — THE — CHEF. 'Did you, now? How'd you manage it?'

I was pretty impatient, but I told him.

He nodded appreciatively. 'Very ingenious. It would've

been better if you'd poisoned that pesky naiad, but no matter.'

'Let my friends go,' I said. 'We had a deal.'

'Ah, I've been thinking about that. The problem is, if I let them go, I don't get paid.'

'You promised!'

Geryon made a *tsk-tsk* noise. 'But did you make me swear on the River Styx? No you didn't. So it's not binding. When you're conducting business, sonny, you should always get a binding oath.'

I drew my sword. Orthus growled. One head leaned down next to Grover's ear and bared its fangs.

'Eurytion,' Geryon said, 'the boy is starting to annoy me. Kill him.'

Eurytion studied me. I didn't like my odds against him and that huge club.

'Kill him yourself,' Eurytion said.

Geryon raised his eyebrows. 'Excuse me?'

'You heard me,' Eurytion grumbled. 'You keep sending me out to do your dirty work. You pick fights for no good reason, and I'm tired of dying for you. You want to fight the kid, do it yourself.'

It was the most un-Ares-like thing I'd ever heard a son of Ares say.

Geryon threw down his spatula. 'You dare defy me? I should fire you right now!'

'And who'd take care of your cattle? Orthus, heel.'

The dog immediately stopped growling at Grover and came to sit by the cowherd's feet.

'Fine!' Geryon snarled. 'I'll deal with you later, after the boy is dead!'

He picked up two carving knives and threw them at me. I deflected one with my sword. The other impaled itself in the picnic table, a millimetre from Eurytion's hand.

I went on the attack. Geryon parried my first strike with a pair of red-hot tongs and lunged at my face with a barbecue fork. I got inside his next thrust and stabbed him right through the middle chest.

'Aghhh!' He crumpled to his knees. I waited for him to disintegrate, the way monsters usually do. But instead he just grimaced and began to stand up. The bleeding slice through his chef's apron started to heal.

'Nice try, sonny,' he said. 'Thing is, I have three hearts. The perfect backup system.'

He tipped over the barbecue, and coals spilled everywhere. One landed next to Annabeth's face, and she let out a muffled scream. Tyson strained against his bonds, but even his strength wasn't enough to break them. I had to end this fight before my friends got hurt.

I jabbed Geryon in the left chest, but he only laughed. I stuck him in the right stomach. No good. I might as well have been sticking a sword in a teddy bear for all the reaction he showed.

Three hearts. The perfect backup system. Stabbing one at a time was no good . . .

I ran into the house.

'Coward!' he cried. 'Come back and die right!'

The living-room walls were decorated with a bunch of gruesome hunting trophies — stuffed deer and dragon heads, a gun case, a sword display and a bow with a quiver.

Geryon threw his barbecue fork, and it thudded into the wall right next to my head. He drew two swords from the wall display. 'Your head's gonna go right there, Jackson! Next to the grizzly bear!'

I had a crazy idea. I dropped Riptide and grabbed the bow off the wall.

I was the worst archery shot in the world. I couldn't hit the targets at camp, much less a bull's eye. But I had no choice. I couldn't win this fight with a sword. I prayed to Artemis and Apollo, the twin archers, hoping they might take pity on me for once. *Please, guys. Just one shot. Please.*

I notched an arrow.

Geryon laughed. 'You fool! One arrow is no better than one sword.'

He raised his swords and charged. I dived sideways. Before he could turn, I shot my arrow into the side of his right chest. I heard *THUMP, THUMP, THUMP,* as the arrow passed clean through each of his chests and flew out his left side, embedding itself in the forehead of the grizzly bear trophy.

Geryon dropped his swords. He turned and stared at me. 'You can't shoot. They told me you couldn't . . .'

His face turned a sickly shade of green. He collapsed to his knees and began crumbling into sand, until all that was left were three cooking aprons and an oversized pair of cowboy boots.

I got my friends untied. Eurytion didn't try to stop me. Then I stoked up the barbecue and threw the food into the flames as a burnt offering to Artemis and Apollo.

'Thanks, guys,' I said. 'I owe you one.'

The sky thundered in the distance, so I figured maybe the burgers smelled okay.

'Yay for Percy!' Tyson said.

'Can we tie up this cowherd now?' Nico asked.

'Yeah!' Grover agreed. 'And that dog almost killed me!'

I looked at Eurytion, who was still sitting, relaxed, at the picnic table. Orthus had both his heads on the cowherd's knees.

'How long will it take Geryon to re-form?' I asked him.

Eurytion shrugged. 'Hundred years? He's not one of those fast re-formers, thank the gods. You've done me a favour.'

'You said you'd died for him before,' I remembered. 'How?'

'I've worked for that creep for thousands of years. Started as a regular half-blood, but I chose immortality when my dad offered it. Worst mistake I ever made. Now I'm stuck here at this ranch. I can't leave. I can't quit. I just tend the cows and fight Geryon's fights. We're kinda tied together.'

'Maybe you can change things,' I said.

Eurytion narrowed his eyes. 'How?'

'Be nice to the animals. Take care of them. Stop selling them for food. And stop dealing with the Titans.'

Eurytion thought about that. 'That'd be all right.'

'Get the animals on your side, and they'll help you. Once Geryon gets back, maybe he'll be working for you this time.'

Eurytion grinned. 'Now *that* I could live with.'

'You won't try to stop us leaving?'

'Shoot, no.'

Annabeth rubbed her bruised wrists. She was still looking at Eurytion suspiciously. 'Your boss said that somebody paid for our safe passage. Who?'

The cowherd shrugged. 'Maybe he was just saying that to fool you.'

'What about the Titans?' I asked. 'Did you Iris-message them about Nico yet?'

'Nope. Geryon was waiting until after the barbecue. They don't know anything about him.'

Nico was glaring at me. I wasn't sure what to do about him. I doubted he would agree to come with us. On the other hand, I couldn't just let him roam around on his own.

'You could stay here until we're done with our quest,' I told him. 'It would be safe.'

'*Safe?*' Nico said. 'What do you care if I'm safe? You got my sister killed!'

'Nico,' Annabeth said, 'that wasn't Percy's fault. And Geryon wasn't lying about Kronos wanting to capture you. If he knew who you were, he'd do anything to get you on his side.'

'I'm not on anyone's side. And I'm not afraid!'

'You should be,' Annabeth said. 'Your sister wouldn't want –'

'If you cared for my sister, you'd help me bring her back!'

'A soul for a soul?' I said.

'Yes!'

'But if you didn't want my soul –'

'I'm not explaining anything to you!' He blinked tears out of his eyes. 'And I *will* bring her back.'

'Bianca wouldn't want to be brought back,' I said. 'Not like that.'

'You didn't know her!' he shouted. 'How do you know what she'd want?'

I stared at the flames in the barbecue pit. I thought about the line in Annabeth's prophecy: *You shall rise or fall by the ghost king's hand.* That had to be Minos, and I *had* to convince Nico not to listen to him. 'Let's ask Bianca.'

The sky seemed to grow darker all of a sudden.

'I've tried,' Nico said miserably. 'She won't answer.'

'Try again. I've got a feeling she'll answer, with me here.'

'Why would she?'

'Because she's been sending me Iris-messages,' I said, suddenly sure of it. 'She's been trying to warn me what you're up to, so I can protect you.'

Nico shook his head. 'That's impossible.'

'One way to find out. You said you're not afraid.' I turned to Eurytion. 'We're going to need a pit, like a grave. And food and drinks.'

'Percy,' Annabeth warned. 'I don't think this is a good —'

'All right,' Nico said. 'I'll try.'

Eurytion scratched his beard. 'There's a hole dug out back for a septic tank. We could use that. Cyclops boy, fetch my ice chest from the kitchen. I hope the dead like root beer.'

WE PLAY THE GAME SHOW OF DEATH

We did our summons after dark, at a seven-metre-long pit in front of the septic tank. The tank was bright yellow, with a smiley face and red words painted on the side: HAPPY FLUSH DISPOSAL CO. It didn't quite go with the mood of summoning the dead.

The moon was full. Silver clouds drifted across the sky.

'Minos should be here by now,' Nico said, frowning. 'It's full dark.'

'Maybe he got lost,' I said hopefully.

Nico poured root beer and tossed barbecue into the pit, then began chanting in Ancient Greek. Immediately, the bugs in the woods stopped chirping. In my pocket, the Stygian ice dog whistle started to grow colder, freezing against the side of my leg.

'Make him stop,' Tyson whispered to me.

Part of me agreed. This was unnatural. The night air felt cold and menacing. But before I could say anything, the first spirits appeared. Sulphurous mist seeped out of the ground. Shadows thickened into human forms. One blue shade drifted to the edge of the pit and knelt to drink.

'Stop him!' Nico said, momentarily breaking his chant. 'Only Bianca may drink!'

I drew Riptide. The ghosts retreated with a collective

hiss at the sight of my celestial bronze blade. But it was too late to stop the first spirit. He had already solidified into the shape of a bearded man in white robes. A circlet of gold wreathed his head, and even in death his eyes were alive with malice.

'Minos!' Nico said. 'What are you doing?'

'My apologies, master,' the ghost said, though he didn't sound very sorry. 'The sacrifice smelled so good, I couldn't resist.' He examined his own hands and smiled. 'It is good to see myself again. Almost in solid form –'

'You are disrupting the ritual!' Nico protested. 'Get –'

The spirits of the dead began shimmering dangerously bright, and Nico had to take up the chant again to keep them at bay.

'Yes, quite right, master,' Minos said with amusement. 'You keep chanting. I've only come to protect you from these *liars* who would deceive you.'

He turned to me as if I were some kind of cockroach. 'Percy Jackson . . . my, my. The sons of Poseidon haven't improved over the centuries, have they?'

I wanted to punch him, but I figured my fist would go right through his face. 'We're looking for Bianca di Angelo,' I said. 'Get lost.'

The ghost chuckled. 'I understand you once killed my Minotaur with your bare hands. But worse things await you in the maze. Do you really believe Daedalus will help you?'

The other spirits stirred in agitation. Annabeth drew her knife and helped me keep them away from the pit. Grover got so nervous he clung to Tyson's shoulder.

'Daedalus cares nothing for you, half-bloods,' Minos

warned. 'You can't trust him. He is old beyond counting, and crafty. He is bitter from the guilt of murder and is cursed by the gods.'

'The guilt of murder?' I asked. 'Who did he kill?'

'Do not change the subject!' the ghost growled. 'You are hindering Nico. You try to persuade him to give up his goal. *I* would make him a lord!'

'Enough, Minos,' Nico commanded.

The ghost sneered. 'Master, these are your enemies. You must not listen to them! Let me protect you. I will turn their minds to madness, as I did the others.'

'The others?' Annabeth gasped. 'You mean Chris Rodriguez? That was *you*?'

'The maze is my property,' the ghost said, 'not Daedalus's! Those who intrude deserve madness.'

'Begone, Minos!' Nico demanded. 'I want to see my sister!'

The ghost bit back his rage. 'As you wish, master. But I warn you. You cannot trust these heroes.'

With that, he faded into mist.

Other spirits rushed forward, but Annabeth and I kept them back.

'Bianca, appear!' Nico intoned. He started chanting faster, and the spirits shifted restlessly.

'Any time now,' Grover muttered.

Then a silvery light flickered in the trees – a spirit that seemed brighter and stronger than the others. It came closer, and something told me to let it pass. It knelt to drink at the pit. When it arose, it was the ghostly form of Bianca di Angelo.

Nico's chanting faltered. I lowered my sword. The other

spirits started to crowd forward, but Bianca raised her arms and they retreated into the woods.

'Hello, Percy,' she said.

She looked the same as she had in life: a green cap set sideways on her thick black hair, dark eyes and olive skin like her brother. She wore jeans and a silvery jacket, the outfit of a Hunter of Artemis. A bow was slung over her shoulder. She smiled faintly, and her whole form flickered.

'Bianca,' I said. My voice was thick. I'd felt guilty about her death for a long time, but seeing her in front of me was five times as bad, like her death was fresh and new. I remembered searching through the wreckage of the giant bronze warrior she'd sacrificed her life to defeat, and not finding any sign of her.

'I'm so sorry,' I said.

'You have nothing to apologize for, Percy. I made my own choice. I don't regret it.'

'Bianca!' Nico stumbled forward like he was just coming out of a daze.

She turned towards her brother. Her expression was sad, as if she'd been dreading this moment. 'Hello, Nico. You've got so tall.'

'Why didn't you answer me sooner?' he cried. 'I've been trying for months!'

'I was hoping you would give up.'

'Give up?' He sounded heartbroken. 'How can you say that? I'm trying to save you!'

'You can't, Nico. Don't do this. Percy is right.'

'No! He let you die! He's not your friend.'

Bianca stretched out a hand as if to touch her brother's

face, but she was made of mist. Her hand evaporated as it got close to living skin.

'You must listen to me,' she said. 'Holding grudges is dangerous for a child of Hades. It is our fatal flaw. You have to forgive. You have to promise me this.'

'I can't. Never.'

'Percy has been worried about you, Nico. He can help. I let him see what you were up to, hoping he would find you.'

'So it *was* you,' I said. 'You sent those Iris-messages.'

Bianca nodded.

'Why are you helping him and not me?' Nico screamed. 'It's not fair!'

'You are close to the truth now,' Bianca told him. 'It's not Percy you're mad at, Nico. It's me.'

'No.'

'You're mad because I left you to become a Hunter of Artemis. You're mad because I died and left you alone. I'm sorry for that, Nico. I truly am. But you must overcome the anger. And stop blaming Percy for my choices. It will be your doom.'

'She's right,' Annabeth broke in. 'Kronos is rising, Nico. He'll twist anyone he can to his cause.'

'I don't care about Kronos,' Nico said. 'I just want my sister back.'

'You can't have that, Nico,' Bianca told him gently.

'I'm the son of Hades! I *can*.'

'Don't try,' she said. 'If you love me, don't . . .'

Her voice trailed off. Spirits had started to gather around us again, and they seemed agitated. Their shadows shifted. Their voices whispered, *Danger!*

'Tartarus stirs,' Bianca said. 'Your power draws the attention of Kronos. The dead must return to the Underworld. It is not safe for us to remain.'

'Wait,' Nico said. 'Please –'

'Goodbye, Nico,' Bianca said. 'I love you. Remember what I said.'

Her form shivered and the ghosts disappeared, leaving us alone with a pit, a HAPPY FLUSH septic tank and a cold full moon.

None of us were anxious to travel that night, so we decided to wait until morning. Grover and I crashed on the leather couches in Geryon's living room, which was a lot more comfortable than a bedroll in the maze, but it didn't make my nightmares any better.

I dreamed I was with Luke, walking through the dark palace on top of Mount Tam. It was a real building now – not some half-finished illusion like I'd seen last winter. Green fires burned in braziers along the walls. The floor was polished black marble. A cold wind blew down the hallway, and above us through the open ceiling the sky swirled with grey storm clouds.

Luke was dressed for battle. He wore camouflage combats, a white T-shirt and a bronze breastplate, but his sword, Backbiter, wasn't at his side – only an empty scabbard. We walked into a large courtyard where dozens of warriors and *dracaenae* were preparing for war. When they saw him, the demigods rose to attention. They beat their swords against their shields.

'Issss it time, my lord?' a *dracaena* asked.

'Soon,' Luke promised. 'Continue your work.'

'My lord,' a voice said behind him. Kelli the *empousa* was smiling at him. She wore a blue dress tonight, and looked wickedly beautiful. Her eyes flickered – sometimes dark brown, sometimes pure red. Her hair was braided down her back and seemed to catch the light of the torches, as if it were anxious to turn back into pure flame.

My heart was pounding. I waited for Kelli to see me, to chase me out of the dream as she had before, but this time she didn't seem to notice me.

'You have a visitor,' she told Luke. She stepped aside, and even Luke seemed stunned by what he saw.

The monster Kampê towered above him. Her snakes hissed around her legs. Animal heads growled at her waist. Her swords were drawn, shimmering with poison, and with her bat wings extended, she took up the entire corridor.

'You.' Luke's voice sounded a little shaky. 'I told you to stay on Alcatraz.'

Kampê's eyelids blinked sideways like a reptile's. She spoke in that weird rumbling language, but this time I understood, somewhere in the back of my mind: *I come to serve. Give me revenge.*

'You're a jailer,' Luke said. 'Your job –'

I will have them dead. No one escapes me.

Luke hesitated. A line of sweat trickled down the side of his face. 'Very well,' he said. 'You will go with us. You may carry Ariadne's string. It is a position of great honour.'

Kampê hissed at the stars. She sheathed her swords and turned, pounding down the hallway on her enormous dragon legs.

'We should have left that one in Tartarus,' Luke mumbled. 'She is too chaotic. Too powerful.'

Kelli laughed softly. 'You should not fear power, Luke. Use it!'

'The sooner we leave, the better,' Luke said. 'I want this over with.'

'Aww,' Kelli sympathized, running a finger down his arm. 'You find it unpleasant to destroy your old camp?'

'I didn't say that.'

'You're not having second thoughts about your own, ah, special part?'

Luke's face turned stony. 'I know my duty.'

'That is good,' the demon said. 'Is our strike force sufficient, do you think? Or will I need to call Mother Hecate for help?'

'We have more than enough,' Luke said grimly. 'The deal is almost complete. All I need now is to negotiate safe passage through the arena.'

'Mmm,' Kelli said. 'That should be interesting. I would hate to see your handsome head on a spike if you fail.'

'I will not fail. And you, demon, don't you have other matters to attend to?'

'Oh, yes.' Kelli smiled. 'I am bringing despair to our eavesdropping enemies. I am doing that right now.'

She turned her eyes directly on me, exposed her talons and ripped through my dream.

Suddenly I was in a different place.

I stood at the top of a stone tower, overlooking rocky cliffs and the ocean below. The old man Daedalus was hunched over a worktable, wrestling with some kind of navigational instrument, like a huge compass. He looked years older than when I'd last seen him. He was stooped and his hands were gnarled. He cursed in Ancient Greek and squinted as if he couldn't see his work, even though it was a sunny day.

'Uncle!' a voice called.

A smiling boy about Nico's age came bounding up the steps, carrying a wooden box.

'Hello, Perdix,' the old man said, though his tone sounded cold. 'Done with your projects already?'

'Yes, Uncle. They were easy!'

Daedalus scowled. 'Easy? The problem of moving water uphill without a pump was easy?'

'Oh, yes! Look!'

The boy dumped his box and rummaged through the junk. He came up with a strip of papyrus and showed the old inventor some diagrams and notes. They didn't make any sense to me, but Daedalus nodded grudgingly. 'I see. Not bad.'

'The king loved it!' Perdix said. 'He said I might be even smarter than you!'

'Did he now?'

'But I don't believe that. I'm so glad Mother sent me to study with you! I want to know everything you do.'

'Yes,' Daedalus muttered. 'So when I die, you can take my place, eh?'

The boy's eyes widened. 'Oh no, Uncle! But I've been thinking . . . why does a man have to die, anyway?'

The inventor scowled. 'It is the way of things, lad. Everything dies but the gods.'

'But *why?*' the boy insisted. 'If you could capture the *animus*, the soul in another form . . . Well, you've told me

[162]

about your automatons, Uncle. Bulls, eagles, dragons, horses of bronze. Why not a bronze form for a man?'

'No, my boy,' Daedalus said sharply. 'You are naive. Such a thing is impossible.'

'I don't think so,' Perdix insisted. 'With the use of a little magic –'

'Magic? Bah!'

'Yes, Uncle! Magic and mechanics together – with a little work, one could make a body that would look exactly human, only better. I've made some notes.'

He handed the old man a thick scroll. Daedalus unfurled it. He read for a long time. His eyes narrowed. He glanced at the boy, then closed the scroll and cleared his throat. 'It would never work, my boy. When you're older, you'll see.'

'Can I fix that astrolabe, then, Uncle? Are your joints swelling up again?'

The old man's jaw clenched. 'No. Thank you. Now why don't you run along?'

Perdix didn't seem to notice the old man's anger. He snatched a bronze beetle from his mound of stuff and ran to the edge of the tower. A low sill ringed the rim, coming just up to the boy's knees. The wind was strong.

Move back, I wanted to tell him. But my voice didn't work.

Perdix wound up the beetle and tossed it into the sky. It spread its wings and hummed away. Perdix laughed with delight.

'Smarter than me,' Daedalus mumbled, too softly for the boy to hear.

'Is it true your son died flying, Uncle? I heard you made him enormous wings, but they failed.'

Daedalus's hands clenched. 'Take my place,' he muttered.

The wind whipped around the boy, tugging at his clothes, making his hair ripple.

'I would like to fly,' Perdix said. 'I'd make my own wings that wouldn't fail. Do you think I could?'

Maybe it was a dream within my dream, but suddenly I imagined the two-headed god Janus shimmering in the air next to Daedalus, smiling as he tossed a silver key from hand to hand. *Choose*, he whispered to the old inventor. *Choose.*

Daedalus picked up another one of the boy's metal bugs. The inventor's old eyes were red with anger.

'Perdix,' he called. 'Catch.'

He tossed the bronze beetle towards the boy. Delighted, Perdix tried to catch it, but the throw was too long. The beetle sailed into open sky, and Perdix reached a little too far. The wind caught him.

Somehow he managed to grab the rim of the tower with his fingers as he fell. 'Uncle!' he screamed. 'Help me!'

The old man's face was a mask. He did not move from his spot.

'Go on, Perdix,' Daedalus said softly. 'Make your own wings. Be quick about it.'

'Uncle!' the boy cried as he lost his grip. He tumbled towards the sea.

There was a moment of deadly silence. The god Janus flickered and disappeared. Then thunder shook the sky. A woman's stern voice spoke from above: *You will pay the price for that, Daedalus.*

I'd heard that voice before. It was Annabeth's mother: Athena.

Daedalus scowled up at the heavens. 'I have always honoured you, Mother. I have sacrificed everything to follow your way.'

Yet the boy had my blessing as well. And you have killed him. For that, you must pay.

'I've paid and paid!' Daedalus growled. 'I've lost everything. I'll suffer in the Underworld, no doubt. But in the meantime . . .'

He picked up the boy's scroll, studied it for a moment and slipped it into his sleeve.

You do not understand, Athena said coldly. *You will pay now and forever.*

Suddenly Daedalus collapsed in agony. I felt what he felt. A searing pain closed around my neck like a molten-hot collar – cutting off my breath, making everything go black.

I woke in the dark, my hands clutching at my throat.

'Percy?' Grover called from the other sofa. 'Are you okay?'

I steadied my breathing. I wasn't sure how to answer. I'd just watched the guy we were looking for, Daedalus, murder his own nephew. How could I be okay? The television was going. Blue light flickered through the room.

'What – what time is it?' I croaked.

'Two in the morning,' Grover said. 'I couldn't sleep. I was watching the Nature Channel.' He sniffled. 'I miss Juniper.'

I rubbed the sleep out of my eyes. 'Yeah, well . . . you'll see her again soon.'

Grover shook his head sadly. 'Do you know what day it is, Percy? I just saw it on TV. It's June thirteenth. Seven days since we left camp.'

'What?' I said. 'That can't be right.'

'Time is faster in the Labyrinth,' Grover reminded me. 'The first time you and Annabeth went down there, you thought you were only gone a few minutes, right? But it was an hour.'

'Oh,' I said. 'Right.' Then it dawned on me what he was saying, and my throat felt searing hot again. 'Your deadline with the Council of Cloven Elders.'

Grover put the TV remote in his mouth and crunched off the end of it. 'I'm out of time,' he said with a mouthful of plastic. 'As soon as I go back, they'll take away my searcher's licence. I'll never be allowed to go out again.'

'We'll talk to them,' I promised. 'Make them give you more time.'

Grover swallowed. 'They'll never go for it. The world is dying, Percy. Every day it gets worse. The wild . . . I can just feel it fading. I *have* to find Pan.'

'You will, man. No doubt.'

Grover looked at me with sad goat eyes. 'You've always been a good friend, Percy. What you did today – saving the ranch animals from Geryon – that was amazing. I – I wish I could be more like you.'

'Hey,' I said. 'Don't say that. You're just as much a hero –'

'No, I'm not. I keep trying, but . . .' He sighed. 'Percy, I can't go back to camp without finding Pan. I just can't.

You understand that, don't you? I can't face Juniper if I fail. I can't even face myself.'

His voice was so unhappy, it hurt to hear. We'd been through a lot together, but I'd never heard him sound this down.

'We'll figure out something,' I said. 'You haven't failed. You're the champion goat boy, all right? Juniper knows that. So do I.'

Grover closed his eyes. 'Champion goat boy,' he muttered dejectedly.

A long time after he had dozed off, I was still awake, watching the blue light of the Nature Channel wash over the stuffed trophy heads on Geryon's walls.

The next morning we walked down to the cattle grid and said our goodbyes.

'Nico, you could come with us,' I blurted out. I guess I was thinking about my dream, and how much the young boy Perdix reminded me of Nico.

He shook his head. I don't think one of us had slept well in the demon ranch house, but Nico looked worse than anybody else. His eyes were red and his face chalky. He was wrapped in a black robe that must've belonged to Geryon, because it was three sizes too big even for a grown man.

'I need time to think.' His eyes wouldn't meet mine, but I could tell from his tone he was still angry. The fact that his sister had come out of the Underworld for me and not for him didn't seem to sit well with him.

'Nico,' Annabeth said. 'Bianca just wants you to be okay.'

She put her hand on his shoulder, but he pulled away and trudged up the road towards the ranch house. Maybe it was my imagination, but the morning mist seemed to cling to him as he walked.

'I'm worried about him,' Annabeth told me. 'If he starts talking to Minos's ghost again –'

'He'll be all right,' Eurytion promised. The cowherd had cleaned up nicely. He was wearing new jeans and a clean Western shirt and he'd even trimmed his beard. He'd put on Geryon's boots. 'The boy can stay here and gather his thoughts as long as he wants. He'll be safe, I promise.'

'What about you?' I asked.

Eurytion scratched Orthus behind one chin, then the other. 'Things are going to be run a little different on this ranch from now on. No more sacred cattle meat. I'm thinking about soya-bean patties. And I'm going to befriend those flesh-eating horses. Might just sign up for the next rodeo.'

The idea made me shudder. 'Well, good luck.'

'Yep.' Eurytion spat into the grass. 'I reckon you'll be looking for Daedalus's workshop now?'

Annabeth's eyes lit up. 'Can you help us?'

Eurytion studied the cattle grid, and I got the feeling the subject of Daedalus's workshop made him uncomfortable. 'Don't know where it is. But Hephaestus probably would.'

'That's what Hera said,' Annabeth agreed. 'But how do we find Hephaestus?'

Eurytion pulled something from under the collar of his shirt. It was a necklace – a smooth silver disc on a silver chain. The disc had a depression on the middle, like a thumbprint. He handed it to Annabeth.

'Hephaestus comes here from time to time,' Eurytion said. 'Studies the animals and such so he can make bronze automaton copies. Last time, I – uh – did him a favour. A little trick he wanted to play on my dad, Ares, and Aphrodite. He gave me that chain in gratitude. Said if I ever needed to find him, the disc would lead me to his forges. But only once.'

'And you're giving it to me?' Annabeth asked.

Eurytion blushed. 'I don't need to see the forges, miss. Got enough to do here. Just press the button and you'll be on your way.'

Annabeth pressed the button and the disc sprang to life. It grew eight metallic legs. Annabeth shrieked and dropped it, much to Eurytion's confusion.

'Spider!' she screamed.

'She's, um, a little scared of spiders,' Grover explained. 'That old grudge between Athena and Arachne.'

'Oh.' Eurytion looked embarrassed. 'Sorry, miss.'

The spider scrambled to the cattle grid and disappeared between the bars.

'Hurry,' I said. 'That thing's not going to wait for us.'

Annabeth wasn't anxious to follow, but we didn't have much choice. We said our goodbyes to Eurytion, Tyson pulled the cattle grid off the hole and we dropped back into the maze.

I wish I could've put the mechanical spider on a leash. It scuttled along the tunnels so fast that most of time I couldn't even see it. If it hadn't been for Tyson's and Grover's excellent hearing, we never would've known which way it was going.

We ran down a marble tunnel, then dashed to the left and almost fell into an abyss. Tyson grabbed me and hauled me back before I could fall. The tunnel continued in front of us, but there was no floor for about thirty metres, just gaping darkness and a series of iron rungs in the ceiling. The mechanical spider was about halfway across, swinging from bar to bar by shooting out metal web fibre.

'Monkey bars,' Annabeth said. 'I'm great at these.'

She leaped onto the first rung and started swinging her way across. She was scared of tiny spiders, but not of plummeting to her death from a set of monkey bars. Go figure.

Annabeth got to the opposite side and ran after the spider. I followed. When I got across, I looked back and saw Tyson giving Grover a piggyback ride (or was it a goatyback ride?). The big guy made it across in three swings, which was a good thing since, just as he landed, the last iron bar ripped free under his weight.

We kept moving and passed a skeleton crumpled in the tunnel. It wore the remains of a dress shirt, trousers and a tie. The spider didn't slow down. I slipped on a pile of wood scraps, but when I shone a light on them I realized they were pencils – hundreds of them, all broken in half.

The tunnel opened up into a large room. A blazing light hit us. Once my eyes adjusted, the first thing I noticed were the skeletons. Dozens littered the floor around us. Some were old and bleached white. Others were more recent and a lot grosser. They didn't smell quite as bad as Geryon's stables, but almost.

Then I saw the monster. She stood on a glittery dais on the opposite side of the room. She had the body of a huge lion and the head of a woman. She would've been pretty, but her hair was tied back in a tight bun and she wore too much makeup, so she kind of reminded me of my third-grade choir teacher. She had a blue ribbon badge pinned to her chest that took me a moment to read: THIS MONSTER HAS BEEN RATED EXEMPLARY!

Tyson whimpered. 'Sphinx.'

I knew exactly why he was scared. When he was small, Tyson had been attacked by a Sphinx in New York. He still had the scars on his back to prove it.

Spotlights blazed on either side of the creature. The only exit was a tunnel right behind the dais. The mechanical spider scuttled between the Sphinx's paws and disappeared.

Annabeth started forward, but the Sphinx roared, showing fangs in her otherwise human face. Bars came down on both tunnel exits, behind us and in front.

Immediately the monster's snarl turned into a brilliant smile.

'Welcome, lucky contestants!' she announced. 'Get ready to play . . . ANSWER THAT RIDDLE!'

Canned applause blasted from the ceiling, as if there were invisible loudspeakers. Spotlights swept across the room and reflected off the dais, throwing disco glitter over the skeletons on the floor.

'Fabulous prizes!' the Sphinx said. 'Pass the test, and you get to advance! Fail, and I get to eat you! Who will be our contestant?'

Annabeth grabbed my arm. 'I've got this,' she whispered. 'I know what she's going to ask.'

I didn't argue too hard. I didn't want Annabeth getting devoured by a monster, but I figured if the Sphinx were going to ask riddles, Annabeth was the best one of us to try.

She stepped forward to the contestant's podium, which had a skeleton in a school uniform hunched over it. She pushed the skeleton out of the way, and it clattered to the floor.

'Sorry,' Annabeth told it.

'Welcome, Annabeth Chase!' the monster cried, though Annabeth hadn't said her name. 'Are you ready for your test?'

'Yes,' she said. 'Ask your riddle.'

'Twenty riddles, actually!' the Sphinx said gleefully.

'What? But back in the old days —'

'Oh, we've raised our standards! To pass, you must show proficiency in all twenty. Isn't that great?'

Applause switched on and off like somebody turning a faucet.

Annabeth glanced at me nervously. I gave her an encouraging nod.

'Okay,' she told the Sphinx. 'I'm ready.'

A drumroll sounded from above. The Sphinx's eyes glittered with excitement. 'What . . . is the capital of Bulgaria?'

Annabeth frowned. For a terrible moment, I thought she was stumped.

'Sofia,' she said, 'but —'

'Correct!' More canned applause. The Sphinx smiled so wide her fangs showed. 'Please be sure to mark your answer clearly on your test sheet with a 2B pencil.'

'What?' Annabeth looked mystified. Then a test booklet appeared on the podium in front of her, along with a sharpened pencil.

'Make sure you bubble each answer clearly and stay inside the circle,' the Sphinx said. 'If you have to erase, erase completely or the machine will not be able to read your answers.'

'What machine?' Annabeth asked.

The Sphinx pointed with her paw. Over by the spotlight was a bronze box with a bunch of gears and levers and a big Greek letter H, Êta, on the side, the mark of Hephaestus.

'Now,' said the Sphinx, 'next question –'

'Wait a second,' Annabeth protested. 'What about "What walks on four legs in the morning?"'

'I beg your pardon?' the Sphinx said, clearly annoyed now.

'The riddle about man. He walks on four legs in morning, like a baby, two legs in the afternoon, like an adult, and three legs in the evening, as an old man with a cane. That's the riddle you used to ask.'

'Exactly why we changed the test!' the Sphinx exclaimed. 'You already knew the answer. Now, second question, what is the square root of sixteen?'

'Four,' Annabeth said, 'but –'

'Correct! Which US president signed the Emancipation Proclamation?'

'Abraham Lincoln, but –'

'Correct! Riddle number four. How much –'

'Hold up!' Annabeth shouted.

I wanted to tell her to stop complaining. She was doing

great! She should just answer the questions so we could leave.

'These aren't riddles,' Annabeth said.

'What do you mean?' the Sphinx snapped. 'Of course they are. This test material is specially designed —'

'It's just a bunch of dumb, random facts,' Annabeth insisted. 'Riddles are supposed to make you think.'

'Think?' The Sphinx frowned. 'How am I supposed to test whether you can think? That's ridiculous! Now, how much force is required —'

'Stop!' Annabeth insisted. 'This is a stupid test.'

'Um, Annabeth,' Grover cut in nervously. 'Maybe you should just, you know, finish first and complain later?'

'I'm a child of Athena,' she insisted. 'And this is an insult to my intelligence. I won't answer these questions.'

Part of me was impressed with her for standing up like that. But part of me thought her pride was going to get us all killed.

The spotlights glared. The Sphinx's eyes glittered pure black.

'Why then, my dear,' the monster said calmly. 'If you won't pass, you fail. And since we can't allow any children to be held back, you'll be EATEN!'

The Sphinx bared her claws, which gleamed like stainless steel. She pounced at the podium.

'No!' Tyson charged. He hates it when people threaten Annabeth, but I couldn't believe he was being so brave, especially since he'd had such a bad experience with a Sphinx before.

He tackled the Sphinx midair and they crashed sideways into a pile of bones. This gave Annabeth just enough time to gather her wits and draw her knife. Tyson got up, his shirt clawed to shreds. The Sphinx growled, looking for an opening.

I drew Riptide and stepped in front of Annabeth.

'Turn invisible,' I told her.

'I can fight!'

'No!' I yelled. 'The Sphinx is after *you*! Let us get it.'

As if to prove my point, the Sphinx knocked Tyson aside and tried to charge past me. Grover poked her in the eye with somebody's leg bone. She screeched in pain. Annabeth put on her cap and vanished. The Sphinx pounced right where she'd been standing, but came up with empty paws.

'No fair!' the Sphinx wailed. 'Cheater!'

With Annabeth no longer in sight, the Sphinx turned on me. I raised my sword but, before I could strike, Tyson ripped the monster's grading machine out of the floor and threw it at the monster's head, ruining her hair bun. It landed in pieces all around her.

'My grading machine!' she cried. 'I can't be exemplary without my test scores!'

The bars lifted from the exits. We all dashed for the far tunnel. I could only hope Annabeth was doing the same.

The Sphinx started to follow, but Grover raised his reed pipes and began to play. Suddenly the pencils remembered they used to be parts of trees. They collected around the Sphinx's paws, grew roots and branches, and began wrapping around the monster's legs. The Sphinx ripped through them, but it bought us just enough time.

Tyson pulled Grover into the tunnel, and the bars slammed shut behind us.

'Annabeth!' I yelled.

'Here!' she said, right next to me. 'Keep moving!'

We ran through the dark tunnels, listening to the roar of the Sphinx behind us as she complained about all the tests she would have to grade by hand.

II   I SET MYSELF ON FIRE

I thought we'd lost the spider until Tyson heard a faint pinging sound. We made a few turns, backtracked a few times and eventually found the spider banging its tiny head on a metal door.

The door looked like one of those old-fashioned submarine hatches — oval, with metal rivets around the edges and a wheel for a doorknob. Where the portal should've been was a big brass plaque, green with age, with a Greek Êta inscribed in the middle.

We all looked at each other.

'Ready to meet Hephaestus?' Grover said nervously.

'No,' I admitted.

'Yes!' Tyson said gleefully, and he turned the wheel.

As soon as the door opened, the spider scuttled inside with Tyson right behind it. The rest of us followed, not quite as anxious.

The room was enormous. It looked like a mechanic's garage, with several hydraulic lifts. Some had cars on them, but others had stranger things: a bronze hippalektryon with its horse head off and a bunch of wires hanging out of its rooster tail, a metal lion that seemed to be hooked up to a battery charger, and a Greek war chariot made entirely of flames.

Smaller projects cluttered a dozen worktables. Tools

hung along the walls. Each had its own outline on a peg-board, but nothing seemed to be in the right place. The hammer was over the screwdriver place. The staple gun was where the hacksaw was supposed to go.

Under the nearest hydraulic lift, which was holding a '98 Toyota Corolla, a pair of legs stuck out – the lower half of a huge man in grubby grey overalls and shoes even bigger than Tyson's. One leg was in a metal brace.

The spider scuttled straight under the car, and the sounds of banging stopped.

'Well, well,' a deep voice boomed from under the Corolla. 'What have we here?'

The mechanic pushed out on a back trolley and sat up. I'd seen Hephaestus once before, briefly, on Olympus, so I thought I was prepared, but his appearance made me gulp.

I guess he'd cleaned up when I saw him on Olympus, or used magic to make his form seem a little less hideous. Here in his own workshop, he apparently didn't care how he looked. He wore overalls smeared with oil and grime. *Hephaestus* was embroidered over the chest pocket. His leg creaked and clicked in its metal brace as he stood, and his left shoulder was lower than his right, so he seemed to be leaning even when he was standing up straight. His head was misshapen and bulging. He wore a permanent scowl. His black beard smoked and hissed. Every once in a while a small wildfire would erupt in his whiskers then die out. His hands were the size of catcher's mitts, but he handled the spider with amazing skill. He disassembled it in two seconds, then put it back together.

'There,' he muttered to himself. 'Much better.'

The spider did a happy flip in his palm, shot a metallic web at the ceiling, and went swinging away.

Hephaestus glowered up at us. 'I didn't make you, did I?'

'Uh,' Annabeth said, 'no, sir.'

'Good,' the god grumbled. 'Shoddy workmanship.'

He studied Annabeth and me. 'Half-bloods,' he grunted. 'Could be automatons, of course, but probably not.'

'We've met, sir,' I told him.

'Have we?' the god asked absently. I got the feeling he didn't care one way or the other. He was just trying to figure out how my jaw worked, whether it was a hinge or lever or what. 'Well then, if I didn't smash you to a pulp the first time we met, I suppose I won't have to do it now.'

He looked at Grover and frowned. 'Satyr.' Then he looked at Tyson, and his eyes twinkled. 'Well, a Cyclops. Good, good. What are you doing travelling with this lot?'

'Uh . . .' said Tyson, staring in wonder at the god.

'Yes, well said,' Hephaestus agreed. 'So, there'd better be a good reason you're disturbing me. The suspension on this Corolla is no small matter, you know.'

'Sir,' Annabeth said hesitantly, 'we're looking for Daedalus. We thought –'

'*Daedalus?*' the god roared. 'You want that old scoundrel? You dare to seek him out!'

His beard burst into flames and his black eyes glowed.

'Uh, yes, sir, please,' Annabeth said.

'Humph. You're wasting your time.' He frowned at

something on his worktable and limped over to it. He picked up a lump of springs and metal plates and tinkered with them. In a few seconds, he was holding a bronze and silver falcon. It spread its metal wings, blinked its obsidian eyes and flew around the room.

Tyson laughed and clapped his hands. The bird landed on Tyson's shoulder and nipped his ear affectionately.

Hephaestus regarded him. The god's scowl didn't change, but I thought I saw a kinder twinkle in his eyes. 'I sense you have something to tell me, Cyclops.'

Tyson's smile faded. 'Y-yes, lord. We met a Hundred-handed One.'

Hephaestus nodded, looking unsurprised. 'Briares?'

'Yes. He – he was scared. He would not help us.'

'And that bothered you.'

'Yes!' Tyson's voice wavered. 'Briares should be strong! He is older and greater than Cyclopes. But he ran away.'

Hephaestus grunted. 'There was a time I admired the Hundred-handed Ones. Back in the days of the first war. But people, monsters, even gods change, young Cyclops. You can't trust 'em. Look at my loving mother, Hera. You met her, didn't you? She'll smile to your face and talk about how important family is, eh? Didn't stop her from pitching me off Mount Olympus when she saw my ugly face.'

'But I thought Zeus did that to you,' I said.

Hephaestus cleared his throat and spat into a bronze spittoon. He snapped his fingers, and the robotic falcon flew back to the worktable.

'Mother likes telling that version of the story,' he grumbled. 'Makes her seem more likeable, doesn't it? Blaming it all on my dad. The truth is, my mother likes families, but she likes a certain kind of family. *Perfect* families. She took one look at me and . . . well, I don't fit the image, do I?'

He pulled a feather from the falcon's back, and the whole automaton fell apart.

'Believe me, young Cyclops,' Hephaestus said, 'you can't trust others. All you can trust is the work of your own hands.'

It seemed like a pretty lonely way to live. Plus, I didn't exactly trust the work of Hephaestus. One time in Denver, his mechanical spiders had almost killed Annabeth and me. And last year it had been a defective Talos statue that cost Bianca her life – another one of Hephaestus's little projects.

He focused on me and narrowed his eyes, as if he were reading my thoughts. 'Oh, this one doesn't like me,' he mused. 'No worries, I'm used to that. What would you ask of me, little demigod?'

'We told you,' I said. 'We need to find Daedalus. There's this guy Luke, and he's working for Kronos. He's trying to find a way to navigate the Labyrinth so he can invade our camp. If we don't get to Daedalus first –'

'And I told *you*, boy. Looking for Daedalus is a waste of time. He won't help you.'

'Why not?'

Hephaestus shrugged. 'Some of us get thrown off mountainsides. Some of us . . . the way we learn not to trust people is even more painful. Ask me for gold. Or a flaming sword. Or a magical steed. These I can grant you easily. But a way to Daedalus? That's an expensive favour.'

'You know where he is, then,' Annabeth pressed.

'It isn't wise to go looking, girl.'

'My mother says looking is the nature of wisdom.'

Hephaestus narrowed his eyes. 'Who's your mother, then?'

'Athena.'

'Figures.' He sighed. 'Fine goddess, Athena. A shame she pledged never to marry. All right, half-blood. I can tell you what you want to know. But there is a price. I need a favour done.'

'Name it,' Annabeth said.

Hephaestus actually laughed – a booming sound like a huge bellows stoking a fire. 'You heroes,' he said, 'always making rash promises. How refreshing!'

He pressed a button on his workbench, and metal shutters opened along the wall. It was either a huge window or a big-screen TV, I couldn't tell which. We were looking at a grey mountain ringed in forests. It must've been a volcano, because smoke rose from its crest.

'One of my forges,' Hephaestus said. 'I have many, but that used to be my favourite.'

'That's Mount St Helens,' Grover said. 'Great forests around there.'

'You've been there?' I asked.

'Looking for . . . you know. Pan.'

'Wait,' Annabeth said, looking at Hephaestus. 'You said it *used* to be your favourite. What happened?'

Hephaestus scratched his smouldering beard. 'Well, that's where the monster Typhon is trapped, you know. Used to be under Mount Etna, but when we moved to America, his force got pinned under Mount St Helens instead. Great source of fire, but a bit dangerous. There's always a chance he will escape. Lots of eruptions these days, smouldering all the time. He's restless with the Titan rebellion.'

'What do you want us to do?' I said. 'Fight him?'

Hephaestus snorted. 'That would be suicide. The gods themselves ran from Typhon when he was free. No, pray you never have to see him, much less fight him. But lately I have sensed intruders in my mountain. Someone or something is using my forges. When I go there, it is empty, but I can tell it is being used. They sense me coming, and they disappear. I send my automatons to investigate, but they do not return. Something . . . ancient is there. Evil. I want to know who dares invade my territory, and if they mean to loose Typhon.'

'You want us to find out who it is,' I said.

'Aye,' Hephaestus said. 'Go there. They may not sense you coming. You are not gods.'

'Glad you noticed,' I muttered.

'Go and find out what you can,' Hephaestus said. 'Report back to me, and I will tell you what you need to know about Daedalus.'

'All right,' Annabeth said. 'How do we get there?'

Hephaestus clapped his hands. The spider came swinging down from the rafters. Annabeth flinched when it landed at her feet.

'My creation will show you the way,' Hephaestus said. 'It is not far through the Labyrinth. And try to stay alive, will you? Humans are much more fragile than automatons.'

We were doing okay until we hit the tree roots. The spider raced along and we were keeping up, but then we spotted a tunnel off to the side that was dug from raw earth, and wrapped in thick roots. Grover stopped dead in his tracks.

'What is it?' I said.

He didn't move. He stared open-mouthed into the dark tunnel. His curly hair rustled in the breeze.

'Come on!' Annabeth said. 'We have to keep moving.'

'This is the way,' Grover muttered in awe. 'This is it.'

'What way?' I asked. 'You mean . . . to Pan?'

Grover looked at Tyson. 'Don't you smell it?'

'Earth,' Tyson said. 'And plants.'

'Yes! This is the way. I'm sure of it!'

Up ahead, the spider was getting further down the stone corridor. A few more seconds and we'd lose it.

'We'll come back,' Annabeth promised. 'On our way back to Hephaestus.'

'The tunnel will be gone by then,' Grover said. 'I have to follow it. A door like this won't stay open!'

'But we can't,' Annabeth said. 'The forges!'

Grover looked at her sadly. 'I have to, Annabeth. Don't you understand?'

She looked desperate, like she didn't understand at all. The spider was almost out of sight. But I thought about my conversation with Grover last night, and I knew what we had to do.

'We'll split up,' I said.

'No!' Annabeth said. 'That's way too dangerous. How will we ever find each other again? And Grover can't go alone.'

Tyson put his hand on Grover's shoulder. 'I – I will go with him.'

I couldn't believe I was hearing this. 'Tyson, are you sure?'

The big guy nodded. 'Goat boy needs help. We will find the god person. I am not like Hephaestus. I trust friends.'

Grover took a deep breath. 'Percy, we'll find each other again. We've still got the empathy link. I just . . . have to.'

I didn't blame him. This was his life's goal. If he didn't find Pan on this journey, the council would never give him another chance.

'I hope you're right,' I said.

'I know I am.' I'd never heard him sound so confident about anything, except maybe that cheese enchiladas were better than chicken enchiladas.

'Be careful,' I told him. Then I looked at Tyson. He gulped back a sob and gave me a hug that just about squeezed my eyes out of their sockets. Then he and Grover disappeared through the tunnel of tree roots and were lost in the darkness.

'This is bad,' Annabeth said. 'Splitting up is a really, really bad idea.'

'We'll see them again,' I said, trying to sound confident. 'Now, come on. The spider is getting away!'

It wasn't long before the tunnel started to get hot.

The stone walls glowed. The air felt as if we were walking through an oven. The tunnel sloped down and I could hear a loud roar, like a river of metal. The spider skittered along, with Annabeth right behind.

'Hey, wait up,' I called to her.

She glanced back at me. 'Yeah?'

'Something Hephaestus said back there . . . about Athena.'

'She swore never to marry,' Annabeth said. 'Like Artemis and Hestia. She's one of the maiden goddesses.'

I blinked. I'd never heard that about Athena before. 'But then —'

'How come she has demigod children?'

I nodded. I was probably blushing, but hopefully it was so hot anyway that Annabeth wouldn't notice.

'Percy, you know how Athena was born?'

'She sprang from the head of Zeus in full battle armour or something.'

'Exactly. She wasn't born in the normal way. She was literally born from thoughts. Her children are born the same way. When Athena falls in love with a mortal man, it's purely intellectual, the way she loved Odysseus in the old stories. It's a meeting of minds. She would tell you that's the purest kind of love.'

'So your dad and Athena . . . so you weren't . . .'

'I was a brain child,' Annabeth said. 'Literally. Children of Athena are sprung from the divine thoughts of our mother and the mortal ingenuity of our father. We are supposed to be a gift, a blessing from Athena on the men she favours.'

'But —'

'Percy, the spider's getting away. Do you really want me to explain the exact details of how I was born?'

'Um . . . no. That's okay.'

She smirked. 'I thought not.' And she ran ahead. I followed, but I wasn't sure I would ever look at Annabeth the same way again. I decided some things were better left as mysteries.

The roaring got louder. After another half-kilometre or so, we emerged in a cavern the size of a Super Bowl stadium. Our spider escort stopped and curled into a ball. We had arrived at the forge of Hephaestus.

There was no floor, just bubbling lava hundreds of metres below. We stood on a rock ridge that circled the cavern. A network of metal bridges spanned across it. At the centre was a huge platform with all sorts of machines, cauldrons, forges and the largest anvil I'd ever seen – a block of iron the size of a house. Creatures moved around the platform – several strange, dark shapes, but they were too far away to make out details.

'We'll never be able to sneak up on them,' I said.

Annabeth picked up the metal spider and slipped it into her pocket. 'I can. Wait here.'

'Hold it!' I said, but before I could argue she put on her Yankees cap and turned invisible.

I didn't dare call after her, but I didn't like the idea of her approaching the forge on her own. If those things out there could sense a god coming, would Annabeth be safe?

I looked back at the Labyrinth tunnel. I missed Grover and Tyson already. Finally I decided I couldn't stay put. I crept along the outer rim of the lava lake, hoping I could get a better angle to see what was happening in the middle.

The heat was horrible. Geryon's ranch had been a winter wonderland compared to this. In no time I was drenched with sweat. My eyes stung from the smoke. I moved along, trying to keep away from the edge, until I found my way blocked by a cart on metal wheels, like the kind they use in mine shafts. I lifted up the tarp and found it was half full of scrap metal. I was about to squeeze my way around it when I heard voices from up ahead, probably from a side tunnel.

'Bring it in?' one asked.

'Yeah,' another said. 'Movie's just about done.'

I panicked. I didn't have time to back up. There was nowhere to hide except . . . the cart. I scrambled inside and pulled the tarp over me, hoping no one had seen me. I curled my fingers around Riptide, just in case I had to fight.

The cart lurched forward.

'Oi,' a gruff voice said. 'Thing weighs a ton.'

'It's celestial bronze,' the other said. 'What did you expect?'

I got pulled along. We turned a corner, and from the sound of the wheels echoing against the walls I guessed we had passed down a tunnel and into a smaller room. Hopefully I was not about to be dumped into a smelting pot. If they started to tip me over, I'd have to fight my way out fast. I heard lots of talking, chattering voices that didn't sound human – somewhere between a seal's bark and a dog's growl. There was another sound, too – like an old-fashioned film projector and a tinny voice narrating.

'Just set it at the back,' a new voice ordered from across the room. 'Now, younglings. Please attend to the film. There will be time for questions afterwards.'

The voices quieted down, and I could hear the film.

As a young sea demon matures, the narrator said, *changes happen in the monster's body. You may notice your fangs getting longer and you*

may have a sudden desire to devour human beings. These changes are
perfectly normal and happen to all young monsters.

Excited snarling filled the room. The teacher – I guess it must have been a teacher – scolded the younglings to be quiet, and the film continued. I didn't understand most of it, and I didn't dare look. The film kept talking about growth spurts and acne problems caused by working in the forges, and proper flipper hygiene, and finally it was over.

'Now, younglings,' the instructor said. 'What is the proper name of our kind?'

'Sea demons!' one of them barked.

'No. Anyone else?'

'Telekhines!' another monster growled.

'Very good,' the instructor said. 'And why are we here?'

'Revenge!' several shouted.

'Yes, yes, but why?'

'Zeus is evil!' one monster said. 'He cast us into Tartarus just because we used magic!'

'Indeed,' the instructor said. 'After we made so many of the gods' finest weapons. The trident of Poseidon, for one. And of course – we made the greatest weapon of the Titans! Nevertheless, Zeus cast us away and relied on those fumbling Cyclopes. That is why we are taking over the forges of the usurper Hephaestus. And soon we will control the undersea furnaces, our ancestral home!'

I clutched my pen-sword. These snarling things had created Poseidon's trident? What were they talking about? I'd never even heard of a telekhine.

'And so, younglings,' the instructor continued, 'who do we serve?'

'Kronos!' they shouted.

'And when you grow to be big telekhines, will you make weapons for his army?'

'Yes!'

'Excellent. Now, we've brought in some scraps for you to practise with. Let's see how ingenious you are.'

There was a rush of movement and excited voices coming towards the cart. I got ready to uncap Riptide. The tarp was thrown back. I jumped up, my bronze sword springing to life in my hands, and found myself facing a bunch of . . . dogs.

Well, their faces were dogs, anyway, with black snouts, brown eyes and pointy ears. Their bodies were sleek and black like sea mammals, with stubby legs that were half flipper, half foot, and humanlike hands with sharp claws. If you blended together a kid, a Dobermann pinscher and a sea lion, you'd get something like what I was looking at.

'A demigod!' one snarled.

'Eat it!' yelled another.

But that's as far as they got before I slashed a wide arc with Riptide and vaporized the entire front row of monsters.

'Back off!' I yelled at the rest, trying to sound fierce. Behind them stood their instructor — a two-metre-tall telekhine with Dobermann fangs, snarling at me. I did my best to stare him down.

'New lesson, class,' I announced. 'Most monsters will vaporize when sliced with a celestial bronze sword. This change is perfectly normal, and will happen to you *right now* if you don't BACK OFF!'

To my surprise, it worked. The monsters backed up, but there were at least twenty of them. My fear factor wasn't going to last long.

I jumped out of the cart, yelled, 'CLASS DISMISSED!' and ran for the exit.

The monsters charged after me, barking and growling. I hoped they couldn't run very fast with those stubby little legs and flippers, but they waddled along pretty well. Thank the gods there was a door in the tunnel leading out to the main cavern. I slammed it shut and turned the wheel handle to lock it, but I doubted it would keep them long.

I didn't know what to do. Annabeth was out here somewhere, invisible. Our chance for a subtle reconnaissance mission had just been blown. I ran towards the platform at the centre of the lava lake.

'Annabeth!' I yelled.

'Shhh!' An invisible hand clamped over my mouth and wrestled me down behind a big bronze cauldron. 'You want to get us killed?'

I found her head and took off her Yankees cap. She shimmered into existence in front of me, scowling, her face streaked with ash and grime.

'Percy, what is your problem?'

'We're going to have company!' I explained quickly about the monster orientation class. Her eyes widened.

'So that's what they are,' she said. 'Telekhines. I should've known. And they're making . . . Well, look.'

We peeked over the cauldron. In the centre of the platform stood four sea demons, but these were fully grown, at least two and a half metres tall. Their black skin glistened in the firelight as they worked, sparks flying as they took turns hammering on a long piece of glowing hot metal.

'The blade is almost complete,' one said. 'It needs another cooling in blood to fuse the metals.'

'Aye,' a second said. 'It shall be even sharper than before.'

'What *is* that?' I whispered.

Annabeth shook her head. 'They keep talking about fusing metals. I wonder –'

'They were talking about the greatest Titan weapon,' I said. 'And they . . . they said they made my father's trident.'

'The telekhines betrayed the gods,' Annabeth said. 'They were practising dark magic. I don't know what, exactly, but Zeus banished them to Tartarus.'

'With Kronos.'

She nodded. 'We have to get out –'

No sooner had she said that than the door to the classroom exploded and young telekhines came pouring out. They stumbled over each other, trying to figure out which way to charge.

'Put your cap back on,' I said. 'Get out!'

'What?' Annabeth shrieked. 'No! I'm not leaving you.'

'I've got a plan. I'll distract them. You can use the metal spider – maybe it'll lead you back to Hephaestus. You have to tell him what's going on.'

'But you'll be killed!'

'I'll be fine. Besides, we've got no choice.'

Annabeth glared at me like she was going to punch me. And then she did something that surprised me even more. She kissed me.

'Be careful, Seaweed Brain.' She put on her hat and vanished.

I probably would've sat there for the rest of the day, staring at the lava and trying to remember what my name was, but the sea demons jarred me back to reality.

'There!' one yelled. The entire class of telekhines charged across the bridge towards me. I ran for the middle of the platform, surprising the four elder sea demons so much they dropped the red-hot blade. It was about two metres long and curved like a crescent moon. I'd seen a lot of terrifying things, but this unfinished whatever-it-was scared me the most.

The elder demons got over their surprise quickly. There were four ramps leading off the platform, and before I could dash in any direction each of them had covered an exit.

The tallest one snarled, 'What do we have here? A son of Poseidon?'

'Yes,' another growled. 'I can smell the sea in his blood.'

I raised Riptide. My heart was pounding.

'Strike down one of us, demigod,' the third demon said, 'and the rest of us shall tear you to shreds. Your father betrayed us. He took our gift and said nothing as we were cast into the pit. We will see *him* sliced to pieces. He and all the other Olympians.'

I wished I had a plan. I wished I hadn't been lying to Annabeth. I'd wanted her to get out safely, and I hoped she'd been sensible enough to do it. But now it was dawning on me that this might be the place I would die. No prophecies for me. I would get overrun in the heart of a volcano by a pack of dog-faced sea-lion people. The young telekhines were at the platform now, too, snarling and waiting to see how their four elders would deal with me.

I felt something burning against the side of my leg. The ice whistle in my pocket was getting colder. If I ever needed help, now was the time. But I hesitated. I didn't trust Quintus's gift.

Before I could make up my mind the tallest telekhine said, 'Let us see how strong he is. Let us see how long it takes him to burn!'

He scooped some lava from the nearest furnace. It set his fingers ablaze, but this didn't seem to bother him at all. The other elder telekhines did the same. The first one threw a glop of molten rock at me and set my trousers on fire. Two more splattered across my chest. I dropped my sword in sheer terror and swatted at my clothes. Fire was engulfing me. Strangely, it felt only warm at first, but it was getting hotter by the instant.

'Your father's nature protects you,' one said. 'Makes you hard to burn. But not impossible, youngling. Not impossible.'

They threw more lava at me and I remember screaming. My whole body was on fire. The pain was worse than anything I'd ever felt. I was being consumed. I crumpled to the metal floor and heard the sea demon children howling in delight.

Then I remembered the voice of the river naiad at the ranch: *The water is within me.*

I needed the sea. I felt a tugging sensation in my gut, but I had nothing around to help me. Not a faucet or a river. Not even a petrified seashell this time. And, besides, the last time I'd unleashed my power at the stables, there'd been that scary moment when it had almost got away from me.

I had no choice. I called to the sea. I reached inside myself and remembered the waves and the currents, the endless power of the ocean. And I let it loose in one horrible scream.

Afterwards, I could never describe what happened. An explosion, a tidal wave, a whirlwind of power simultaneously catching me up and blasting me downwards into the lava. Fire and water collided, superheated steam, and I shot up from the heart of the volcano in a huge explosion, just one piece of flotsam thrown free by a million pounds of pressure. The last thing I remember before losing consciousness was flying, flying so high Zeus would never have forgiven me, and then beginning to fall, smoke and fire and water streaming from me. I was a comet hurtling towards the earth.

12 I TAKE A PERMANENT VACATION

I woke up feeling like I was still on fire. My skin stung. My throat felt as dry as sand.

I saw blue sky and trees above me. I heard a fountain gurgling, and smelled juniper and cedar and a bunch of other sweet-scented plants. I heard waves, too, gently lapping on a rocky shore. I wondered if I were dead, but I knew better. I'd been to the Land of the Dead, and there was no blue sky.

I tried to sit up. My muscles felt like they were melting.

'Stay still,' a girl's voice said. 'You're too weak to rise.'

She laid a cool cloth across my forehead. A bronze spoon hovered over me and liquid was dribbled into my mouth. The drink soothed my throat and left a warm chocolatey aftertaste. Nectar of the gods. Then the girl's face appeared above me.

She had almond eyes and caramel-colour hair, braided over one shoulder. She was . . . fifteen? Sixteen? It was hard to tell. She had one of those faces that just seemed timeless. She began singing, and my pain dissolved. She was working magic. I could feel her music sinking into my skin, healing and repairing my burns.

'Who?' I croaked.

'Shhh, brave one,' she said. 'Rest and heal. No harm will come to you here. I am Calypso.'

The next time I woke I was in a cave, but as far as caves go I'd been in a lot worse. The ceiling glittered with different-colour crystal formations – white and purple and green, like I was inside one of those cut geodes you see in souvenir shops. I was lying on a comfortable bed with feather pillows and white cotton sheets. The cave was divided into sections by white silk curtains. Against one wall stood a large loom and a harp. Against the other wall were shelves neatly stacked with jars of fruit preserves. Dried herbs hung from the ceiling: rosemary, thyme and a bunch of other stuff. My mother could've named them all.

There was a fireplace built into the cave wall, and a pot bubbling over the flames. It smelled great, like beef stew.

I sat up, trying to ignore the throbbing pain in my head. I looked at my arms, sure that they would be hideously scarred, but they seemed fine. A little pinker than usual, but not bad. I was wearing a white cotton T-shirt and cotton drawstring trousers that weren't mine. My feet were bare. In a moment of panic, I wondered what had happened to Riptide, but I felt in my pocket and there was my pen, right where it always reappeared.

Not only that but the Stygian-ice dog whistle was back in my pocket, too. Somehow it had followed me. And that didn't exactly reassure me.

With difficulty, I stood. The stone floor was freezing under my feet. I turned and found myself staring into a polished bronze mirror.

'Holy Poseidon,' I muttered. I looked as if I'd lost ten kilos I couldn't afford to lose. My hair was a rat's nest. It was singed at the edges like Hephaestus's beard. If I saw that face on somebody walking down a highway intersection asking for money, I would've locked the car doors.

I turned away from the mirror. The cave entrance was to my left. I headed towards the daylight.

The cave opened onto a green meadow. On the left was grove of cedar trees and on the right a huge flower garden. Four fountains gurgled in the meadow, each shooting water from the pipes of stone satyrs. Straight ahead, the grass sloped down to a rocky beach. The waves of a lake lapped against the stones. I could tell it was a lake because . . . well, I just could. Fresh water. Not salt. The sun sparkled on the water, and the sky was pure blue. It seemed like a paradise, which immediately made me nervous. You deal with mythological stuff for a few years, you learn that paradises are usually places where you get killed.

The girl with the braided caramel hair, the one who'd called herself Calypso, was standing at the beach, talking to someone. I couldn't see him very well in the shimmer from the sunlight off the water, but they appeared to be arguing. I tried to remember what I knew about Calypso from the old myths. I'd heard the name before, but . . . I couldn't remember. Was she a monster? Did she trap heroes and kill them? But if she were evil, why was I still alive?

I walked towards her slowly because my legs were still stiff. When the grass changed to gravel, I looked down to keep my balance, and when I looked up again, the girl was alone. She wore a white sleeveless Greek dress with a low circular neckline trimmed in gold. She brushed at her eyes like she'd just been crying.

'Well,' she said, trying for a smile, 'the sleeper finally awakes.'

'Who were you talking to?' My voice sounded like a frog that had spent time in a microwave.

'Oh . . . just a messenger,' she said. 'How do you feel?'

'How long have I been out?'

'Time,' Calypso mused. 'Time is always difficult here. I honestly don't know, Percy.'

'You know my name?'

'You talk in your sleep.'

I blushed. 'Yeah. I've been . . . uh, told that before.'

'Yes. Who is Annabeth?'

'Oh, uh. A friend. We were together when – wait, how did I get here? Where am I?'

Calypso reached up and ran her fingers through my mangled hair. I stepped back nervously.

'I'm sorry,' she said. 'I've just grown used to caring for you. As to how you got here, you fell from the sky. You landed in the water, just there.' She pointed across the beach. 'I do not know how you survived. The water seemed to cushion your fall. As to where you are, you are in Ogygia.'

She pronounced it like *oh-jee-jee-ah*.

'Is that near Mount St Helens?' I asked, because my geography was pretty terrible.

Calypso laughed. It was a small, restrained laugh, like she found me really funny but didn't want to embarrass me. She was cute when she laughed.

'It isn't near anything, brave one,' she said. 'Ogygia is my phantom island. It exists by itself, anywhere and nowhere. You can heal here in safety. Never fear.'

'But my friends –'

'Annabeth,' she said. 'And Grover and Tyson?'

'Yes!' I said. 'I have to get back to them. They're in danger.'

She touched my face, and I didn't back away this time. 'Rest first. You are no good to your friends until you heal.'

As soon as she said it, I realized how tired I was. 'You're not . . . you're not an evil sorceress, are you?'

She smiled coyly. 'Why would you think that?'

'Well, I met Circe once, and she had a pretty nice island, too. Except she liked to turn men into guinea pigs.'

Calypso gave me that laugh again. 'I promise I will not turn you into a guinea pig.'

'Or anything else?'

'I am no evil sorceress,' Calypso said. 'And I am not your enemy, brave one. Now rest. Your eyes are already closing.'

She was right. My knees buckled, and I would've landed face-first in the gravel if Calypso hadn't caught me. Her hair smelled like cinnamon. She was very strong, or maybe I was just really weak and thin. She walked me back to a cushioned bench by a fountain and helped me lie down.

'Rest,' she ordered. And I fell asleep to the sound of the fountains and the smell of cinnamon and juniper.

The next time I awoke it was night, but I wasn't sure if it was the same night or many nights later. I was in the bed in the cave, but I rose and wrapped a robe around myself and padded outside. The stars were brilliant – thousands of them, like you only see way out in the country. I could make out all the constellations Annabeth had taught me: Capricorn, Pegasus, Sagittarius. And there, near the southern horizon, was a new constellation: the Huntress, a tribute to a friend of ours who had died last winter.

'Percy, what do you see?'

I brought my eyes back to earth. However amazing the stars were, Calypso was twice as brilliant. I mean, I've seen the goddess of love herself, Aphrodite, and I would never say this out loud or she'd blast me to ashes, but, for my money, Calypso was a lot more beautiful, because she just seemed so natural, like she wasn't trying to be beautiful and didn't even care about that. She just *was*. With her braided hair and white dress, she seemed to glow in the moonlight. She was holding a tiny plant in her hands. Its flowers were silver and delicate.

'I was just looking at . . .' I found myself staring at her face. 'Uh . . . I forgot.'

She laughed gently. 'Well, as long as you're up, you can help me plant these.'

She handed me a plant, which had a clump of earth and roots at the base. The flowers glowed as I held them. Calypso picked up her gardening spade and directed me to the edge of the garden, where she began to dig.

'That's moonlace,' Calypso explained. 'It can only be planted at night.'

I watched the silvery light flicker around the petals. 'What does it do?'

'Do?' Calypso mused. 'It doesn't really *do* anything, I

suppose. It lives, it gives light, it provides beauty. Does it have to do anything else?'

'I suppose not,' I said.

She took the plant, and our hands met. Her fingers were warm. She planted the moonlace and stepped back, surveying her work. 'I love my garden.'

'It's awesome,' I agreed. I mean, I wasn't exactly a gardening type, but Calypso had arbours covered with six different colours of roses, lattices filled with honeysuckle, rows of grapevines bursting with red and purple grapes that would've made Dionysus sit up and beg.

'Back home,' I said, 'my mom always wanted a garden.'

'Why did she not plant one?'

'Well, we live in Manhattan. In an apartment.'

'Manhattan? Apartment?'

I stared at her. 'You don't know what I'm talking about, do you?'

'I fear not. I haven't left Ogygia in . . . a long time.'

'Well, Manhattan's a big city, with not much gardening space.'

Calypso frowned. 'That is sad. Hermes visits from time to time. He tells me the world outside has changed greatly. I did not realize it had changed so much you cannot have gardens.'

'Why haven't you left your island?'

She looked down. 'It is my punishment.'

'Why? What did you do?'

'I? Nothing. But I'm afraid my father did a great deal. His name is Atlas.'

The name sent a shiver down my back. I'd met the

Titan Atlas last winter, and it had not been a happy time. He'd tried to kill pretty much everyone I cared about.

'Still,' I said hesitantly, 'it's not fair to punish you for what your father's done. I knew another daughter of Atlas. Her name was Zoë. She was one of the bravest people I've ever met.'

Calypso studied me for a long time. Her eyes were sad.

'What is it?' I asked.

'Are – are you healed yet, my brave one? Do you think you'll be ready to leave soon?'

'What?' I asked. 'I don't know.' I moved my legs. They were still stiff. I was already getting dizzy from standing up so long. 'You want me to go?'

'I . . .' Her voice broke. 'I'll see you in the morning. Sleep well.'

She ran off towards the beach. I was too confused to do anything but watch until she disappeared in the dark.

I don't know exactly how much time passed. Like Calypso said, it was hard to keep track on the island. I knew I should be leaving. At the very least, my friends would be worried. At worst, they could be in serious danger. I didn't even know if Annabeth had made it out of the volcano. I tried to use my empathy link with Grover several times, but I couldn't make contact. I hated not knowing if they were all right.

On the other hand, I really was weak. I couldn't stay on my feet more than a few hours. Whatever I'd done in Mount St Helens had drained me like nothing else I'd ever experienced.

I didn't feel like a prisoner or anything. I remembered the Lotus Hotel and Casino in Vegas, where I'd been lured into this amazing game world until I almost forgot everything I cared about. But the island of Ogygia wasn't like that at all. I thought about Annabeth, Grover and Tyson constantly. I remembered exactly why I needed to leave. I just . . . couldn't. And then there was Calypso.

She never talked much about herself, but that just made me want to know more. I would sit in the meadow, sipping nectar, and I would try to concentrate on the flowers or the clouds or the reflections on the lake, but I was really staring at Calypso as she worked, the way she brushed her hair over her shoulder, and the little strand that fell in her face whenever she knelt to dig in the garden. Sometimes she would hold out her hand and birds would fly out of the woods to settle on her arm – lorikeets, parrots, doves. She would say good morning to them, ask how it was going back at the nest, and they would chirp for a while, then fly off cheerfully. Calypso's eyes gleamed. She would look at me and we'd share a smile, but almost immediately she'd get that sad expression again and turn away. I didn't understand what was bothering her.

One night we were eating dinner together at the beach. Invisible servants had set up a table with beef stew and apple cider, which may not sound all that exciting, but that's because you haven't tasted it. I hadn't even noticed the invisible servants when I first got to the island, but after a while I became aware of the beds making themselves, meals cooking on their own, clothes being washed and folded by unseen hands.

Anyway, Calypso and I were sitting at dinner, and she looked beautiful in the candlelight. I was telling her about

New York and Camp Half-Blood, and then I starting telling her about the time Grover had eaten an apple while we were playing Hacky Sack with it. She laughed, showing off her amazing smile, and our eyes met. Then she dropped her gaze.

'There it is again,' I said.

'What?'

'You keep pulling away, like you're trying not to enjoy yourself.'

She kept her eyes on her glass of cider. 'As I told you, Percy, I have been punished. Cursed, you might say.'

'How? Tell me. I want to help.'

'Don't say that. Please don't say that.'

'Tell me what the punishment is.'

She covered her half-finished stew with a napkin, and immediately an invisible servant whisked the bowl away. 'Percy, this island, Ogygia, is my home, my birthplace. But it is also my prison. I am under . . . house arrest, I guess you would call it. I will never visit this Manhattan of yours. Or anywhere else. I am alone here.'

'Because your father was Atlas.'

She nodded. 'The gods do not trust their enemies. And rightly so. I should not complain. Some of the prisons are not nearly as nice as mine.'

'But that's not fair,' I said. 'Just because you're related doesn't mean you support him. This other daughter I knew, Zoë Nightshade – she fought against him. She wasn't imprisoned.'

'But, Percy,' Calypso said gently, 'I *did* support him in the first war. He is my father.'

'*What?* But the Titans are evil!'

[205]

'Are they? All of them? All the time?' She pursed her lips. 'Tell me, Percy. I have no wish to argue with you. But do you support the gods because they are good, or because they are your family?'

I didn't answer. She had a point. Last winter, after Annabeth and I had saved Olympus, the gods had had a debate about whether or not they should kill me. That hadn't been exactly good. But, still, I felt like I supported them because Poseidon was my dad.

'Perhaps I was wrong in the war,' Calypso said. 'And, in fairness, the gods have treated me well. They visit me from time to time. They bring me word of the outside world. But they can leave. And I cannot.'

'You don't have any friends?' I asked. 'I mean . . . wouldn't anyone else live here with you? It's a nice place.'

A tear trickled down her cheek. 'I . . . I promised myself I wouldn't speak of this. But –'

She was interrupted by a rumbling sound somewhere out on the lake. A glow appeared on the horizon. It got brighter and brighter, until I could see a column of fire moving across the surface of the water, coming towards us.

I stood and reached for my sword. 'What is that?'

Calypso sighed. 'A visitor.'

As the column of fire reached the beach, Calypso stood and bowed to it formally. The flames dissipated, and standing before us was a tall man in grey overalls and a metal leg brace, his beard and hair smouldering with fire.

'Lord Hephaestus,' Calypso said. 'This is a rare honour.'

The fire god grunted. 'Calypso. Beautiful as always.

Would you excuse us, please, my dear? I need to have a word with our young Percy Jackson.'

Hephaestus sat down clumsily at the dinner table and ordered a Pepsi. The invisible servant brought him one, opened it too suddenly and sprayed soda all over the god's work clothes. Hephaestus roared and spat a few curses and swatted the can away.

'Stupid servants,' he muttered. 'Good automatons are what she needs. They never act up!'

'Hephaestus,' I said, 'what's going on? Is Annabeth –'

'She's fine,' he said. 'Resourceful girl, that one. Found her way back, told me the whole story. She's worried sick, you know.'

'You haven't told her I'm okay?'

'That's not for me to say,' Hephaestus said. 'Everyone thinks you're dead. I had to be sure you were coming back before I started telling everyone where you were.'

'What do you mean?' I said. 'Of course I'm coming back!'

Hephaestus studied me sceptically. He fished something out of his pocket – a metal disc the size of an iPod. He clicked a button and it expanded into a miniature bronze TV. On the screen was news footage of Mount St Helens, a huge plume of fire and ash trailing into the sky.

'*Still uncertain about further eruptions,*' the newscaster was saying, '*authorities have ordered the evacuation of almost half a million people as a precaution. Meanwhile, ash has fallen as far away as Lake Tahoe and Vancouver, and the entire Mount St Helens area is closed to traffic within a hundred-mile radius. While no deaths have been reported, minor injuries and illnesses include –*'

Hephaestus switched it off. 'You caused quite an explosion.'

I stared at the blank bronze screen. Half a million people evacuated? Injuries. Illness. What had I done?

'The telekhines were scattered,' the god told me. 'Some vaporized. Some got away, no doubt. I don't think they'll be using my forge any time soon. On the other hand, neither will I. The explosion caused Typhon to stir in his sleep. We'll have to wait and see —'

'I couldn't release him, could I? I mean, I'm not that powerful!'

The god grunted. 'Not that powerful, eh? Could have fooled me. You're the son of the Earthshaker, lad. You don't know your own strength.'

That's the last thing I wanted him to say. I hadn't been in control of myself in that mountain. I'd released so much energy I'd almost vaporized myself, drained all the life out of me. Now I found out I'd nearly destroyed the Northwest US and almost woken the most horrible monster ever imprisoned by the gods. Maybe I was too dangerous. Maybe it was safer for my friends to think I was dead.

'What about Grover and Tyson?' I asked.

Hephaestus shook his head. 'No word, I'm afraid. I suppose the Labyrinth has them.'

'So what am I supposed to do?'

Hephaestus winced. 'Don't ever ask an old cripple for advice, lad. But I'll tell you this. You've met my wife?'

'Aphrodite.'

'That's her. She's a tricky one, lad. Be careful of love. It'll twist your brain around and leave you thinking up is down and right is wrong.'

I thought about my meeting with Aphrodite, in the back of a white Cadillac in the desert last winter. She'd told me that she had taken a special interest in me, and she'd be making things hard for me in the romance department, just because she liked me.

'Is this part of her plan?' I asked. 'Did she land me here?'

'Possibly. Hard to say with her. But if you decide to leave this place – and I don't say what's right or wrong – then I promised you an answer to your quest. I promised you the way to Daedalus. Well now, here's the thing. It has nothing to do with Ariadne's string. Not really. Sure, the string works. That's what the Titans' army will be after. But the best way through the maze . . . Theseus had the princess's help. And the princess was a regular mortal. Not a drop of god blood in her. But she was clever, and she could see, lad. She could see very clearly. So what I'm saying – I think you know how to navigate the maze.'

It finally sank in. Why hadn't I seen it before? Hera had been right. The answer was there all the time.

'Yeah,' I said. 'Yeah, I know.'

'Then you'll need to decide whether or not you're leaving.'

'I . . .' I wanted to say yes. Of course I would. But the words stuck in my throat. I found myself looking out at the lake, and suddenly the idea of leaving seemed very hard.

'Don't decide yet,' Hephaestus advised. 'Wait until daybreak. Daybreak is a good time for decisions.'

'Will Daedalus even help us?' I asked. 'I mean, if he gives Luke a way to navigate the Labyrinth, we're dead. I saw dreams about . . . Daedalus killed his nephew. He turned bitter and angry and –'

'It isn't easy being a brilliant inventor,' Hephaestus rumbled. 'Always alone. Always misunderstood. Easy to turn bitter, make horrible mistakes. People are more difficult to work with than machines. And when you break a person, he can't be fixed.'

Hephaestus brushed the last drops of Pepsi off his work clothes. 'Daedalus started well enough. He helped the Princess Ariadne and Theseus because he felt sorry for them. He tried to do a good deed. And everything in his life went bad because of it. Was that fair?' The god shrugged. 'I don't know if Daedalus will help you, lad, but don't judge someone until you've stood at his forge and worked with his hammer, eh?'

'I'll – I'll try.'

Hephaestus stood. 'Goodbye, lad. You did well, destroying the telekhines. I'll always remember you for that.'

It sounded very final, that goodbye. Then he erupted into a column of flame, and the fire moved over the water, heading back to the world outside.

I walked along the beach for several hours. When I finally came back to the meadow, it was very late, maybe four or five in the morning, but Calypso was still in her garden, tending the flowers by starlight. Her moonlace glowed silver, and the other plants responded to the magic, glowing red and yellow and blue.

'He has ordered you to return,' Calypso guessed.

'Well, not ordered. He gave me a choice.'

Her eyes met mine. 'I promised I would not offer.'

'Offer what?'

'For you to stay.'

'Stay,' I said. 'Like . . . forever?'

'You would be immortal on this island,' she said quietly. 'You would never age or die. You could leave the fight to others, Percy Jackson. You could escape your prophecy.'

I stared at her, stunned. 'Just like that?'

She nodded. 'Just like that.'

'But . . . my friends.'

Calypso rose and took my hand. Her touch sent a warm current through my body. 'You asked about my curse, Percy. I did not want to tell you. The truth is, the gods send me companionship from time to time. Every thousand years or so, they allow a hero to wash up on my shores, someone who needs my help. I tend to him and befriend him, but it is never random. The Fates make sure that the sort of hero they send . . .'

Her voice trembled, and she had to stop.

I squeezed her hand tighter. 'What? What have I done to make you sad?'

'They send a person who can never stay,' she whispered. 'Who can never accept my offer of companionship for more than a little while. They send me a hero I can't help . . . just the sort of person I can't help falling in love with.'

The night was quiet except for the gurgle of the fountains and waves lapping on the shore. It took me a long time to realize what she was saying.

'Me?' I asked.

'If you could see your face.' She suppressed a smile, though her eyes were still teary. 'Of course, you.'

'That's why you've been pulling away all this time?'

'I tried very hard. But I can't help it. The Fates are

cruel. They sent you to me, my brave one, knowing that you would break my heart.'

'But . . . I'm just . . . I mean, I'm just *me*.'

'That is enough,' Calypso promised. 'I told myself I would not even speak of this. I would let you go without even offering. But I can't. I suppose the Fates knew that, too. You could stay with me, Percy. I'm afraid that is the only way you could help me.'

I stared at the horizon. The first red streaks of dawn were lightening the sky. I could stay here forever, disappear from the earth. I could live with Calypso, with invisible servants tending to my every need. We could grow flowers in the garden and talk to songbirds and walk on the beach under perfect blue skies. No war. No prophecy. No more taking sides.

'I can't,' I told her.

She looked down sadly.

'I would never do anything to hurt you,' I said, 'but my friends need me. I know how to help them now. I have to get back.'

She picked a flower from her garden – a sprig of silver moonlace. Its glow faded as the sunrise came up. *Daybreak is a good time for decisions*, Hephaestus had said. Calypso tucked the flower into my T-shirt pocket.

She stood on her tiptoes and kissed me on the forehead, like a blessing. 'Then come to the beach, my hero. And we will send you on your way.'

The raft was a three-metre square of logs lashed together with a pole for a mast and a simple white linen sail. It didn't look like it would be very seaworthy, or lakeworthy.

'This will take you wherever you desire,' Calypso promised. 'It is quite safe.'

I took her hand, but she let it slip out of mine.

'Maybe I can visit you,' I said.

She shook her head. 'No man ever finds Ogygia twice, Percy. When you leave, I will never see you again.'

'But –'

'Go, please.' Her voice broke. 'The Fates are cruel, Percy. Just remember me.' Then a little trace of her smile returned. 'Plant a garden in Manhattan for me, will you?'

'I promise.' I stepped onto the raft. Immediately it began to sail from the shore.

As I sailed into the lake I realized the Fates really were cruel. They sent Calypso someone she couldn't help but love. But it worked both ways. For the rest of my life I would be thinking about her. She would always be my biggest *what if*.

Within minutes the island of Ogygia was lost in the mist. I was sailing alone over the water towards the sunrise.

Then I told the raft what to do. I said the only place I could think of, because I needed comfort and friends.

'Camp Half-Blood,' I said. 'Sail me home.'

13 WE HIRE A NEW GUIDE

Hours later, my raft washed up at Camp Half-Blood. How I got there, I have no idea. At some point the lake water just changed to salt water. The familiar shoreline of Long Island appeared up ahead, and a couple of friendly great white sharks surfaced and steered me towards the beach.

When I landed, the camp seemed deserted. It was late afternoon, but the archery range was empty. The climbing wall poured lava and rumbled all by itself. Pavilion: nothing. Cabins: all vacant. Then I noticed smoke rising from the amphitheatre. Too early for a campfire, and I didn't think they were roasting marshmallows. I ran towards it.

Before I even got there I heard Chiron making an announcement. When I realized what he was saying, I stopped in my tracks.

'– assume he is dead,' Chiron said. 'After so long a silence, it is unlikely our prayers will be answered. I have asked his best surviving friend to do the final honours.'

I crept up the back of the amphitheatre. Nobody noticed me. They were all looking forward, watching as Annabeth took a long green silk burial cloth, embroidered with a trident, and set it on the flames. They were burning my shroud.

Annabeth turned to face the audience. She looked

terrible. Her eyes were puffy from crying, but she managed to say, 'He was probably the bravest friend I've ever had. He . . .' Then she saw me. Her face went blood red. 'He's right there!'

Heads turned. People gasped.

'Percy!' Beckendorf grinned. A bunch of other kids crowded around me and clapped me on the back. I heard a few curses from the Ares cabin, but Clarisse just rolled her eyes, like she couldn't believe I'd had the nerve to survive. Chiron cantered over and everyone made way for him.

'Well,' he sighed with obvious relief. 'I don't believe I've ever been happier to see a camper return. But you must tell me –'

'WHERE HAVE YOU BEEN?' Annabeth interrupted, shoving aside the other campers. I thought she was going to punch me, but instead she hugged me so fiercely she nearly cracked my ribs. The other campers fell silent. Annabeth seemed to realize she was making a scene and pushed me away. 'I – we thought you were dead, Seaweed Brain!'

'I'm sorry,' I said. 'I got lost.'

'LOST?' she yelled. 'Two weeks, Percy? Where in the world –'

'Annabeth,' Chiron interrupted. 'Perhaps we should discuss this somewhere more private, shall we? The rest of you, back to your normal activities!'

Without waiting for us to protest, he picked up Annabeth and me as easily as if we were kittens, slung us both onto his back and galloped off towards the Big House.

* * *

I didn't tell them the whole story. I just couldn't bring myself to talk about Calypso. I explained how I'd caused the explosion at Mount St Helens and got blasted out of the volcano. I told them I'd been marooned on an island. Then Hephaestus had found me and told me I could leave. A magic raft had carried me back to camp.

All that was true, but as I said it my palms felt sweaty.

'You've been gone two weeks.' Annabeth's voice was steadier now, but she still looked pretty shaken up. 'When I heard the explosion, I thought —'

'I know,' I said. 'I'm sorry. But I figured out how to get through the Labyrinth. I talked to Hephaestus.'

'He told you the answer?'

'Well, he sort of told me that I already knew. And I do. I understand now.'

I told them my idea.

Annabeth's jaw dropped. 'Percy, that's crazy!'

Chiron sat back in his wheelchair and stroked his beard. 'There is a precedent, however. Theseus had the help of Ariadne. Harriet Tubman, daughter of Hermes, used many mortals on her Underground Railroad for just this reason.'

'But this is *my* quest,' Annabeth said. '*I* need to lead it.'

Chiron looked uncomfortable. 'My dear, it is your quest. But you need help.'

'And *this* is supposed to help? Please! It's wrong. It's cowardly. It's —'

'Hard to admit we need a mortal's help,' I said. 'But it's true.'

Annabeth glared at me. 'You are the single *most annoying*

person I have ever met!' And she stormed out of the room.

I stared at the doorway. I felt like hitting something. 'So much for being the bravest friend she's ever had.'

'She will calm down,' Chiron promised. 'She's jealous, my boy.'

'That's stupid. She's not . . . it's not like . . .'

Chiron chuckled. 'It hardly matters. Annabeth is very territorial about her friends, in case you haven't noticed. She was quite worried about you. And now that you're back, I think she suspects where you were marooned.'

I met his eyes, and I knew Chiron had guessed about Calypso. It was hard to hide anything from a guy who's been training heroes for three thousand years. He's pretty much seen it all.

'We won't dwell on your choices,' Chiron said. 'You came back. That is what matters.'

'Tell that to Annabeth.'

Chiron smiled. 'In the morning I will have Argus take the two of you into Manhattan. You might stop by your mother's, Percy. She is . . . understandably distraught.'

My heart skipped a beat. All that time on Calypso's island, I'd never even thought how my mom would be feeling. She'd think I was dead. She'd be devastated. What was wrong with me that I hadn't even considered her?

'Chiron,' I said, 'what about Grover and Tyson? Do you think –'

'I don't know, my boy.' Chiron gazed into the empty fireplace. 'Juniper is quite distressed. All her branches are turning yellow. The Council of Cloven Elders have revoked Grover's searcher's licence *in absentia*. Assuming he comes back alive, they will force him into a shameful exile.' He sighed. 'Grover and Tyson are very resourceful, however. We can still hope.'

'I shouldn't have let them run off.'

'Grover has his own destiny, and Tyson was brave to follow him. You would know if Grover was in mortal danger, don't you think?'

'I suppose. The empathy link. But –'

'There is something else I should tell you, Percy,' he said. 'Actually two unpleasant things.'

'Great.'

'Chris Rodriguez, our guest . . .'

I remembered what I'd seen in the basement, Clarisse trying to talk to him while he babbled about the Labyrinth. 'Is he dead?'

'Not yet,' Chiron said grimly. 'But he's much worse. He's in the infirmary now, too weak to move. I had to order Clarisse back to her regular schedule, because she was at his bedside constantly. He doesn't respond to anything. He won't take food or drink. None of my medicines help. He has simply lost the will to live.'

I shuddered. Despite all the run-ins I'd had with Clarisse, I felt horrible for her. She'd tried so hard to help him. And now that I'd been in the Labyrinth, I could understand why it had been so easy for the ghost of Minos to drive Chris mad. If I'd been wandering around down there alone, without my friends to help, I'd never have made it out.

'I'm sorry to say,' Chiron continued, 'the other news is less pleasant still. Quintus has disappeared.'

'Disappeared? How?'

'Three nights ago he slipped into the Labyrinth. Juniper

watched him go. It appears you may have been right about him.'

'He's a spy for Luke.' I told Chiron about the Triple G Ranch – how Quintus had bought his scorpions there and Geryon had been supplying Kronos's army. 'It can't be a coincidence.'

Chiron sighed heavily. 'So many betrayals. I had hoped Quintus would prove a friend. It seems my judgement was bad.'

'What about Mrs O'Leary?' I asked.

'The hellhound is still in the arena. It won't let anyone approach. I did not have the heart to force it into a cage . . . or destroy it.'

'Quintus wouldn't just leave her.'

'As I said, Percy, we seem to have been wrong about him. Now, you should prepare yourself for the morning. You and Annabeth still have much to do.'

I left him in his wheelchair, staring sadly into the fireplace. I wondered how many times he'd sat here, waiting for heroes that never came back.

Before dinner I stopped by the sword arena. Sure enough, Mrs O'Leary was curled up in an enormous black furry mound in the middle of the stadium, chewing halfheartedly on the head of a warrior dummy.

When she saw me, she barked and came bounding towards me. I thought I was dead meat. I just had time to say, 'Whoa!' before she bowled me over and started licking my face. Now usually, being the son of Poseidon and all, I only get wet if I want to, but my powers apparently did not extend to dog saliva, because I got a pretty good bath.

'Whoa, girl!' I yelled. 'Can't breathe. Lemme up!'

Eventually I managed to get her off me. I scratched her ears and found her an extra-gigantic dog biscuit.

'Where's your master?' I asked her. 'How could he just leave you, huh?'

She whimpered like she wanted to know that, too. I was ready to believe Quintus was an enemy, but still I couldn't understand why he'd leave Mrs O'Leary behind. If there was one thing I was sure of, it was that he really cared for his megadog.

I was thinking about that and towelling the dog spit off my face when a girl's voice said, 'You're lucky she didn't bite your head off.'

Clarisse was standing at the other end of the arena with her sword and shield. 'Came here to practise yesterday,' she grumbled. 'Dog tried to chew me up.'

'She's an intelligent dog,' I said.

'Funny.'

She walked towards us. Mrs O'Leary growled, but I patted her on the head and calmed her down.

'Stupid hellhound,' Clarisse said. 'Not going to keep me from practising.'

'I heard about Chris,' I said. 'I'm sorry.'

Clarisse paced a circle around the arena. When she came to the nearest dummy, she attacked viciously, chopping its head off with a single blow and driving her sword through its guts. She pulled the sword out and kept walking.

'Yeah, well. Sometimes things go wrong.' Her voice was shaky. 'Heroes get hurt. They . . . they die, and the monsters just keep coming back.'

She picked up a javelin and threw it across the arena.

It nailed a dummy straight between the eyeholes of its helmet.

She had called Chris a hero, like he had never gone over to the Titans' side. It reminded me of the way Annabeth sometimes talked about Luke. I decided not to bring that up.

'Chris was brave,' I said. 'I hope he gets better.'

She glared at me as if I were her next target. Mrs O'Leary growled.

'Do me a favour,' Clarisse told me.

'Yeah, sure.'

'If you find Daedalus, don't trust him. Don't ask him for help. Just kill him.'

'Clarisse —'

'Because anybody who can make something like the Labyrinth, Percy? That person is evil. Plain evil.'

For a second she reminded me of Eurytion the cowherd, her much older half-brother. She had the same hard look in her eyes, as if she'd been used for the past two thousand years and was getting tired of it. She sheathed her sword. 'Practice time is over. From now on, it's for real.'

That night I slept in my own bunk, and for the first time since Calypso's Island, dreams found me.

I was in a king's courtroom — a big white chamber with marble columns and a wooden throne. Sitting on it was a plump guy with curly red hair and a crown of laurels. At his side stood three girls who looked like his daughters. They all had his red hair and were dressed in blue robes.

The doors creaked open and a herald announced, 'Minos, King of Crete!'

I tensed, but the man on the throne just smiled at his daughters. 'I can't wait to see the expression on his face.'

Minos, the royal creep himself, swept into the room. He was so tall and serious he made the other king look silly. Minos's pointed beard had gone grey. He looked thinner than the last time I'd dreamed of him, and his sandals were spattered with mud, but the same cruel light shone in his eyes.

He bowed stiffly to the man on the throne. 'King Cocalus. I understand you have solved my little riddle?'

Cocalus smiled. 'Hardly *little*, Minos. Especially when you advertise across the world that you are willing to pay a thousand gold talents to the one who can solve it. Is the offer genuine?'

Minos clapped his hands. Two buff guards walked in, struggling with a big wooden crate. They set it at Cocalus's feet and opened it. Stacks of gold bars glittered. It had to be worth, like, a gazillion dollars.

Cocalus whistled appreciatively. 'You must have bankrupted your kingdom for such a reward, my friend.'

'That is not your concern.'

Cocalus shrugged. 'The riddle was quite simple, really. One of my retainers solved it.'

'Father,' one of the girls warned. She looked like the oldest – a little taller than her sisters.

Cocalus ignored her. He took a spiral seashell from the folds of his robe. A silver string had been threaded through it, so it hung like a huge bead on a necklace.

Minos stepped forward and took the shell. 'One of your retainers, you say? How did he thread the string without breaking the shell?'

'He used an ant, if you can believe it. Tied a silk string to the little creature and coaxed it through the shell by putting honey at the far end.'

'Ingenious man,' Minos said.

'Oh, indeed. My daughters' tutor. They are quite fond of him.'

Minos's eyes turned cold. 'I would be careful of that.'

I wanted to warn Cocalus: *Don't trust this guy! Throw him in the dungeon with some man-eating lions or something!* But the redheaded king just chuckled. 'Not to worry, Minos. My daughters are wise beyond their years. Now, about my gold –'

'Yes,' Minos said. 'But, you see, the gold is for the man who solved the riddle. And there can be only one such man. You are harbouring Daedalus.'

Cocalus shifted uncomfortably on his throne. 'How is it that you know his name?'

'He is a thief,' Minos said. 'He once worked in my court, Cocalus. He turned my own daughter against me. He helped a usurper make a fool of me in my own palace. And then he escaped justice. I have been pursuing him for ten years.'

'I knew nothing of this. But I have offered the man my protection. He has been a most useful –'

'I offer you a choice,' Minos said. 'Turn over the fugitive to me, and this gold is yours. Or risk making me your enemy. You do not want Crete as your enemy.'

Cocalus paled. I thought it was stupid for him to look so scared in the middle of his own throne room. He should've summoned his army or something. Minos only had two guards. But Cocalus just sat there, sweating, on his throne.

'Father,' his oldest daughter said, 'you can't –'

'Silence, Aelia.' Cocalus twisted his beard. He looked again at the glittering gold. 'This pains me, Minos. The gods do not love a man who breaks his oath of hospitality.'

'The gods do not love those who harbour criminals, either.'

Cocalus nodded. 'Very well. You shall have your man in chains.'

'Father!' Aelia said again. Then she caught herself, and changed her voice to a sweeter tone. 'At – at least let us feast with our guest first. After his long journey, he should be treated to a hot bath, new clothes and a decent meal. I would be honoured to draw the bath myself.'

She smiled prettily at Minos, and the old king grunted. 'I suppose a bath would not be amiss.' He looked at Cocalus. 'I will see you at dinner, my lord. With the prisoner.'

'This way, Your Majesty,' said Aelia. She and her sisters led Minos out of the chamber.

I followed them into a bath chamber decorated with mosaic tiles. Steam filled the air. A running-water faucet poured hot water into the tub. Aelia and her sisters filled it with rose petals and something that must've been Ancient Greek Mr Bubble, because soon the water was covered with multicoloured foam. The girls turned aside as Minos dropped his robes and slipped into the bath.

'Ahh.' He smiled. 'An excellent bath. Thank you, my dears. The journey has been long indeed.'

'You have been chasing your prey ten years, my lord?'

Aelia asked, batting her eyelashes. 'You must be very determined.'

'I never forget a debt.' Minos grinned. 'Your father was wise to agree to my demands.'

'Oh, indeed, my lord!' Aelia said. I thought she was laying on the flattery pretty thick, but the old guy was eating it up. Aelia's sisters trickled scented oil over the king's head.

'You know, my lord,' Aelia said, 'Daedalus thought you would come. He thought the riddle might be a trap, but he couldn't resist solving it.'

Minos frowned. 'Daedalus spoke to you about me?'

'Yes, my lord.'

'He is a bad man, princess. My own daughter fell under his spell. Do not listen to him.'

'He is a genius,' Aelia said. 'And he believes a woman is just as smart as a man. He was the first ever to teach us as if we had minds of our own. Perhaps your daughter felt the same way.'

Minos tried to sit up, but Aelia's sisters pushed him back into the water. Aelia came up behind him. She held three tiny orbs in her palm. At first I thought they were bath beads, but she threw them in the water and the beads sprouted bronze threads that began wrapping themselves around the king, tying him up at the ankles, binding his wrists to his sides, circling his neck. Even though I hated Minos, it was pretty horrible to watch. He thrashed and cried out, but the girls were much stronger. Soon he was helpless, lying in the bath with his chin just above the water. The bronze strands were still wrapping themselves around him like a cocoon, tightening across his body.

'What do you want?' Minos demanded. 'Why do you do this?'

Aelia smiled. 'Daedalus has been kind to us, Your Majesty. And I do not like you threatening our father.'

'You tell Daedalus,' Minos growled. 'You tell him I will hound him even after death! If there is any justice in the Underworld, my soul will haunt him for eternity!'

'Brave words, Your Majesty,' Aelia said. 'I wish you luck finding your justice in the Underworld.'

And with that, the bronze threads wrapped themselves around Minos's face, making him a bronze mummy.

The door of the bathhouse opened. Daedalus stepped in, carrying a traveller's bag.

He'd trimmed his hair short. His beard was pure white. He looked frail and sad, but he reached down and touched the mummy's forehead. The threads unravelled and sank to the bottom of the tub. There was nothing inside them. It was as if King Minos had just dissolved.

'A painless death,' Daedalus mused. 'More than he deserved. Thank you, my princesses.'

Aelia hugged him. 'You cannot stay here, teacher. When our father finds out –'

'Yes,' Daedalus said. 'I fear I have brought you trouble.'

'Oh, do not worry for us. Father will be happy enough taking that old man's gold. And Crete is a very long way away. But he will blame you for Minos's death. You must flee to somewhere safe.'

'Somewhere safe,' the old man repeated. 'For years I have fled from kingdom to kingdom, looking for somewhere safe. I fear Minos told the truth. Death will not stop him from hounding me. There is no place under the sun that will harbour me, once word of this crime gets out.'

'Then where will you go?' Aelia said.

'A place I swore never to enter again,' Daedalus said. 'My prison may be my only sanctuary.'

'I do not understand,' Aelia said.

'It's best you do not.'

'But what of the Underworld?' one of her sisters asked. 'Terrible judgement will await you! Every man must die.'

'Perhaps,' Daedalus said. Then he brought a scroll from his travelling bag – the same scroll I'd seen in my last dream, with his nephew's notes. 'Or perhaps not.'

He patted Aelia's shoulder, then blessed her and her sisters. He looked down once more at the coppery threads glinting in the bottom of the bath. 'Find me if you dare, king of ghosts.'

He turned towards the mosaic wall and touched a tile. A glowing mark appeared – a Greek Δ – and the wall slid aside. The princesses gasped.

'You never told us of secret passages!' Aelia said. 'You have been busy.'

'The *Labyrinth* has been busy,' Daedalus corrected her. 'Do not try to follow me, my dears, if you value your sanity.'

My dream shifted. I was underground in a stone chamber. Luke and another half-blood warrior were studying a map by flashlight.

Luke cursed. 'It should've been the last turn.' He crumpled up the map and tossed it aside.

'Sir!' his companion protested.

'Maps are useless here,' Luke said. 'Don't worry. I'll find it.'

'Sir, is it true that the larger the group —'

'The more likely you'll get lost? Yes, that's true. Why do you think we sent out solo explorers to begin with? But don't worry. As soon as we have the thread, we can lead the vanguard through.'

'But how will we *get* the thread?'

Luke stood, flexing his fingers. 'Oh, Quintus will come through. All we have to do is reach the arena, and it's at a juncture. Impossible to get anywhere without passing it. That's why we must have a truce with its master. We just have to stay alive until —'

'Sir!' a new voice came from the corridor. Another guy in Greek armour ran forward, carrying a torch. 'The *dracaenae* found a half-blood!'

Luke scowled. 'Alone? Wandering the maze?'

'Yes, sir! You'd better come quick. They're in the next chamber. They've got him cornered.'

'Who is it?'

'No one I've ever seen before, sir.'

Luke nodded. 'A blessing from Kronos. We may be able to use this half-blood. Come!'

They ran down the corridor, and I woke with a start, staring into the dark. *A lone half-blood, wandering in the maze.* It was a long time before I got to sleep again.

The next morning I made sure Mrs O'Leary had enough dog biscuits. I asked Beckendorf to keep an eye on her, which he didn't seem too happy about. Then I hiked over Half-Blood Hill and met Annabeth and Argus on the road.

Annabeth and I didn't talk much in the van. Argus never spoke, probably because he had eyes all over his body, including — so I'd heard — at the tip of his tongue, and he didn't like to show that off.

Annabeth looked queasy, as if she'd slept even worse than me.

'Bad dreams?' I asked at last.

She shook her head. 'An Iris-message from Eurytion.'

'Eurytion! Is something wrong with Nico?'

'He left the ranch last night, heading back into the maze.'

'*What?* Didn't Eurytion try to stop him?'

'Nico was gone before he woke up. Orthus tracked his scent as far as the cattle grid. Eurytion said he'd been hearing Nico talk to himself the last few nights. Only now he thinks Nico was talking with the ghost again, Minos.'

'He's in danger,' I said.

'No kidding. Minos is one of the judges of the dead, but he's got a vicious streak a mile wide. I don't know what he wants with Nico, but —'

'That's not what I meant,' I said. 'I had this dream last night . . .' I told her about Luke, how he'd mentioned Quintus, and how his men had found a half-blood alone in the maze.

Annabeth's jaw clenched. 'That's very, very bad.'

'So what do we do?'

She raised an eyebrow. 'Well, it's a good thing you have a plan to guide us, huh?'

It was Saturday, and traffic was heavy going into the city. We arrived at my mom's apartment around noon. When she answered the door, she gave me a hug only a little less overwhelming than having a hellhound jump on you.

'I *told* them you were all right,' my mom said, but she sounded like the weight of the sky had just been lifted off her shoulders – and, believe me, I know first hand how that feels.

She sat us down at the kitchen table and insisted on feeding us her special blue chocolate-chip cookies while we filled her in on the quest. As usual, I tried to water down the frightening parts (which was pretty much everything), but somehow that just made it sound more dangerous.

When I got to the part about Geryon and the stables, my mom pretended like she was going to strangle me. 'I can't get him to clean his room, but he'll clean a hundred tons of horse manure out of some monster's stables!'

Annabeth laughed. It was the first time I'd heard her laugh in a long time, and it was nice to hear.

'So,' my mom said when I was done with the story, 'you wrecked Alcatraz Island, made Mount St Helens explode and displaced half a million people, but at least you're safe.' That's my mom, always looking on the bright side.

'Yep,' I agreed. 'That pretty much covers it.'

'I wish Paul were here,' she said, half to herself. 'He wanted to talk to you.'

'Oh, right. The school.'

So much had happened since then that I'd almost forgotten about the high school orientation at Goode – the fact I'd left the band hall in flames, and my mom's boyfriend had last seen me jumping through a window like a fugitive.

'What did you tell him?' I asked.

My mom shook her head. 'What could I say? He knows something is different about you, Percy. He's a smart man. He believes that you're not a bad person. He doesn't know what's going on, but the school is pressuring him. After all, he got you admitted there. He needs to convince them the fire wasn't your fault, and, since you ran away, that looks bad.'

Annabeth was studying me. She looked pretty sympathetic. I knew she'd been in similar situations. It's never easy for a half-blood in the mortal world.

'I'll talk to him,' I promised. 'After we're done with the quest. I'll even tell him the truth if you want.'

My mom put her hand on my shoulder. 'You would do that?'

'Well, yeah. I mean, he'll think we're crazy.'

'He already thinks that.'

'Then there's nothing to lose.'

'Thank you, Percy. I'll tell him you'll be home . . .' She frowned. 'When? What happens now?'

Annabeth broke her cookie in half. 'Percy has this *plan*.'

Reluctantly I told my mom.

She nodded slowly. 'It sounds very dangerous. But it might work.'

'You have the same abilities, don't you?' I asked. 'You can see through the Mist.'

My mom sighed. 'Not so much now. When I was younger it was easier. But, yes, I've always been able to see more than was good for me. It's one of the things that caught your father's attention, when we first met. Just be careful. Promise me you'll be safe.'

'We'll try, Ms Jackson,' Annabeth said. 'Keeping your son safe is a big job, though.' She folded her arms and glared out of the kitchen window. I picked at my napkin and tried not to say anything.

My mom frowned. 'What's going on with you two? Have you been fighting?'

Neither of us said anything.

'I see,' my mom said, and I wondered if she could see through more than just the Mist. It sounded like she understood what was going on with Annabeth and me, but I sure as heck didn't. 'Well, remember,' she said, 'Grover and Tyson are counting on you two.'

'I know,' Annabeth and I said at the same time, which embarrassed me even more.

My mom smiled. 'Percy, you'd better use the phone in the hall. Good luck.'

I was relieved to get out of the kitchen, even though I was nervous about what I was about to do. I went to the phone and placed the call. The number had washed off my hand a long time ago, but that was okay. Without meaning to, I'd memorized it.

We arranged a meeting in Times Square. We found Rachel Elizabeth Dare in front of the Marriott Marquis, and she was painted gold completely.

I mean her face, her hair, her clothes – everything. She looked like she'd been touched by King Midas. She was standing like a statue with five other kids all painted metallic – copper, bronze, silver. They were frozen in different poses while tourists hustled past or stopped to stare. Some passers-by threw money at the tarp on the sidewalk.

The sign at Rachel's feet said, URBAN ART FOR KIDS, *donations appreciated.*

Annabeth and I stood there for, like, five minutes, staring at Rachel, but if she noticed us she didn't let on. She didn't move or even blink as far as I could see. Being ADHD and all, I could not have done that. Standing still that long would've driven me crazy. It was weird to see Rachel in gold, too. She looked like a statue of somebody famous, an actress or something. Only her eyes were normal green.

'Maybe if we push her over,' Annabeth suggested.

I thought that was a little mean, but Rachel didn't respond. After another few minutes, a kid in silver walked up from the hotel taxi stand, where he'd been taking a break. He took a pose like he was lecturing the crowd, right next to Rachel. Rachel unfroze and stepped off the tarp.

'Hey, Percy.' She grinned. 'Good timing! Let's get some coffee.'

We walked down to a place called the Java Moose on West 43rd. Rachel ordered an Espresso Extreme, the kind of stuff Grover would like. Annabeth and I got fruit smoothies and we sat at a table right under the stuffed moose. Nobody even looked twice at Rachel in her golden outfit.

'So,' she said. 'It's Annabelle, right?'

'Annabeth,' Annabeth corrected her. 'Do you always dress in gold?'

'Not usually,' Rachel said. 'We're raising money for our group. We do volunteer art projects for elementary kids 'cause they're cutting art from the schools, you know? We do this once a month, take in about five hundred dollars on a good weekend. But I'm guessing you don't want to talk about that. You're a half-blood, too?'

'Shhh!' Annabeth said, looking around. 'Just announce it to the world, how about?'

'Okay.' Rachel stood up and said, really loud, 'Hey, everybody! These two aren't human! They're half Greek god!'

Nobody even looked over. Rachel shrugged and sat down. 'They don't seem to care.'

'That's not funny,' Annabeth said. 'This isn't a joke, mortal girl.'

'Hold it, you two,' I said. 'Just calm down.'

'I'm calm,' Rachel insisted. 'Every time I'm around you, some monster attacks us. What's to be nervous about?'

'Look,' I said, 'I'm sorry about the band room. I hope they didn't kick you out or anything.'

'Nah. They asked me a lot of questions about you. I played dumb.'

'Was it hard?' Annabeth asked.

'Okay, stop!' I intervened. 'Rachel, we've got a problem. And we need your help.'

Rachel narrowed her eyes at Annabeth. 'You need my help?'

Annabeth stirred her straw in her smoothie. 'Yeah,' she said sullenly. 'Maybe.'

I told Rachel about the Labyrinth, and how we needed to find Daedalus. I told her what had happened the last few times we'd gone in.

'So you want me to guide you,' she said. 'Through a place I've never been.'

'You can see through the Mist,' I said. 'Just like Ariadne. I'm betting you can see the right path. The Labyrinth won't be able to fool you as easily.'

'And if you're wrong?'

'Then we'll get lost. Either way, it'll be dangerous. Very, very dangerous.'

'I could die?'

'Yeah.'

'I thought you said monsters don't care about mortals. That sword of yours —'

'Yeah,' I said. 'Celestial bronze doesn't hurt mortals. Most monsters would ignore you. But Luke . . . he doesn't care. He'll use mortals, demigods, monsters, whatever. And he'll kill anyone who gets in his way.'

'Nice guy,' Rachel said.

'He's under the influence of a Titan,' Annabeth said defensively. 'He's been deceived.'

Rachel looked back and forth between us. 'Okay,' she said, 'I'm in.'

I blinked. I hadn't figured it would be so easy. 'Are you sure?'

'Hey, my summer was going to be boring. This is the best offer I've had yet. So what do I look for?'

'We have to find an entrance to the Labyrinth,' Annabeth said. 'There's an entrance at Camp Half-Blood, but you can't go there. It's off-limits to mortals.'

She said *mortals* like it was some sort of terrible condition, but Rachel just nodded. 'Okay. What does an entrance to the Labyrinth look like?'

'It could be anything,' Annabeth said. 'A section of wall. A boulder. A doorway. A sewer entrance. But it would have the mark of Daedalus on it. A Greek Delta, glowing in blue.'

'Like this?' Rachel drew the symbol Δ in water on our table.

'That's it,' Annabeth said. 'You know Greek?'

'No,' Rachel said. She pulled a big blue plastic hairbrush from her pocket and started brushing the gold out of her hair. 'Let me get changed. You'd better come with me to the Marriott.'

'Why?' Annabeth asked.

'Because there's an entrance like that in the hotel basement, where we store our costumes. It's got the mark of Daedalus.'

14 MY BROTHER DUELS ME TO THE DEATH

The metal door was half hidden behind a laundry bin full of dirty hotel towels. I didn't see anything strange about it, but Rachel showed me where to look, and I recognized the faint blue symbol etched in the metal.

'It hasn't been used in a long time,' Annabeth said.

'I tried to open it once,' Rachel said, 'just out of curiosity. It's rusted shut.'

'No.' Annabeth stepped forward. 'It just needs the touch of a half-blood.'

Sure enough, as soon as Annabeth put her hand on the mark, it glowed blue. The metal door unsealed and creaked open, revealing a dark staircase leading down.

'Wow.' Rachel looked calm, but I couldn't tell if she was pretending or not. She'd changed into a ratty Museum of Modern Art T-shirt and her regular marker-coloured jeans, her blue plastic hairbrush sticking out of her pocket. Her red hair was tied back, but she still had flecks of gold in it, and traces of the gold glitter on her face. 'So . . . after you?'

'You're the guide,' Annabeth said with mock politeness. 'Lead on.'

The stairs led down to a large brick tunnel. It was so dark I couldn't see further than a metre in front of us, but Annabeth and I had restocked on flashlights. As soon as we switched them on, Rachel yelped.

A skeleton was grinning at us. It wasn't human. It was huge, for one thing – at least two and a half metres tall. It had been strung up, chained by its wrists and ankles so it made a kind of giant X over the tunnel. But what really sent a shiver down my back was the single black eye socket in the centre of its skull.

'A Cyclops,' Annabeth said. 'It's very old. It's not . . . anybody we know.'

It wasn't Tyson, she meant. But that didn't make me feel much better. I still felt like it had been put here as a warning. Whatever could kill a grown Cyclops, I didn't want to meet.

Rachel swallowed. 'You have a friend who's a Cyclops?'

'Tyson,' I said. 'My half-brother.'

'Your *half-brother*?'

'Hopefully we'll find him down here,' I said. 'And Grover. He's a satyr.'

'Oh.' Her voice was small. 'Well then, we'd better keep moving.'

She stepped under the skeleton's left arm and kept walking. Annabeth and I exchanged looks. Annabeth shrugged. We followed Rachel deeper into the maze.

After fifteen metres we came to a crossroads. Ahead, the brick tunnel continued. To the right, the walls were made of ancient marble slabs. To the left, the tunnel was earth and tree roots.

I pointed left. 'That looks like the tunnel Tyson and Grover took.'

Annabeth frowned. 'Yeah, but the architecture to the right – those old stones – that's more likely to lead to an ancient part of the maze, towards Daedalus's workshop.'

'We need to go straight,' Rachel said.

Annabeth and I both looked at her.

'That's the least likely choice,' Annabeth said.

'You don't see it?' Rachel asked. 'Look at the floor.'

I saw nothing except well-worn bricks and mud.

'There's a brightness there,' Rachel insisted. 'Very faint. But forward is the correct way. To the left, further down the tunnel, those tree roots are moving like feelers. I don't like that. To the right, there's a trap about seven metres down. Holes in the walls, maybe for spikes. I don't think we should risk it.'

I didn't see anything like what she was describing, but I nodded. 'Okay. Forward.'

'You believe her?' Annabeth asked.

'Yeah,' I said. 'Don't you?'

Annabeth looked like she wanted to argue, but she waved at Rachel to lead on. Together we kept walking down the brick corridor. It twisted and turned, but there were no more side tunnels. We seemed to be angling down, heading deeper underground.

'No traps?' I asked anxiously.

'Nothing.' Rachel knitted her eyebrows. 'Should it be this easy?'

'I don't know,' I said. 'It never was before.'

'So, Rachel,' Annabeth said, 'where are you from, exactly?'

She said it like, *What planet are you from?* But Rachel didn't look offended.

'Brooklyn,' she said.

'Aren't your parents going to be worried if you're out late?'

Rachel exhaled. 'Not likely. I could be gone a week and they'd never notice.'

'Why not?' This time Annabeth didn't sound as sarcastic. Having trouble with parents was something she understood.

Before Rachel could answer, there was a creaking noise in front of us, like huge doors opening.

'What was that?' Annabeth asked.

'I don't know,' Rachel said. 'Metal hinges.'

'Oh, that's very helpful. I mean, *what is it?*'

Then I heard heavy footsteps shaking the corridor — coming towards us.

'Run?' I asked.

'Run,' Rachel agreed.

We turned and fled the way we'd come, but we hadn't made it six metres before we ran straight into some old friends. Two *dracaenae* — snake women in Greek armour — levelled their javelins at our chests. Standing between them was Kelli, the *empousa* cheerleader.

'Well, well,' Kelli said.

I uncapped Riptide, and Annabeth pulled her knife, but before my sword was even out of pen form Kelli pounced on Rachel. Her hand turned into a claw and she spun Rachel around, holding her tight, with her talons at Rachel's neck.

'Taking your little mortal pet for a walk?' Kelli asked me. 'They're such fragile things. So easy to break!'

Behind us, the footsteps came closer. A huge form appeared out of the gloom — a three-metre-tall Laistrygonian giant with red eyes and fangs.

The giant licked his lips when he saw us. 'Can I eat them?'

'No,' Kelli said. 'Your master will want these. They will provide a great deal of entertainment.' She smiled at me. 'Now march, half-bloods. Or you all die here, starting with the mortal girl.'

It was pretty much my worst nightmare. And believe me I've had plenty of nightmares. We were marched down the tunnel flanked by *dracaenae*, with Kelli and the giant at the back, just in case we tried to run for it. Nobody seemed to worry about us running forward. That was the direction they wanted us to go.

Up ahead I could see bronze doors. They were about three and a half metres tall, emblazoned with a pair of crossed swords. From behind them came a muffled roar, like a crowd.

'Oh, yessssss,' said the snake woman on my left. 'You'll be very popular with our hossssst.'

I'd never got to look at a *dracaena* up close before, and I wasn't thrilled to have the opportunity. She would've had a beautiful face, except her tongue was forked and her eyes were yellow with black slits for pupils. She wore bronze armour that stopped at her waist. Below that, where her legs should've been, were two massive snake trunks, mottled bronze and green. She moved by a combination of slithering and walking, as if she were on living skis.

'Who's your host?' I asked.

She hissed, which might have been a laugh. 'Oh, you'll sssssee. You'll get along famousssly. He'ssss your brother, after all.'

'My what?' Immediately I thought of Tyson, but that was impossible. What was she talking about?

The giant pushed past us and opened the doors. He picked up Annabeth by her shirt and said, 'You stay here.'

'Hey!' she protested, but the guy was twice her size and he'd already confiscated her knife and my sword.

Kelli laughed. She still had her claws at Rachel's neck. 'Go on, Percy. Entertain us. We'll wait here with your friends to make sure you behave.'

I looked at Rachel. 'I'm sorry. I'll get you out of this.'

She nodded as much as she could with a demon at her throat. 'That would be nice.'

The *dracaenae* prodded me towards the doorway at javelin-point, and I walked out onto the floor of an arena.

I guess it wasn't the largest arena I'd ever been in, but it seemed pretty spacious considering the whole place was underground. The dirt floor was circular, just big enough that you could drive a car around the rim if you pulled it really tight. In the centre of the arena, a fight was going on between a giant and a centaur. The centaur looked panicked. He was galloping around his enemy, using sword and shield, while the giant swung a javelin the size of a telephone pole and the crowd cheered.

The first tier of seats was four metres above the arena floor. Plain stone benches wrapped all the way around, and every seat was full. There were giants, *dracaenae*, demigods, telekhines and stranger things: bat-winged demons and creatures that seemed half human and half you name it – bird, reptile, insect, mammal.

But the creepiest things were the skulls. The arena was full of them. They ringed the edge of the railing. Metre-high piles of them decorated the steps between the benches. They grinned from pikes at the back of the stands and hung on chains from the ceiling like horrible chandeliers. Some of them looked very old — nothing but bleached-white bone. Others looked a lot fresher. I'm not going to describe them. Believe me, you don't want me to.

In the middle of all this, proudly displayed on the side of the spectators' wall, was something that made no sense to me — a green banner with the trident of Poseidon in the centre. What was *that* doing in a horrible place like this?

Above the banner, sitting in a seat of honour, was an old enemy.

'Luke,' I said.

I'm not sure he could hear me over the roar of the crowd, but he smiled coldly. He was wearing camouflage combat trousers, a white T-shirt and a bronze breastplate, just like I'd seen in my dream. But he still wasn't wearing his sword, which I thought was strange. Next to him sat the largest giant I'd ever seen, much larger than the one on the floor fighting the centaur. The giant next to Luke must've been five metres tall, easy, and so wide he took up three seats. He wore only a loincloth, like a sumo wrestler. His skin was dark red and tattooed with blue wave designs. I figured he must be Luke's new bodyguard or something.

There was a cry from the arena floor, and I jumped back as the centaur crashed to the ground beside me.

He met my eyes pleadingly. 'Help!'

I reached for my sword, but it had been taken from me and hadn't reappeared in my pocket yet.

The centaur struggled to get up as the giant approached, his javelin ready.

A taloned hand gripped my shoulder. 'If you value your friendsss' livesss,' my *dracaena* guard said, 'you won't interfere. This isssn't your fight. Wait your turn.'

The centaur couldn't get up. One of his legs was broken. The giant put his huge foot on the horseman's chest and raised the javelin. He looked up at Luke. The crowd cheered, 'DEATH! DEATH!'

Luke didn't do anything, but the tattooed sumo dude sitting next to him rose. He smiled down at the centaur, who was whimpering, 'Please! No!'

Then the sumo dude held out his hand and gave the 'thumbs down' sign.

I closed my eyes as the gladiator giant thrust his javelin. When I looked again, the centaur was gone, disintegrated to ashes. All that was left was a single hoof, which the giant took up as a trophy and showed to the crowd. They roared their approval.

A gate opened at the opposite end of the stadium and the giant marched out in triumph.

In the stands, the sumo dude raised his hands for silence.

'Good entertainment!' he bellowed. 'But nothing I haven't seen before. What else do you have, Luke, son of Hermes?'

Luke's jaw tightened. I could tell he didn't like being called *son of Hermes*. He hated his father. But he rose calmly to his feet. His eyes glittered. In fact, he seemed to be in a pretty good mood.

'Lord Antaeus,' Luke said, loud enough for the crowd to hear, 'you have been an excellent host! We would be happy to amuse you, to repay the favour of passing through your territory.'

'A favour I have not yet granted,' Antaeus growled. 'I want entertainment!'

Luke bowed. 'I believe I have something better than centaurs to fight in your arena now. I have a brother of yours.' He pointed at me. 'Percy Jackson, son of Poseidon.'

The crowd began jeering at me and throwing stones, most of which I dodged, but one caught me on the cheek and made a good-sized cut.

Antaeus's eyes lit up. 'A son of Poseidon? Then he should fight well! Or die well!'

'If his death pleases you,' Luke said, 'will you let our armies cross your territory?'

'Perhaps!' Antaeus said.

Luke didn't look too pleased about the 'perhaps'. He glared down at me, as if warning me that I'd better die in a really spectacular way or I'd be in big trouble.

'Luke!' Annabeth yelled. 'Stop this. Let us go!'

Luke seemed to notice her for the first time. He looked stunned for a moment. 'Annabeth?'

'Enough time for the females to fight afterwards,' Antaeus interrupted. 'First, Percy Jackson, what weapons will you choose?'

The *dracaenae* pushed me into the middle of the arena.

I stared up at Antaeus. 'How can you be a son of Poseidon?'

Antaeus laughed, and the rest of the crowd laughed, too.

'I am his favourite son!' Antaeus boomed. 'Behold, my temple to the Earthshaker, built from the skulls of all those I've killed in his name! Your skull shall join them!'

I stared in horror at all the skulls — hundreds of them, and the banner of Poseidon. How could this be a temple for my dad? My dad was a nice guy. He'd never asked me for a Father's Day card, much less somebody's skull.

'Percy!' Annabeth yelled at me. 'His mother is Gaea! Gae—'

Her Laistrygonian captor clamped his hand over her mouth. *His mother is Gaea.* The earth goddess. Annabeth was trying to tell me that this was important, but I didn't know why. Maybe just because the guy had two godly parents. That would make him even harder to kill.

'You're crazy, Antaeus,' I said. 'If you think this is a good tribute, you know nothing about Poseidon.'

The crowd screamed insults at me, but Antaeus raised his hand for silence.

'Weapons,' he insisted. 'And then we will see how you die. Will you have axes? Shields? Nets? Flamethrowers?'

'Just my sword,' I said.

Laughter erupted from the monsters, but immediately Riptide appeared in my hands, and some of the voices in the crowd turned nervous. The bronze blade glowed with a faint light.

'Round one!' Antaeus announced. The gates opened, and a *dracaena* slithered out. She had a trident in one hand and a weighted net in the other — classic gladiator style. I'd trained against those weapons at camp for years.

She jabbed at me experimentally. I stepped away. She threw her net, hoping to tangle my sword hand, but I sidestepped easily, sliced her spear in half and stabbed Riptide through a chink in her armour. With a painful wail, she vaporized into nothing, and the cheering of the crowd died.

'No!' Antaeus bellowed. 'Too fast! You must wait for the kill. Only I give that order!'

I glanced over at Annabeth and Rachel. I had to find a way to get them free, maybe distract their guards.

'Nice job, Percy.' Luke smiled. 'You've got better with the sword. I'll grant you that.'

'Round two!' Antaeus yelled. 'And slower this time! More entertainment! Wait for my call before killing anybody, OR ELSE!'

The gates opened again, and this time a young warrior came out. He was a little older than me, about sixteen. He had glossy black hair, and his left eye was covered with an eye patch. He was thin and wiry so his Greek armour hung on him loosely. He stabbed his sword into the ground, adjusted his shield straps and pulled on his horsehair helmet.

'Who are you?' I asked.

'Ethan Nakamura,' he said. 'I have to kill you.'

'Why are you doing this?'

'Hey!' a monster jeered from the stands. 'Stop talking and fight already!' The others took up the call.

'I have to prove myself,' Ethan told me. 'Only way to join up.'

And with that he charged. Our swords met in midair and the crowd roared. It didn't seem right. I didn't want to fight to entertain a bunch of monsters, but Ethan Nakamura wasn't giving me much choice.

He pressed forward. He was good. He'd never been at Camp Half-Blood, as far as I knew, but he'd been trained. He parried my strike and almost slammed me with his shield, but I jumped back. He slashed. I rolled to one side. We exchanged thrusts and parries, getting a feel for each other's fighting style. I tried to keep to Ethan's blind side, but it didn't help much. He'd apparently been fighting with only one eye for a long time, because he was excellent at guarding his left.

'Blood!' the monsters cried.

My opponent glanced up at the stands. That was his weakness, I realized. He needed to impress them. I didn't.

He yelled an angry battle cry and charged me, but I parried his blade and backed away, letting him come after me.

'Booo!' Antaeus said. 'Stand and fight!'

Ethan pressed me, but I had no trouble defending, even without a shield. He was dressed for defence – heavy armour and shield – which made it very tiring to play offence. I was a softer target, but I was also lighter and faster. The crowd went nuts, yelling complaints and throwing rocks. We'd been fighting for almost five minutes and there was no blood.

Finally Ethan made his mistake. He tried to jab at my stomach and I locked his sword hilt in mine and twisted. His sword dropped into the dirt. Before he could recover I slammed the butt of my sword into his helmet and pushed him down. His heavy armour helped me more than him.

He fell on his back, dazed and tired. I put the tip of my sword on his chest.

'Get it over with,' Ethan groaned.

I looked up at Antaeus. His red face was stony with displeasure, but he held up his hand and put it 'thumbs down'.

'Forget it.' I sheathed my sword.

'Don't be a fool,' Ethan groaned. 'They'll just kill us both.'

I offered him my hand. Reluctantly, he took it. I helped him up.

'No one dishonours the games!' Antaeus bellowed. 'Your heads shall both be tributes to Poseidon!'

I looked at Ethan. 'When you see your chance, run.' Then I turned back to Antaeus. 'Why don't you fight me yourself? If you've got Dad's favour, come down here and prove it!'

The monsters grumbled in the stands. Antaeus looked around, and apparently realized he had no choice. He couldn't say no without looking like a coward.

'I am the greatest wrestler in the world, boy,' he warned. 'I have been wrestling since the first *pankration!*'

'*Pankration?*' I asked.

'He means fighting to the death,' Ethan said. 'No rules. No holds barred. It used to be an Olympic sport.'

'Thanks for the tip,' I said.

'Don't mention it.'

Rachel was watching me with wide eyes. Annabeth shook her head emphatically, the Laistrygonian's hand still clamped over her mouth.

I pointed my sword at Antaeus. 'Winner takes all! I

win, we all go free. You win, we die. Swear upon the River Styx.'

Antaeus laughed. 'This shouldn't take long. I swear to your terms!'

He leaped off the railing into the arena.

'Good luck,' Ethan told me. 'You'll need it.' Then he backed up quickly.

Antaeus cracked his knuckles. He grinned, and I saw that even his teeth were etched in wave patterns, which must've made brushing after meals a real pain.

'Weapons?' he asked.

'I'll stick with my sword. You?'

He held up his huge hands and wiggled his fingers. 'I don't need anything else! Master Luke, you will referee this one.'

Luke smiled down at me. 'With pleasure.'

Antaeus lunged. I rolled under his legs and stabbed him in the back of his thigh.

'Argggh!' he yelled. But where blood should've come out, there was a spout of sand, like I'd busted the side of an hourglass. It spilled to the ground, and the earth rose up to collect around his leg, almost like a cast. When it fell away, the wound was gone.

He charged again. Fortunately I'd had some experience fighting giants. I dodged sideways this time and stabbed him under the arm. Riptide's blade was buried to the hilt in his ribs. That was the good news. The bad news was that it wrenched out of my hand when the giant turned, and I was thrown across the arena, weaponless.

Antaeus bellowed in pain. I waited for him to disintegrate. No monster had ever withstood a direct hit like that from my sword. The celestial bronze blade had to be destroying his essence. But Antaeus groped for the hilt, pulled out the sword and tossed it behind him. More sand poured from the wound, but again the earth rose up to cover him. Dirt coated his body all the way to his shoulders. As soon as the dirt spilled away, Antaeus was fine.

'Now you see why I never lose, demigod!' Antaeus gloated. 'Come here and let me crush you. I'll make it quick!'

Antaeus stood between me and my sword. Desperately, I glanced to either side, and I caught Annabeth's eye.

The earth, I thought. What had Annabeth been trying to tell me? Antaeus's mother was Gaea the earth mother, the most ancient goddess of all. Antaeus's father might have been Poseidon, but Gaea was keeping him alive. I couldn't hurt him as long as he was touching the ground.

I tried to skirt around him, but Antaeus anticipated my move. He blocked my path, chuckling. He was just toying with me now. He had me cornered.

I looked up at the chains hanging from the ceiling, dangling the skulls of his enemies on hooks. Suddenly I had an idea.

I feinted to the other side. Antaeus blocked me. The crowd jeered and screamed at Antaeus to finish me off, but he was having too much fun.

'Puny boy,' he said. 'Not a worthy son of the sea god!'

I felt my pen return to my pocket, but Antaeus wouldn't know about that. He would think Riptide was still in the dirt behind him. He would think my goal was to get my sword. It wasn't much of an advantage, but it was all I had.

I charged straight ahead, crouching low so he would think I was going to roll between his legs again. While he was stooping, ready to catch me like a grounder, I jumped for all I was worth – kicking off his forearm, scrambling up his shoulder like it was a ladder, placing my shoe on his head. He did the natural thing. He straightened up indignantly and yelled 'HEY!' I pushed off, using his force to catapult me towards the ceiling. I caught the top of a chain, and the skulls and hooks jangled beneath me. I wrapped my legs around the chain, just like I used to do at the ropes course in gym class. I drew Riptide and sawed off the chain next to me.

'Come down here, coward!' Antaeus bellowed. He tried to grab me, but I was just out of reach. Hanging on for dear life, I yelled, 'Come up and get me! Or are you too slow and fat?'

He howled and made another grab for me. He caught a chain and tried to pull himself up. While he was struggling, I lowered my sawn-off chain, hook first. It took me two tries, but finally I snagged Antaeus's loincloth.

'WAAA!' he yelled. Quickly I slipped the free chain through the fastening link on my own chain, pulled it taut and secured it the best I could. Antaeus tried to slip back to the ground, but his butt stayed suspended by his loincloth. He had to hold on to the other chains with both hands to avoid getting flipped upside down. I prayed the loincloth and the chain would hold up for a few more seconds. While Antaeus cursed and flailed, I scrambled around the chains, swinging and cutting like I was some kind of crazed monkey. I made loops with hooks and metal links. I don't know how I did it. My mom always said I have a gift for getting stuff tangled up. Plus I was desperate to save my friends. Anyway, within a couple of minutes the giant was suspended above the ground, hopelessly snarled in chains and hooks.

I dropped to the floor, panting and sweaty. My hands were raw from climbing.

'Get me down!' Antaeus demanded.

'Free him!' Luke ordered. 'He is our host!'

I uncapped Riptide. 'I'll free him.'

And I stabbed the giant in the stomach. He bellowed, and sand poured out, but he was too far up to touch the earth, and the dirt did not rise to help him. Antaeus just dissolved, pouring out bit by bit, until there was nothing left but empty swinging chains, a really big loincloth on a hook and a bunch of grinning skulls dancing above me like they finally had something to smile about.

'Jackson!' Luke yelled. 'I should have killed you long ago!'

'You tried,' I reminded him. 'Let us go, Luke. We had a sworn agreement with Antaeus. I'm the winner.'

He did just what I expected. He said, 'Antaeus is dead. His oath dies with him. But since I'm feeling merciful today, I'll have you killed quickly.'

He pointed at Annabeth. 'Spare the girl.' His voice quavered just a little. 'I would speak to her before — before our great triumph.'

Every monster in the audience drew a weapon or extended its claws. We were trapped. Hopelessly outnumbered.

Then I felt something in my pocket – a freezing sensation, growing colder and colder. *The dog whistle.* My fingers closed around it. For days I'd avoided using Quintus's gift. It had to be a trap. But now . . . I had no choice. I took it out of my pocket and blew. It made no audible sound as it shattered into shards of ice, melting in my hand.

Luke laughed. 'What was that supposed to do?'

From behind me came a surprised yelp. The Laistrygonian giant who'd been guarding Annabeth flew past me and smashed into the wall.

'AROOOOF!'

Kelli the *empousa* screamed as a two-hundred-kilogram black mastiff picked her up like a chew toy and tossed her through the air, straight into Luke's lap. Mrs O'Leary snarled, and the two *dracaenae* guards backed away. For a moment the monsters in the audience were caught completely by surprise.

'Let's go!' I yelled at my friends. 'Heel, Mrs O'Leary!'

'The far exit!' Rachel cried. 'That's the right way!'

Ethan Nakamura took his cue. Together we raced across the arena and out the far exit, Mrs O'Leary right behind us. As we ran, I could hear the disorganized sounds of an entire army trying to jump out of the stands and follow us.

15 WE STEAL SOME SLIGHTLY USED WINGS

'This way!' Rachel yelled.

'Why should we follow you?' Annabeth demanded. 'You led us straight into that death trap!'

'It was the way you needed to go,' Rachel said. 'And so is this. Come on!'

Annabeth didn't look happy about it, but she ran along with the rest of us. Rachel seemed to know exactly where she was going. She whipped around corners and didn't even hesitate at crossroads. Once she said, 'Duck!' and we all crouched as a huge axe swung over our heads. Then we kept going as if nothing had happened.

I lost track of how many turns we made. We didn't stop to rest until we came to a room the size of a gymnasium with old marble columns holding up the roof. I stood at the doorway, listening for sounds of pursuit, but I heard nothing. Apparently, we'd lost Luke and his minions in the maze.

Then I realized something else: Mrs O'Leary was gone. I didn't know when she'd disappeared. I didn't know if she'd got lost or been overrun by monsters, or what. My heart turned to lead. She'd saved our lives, and I hadn't even waited to make sure she was following us.

Ethan collapsed on the floor. 'You people are crazy.' He pulled off his helmet. His face gleamed with sweat.

Annabeth gasped. 'I remember you! You were one of the undetermined kids in Hermes cabin, years ago.'

He glared at her. 'Yeah, and you're Annabeth. I remember.'

'What — what happened to your eye?'

Ethan looked away, and I got the feeling that was one subject he would *not* discuss.

'You must be the half-blood from my dream,' I said. 'The one Luke's people cornered. It wasn't Nico after all.'

'Who's Nico?'

'Never mind,' Annabeth said quickly. 'Why were you trying to join up with the wrong side?'

Ethan sneered. 'There's no right side. The gods never cared about us. Why shouldn't I —'

'Sign up with an army that makes you fight to the death for entertainment?' Annabeth said. 'Gee, I wonder.'

Ethan struggled to his feet. 'I'm not going to argue with you. Thanks for the help, but I'm out of here.'

'We're going after Daedalus,' I said. 'Come with us. Once we get through, you'd be welcome back at camp.'

'You really *are* crazy if you think Daedalus will help you.'

'He has to,' Annabeth said. 'We'll make him listen.'

Ethan snorted. 'Yeah, well. Good luck with that.'

I grabbed his arm. 'You're just going to head off alone into the maze? That's suicide.'

He looked at me with barely controlled anger. His eye patch was frayed around the edges and the black cloth was faded, like he'd been wearing it a long, long time. 'You shouldn't have spared me, Jackson. Mercy has no place in this war.'

Then he ran off into the darkness, back the way we'd come.

Annabeth, Rachel and I were so exhausted we made camp right there in the huge room. I found some scrap wood and we started a fire. Shadows danced off the columns rising around us like trees.

'Something was wrong with Luke,' Annabeth muttered, poking at the fire with her knife. 'Did you notice the way he was acting?'

'He looked pretty pleased to me,' I said. 'Like he'd spent a nice day torturing heroes.'

'That's not true! There was something wrong with him. He looked . . . nervous. He told his monsters to spare me. He wanted to tell me something.'

'Probably, *Hi, Annabeth! Sit here with me and watch while I tear your friends apart. It'll be fun!*'

'You're impossible,' Annabeth grumbled. She sheathed her dagger and looked at Rachel. 'So which way now, Sacagawea?'

Rachel didn't respond right away. She'd become quieter since the arena. Now, whenever Annabeth made a sarcastic comment, Rachel hardly bothered to answer. She'd burned the tip of a stick in the fire and was using it to draw ash figures on the floor, images of the monsters we'd seen. With a few strokes she caught the likeness of a *dracaena* perfectly.

'We'll follow the path,' she said. 'The brightness on the floor.'

'The brightness that led us straight into a trap?' Annabeth asked.

'Lay off her, Annabeth,' I said. 'She's doing the best she can.'

Annabeth stood. 'The fire's getting low. I'll go look for some more scraps while *you* guys talk strategy.' And she marched off into the shadows.

Rachel drew another figure with her stick – an ashy Antaeus dangling from his chains.

'Annabeth's usually not like this,' I told her. 'I don't know what her problem is.'

Rachel raised her eyebrows. 'Are you sure you don't know?'

'What do you mean?'

'Boys,' she muttered. 'Totally blind.'

'Hey, don't you get on my case, too! Look, I'm sorry I got you involved in this.'

'No, you were right,' she said. 'I can see the path. I can't explain it, but it's really clear.' She pointed towards the other end of the room, into the darkness. 'The workshop is that way. The heart of the maze. We're very close now. I don't know why the path led through that arena. I – I'm sorry about that. I thought you were going to die.'

She sounded like she was close to crying.

'Hey, I'm usually about to die,' I promised. 'Don't feel bad.'

She studied my face. 'So you do this every summer? Fight monsters? Save the world? Don't you ever get to do just, you know, normal stuff?'

I'd never really thought about it like that. The last time I'd had something like a normal life had been . . . well, never. 'Half-bloods get used to it, I guess. Or maybe not used to it, but . . .' I shifted uncomfortably. 'What about you? What do you do normally?'

Rachel shrugged. 'I paint. I read a lot.'

Okay, I thought. *So far we are scoring a zero on the similarities chart.* 'What about your family?'

I could sense her mental shields going up, like this was not a safe subject. 'Oh . . . they're just, you know, family.'

'You said they wouldn't notice if you were gone.'

She set down her drawing stick. 'Wow, I'm really tired. I may sleep for a while, okay?'

'Oh, sure. Sorry if . . .'

But Rachel was already curling up, using her backpack as a pillow. She closed her eyes and lay very still, but I got the feeling she wasn't really asleep.

A few minutes later, Annabeth came back. She tossed some more sticks on the fire. She looked at Rachel, then at me.

'I'll take first watch,' she said. 'You should sleep, too.'

'You don't have to act like that.'

'Like what?'

'Like . . . never mind.' I lay down, feeling miserable. I was so tired I fell asleep as soon as my eyes closed.

In my dreams, I heard laughter. Cold, harsh laughter, like knives being sharpened.

I was standing at the edge of a pit in the depths of Tartarus. Below me, the darkness seethed like inky soup.

'So close to your own destruction, little hero,' the voice of Kronos chided. 'And still you are blind.'

The voice was different than it had been before. It

seemed almost physical now, as if it were speaking from a real body instead of . . . whatever he'd been in his chopped-up condition.

'I have much to thank you for,' Kronos said. 'You have assured my rise.'

The shadows in the cavern became deeper and heavier. I tried to back away from the edge of the pit, but it was like swimming through oil. Time slowed down. My breathing almost stopped.

'A favour,' Kronos said. 'The Titan lord always pays his debts. Perhaps a glimpse of the friends you abandoned . . .'

The darkness rippled around me, and I was in a different cave.

'Hurry!' Tyson said. He came barrelling into the room. Grover stumbled along behind him. There was a rumbling in the corridor they'd come from, and the head of an enormous snake burst into the cave. I mean, this thing was so big its body barely fitted through the tunnel. Its scales were coppery, its head was diamond-shaped like a rattler and its yellow eyes glowed with hatred. When it opened its mouth, its fangs were as tall as Tyson.

It lashed at Grover, but Grover scampered out of the way. The snake got a mouthful of dirt. Tyson picked up a boulder and threw it at the monster, smacking it between the eyes, but the snake just recoiled and hissed.

'It's going to eat you!' Grover yelled at Tyson.

'How do you know?'

'It just told me! Run!'

Tyson darted to one side, but the snake used its head like a club and knocked him off his feet.

'No!' Grover yelled. But before Tyson could regain his

balance the snake wrapped around him and started to squeeze.

Tyson strained, pushing with all his immense strength, but the snake squeezed tighter. Grover frantically hit the snake with his reed pipes, but he might as well have been banging on a stone wall.

The whole room shook as the snake flexed its muscles, shuddering to overcome Tyson's strength.

Grover began to play the pipes, and stalactites rained down from the ceiling. The whole cave seemed about to collapse . . .

I woke with Annabeth shaking my shoulder. 'Percy, wake up!'

'Tyson — Tyson's in trouble!' I said. 'We have to help him!'

'First things first,' she said. 'Earthquake!'

Sure enough, the room was rumbling. 'Rachel!' I yelled.

Her eyes opened instantly. She grabbed her pack, and the three of us ran. We were almost to the far tunnel when a column next to us groaned and buckled. We kept going as a hundred tons of marble crashed down behind us.

We made it to the corridor and turned just in time to see the other columns toppling. A cloud of white dust billowed over us, and we kept running.

'You know what?' Annabeth said. 'I like this way after all.'

It wasn't long before we saw light up ahead — like regular electric lighting.

'There,' Rachel said.

We followed her into a stainless-steel hallway, like I

imagined they'd have on a space station or something. Fluorescent lights glowed from the ceiling. The floor was a metal grate.

I was so used to being in the darkness that I had to squint. Annabeth and Rachel both looked pale in the harsh illumination.

'This way,' Rachel said, beginning to run. 'We're close!'

'This is so wrong!' Annabeth said. 'The workshop should be in the oldest section of the maze. This can't —'

She faltered, because we'd arrived at a set of metal double doors. Inscribed in the steel, at eye level, was a large blue Greek Δ.

'We're here,' Rachel announced. 'Daedalus's workshop.'

Annabeth pressed the symbol on the doors and they hissed open.

'So much for ancient architecture,' I said.

Annabeth scowled. Together we walked inside.

The first thing that struck me was the daylight — blazing sun coming through giant windows. Not the kind of thing you expect in the heart of a dungeon. The workshop was like an artist's studio, with ten-metre ceilings and industrial lighting, polished stone floors and workbenches. A spiral staircase led up to a second-storey loft. Half a dozen easels displayed hand-drawn diagrams for buildings and machines that looked like Leonardo da Vinci sketches. Several laptop computers were scattered around on the tables. Glass jars of green oil — Greek fire — lined one shelf. There were inventions, too — weird metal machines I couldn't make sense of. One was a bronze chair with a bunch of electrical wires attached to it, like some kind of torture device. In another corner stood a giant metal egg about the size of a man. There was a grandfather clock that appeared to be made entirely of glass, so you could see all the gears turning. And hanging on the wall were several sets of bronze and silver wings.

'*Di immortales,*' Annabeth muttered. She ran to the nearest easel and looked at the sketch. 'He's a genius. Look at the curves on this building!'

'And an artist,' Rachel said in amazement. 'These wings are amazing!'

The wings looked more advanced than the ones I'd seen in my dreams. The feathers were more tightly interwoven. Instead of wax seals, self-adhesive strips ran down the sides.

I kept my hand on Riptide. Apparently Daedalus was not at home, but the workshop looked like it had been used recently. The laptops were running their screen savers. A half-eaten blueberry muffin and a coffee cup sat on a workbench.

I walked to the window. The view outside was amazing. I recognized the Rocky Mountains in the distance. We were high up in the foothills, at least one hundred and fifty metres, and, down below, a valley spread out, filled with a tumbled collection of red mesas and boulders and spires of stone. It looked like some huge kid had been building a toy city with skyscraper-size blocks, and then decided to knock it over.

'Where are we?' I wondered.

'Colorado Springs,' a voice said behind us. 'The Garden of the Gods.'

Standing on the spiral staircase above us, with his weapon drawn, was our missing sword master, Quintus.

✷　✷　✷

'*You*,' Annabeth said. 'What have you done with Daedalus?'

Quintus smiled faintly. 'Trust me, my dear. You don't want to meet him.'

'Look, Mr Traitor,' she growled, 'I didn't fight a dragon woman and a three-bodied man and a psychotic Sphinx to see *you*. Now where is DAEDALUS?'

Quintus came down the stairs, holding his sword at his side. He was dressed in jeans and boots and his counsellor's T-shirt from Camp Half-Blood, which seemed like an insult now that we knew he was a spy. I didn't know if I could beat him in a sword fight. He was pretty good. But I figured I would have to try.

'You think I'm an agent of Kronos,' he said. 'That I work for Luke.'

'Well, duh,' said Annabeth.

'You're an intelligent girl,' he said. 'But you're wrong. I work only for myself.'

'Luke mentioned you,' I said. 'Geryon knew about you, too. You've been to his ranch.'

'Of course,' he said. 'I've been almost everywhere. Even here.'

He walked past me like I was no threat at all and stood by the window. 'The view changes from day to day,' he mused. 'It's always some place high up. Yesterday it was from a skyscraper overlooking Manhattan. The day before that, there was a beautiful view of Lake Michigan. But it keeps coming back to the Garden of the Gods. I think the Labyrinth likes it here. A fitting name, I suppose.'

'You've been here before,' I said.

'Oh, yes.'

'That's an illusion out there?' I asked. 'A projection or something?'

'No,' Rachel murmured. 'It's real. We're really in Colorado.'

Quintus regarded her. 'You have clear vision, don't you? You remind me of another mortal girl I once knew. Another princess who came to grief.'

'Enough games,' I said. 'What have you done with Daedalus?'

Quintus stared at me. 'My boy, you need lessons from your friend on seeing clearly. I *am* Daedalus.'

There were a lot of answers I might've given, from 'I knew that' to 'LIAR!' to 'Yeah right, and I'm Zeus.'

The only thing I could think to say was, 'But you're not an inventor! You're a swordsman!'

'I am both,' Quintus said. 'And an architect. And a scholar. I also play basketball pretty well for a guy who didn't start until he was two thousand years old. A real artist must be good at many things.'

'That's true,' Rachel said. 'Like I can paint with my feet as well as my hands.'

'You see?' Quintus said. 'A girl of many talents.'

'But you don't even look like Daedalus,' I protested. 'I saw him in a dream, and . . .' Suddenly a horrible thought dawned on me.

'Yes,' Quintus said. 'You've finally guessed the truth.'

'You're an automaton. You made yourself a new body.'

'Percy,' Annabeth said uneasily, 'that's not possible. That – that can't be an automaton.'

Quintus chuckled. 'Do you know what Quintus means, my dear?'

'The fifth, in Latin. But —'

'This is my fifth body.' The swordsman held out his forearm. He pressed his elbow and part of his wrist popped open — a rectangular hatch in his skin. Underneath, bronze gears whirred. Wires glowed.

'That's amazing!' Rachel said.

'That's weird,' I said.

'You found a way to transfer your *animus* into a machine?' Annabeth said. 'That's . . . not natural.'

'Oh, I assure you, my dear, it's still me. I'm still very much Daedalus. Our mother, Athena, makes sure I never forget that.' He tugged back the collar of his shirt. At the base of his neck was the mark I'd seen before — the dark shape of a bird grafted to his skin.

'A murderer's brand,' Annabeth said.

'For your nephew, Perdix,' I guessed. 'The boy you pushed off the tower.'

Quintus's face darkened. 'I did not push him. I simply —'

'Made him lose his balance,' I said. 'Let him die.'

Quintus gazed out of the windows at the purple mountains. 'I regret what I did, Percy. I was angry and bitter. But I cannot take it back, and Athena never lets me forget. As Perdix died, she turned him into a small bird — a partridge. She branded the bird's shape on my neck as a reminder. No matter what body I take, the brand appears on my skin.'

I looked into his eyes, and I realized he was the same man I'd seen in my dreams. His face might be totally different, but the same soul was in there — the same intelligence and all the sadness.

'You really are Daedalus,' I decided. 'But why did you come to the camp? Why spy on us?'

'To see if your camp was worth saving. Luke had given me one story. I preferred to come to my own conclusions.'

'So you *have* talked to Luke.'

'Oh, yes. Several times. He is quite persuasive.'

'But now you've seen the camp!' Annabeth persisted. 'So you know we need your help. You can't let Luke through the maze!'

Daedalus set his sword on the workbench. 'The maze is no longer mine to control, Annabeth. I created it, yes. In fact, it is tied to my life force. But I have allowed it to live and grow on its own. That is the price I paid for privacy.'

'Privacy from what?'

'The gods,' he said. 'And death. I have been alive for two millennia, my dear, hiding from death.'

'But how can you hide from Hades?' I asked. 'I mean . . . Hades has the Furies.'

'They do not know everything,' he said. 'Or see everything. You have encountered them, Percy. You know this is true. A clever man can hide quite a long time, and I have buried myself very deep. Only my greatest enemy has kept after me, and even him I have thwarted.'

'You mean Minos,' I said.

Daedalus nodded. 'He hunts for me relentlessly. Now that he is a judge of the dead, he would like nothing better than for me to come before him so he can punish me for my crimes. After the daughters of Cocalus killed him, Minos's ghost began torturing me in my dreams. He promised that he would hunt me down. I did the only thing I could. I retreated from the world completely. I descended into my Labyrinth. I decided this would be my ultimate accomplishment: I would cheat death.'

'And you did,' Annabeth marvelled, 'for two thousand years.' She sounded kind of impressed, despite the horrible things Daedalus had done.

Just then a loud bark echoed from the corridor. I heard the ba-BUMP, ba-BUMP, ba-BUMP of huge paws, and Mrs O'Leary bounded into the workshop. She licked my face once, then almost knocked Daedalus over with an enthusiastic leap.

'There is my old friend!' Daedalus said, scratching Mrs O'Leary behind the ears. 'My only companion all these long lonely years.'

'You let her save me,' I said. 'That whistle actually worked.'

Daedalus nodded. 'Of course it did, Percy. You have a good heart. And I knew Mrs O'Leary liked you. I wanted to help you. Perhaps I – I felt guilty, as well.'

'Guilty about what?'

'That your quest would be in vain.'

'What?' Annabeth said. 'But you can still help us. You have to! Give us Ariadne's string so Luke can't get it.'

'Yes . . . the string. I told Luke that the eyes of a clear-sighted mortal are the best guide, but he did not trust me. He was so focused on the idea of a magic item. And the string works. It's not as accurate as your mortal friend here, perhaps. But good enough. Good enough.'

'Where is it?' Annabeth said.

'With Luke,' Daedalus said sadly. 'I'm sorry, my dear. But you are several hours too late.'

With a chill I realized why Luke had been in such a good mood in the arena. He'd already got the string from Daedalus. His only obstacle had been the arena master, and I'd taken care of that for him by killing Antaeus.

'Kronos promised me freedom,' Quintus said. 'Once Hades is overthrown, he will set me over the Underworld. I will reclaim my son Icarus. I will make things right with poor young Perdix. I will see Minos's soul cast into Tartarus, where it cannot bother me again. And I will no longer have to run from death.'

'That's your brilliant idea?' Annabeth yelled. 'You're going to let Luke destroy our camp, kill hundreds of demigods and then attack Olympus? You're going to bring down the entire world so you can get what you want?'

'Your cause is doomed, my dear. I saw that as soon as I began to work at your camp. There is no way you can hold back the might of Kronos.'

'That's not true!' she cried.

'I am doing what I must, my dear. The offer was too sweet to refuse. I'm sorry.'

Annabeth pushed over an easel. Architectural drawings scattered across the floor. 'I used to respect you. You were my hero! You — you built amazing things. You solved problems. Now . . . I don't know what you are. Children of Athena are supposed to be *wise*, not just clever. Maybe you *are* just a machine. You should have died two thousand years ago.'

Instead of getting mad, Daedalus hung his head. 'You should go warn your camp. Now that Luke has the string —'

Suddenly Mrs O'Leary pricked up her ears.

'Someone's coming!' Rachel warned.

The doors of the workshop burst open, and Nico was pushed inside, his hands in chains. Then Kelli and two Laistrygonians marched in behind him, followed by the ghost of Minos. He looked almost solid now – a pale bearded king with cold eyes and tendrils of Mist coiling off his robes.

He fixed his gaze on Daedalus. 'There you are, my old friend.'

Daedalus's jaw clenched. He looked at Kelli. 'What is the meaning of this?'

'Luke sends his compliments,' Kelli said. 'He thought you might like to see your old employer, Minos.'

'This was not part of our agreement,' Daedalus said.

'No indeed,' Kelli said. 'But we already have what we want from you, and we have other agreements to honour. Minos required something else from us, in order to turn over this fine young demigod.' She ran a finger under Nico's chin. 'He'll be quite useful. And all Minos asked in return was your head, old man.'

Daedalus paled. 'Treachery.'

'Get used to it,' Kelli said.

'Nico,' I said. 'Are you okay?'

He nodded morosely. 'I – I'm sorry, Percy. Minos told me you were in danger. He convinced me to go back into the maze.'

'You were trying to *help* us?'

'I was tricked,' he said. 'He tricked all of us.'

I glared at Kelli. 'Where's Luke? Why isn't he here?'

The she-demon smiled like we were sharing a private

joke. 'Luke is . . . busy. He is preparing for the assault. But don't worry. We have more friends on the way. And in the meantime, I think I'll have a wonderful snack!' Her hands changed to claws. Her hair burst into flame and her legs turned to their true form – one donkey leg, one bronze.

'Percy,' Rachel whispered, 'the wings. Do you think –'

'Get them,' I said. 'I'll try to buy you some time.'

And with that, all Hades broke loose. Annabeth and I charged at Kelli. The giants came right at Daedalus, but Mrs O'Leary leaped to his defence. Nico got pushed to the ground and struggled with his chains while the spirit of Minos wailed, 'Kill the inventor! Kill him!'

Rachel grabbed the wings off the wall. Nobody paid her any attention. Kelli slashed at Annabeth. I tried to get to her, but the demon was quick and deadly. She turned over tables, smashed inventions and wouldn't let us get close. Out of the corner of my eye, I saw Mrs O'Leary chomp her fangs into a giant's arm. He wailed in pain and flung her around, trying to shake her off. Daedalus grabbed for his sword, but the second giant smashed the workbench with his fist, and the sword went flying. A clay jar of Greek fire broke on the floor and began to burn, green flames spreading quickly.

'To me!' Minos cried. 'Spirits of the dead!' He raised his ghostly hands and the air began to hum.

'No!' Nico cried. He was on his feet now. He'd somehow managed to remove his shackles.

'You do not control me, young fool,' Minos sneered. 'All this time, I have been controlling you! A soul for a soul, yes. But it is not your sister who will return from the dead. It is I, as soon as I slay the inventor!'

Spirits began to appear around Minos – shimmering forms that slowly multiplied, solidifying into Cretan soldiers.

'I am the son of Hades,' Nico insisted. 'Begone!'

Minos laughed. 'You have no power over me. I am the lord of spirits! The ghost king!'

'No.' Nico drew his sword. '*I* am.'

He stabbed his black blade into the floor, and it cleaved through the stone like butter.

'Never!' Minos's form rippled. 'I will not –'

The ground rumbled. The windows cracked and shattered to pieces, letting in a blast of fresh air. A fissure opened in the stone floor of the workshop, and Minos and all his spirits were sucked into the void with a horrible wail.

The bad news: the fight was still going on all around us, and I let myself get distracted. Kelli pounced on me so fast I had no time to defend myself. My sword skittered away and I hit my head hard on a worktable as I fell. My eyesight went fuzzy. I couldn't raise my arms.

Kelli laughed. 'You will taste wonderful!'

She bared her fangs. Then suddenly her body went rigid. Her red eyes widened. She gasped, 'No . . . school . . . spirit . . .'

And Annabeth took her knife out of the *empousa*'s back. With an awful screech, Kelli dissolved into yellow vapour.

Annabeth helped me up. I still felt dizzy, but we had no time to lose. Mrs O'Leary and Daedalus were still locked in combat with the giants, and I could hear shouting in the tunnel. More monsters were coming towards the workshop.

'We have to help Daedalus!' I said.

'No time,' Rachel said. 'Too many coming!'

She'd already fitted herself with wings and was working on Nico, who looked pale and sweaty from his struggle with Minos. The wings grafted instantly to his back and arms.

'Now you!' she told me.

In seconds, Nico, Annabeth, Rachel and I had fitted ourselves with coppery wings. Already I could feel myself being lifted by the wind coming through the window. Greek fire was burning the tables and furniture, spreading up the circular stairs.

'Daedalus!' I yelled. 'Come on!'

He was cut in a hundred places – but he was bleeding golden oil instead of blood. He'd found his sword and was using part of a smashed table as a shield against the giants. 'I won't leave Mrs O'Leary!' he said. 'Go!'

There was no time to argue. Even if we stayed, I wasn't sure we could help.

'None of us know how to fly!' Nico protested.

'Great time to find out,' I said. And together the four of us jumped out of the window into open sky.

16 I OPEN A COFFIN

Jumping out of a window one hundred and fifty metres above ground is not usually my idea of fun. Especially when I'm wearing bronze wings and flapping my arms like a duck.

I plummeted towards the valley and the red rocks below. I was pretty sure I was going to become a grease spot in the Garden of the Gods, as Annabeth yelled from somewhere above me, 'Spread your arms! Keep them extended.'

The small part of my brain that wasn't engulfed in panic heard her, and my arms responded. As soon as I spread them out, the wings stiffened, caught the wind and my descent slowed. I soared downwards, but at a controlled angle, like a kite in a dive.

Experimentally, I flapped my arms once. I arced into the sky, the wind whistling in my ears.

'Yeah!' I yelled. The feeling was unbelievable. After getting the hang of it, I felt like the wings were part of my body. I could soar and swoop and dive anywhere I wanted to.

I turned and saw my friends – Rachel, Annabeth and Nico – spiralling above me, glinting in the sunlight. Behind them, smoke billowed from the windows of Daedalus's workshop.

'Land!' Annabeth yelled. 'These wings won't last forever.'

'How long?' Rachel cried.

'I don't want to find out!' Annabeth said.

We swooped down towards the Garden of the Gods. I did a complete circle around one of the rock spires and freaked out a couple of climbers. Then the four of us soared across the valley, over a road, and landed on the terrace of the visitor centre. It was late afternoon and the place looked pretty empty, but we ripped off our wings as quickly as we could. Looking at them, I could see Annabeth was right. The self-adhesive seals that bound the wings to our backs were already melting, and we were shedding bronze feathers. It seemed a shame, but we couldn't fix them, and couldn't leave them around for the mortals, so we stuffed the wings in the bin outside the cafeteria.

I used the tourist binocular camera to look up at the hill where Daedalus's workshop had been, but it had vanished. No more smoke. No broken windows. Just the side of a hill.

'The workshop moved,' Annabeth guessed. 'There's no telling where.'

'So what do we do now?' I asked. 'How do we get back in the maze?'

Annabeth gazed at the summit of Pikes Peak in the distance. 'Maybe we can't. If Daedalus died . . . he said his life force was tied to the Labyrinth. The whole thing might've been destroyed. Maybe that will stop Luke's invasion.'

I thought about Grover and Tyson, still down there somewhere. And Daedalus . . . even though he'd done some terrible things and put everybody I cared about at risk, it still seemed like a pretty horrible way to die.

'No,' Nico said. 'He isn't dead.'

'How can you be sure?' I asked.

'I *know* when people die. It's this feeling I get, like a buzzing in my ears.'

'What about Tyson and Grover, then?'

Nico shook his head. 'That's harder. They're not humans or half-bloods. They don't have mortal souls.'

'We have to get into town,' Annabeth decided. 'Our chances of finding an entrance to the Labyrinth will be better. We have to make it back to camp before Luke and his army.'

'We could just take a plane,' Rachel said.

I shuddered. 'I don't fly.'

'But you just did.'

'That was low flying,' I said, 'and even that's risky. Flying up really high – that's Zeus's territory. I can't do it. Besides, we don't even have time for a flight. The Labyrinth is the quickest way back.'

I didn't want to say it, but I was also hoping that maybe, just maybe, we would find Grover and Tyson along the way.

'So we need a car to take us into the city,' Annabeth said.

Rachel looked down into the parking lot. She grimaced, as if she were about to do something she regretted. 'I'll take care of it.'

'How?' Annabeth asked.

'Just trust me.'

Annabeth looked uneasy, but she nodded. 'Okay, I'm going to buy a prism in the gift shop, try to make a rainbow and send an Iris-message to camp.'

'I'll go with you,' Nico said. 'I'm hungry.'

'I'll stick with Rachel, then,' I said. 'Meet you guys in the parking lot.'

Rachel frowned like she didn't want me with her. That made me feel kind of bad, but I followed her down to the parking lot anyway.

She headed towards a big black car parked at the edge of the lot. It was a chauffeured Lexus, like the kind I always saw driving around Manhattan. The driver was out at the front, reading a newspaper. He wore a dark suit and tie.

'What are you going to do?' I asked Rachel.

'Just wait here,' she said miserably. 'Please.'

Rachel marched straight up to the driver and talked to him. He frowned. Rachel said something else. He turned pale and hastily folded up his magazine. He nodded and fumbled for his cell phone. After a brief call, he opened the back door of the car for Rachel to get in. She pointed back in my direction, and the driver bobbed his head some more, like *Yes, ma'am. Whatever you want.*

I couldn't figure out why he was acting so flustered.

Rachel came back to get me just as Nico and Annabeth appeared from the gift shop.

'I talked to Chiron,' Annabeth said. 'They're doing their best to prepare for battle, but he still wants us back. They're going to need every hero they can get. Did we find a ride?'

'The driver's ready when we are,' Rachel said.

The chauffeur was now talking to another guy in khakis and a polo shirt, probably his client who'd rented the car. The client was complaining, but I could hear the driver saying, 'I'm sorry, sir. Emergency. I've ordered another car for you.'

'Come on,' Rachel said. She led us to the car and got

in without even looking at the annoyed guy who'd rented it. A minute later we were cruising down the road. The seats were leather. There was plenty of leg room. The back seat had flat-panel TVs built into the headrests and a mini-fridge stocked with bottled water, drinks and snacks. We started pigging out.

'Where to, Miss Dare?' the driver asked.

'I'm not sure yet, Robert,' she said. 'We just need to drive through town and, uh, look around.'

'Whatever you say, miss.'

I looked at Rachel. 'Do you know this guy?'

'No.'

'But he dropped everything to help you. Why?'

'Just keep your eyes peeled,' she said. 'Help me look.'

Which didn't exactly answer my question.

We drove through Colorado Springs for about half an hour and saw nothing that Rachel considered a possible Labyrinth entrance. I was very aware of Rachel's shoulder pressing against mine. I kept wondering who she was exactly, and how she could walk up to some random chauffeur and immediately get a ride.

After about an hour we decided to head north towards Denver, thinking that maybe a bigger city would be more likely to have a Labyrinth entrance, but we were all getting nervous. We were losing time.

Then, right as we were leaving Colorado Springs, Rachel sat bolt upright. 'Get off the highway!'

The driver glanced back. 'Miss?'

'I saw something, I think. Get off here.'

The driver swerved across traffic and took the exit.

'What did you see?' I asked, because we were pretty

much out of the city now. There wasn't anything around except hills, grassland and some scattered farm buildings.

Rachel had the driver turn down this unpromising dirt road. We drove by a sign too fast for me to read it, but Rachel said, 'Western Museum of Mining and Industry.'

For a museum, it didn't look like much – a little house like an old-fashioned railroad station, some drills and pumps and old steam shovels on display outside.

'There.' Rachel pointed to a hole in the side of a nearby hill – a tunnel that was boarded up and chained. 'An old mine entrance.'

'A door to the Labyrinth?' Annabeth asked. 'How can you be sure?'

'Well, look at it!' Rachel said. 'I mean . . . *I* can see it, okay?'

She thanked the driver and we all got out. He didn't ask for money or anything. 'Are you sure you'll be all right, Miss Dare? I'd be happy to call your –'

'No!' Rachel said. 'No, really. Thanks, Robert. But we're fine.'

The museum seemed to be closed, so nobody bothered us as we climbed the hill to the mine shaft. When we got to the entrance, I saw the mark of Daedalus engraved on the padlock, though how Rachel had seen something so tiny all the way from the highway I had no idea. I touched the padlock and the chains fell away. We kicked down a few boards and walked inside. For better or worse, we were back in the Labyrinth.

The dirt tunnels turned to stone. They wound around and split off and basically tried to confuse us, but Rachel had no trouble guiding us. We told her we needed to get back to New York, and she hardly even paused when the tunnels offered a choice.

To my surprise, Rachel and Annabeth started up a conversation as we walked. Annabeth asked her more about her background, but Rachel was evasive so they started talking about architecture. It turned out that Rachel knew something about it from studying art. They talked about different facades on buildings around New York – 'Have you seen this one,' blah, blah, blah, so I hung back and walked next to Nico in uncomfortable silence.

'Thanks for coming after us,' I told him at last.

Nico's eyes narrowed. He didn't seem as angry as he used to – just suspicious, careful. 'I owed you for the ranch, Percy. Plus . . . I wanted to see Daedalus for myself. Minos was right, in a way. Daedalus *should* die. Nobody should be able to avoid death that long. It's not natural.'

'That's what you were after all along,' I said. 'Trading Daedalus's soul for your sister's.'

Nico walked for another fifty metres before answering. 'It hasn't been easy, you know. Having only the dead for company. Knowing that I'll never be accepted by the living. Only the dead respect me, and they only do that out of fear.'

'You could be accepted,' I said. 'You could have friends at camp.'

He stared at me. 'Do you really believe that, Percy?'

I didn't answer. The truth was, I didn't know. Nico had always been a little different, but since Bianca's death, he'd become almost . . . scary. He had his father's eyes – that intense, manic fire that made you suspect he was either a genius or a madman. And the way he'd banished Minos, and called *himself* the king of ghosts – it was kind of impressive, but it made me uncomfortable, too.

Before I could figure out what to tell him, I ran into Rachel, who'd stopped in front of me. We'd come to a crossroads. The tunnel continued straight ahead, but a side tunnel T'd off to the right – a circular shaft carved from black volcanic rock.

'What is it?' I asked.

Rachel stared down the dark tunnel. In the dim flashlight beam, her face looked like one of Nico's spectres.

'Is that the way?' Annabeth asked.

'No,' Rachel said nervously. 'Not at all.'

'Why are we stopping, then?' I asked.

'Listen,' Nico said.

I heard wind coming down the tunnel, as if the exit were close. And I smelled something vaguely familiar – something that brought back bad memories.

'Eucalyptus trees,' I said. 'Like in California.'

Last winter, when we'd faced Luke and the Titan Atlas on top of Mount Tamalpais, the air had smelled just like that.

'There's something evil down that tunnel,' Rachel said. 'Something very powerful.'

'And the smell of death,' Nico added, which made me feel a whole lot better.

Annabeth and I exchanged glances.

'Luke's entrance,' she guessed. 'The one to Mount Othrys – the Titans' palace.'

'I have to check it out,' I said.

'Percy, no.'

'Luke could be right there,' I said. 'Or . . . or Kronos. I have to find out what's going on.'

Annabeth hesitated. 'Then we'll all go.'

'No,' I said. 'It's too dangerous. If they got hold of Nico, or Rachel for that matter, Kronos could use them. You stay here and guard them.'

What I didn't say: I was also worried about Annabeth. I didn't trust what she would do if she saw Luke again. He had fooled her and manipulated her too many times before.

'Percy, don't,' Rachel said. 'Don't go up there alone.'

'I'll be quick,' I promised. 'I won't do anything stupid.'

Annabeth took her Yankees cap out of her pocket. 'At least take this. And be careful.'

'Thanks.' I remembered the last time Annabeth and I had parted ways, when she'd given me a kiss for luck in Mount St Helens. This time, all I got was the hat.

I put it on. 'Here goes nothing.' And I sneaked invisibly down the dark stone tunnel.

Before I even got to the exit I heard voices: the growling, barking sounds of sea-demon smiths, the telekhines.

'At least we salvaged the blade,' one said. 'The master will still reward us.'

'Yes! Yes!' a second shrieked. 'Rewards beyond measure!'

Another voice, this one more human, said: 'Um, yeah, well that's great. Now, if you're done with me —'

'No, half-blood!' a telekhine said. 'You must help us make the presentation. It is a great honour!'

'Gee, thanks,' the half-blood said, and I realized it was Ethan Nakamura, the guy who'd run away after I'd saved his sorry life in the arena.

I crept towards the end of the tunnel. I had to remind myself I was invisible. They shouldn't be able to see me.

A blast of cold air hit me as I emerged. I was standing near the top of Mount Tam. The Pacific Ocean spread out below, grey under a cloudy sky. About six metres downhill, two telekhines were placing something on a big rock — something long and thin and wrapped in black cloth. Ethan was helping them open it.

'Careful, fool,' the telekhine scolded. 'One touch, and the blade will sever your soul from your body.'

Ethan swallowed nervously. 'Maybe I'll let you unwrap it, then.'

I glanced up at the mountain's peak, where a black marble fortress loomed, just like I'd seen in my dreams. It reminded me of an oversized mausoleum, with walls fifteen metres high. I had no idea how mortals could miss the fact that it was here. But, then again, everything below the summit seemed fuzzy to me, as if there were a thick veil between me and the lower half of the mountain. There was magic going on here — really powerful Mist. Above me, the sky swirled into a huge funnel cloud. I couldn't see Atlas, but I could hear him groaning in the distance, still labouring under the weight of the sky, just beyond the fortress.

'There!' the telekhine said. Reverently, he lifted the weapon, and my blood turned to ice.

It was a scythe — a two-metre-long blade curved like a crescent moon, with a wooden handle wrapped in leather.

The blade glinted two different colours – steel and bronze. It was the weapon of Kronos, the one he'd used to slice up his father, Ouranos, before the gods had taken it away from him and cut *Kronos* to pieces, casting him into Tartarus. Now the weapon was reforged.

'We must sanctify it in blood,' the telekhine said. 'Then you, half-blood, shall help present it when the lord awakes.'

I ran towards the fortress, my pulse pounding in my ears. I didn't want to get anywhere close to that horrible black mausoleum, but I knew what I had to do. I had to stop Kronos from rising. This might be my only chance.

I dashed through a dark foyer and into the main hall. The floor shone like a mahogany piano – pure black and yet full of light. Black marble statues lined the walls. I didn't recognize the faces, but I knew I was looking at images of the Titans who'd ruled before the gods. At the end of the room, between two bronze braziers, was a dais. And on the dais, the golden sarcophagus.

The room was silent except for the crackle of the fires. Luke wasn't here. No guards. Nothing.

It was too easy, but I approached the dais.

The sarcophagus was just like I remembered – about three metres long, much too big for a human. It was carved with elaborate scenes of death and destruction, pictures of the gods being trampled under chariots, temples and famous world landmarks being smashed and burned. The whole coffin gave off an aura of extreme cold, like I was walking into a freezer. My breath began to steam.

I drew Riptide and took a little comfort from the familiar weight of the sword in my hand.

Whenever I'd approached Kronos before, his evil voice had spoken in my mind. Why was he silent now? He'd been shredded into a thousand pieces, cut with his own scythe. What would I find if I opened that lid? How could they make a new body for him?

I had no answers. I just knew that if he was about to rise, I had to strike him down before he got his scythe. I had to figure out a way to stop him.

I stood over the coffin. The lid was decorated even more intricately than the sides – with scenes of carnage and power. In the middle was an inscription carved in letters even older than Greek, a language of magic. I couldn't read it, exactly, but I knew what it said: KRONOS, LORD OF TIME.

My hand touched the lid. My fingertips turned blue. Frost gathered on my sword.

Then I heard noises behind me – voices approaching. It was now or never. I pushed back the golden lid and it fell to the floor with a huge WHOOOOM!

I lifted my sword, ready to strike. But when I looked inside I didn't comprehend what I was seeing. Mortal legs, dressed in grey trousers. A white T-shirt, hands folded over his stomach. One piece of his chest was missing – a clean black hole about the size of a bullet wound, right where his heart should've been. His eyes were closed. His skin was pale. Blond hair . . . and a scar running along the left side of his face.

The body in the coffin was Luke's.

I should have stabbed him right then. I should've brought the point of Riptide down with all my strength.

But I was too stunned. I didn't understand. As much as I hated Luke, as much as he had betrayed me, I just didn't get why he was in the coffin, and why he looked so very, very dead.

Then the voices of the telekhines were right behind me.

'What has happened!' one of the demons screamed when he saw the lid. I stumbled away from the dais, forgetting that I was invisible, and hid behind a column as they approached.

'Careful!' the other demon warned. 'Perhaps he stirs. We must present the gifts now. Immediately!'

The two telekhines shuffled forward and knelt, holding up the scythe on its wrapping cloth. 'My lord,' one said. 'Your symbol of power is remade.'

Silence. Nothing happened in the coffin.

'You fool,' the other telekhine muttered. 'He requires the half-blood first.'

Ethan stepped back. 'Whoa, what do you mean, he requires me?'

'Don't be a coward!' the first telekhine hissed. 'He does not require your death. Only your allegiance. Pledge him your service. Renounce the gods. That is all.'

'No!' I yelled. It was a stupid thing to do, but I charged into the room and took off the cap. 'Ethan, don't!'

'Trespasser!' The telekhines bared their seal teeth. 'The master will deal with you soon enough. Hurry, boy!'

'Ethan,' I pleaded, 'don't listen to them. Help me destroy it.'

Ethan turned towards me, his eye patch blending in

with the shadows on his face. His expression was something like pity. 'I told you not to spare me, Percy. "An eye for an eye." You ever hear that saying? I learned what it means the hard way – when I discovered my godly parent. I'm the child of Nemesis, Goddess of Revenge. And this is what I was made to do.'

He turned towards the dais. 'I renounce the gods! What have they ever done for me? I will see them destroyed. I will serve Kronos.'

The building rumbled. A wisp of blue light rose from the floor at Ethan Nakamura's feet. It drifted towards the coffin and began to shimmer, like a cloud of pure energy. Then it descended into the sarcophagus.

Luke sat bolt upright. His eyes opened, and they were no longer blue. They were golden, the same colour as the coffin. The hole in his chest was gone. He was complete. He leaped out of the coffin with ease, and where his feet touched the floor, the marble froze like craters of ice.

He looked at Ethan and the telekhines with those horrible golden eyes, as if he were a newborn baby, not sure what he was seeing. Then he looked at me, and a smile of recognition crept across his mouth.

'This body has been well prepared.' His voice was like a razor blade running over my skin. It was Luke's, but not Luke's. Underneath his voice was another, more horrible sound – an ancient, cold sound like metal scraping against rock. 'Don't you think so, Percy Jackson?'

I couldn't move. I couldn't answer.

Kronos threw back his head and laughed. The scar on his face rippled.

'Luke feared you,' the Titan's voice said. 'His jealousy

and hatred have been powerful tools. It has kept him obedient. For that I thank you.'

Ethan collapsed in terror. He covered his face with his hands. The telekhines trembled, holding up the scythe.

Finally I found my nerve. I lunged at the thing that used to be Luke, thrusting my blade straight at his chest, but his skin deflected the blow like he was made of pure steel. He looked at me with amusement. Then he flicked his hand, and I flew across the room.

I slammed against a pillar. I struggled to my feet, blinking the stars out of my eyes, but Kronos had already grasped the handle of his scythe.

'Ah . . . much better,' he said. 'Backbiter, Luke called it. An appropriate name. Now that it is reforged completely, it shall indeed *bite back*.'

'What have you done to Luke?' I groaned.

Kronos raised his scythe. 'He serves me with his whole being, as I require. The difference is, he feared you, Percy Jackson. I do not.'

That's when I ran. There wasn't even any thought to it. No debate in my mind about — gee, should I stand up to him and try to fight again? Nope. I simply ran.

But my feet felt like lead. Time slowed down around me, like the world was turning to Jell-O. I'd had this feeling once before, and I knew it was the power of Kronos. His presence was so strong it could bend time itself.

'Run, little hero,' he laughed. 'Run!'

I glanced back and saw him approaching leisurely, swinging his scythe as if he were enjoying the feel of having it in his hands again. No weapon in the world could stop him. No amount of celestial bronze.

He was three metres away when I heard, 'PERCY!'
Rachel's voice.

Something flew past me, and a blue plastic hairbrush
hit Kronos in the eye.

'Ow!' he yelled. For a moment it was only Luke's voice,
full of surprise and pain. My limbs were freed and I ran
straight into Rachel, Nico and Annabeth, who were standing
in the entry hall, their eyes wide with dismay.

'Luke?' Annabeth called. 'What –'

I grabbed her by the shirt and hauled her after me. I
ran as fast as I've ever run, straight out of the fortress. We
were almost back to the Labyrinth entrance when I heard
the loudest bellow in the world – the voice of Kronos,
coming back into control. 'AFTER THEM!'

'No!' Nico yelled. He clapped his hands together, and
a jagged spire of rock the size of an eighteen-wheeler
erupted from the ground right in front of the fortress.
The tremor it caused was so powerful, the front columns
of the building came crashing down. I heard muffled screams
from the telekhines inside. Dust billowed everywhere.

We plunged into the Labyrinth and kept running, the
howl of the Titan lord shaking the entire world behind
us.

17 THE LOST GOD SPEAKS

We ran until we were exhausted. Rachel steered us away from traps, but we had no destination in mind – only *away* from that dark mountain and the roar of Kronos.

We stopped in a tunnel of wet white rock, like part of a natural cave. I couldn't hear anything behind us, but I didn't feel any safer. I could still remember those unnatural golden eyes staring out of Luke's face, and the feeling that my limbs were slowly turning to stone.

'I can't go any further,' Rachel gasped, hugging her chest.

Annabeth had been crying the entire time we'd been running. Now she collapsed and put her head between her knees. Her sobs echoed in the tunnel. Nico and I sat next to each other. He dropped his sword next to mine and took a shaky breath.

'That sucked,' he said, which I thought summed things up pretty well.

'You saved our lives,' I said.

Nico wiped the dust off his face. 'Blame the girls for dragging me along. That's the only thing they could agree on. We needed to help you or you'd mess things up.'

'Nice that they trust me so much.' I shone my flashlight across the cavern. Water dripped from the stalactites like a slow-motion rain. 'Nico . . . you, uh, kind of gave yourself away.'

'What do you mean?'

'That wall of black stone? That was pretty impressive. If Kronos didn't know who you were before, he does now – a child of the Underworld.'

Nico frowned. 'Big deal.'

I let it drop. I figured he was just trying to hide how scared he was, and I couldn't blame him.

Annabeth lifted her head. Her eyes were red from crying. 'What . . . what was wrong with Luke? What did they do to him?'

I told her what I'd seen in the coffin, the way the last piece of Kronos's spirit had entered Luke's body when Ethan Nakamura pledged his service.

'No,' Annabeth said. 'That can't be true. He couldn't –'

'He gave himself over to Kronos,' I said. 'I'm sorry, Annabeth. But Luke is gone.'

'No!' she insisted. 'You saw when Rachel hit him.'

I nodded, looking at Rachel with respect. 'You hit the Lord of the Titans in the eye with a blue plastic hairbrush.'

Rachel looked embarrassed. 'It was the only thing I had.'

'But you *saw*,' Annabeth insisted. 'When it hit him, just for a second, he was dazed. He came back to his senses.'

'So maybe Kronos wasn't completely settled in the body, or whatever,' I said. 'It doesn't mean Luke was in control.'

'You *want* him to be evil, is that it?' Annabeth yelled. 'You didn't know him before, Percy. I did!'

'What is it with you?' I snapped. 'Why do you keep defending him?'

'Whoa, you two,' Rachel said. 'Knock it off.'

Annabeth turned on her. 'Stay out of it, mortal girl! If it wasn't for you . . .'

Whatever she was going to say, her voice broke. She put her head down again and sobbed miserably. I wanted to comfort her, but I didn't know how. I still felt stunned, like Kronos's time-slowing effect had affected my brain. I just couldn't comprehend what I'd seen. Kronos was alive. He was armed. And the end of the world was probably close at hand.

'We have to keep moving,' Nico said. 'He'll send monsters after us.'

Nobody was in any shape to run, but Nico was right. I hauled myself up and helped Rachel to her feet.

'You were great back there,' I told her.

She managed a weak smile. 'Yeah, well. I didn't want you to die.' She blushed. 'I mean . . . just because, you know. You owe me too many favours. How am I going to collect if you die?'

I knelt next to Annabeth. 'Hey, I'm sorry. We need to move.'

'I know,' she said. 'I'm . . . I'm all right.'

She was clearly *not* all right. But she got to her feet, and we started straggling through the Labyrinth again.

'Back to New York,' I said. 'Rachel, can you –'

I froze. A few metres in front of us, my flashlight beam fixed on a trampled clump of red fabric lying on the ground. It was a Rasta cap: the one Grover always wore.

* * *

My hands shook as I picked up the cap. It looked like it had been stepped on by a huge muddy boot. After all that I'd gone through today, I couldn't stand the thought that something might've happened to Grover, too.

Then I noticed something else. The cave floor was mushy and wet from the water dripping off the stalactites. There were large footprints like Tyson's, and smaller ones – goat hooves – leading off to the left.

'We have to follow them,' I said. 'They went that way. It must have been recently.'

'What about Camp Half-Blood?' Nico said. 'There's no time.'

'We have to find them,' Annabeth insisted. 'They're our friends.'

She picked up Grover's smashed cap and forged ahead.

I followed, bracing myself for the worst. The tunnel was treacherous. It sloped at weird angles and was slimy with moisture. Half the time we were slipping and sliding rather than walking.

Finally we got to the bottom of a slope and found ourselves in a large cave with huge stalagmite columns. Through the centre of the room ran an underground river, and Tyson was sitting by the bank, cradling Grover in his lap. Grover's eyes were closed. He wasn't moving.

'Tyson!' I yelled.

'Percy! Come quick!'

We ran over to him. Grover wasn't dead, thank the gods, but his whole body trembled like he was freezing to death.

'What happened?' I asked.

'So many things,' Tyson murmured. 'Large snake. Large dogs. Men with swords. But then . . . we got close to here. Grover was excited. He ran. Then we reached this room, and he fell. Like this.'

'Did he say anything?' I asked.

'He said, 'We're close.' Then he hit his head on rocks.'

I knelt next to him. The only other time I'd seen Grover pass out was in New Mexico, when he'd felt the presence of Pan.

I shone my flashlight around the cavern. The rocks glittered. At the far end was the entrance to another cave, flanked by gigantic columns of crystal that looked like diamonds. And beyond that entrance . . .

'Grover,' I said. 'Wake up.'

'Uhhhhhhhh.'

Annabeth knelt next to him and splashed icy cold river water in his face.

'Splurg!' His eyelids fluttered. 'Percy? Annabeth? Where . . .'

'It's okay,' I said. 'You passed out. The presence was too much for you.'

'I – I remember. Pan.'

'Yeah,' I said. 'Something powerful is just beyond that doorway.'

I made quick introductions, since Tyson and Grover had never met Rachel. Tyson told Rachel she was pretty, which made Annabeth's nostrils flare like she was going to blow fire.

'Anyway,' I said. 'Come on, Grover. Lean on me.'

Annabeth and I helped him up, and together we waded across the underground river. The current was strong. The water came up to our waists. I willed myself to stay dry, which is a handy little ability, but that didn't help the others, and I could still feel the cold, like wading through a snowdrift.

'I think we're in Carlsbad Caverns,' Annabeth said, her teeth chattering. 'Maybe an unexplored section.'

'How do you know?'

'Carlsbad is in New Mexico,' she said. 'That would explain last winter.'

I nodded. Grover's swooning episode had happened when we passed through New Mexico. That's where he'd felt closest to the power of Pan.

We got out of the water and kept walking. As the crystal pillars loomed larger, I started to feel the power emanating from the next room. I'd been in the presence of gods before, but this was different. My skin tingled with living energy. My weariness fell away, as if I'd just had a good night's sleep. I could feel myself growing stronger, like one of those plants in a time-lapse video. And the scent coming from the cave was nothing like the dank wet underground. It smelled of trees and flowers and a warm summer day.

Grover whimpered with excitement. I was too stunned to talk. Even Nico seemed speechless. We stepped into the cave, and Rachel said, 'Oh, wow.'

The walls glittered with crystals — red, green and blue. In the strange light, beautiful plants grew — giant orchids, star-shaped flowers, vines bursting with orange and purple berries that crept among the crystals. The cave floor was covered with soft green moss. Overhead, the ceiling was higher than a cathedral, sparkling like a galaxy of stars. In the centre of the cave stood a Roman-style bed, gilded wood shaped like a curly U, with velvet cushions. Animals lounged around it – but they were animals that shouldn't have been alive. There was a dodo bird, something that looked like a cross between a wolf and a tiger, a huge rodent like the mother of all guinea pigs and, roaming behind the bed, picking berries with its trunk, was a woolly mammoth.

On the bed lay an old satyr. He watched us as we approached, his eyes as blue as the sky. His curly hair was white and so was his pointed beard. Even the goat fur on his legs was frosted with grey. His horns were enormous – glossy brown and curved. There was no way he could've hidden those under a hat, the way Grover did. Around his neck hung a set of reed pipes.

Grover fell to his knees in front of the bed. 'Lord Pan!'

The god smiled kindly, but there was sadness in his eyes. 'Grover, my dear, brave satyr. I have waited a very long time for you.'

'I . . . got lost,' Grover apologized.

Pan laughed. It was a wonderful sound, like the first breeze of springtime, filling the whole cavern with hope. The tiger-wolf sighed and rested his head on the god's knee. The dodo bird pecked affectionately at the god's hooves, making a strange sound in the back of its bill. I could swear it was humming 'It's a Small World'.

Still, Pan looked tired. His whole form shimmered as if he were made of Mist.

I noticed my other friends were kneeling. They had awed looks on their faces. I got to my knees.

'You have a humming dodo bird,' I said stupidly.

The god's eyes twinkled. 'Yes, that's Dede. My little actress.'

Dede the dodo looked offended. She pecked at Pan's knee and hummed something that sounded like a funeral dirge.

'This is the most beautiful place!' Annabeth said. 'It's better than any building ever designed.'

'I'm glad you like it, dear,' Pan said. 'It is one of the last wild places. My realm above is gone, I'm afraid. Only pockets remain. Tiny pieces of life. This one shall stay undisturbed . . . for a little longer.'

'My lord,' Grover said, 'please, you must come back with me! The Elders will never believe it! They'll be overjoyed! You can save the wild!'

Pan placed his hand on Grover's head and ruffled his curly hair. 'You are so young, Grover. So good and true. I think I chose well.'

'Chose?' Grover said. 'I – I don't understand.'

Pan's image flickered, momentarily turning to smoke. The giant guinea pig scuttled under the bed with a terrified squeal. The woolly mammoth grunted nervously. Dede stuck her head under her wing. Then Pan re-formed.

'I have slept many aeons,' the god said forlornly. 'My dreams have been dark. I wake fitfully, and each time my waking is shorter. Now we are near the end.'

'What?' Grover cried. 'But no! You're right here!'

'My dear satyr,' Pan said. 'I tried to tell the world, two thousand years ago. I announced it to Lysas, a satyr very much like you. He lived in Ephesos, and he tried to spread the word.'

Annabeth's eyes widened. 'The old story. A sailor

[297]

passing by the coast of Ephesos heard a voice crying from the shore, "Tell them the great god Pan is dead."'

'But that wasn't true!' Grover said.

'Your kind never believed it,' Pan said. 'You sweet, stubborn satyrs refused to accept my passing. And I love you for that, but you only delayed the inevitable. You only prolonged my long, painful passing, my dark twilight sleep. It must end.'

'No!' Grover's voice trembled.

'Dear Grover,' Pan said. 'You must accept the truth. Your companion, Nico, he understands.'

Nico nodded slowly. 'He's dying. He should have died long ago. This . . . this is more like a memory.'

'But gods can't die,' Grover said.

'They can fade,' Pan said, 'when everything they stood for is gone. When they cease to have power, and their sacred places disappear. The wild, my dear Grover, is so small now, so shattered, that no god can save it. My realm is gone. That is why I need you to carry a message. You must go back to the council. You must tell the satyrs, and the dryads, and the other spirits of nature, that the great god Pan *is* dead. Tell them of my passing. Because they must stop waiting for me to save them. I cannot. The only salvation you must make yourself. Each of you must –'

He stopped and frowned at the dodo bird, who had started humming again.

'Dede, what are you doing?' Pan demanded. 'Are you singing "Kumbaya" again?'

Dede looked up innocently and blinked her yellow eyes.

Pan sighed. 'Everybody's a cynic. But as I was saying, my dear Grover, each of you must take up my calling.'

'But . . . no!' Grover whimpered.

'Be strong,' Pan said. 'You have found me. And now you must release me. You must carry on my spirit. It can no longer be carried by a god. It must be taken up by all of you.'

Pan looked straight at me with his clear blue eyes, and I realized he wasn't just talking about the satyrs. He meant half-bloods, too, and humans. Everyone.

'Percy Jackson,' the god said. 'I know what you have seen today. I know your doubts. But I give you this news: when the time comes, you will not be ruled by fear.'

He turned to Annabeth. 'Daughter of Athena, your time is coming. You will play a great role, though it may not be the role you imagined.'

Then he looked at Tyson. 'Master Cyclops, do not despair. Heroes rarely live up to our expectations. But you, Tyson – your name shall live among the Cyclopes for generations. And Miss Rachel Dare . . .'

Rachel flinched when he said her name. She backed away like she was guilty of something, but Pan only smiled. He raised his hand in a blessing.

'I know you believe you cannot make amends,' he said. 'But you are just as important as your father.'

'I –' Rachel faltered. A tear traced her cheek.

'I know you don't believe this now,' Pan said. 'But look for opportunities. They will come.'

Finally he turned back towards Grover. 'My dear satyr,' Pan said kindly. 'Will you carry my message?'

'I – I can't.'

'You can,' Pan said. 'You are the strongest and bravest. Your heart is true. You have believed in me more than anyone ever has, which is why you must bring the message, and why you must be the first to release me.'

'I don't want to.'

'I know,' the god said. 'But my name, *Pan* . . . originally it meant *rustic*. Did you know that? But over the years it has come to mean *all*. The spirit of the wild must pass to all of you now. You must tell each one you meet: if you would find Pan, take up Pan's spirit. Remake the wild, a little at a time, each in your own corner of the world. You cannot wait for anyone else, even a god, to do that for you.'

Grover wiped his eyes. Then slowly he stood. 'I've spent my whole life looking for you. Now . . . I release you.'

Pan smiled. 'Thank you, dear satyr. My final blessing.'

He closed his eyes, and the god dissolved. White mist divided into wisps of energy, but this kind of energy wasn't scary like the blue power I'd seen from Kronos. It filled the room. A curl of smoke went straight into my mouth, and Grover's, and the others'. But I think a little more of it went into Grover. The crystals dimmed. The animals gave us a sad look. Dede the dodo sighed. Then they all turned grey and crumbled to dust. The vines withered. And we were alone in a dark cave, with an empty bed.

I switched on my flashlight.

Grover took a deep breath.

'Are . . . are you okay?' I asked him.

He looked older and sadder. He took his cap from Annabeth, brushed off the mud, and stuck it firmly on his curly head.

'We should go now,' he said, 'and tell them. The great god Pan is dead.'

18 GROVER CAUSES A STAMPEDE

Distance was shorter in the Labyrinth. Still, by the time Rachel got us back to Times Square, I felt like we'd pretty much run all the way from New Mexico. We climbed out of the Marriott basement and stood on the sidewalk in the bright summer daylight, squinting at the traffic and crowds.

I couldn't decide which seemed less real – New York or the crystal cave where I'd watched a god die.

I led the way into an alley, where I could get a nice echo. Then I whistled as loud as I could, five times.

A minute later, Rachel gasped. 'They're beautiful!'

A flock of pegasi descended from the sky, swooping between the skyscrapers. Blackjack was in the lead, followed by four of his white friends.

Yo, boss! He spoke in my mind. *You lived!*

'Yeah,' I told him. 'I'm lucky that way. Listen, we need a ride to camp *quick.*'

That's my speciality! Oh man, you got that Cyclops with you? Yo, Guido! How's your back holding up?

The pegasus Guido groaned and complained, but eventually he agreed to carry Tyson. Everybody started saddling up – except Rachel.

'Well,' she told me, 'I guess this is it.'

I nodded uncomfortably. We both knew she couldn't

go to camp. I glanced at Annabeth, who was pretending to be very busy with her pegasus.

'Thanks, Rachel,' I said. 'We couldn't have done it without you.'

'I wouldn't have missed it. I mean, except for almost dying, and Pan . . .' Her voice faltered.

'He said something about your father,' I remembered. 'What did he mean?'

Rachel twisted the strap on her backpack. 'My dad . . . My dad's job. He's kind of a famous businessman.'

'You mean . . . you're *rich*?'

'Well, yeah.'

'So that's how you got the chauffeur to help us? You just said your dad's name and –'

'Yes,' Rachel cut me off. 'Percy . . . my dad's a land developer. He flies all over the world, looking for tracts of undeveloped land.' She took a shaky breath. 'The wild. He – he buys it up. I hate it, but he ploughs it down and builds ugly subdivisions and shopping centres. And now that I've seen Pan . . . Pan's death –'

'Hey, you can't blame yourself for that.'

'You don't know the worst of it. I – I don't like to talk about my family. I didn't want you to know. I'm sorry. I shouldn't have said anything.'

'No,' I said. 'It's cool. Look, Rachel, you were awesome. You led us through the maze. You were so brave. That's the only thing I'm going to judge you on. I don't care what your dad does.'

Rachel looked at me gratefully. 'Well . . . if you ever feel like hanging out with a mortal again . . . you could call me or something.'

'Uh, yeah. Sure.'

She knitted her eyebrows. I guess I sounded unenthusiastic or something, but that's not how I meant it. I just wasn't sure what to say with all my friends standing around. And I guess my feelings had got pretty mixed up, the last couple of days.

'I mean . . . I'd like that,' I said.

'My number's not in the book,' she said.

'I've got it.'

'Still on your hand? No way.'

'No. I kinda . . . memorized it.'

Her smile came back slowly, but a lot happier. 'See you later, Percy Jackson. Go save the world for me, okay?'

She walked off down Seventh Avenue and disappeared into the crowds.

When I got back to the horses, Nico was having trouble. His pegasus kept shying away from him, reluctant to let him mount.

He smells like dead people! the pegasus complained.

Hey now, Blackjack said. *Come on, Porkpie. Lotsa demigods smell weird. It ain't their fault. Oh — uh, I didn't mean you, boss.*

'Go without me!' Nico said. 'I don't want to go back to that camp anyway.'

'Nico,' I said, 'we need your help.'

He folded his arms and scowled. Then Annabeth put her hand on his shoulder.

'Nico,' she said. 'Please.'

Slowly, his expression softened. 'All right,' he said reluctantly. 'For *you.* But I'm not staying.'

I raised an eyebrow at Annabeth, like, *How come all of a*

sudden Nico listens to you? She stuck her tongue out at me.

At last we got everybody on a pegasus. We shot into the air, and soon we were over the East River, with Long Island spread out before us.

We landed in the middle of the cabin area and were immediately met by Chiron, the potbellied satyr Silenus and a couple of Apollo cabin archers. Chiron raised an eyebrow when he saw Nico, but if I expected him to be surprised by our latest news about Quintus being Daedalus, or Kronos rising, I was mistaken.

'I feared as much,' Chiron said. 'We must hurry. Hopefully you have slowed down the Titan lord, but his vanguard will still be coming through. They will be anxious for blood. Most of our defenders are already in place. Come!'

'Wait a moment,' Silenus demanded. 'What of the search for Pan? You are almost three weeks overdue, Grover Underwood! Your searcher's licence is revoked!'

Grover took a deep breath. He stood up straight and looked Silenus in the eye. 'Searchers' licences don't matter any more. The great god Pan is dead. He has passed on and left us his spirit.'

'*What?*' Silenus's face turned bright red. 'Sacrilege and lies! Grover Underwood, I will have you exiled for speaking thus!'

'It's true,' I said. 'We were there when he died. All of us.'

'Impossible! You are all liars! Nature-destroyers!'

Chiron studied Grover's face. 'We will speak of this later.'

'We will speak of it now!' Silenus said. 'We must deal with this —'

'Silenus,' Chiron cut in. 'My camp is under attack. The matter of Pan has waited two thousand years. I fear it will have to wait a bit longer. Assuming we are still here this evening.'

And on that happy note, he readied his bow and galloped towards the woods, leaving us to follow as best we could.

It was the biggest military operation I'd ever seen at camp. Everyone was at the clearing, dressed in full battle armour, but this time it wasn't for capture the flag. The Hephaestus cabin had set up traps around the entrance to the Labyrinth — razor wire, pits filled with pots of Greek fire, rows of sharpened sticks to deflect a charge. Beckendorf was manning two catapults the size of pickup trucks, already primed and aimed at Zeus's Fist. The Ares cabin was on the front line, drilling in phalanx formation with Clarisse calling orders. Apollo's and Hermes's cabins were scattered in the woods with bows ready. Many had taken up positions in the trees. Even the dryads were armed with bows, and the satyrs trotted around with wooden cudgels and shields made of rough tree bark.

Annabeth went to join her brethren from the Athena cabin, who had set up a command tent and were directing operations. A grey banner with an owl fluttered outside the tent. Our security chief, Argus, stood guard at the door. Aphrodite's children were running around, straightening everybody's armour and offering to comb the tangles out of our horsehair plumes. Even Dionysus's kids had found something to do. The god himself was still nowhere to be seen, but his two blond twin sons were running around, providing all the sweaty warriors with water bottles and juice boxes.

It looked like a pretty good set-up, but Chiron muttered next to me, 'It isn't enough.'

I thought about what I'd seen in the Labyrinth, all the monsters in Antaeus's stadium and the power of Kronos I'd felt on Mount Tam. My heart sank. Chiron was right, but it was all we could muster. For once I wished Dionysus were here, but even if he had been, I didn't know if he could have done anything. When it came to war, gods were forbidden to interfere directly. Apparently, the Titans didn't believe in restrictions like that.

Over at the edge of the clearing, Grover was talking to Juniper. She held his hands while he told her our story. Green tears formed in her eyes as he delivered the news about Pan.

Tyson helped the Hephaestus kids prepare the defences. He picked up boulders and piled them next to the catapults for firing.

'Stay with me, Percy,' Chiron said. 'When the fighting begins, I want you to wait until we know what we're dealing with. You must go where we most need reinforcements.'

'I saw Kronos,' I said, still stunned by the fact. 'I looked straight into his eyes. It was Luke . . . but it wasn't.'

Chiron ran his fingers along his bowstring. 'He had golden eyes, I would guess. And in his presence, time seemed to turn to liquid.'

I nodded. 'How could he take over a mortal body?'

'I do not know, Percy. Gods have assumed the shapes of mortals for ages, but to actually become one . . . to merge the divine form with the mortal. I don't know how this could be done without Luke's form turning to ashes.'

'Kronos said his body had been prepared.'

'I shudder to think what that means. But perhaps it will limit Kronos's power. For a time, at least, he is confined to a human form. It binds him together. Hopefully it also restricts him.'

'Chiron, if he leads this attack —'

'I do not think so, my boy. I would sense if he were drawing near. No doubt he planned to, but I believe you inconvenienced him when you pulled his throne room down on top of him.' He looked at me reproachfully. 'You and your friend Nico, son of Hades.'

A lump formed in my throat. 'I'm sorry, Chiron. I know I should've told you. It's just —'

Chiron raised his hand. 'I understand why you did it, Percy. You felt responsible. You sought to protect him. But, my boy, if we are to survive this, we must trust each other. We must . . .'

His voice wavered. The ground underneath us was trembling.

Everyone in the clearing stopped what they were doing. Clarisse barked a single order: 'Lock shields!'

Then the Titan lord's army exploded from the Labyrinth.

I'd been in fights before, but this was a full-scale battle. The first thing I saw were a dozen Laistrygonian giants erupting from the ground, yelling so loudly my ears felt like bursting. They carried shields made from flattened cars, and clubs that were tree trunks with rusty spikes bristling at the end.

One of the giants bellowed at the Ares phalanx, smashed it sideways with his club, and the entire cabin was thrown aside, a dozen warriors tossed to the wind like rag dolls.

'Fire!' Beckendorf yelled. The catapults swung into action. Two boulders hurtled towards the giants. One deflected off a car shield with hardly a dent, but the other caught a Laistrygonian in the chest, and the giant went down. Apollo's archers fired a volley, dozens of arrows sticking in the thick armour of the giants like porcupine quills. Several found chinks in armour, and some of the giants vaporized at the touch of celestial bronze.

But just when it looked like the Laistrygonians were about to get overwhelmed, the next wave surged out of the maze: thirty, maybe forty *dracaenae* in full battle armour, wielding spears and nets. They dispersed in all directions. Some hit the traps the Hephaestus cabin had laid. One got stuck on the spikes and became an easy target for archers. Another triggered a trip wire, and pots of Greek fire exploded into green flames, engulfing several of the snake women. But many more kept coming. Argus and Athena's warriors rushed forward to meet them. I saw Annabeth draw a sword and engage one of them. Nearby, Tyson was riding a giant. Somehow he'd managed to climb onto the giant's back and was hitting him on the head with a bronze shield – BONG! BONG! BONG!

Chiron calmly aimed arrow after arrow, taking down a monster with every shot. But more enemies just kept climbing out of the maze. Finally a hellhound – not Mrs O'Leary – leaped out of the tunnel and barrelled straight towards the satyrs.

'GO!' Chiron yelled to me.

I drew Riptide and charged.

As I raced across the battlefield, I saw horrible things. An enemy half-blood was fighting with a son of Dionysus, but it wasn't much of a contest. The enemy stabbed him in the arm then clubbed him over the head with the butt of his sword, and Dionysus's son went down. Another enemy warrior shot flaming arrows into the trees, sending our archers and dryads into a panic.

A dozen *dracaenae* suddenly broke away from the main fight and slithered down the path that led towards camp, like they knew where they were going. If they got out, they could burn down the entire place, completely unopposed.

The only person anywhere near was Nico di Angelo. He stabbed a telekhine, and his black Stygian blade absorbed the monster's essence, drinking its energy until there was nothing left but dust.

'Nico!' I yelled.

He looked where I was pointing, saw the serpent women, and immediately understood.

He took a deep breath and held out his black sword. 'Serve me,' he called.

The earth trembled. A fissure opened in front of the *dracaenae* and a dozen undead warriors crawled from the earth – horrible corpses in military uniforms from all different time periods – US Revolutionaries, Roman centurions, Napoleonic cavalry on skeletal horses. As one, they drew their swords and engaged the *dracaenae*. Nico crumpled to his knees, but I didn't have time to make sure he was okay.

I closed on the hellhound, which was now pushing the satyrs back towards the woods. The beast snapped at one satyr, who danced out of its way, but then it pounced on another who was too slow. The satyr's tree-bark shield cracked as he fell.

'Hey!' I yelled.

The hellhound turned. It snarled at me and leaped. It would've clawed me to pieces, but as I fell backwards my fingers closed around a clay jar – one of Beckendorf's containers of Greek fire. I tossed it into the hellhound's maw, and the creature went up in flames. I scrambled away, breathing heavily.

The satyr who'd been trampled wasn't moving. I rushed over to check on him, but then I heard Grover's voice: 'Percy!'

A forest fire had started. Flames roared within three metres of Juniper's tree, and Juniper and Grover were going nuts trying to save it. Grover played a rain song on his pipes. Juniper desperately tried to beat out the flames with her green shawl, but it was only making things worse.

I ran towards them, jumping past duels, weaving between the legs of giants. The nearest water was the creek, half a kilometre away . . . but I had to do something. I concentrated. There was a pull in my gut, a roar in my ears. Then a wall of water came rushing through the trees. It doused the fire, Juniper, Grover and pretty much everything else.

Grover blew a spout of water. 'Thanks, Percy!'

'No problem!' I ran back towards the fight, and Grover and Juniper followed. Grover had a cudgel in his hand and Juniper held a stick – like an old-fashioned whipping switch. She looked really angry, like she was going to tan somebody's backside.

Just when it seemed like the battle had balanced out

again – like we might stand a chance – an unearthly shriek echoed out of the Labyrinth, a sound I had heard before.

Kampê shot into the sky, her bat wings fully extended. She landed on the top of Zeus's Fist and surveyed the carnage. Her face was filled with evil glee. The mutant animal heads growled at her waist. Snakes hissed and swirled around her legs. In her right hand she held a glittering ball of thread – Ariadne's string – but she popped it into a lion's mouth at her waist and drew her curved swords. The blades glowed green with poison. Kampê screeched in triumph, and some of the campers screamed. Others tried to run and got trampled by hellhounds or giants.

'*Di immortales!*' Chiron yelled. He quickly aimed an arrow, but Kampê seemed to sense his presence. She took flight with amazing speed, and Chiron's arrow whizzed harmlessly past her head.

Tyson untangled himself from the giant whom he'd pummelled into unconsciousness. He ran at our lines, shouting, 'Stand! Do not run from her! Fight!'

But then a hellhound leaped on him, and Tyson and the hound went rolling away.

Kampê landed on the Athena command tent, smashing it flat. I ran after her and found Annabeth at my side, keeping pace, her sword in her hand.

'This might be it,' she said.

'Could be.'

'Nice fighting with you, Seaweed Brain.'

'Ditto.'

Together we leaped into the monster's path. Kampê hissed and sliced at us. I dodged, trying to distract her, while Annabeth went in for a strike, but the monster seemed

able to fight with both hands independently. She blocked
Annabeth's sword, and Annabeth had to jump back to avoid
the cloud of poison. Just being near the thing was like
standing in an acid fog. My eyes burned. My lungs couldn't
get enough air. I knew we couldn't stand our ground for
more than a few seconds.

'Come on!' I shouted. 'We need help!'

But no help came. Everyone was either down, or fighting
for their lives, or too scared to move forward. Three of
Chiron's arrows sprouted from Kampê's chest, but she just
roared louder.

'Now!' Annabeth said.

Together we charged, dodged the monster's slashes, got
inside her guard and almost . . . *almost* managed to stab
Kampê in the chest, but a huge bear's head lashed out from
the monster's waist, and we had to stumble backwards to
avoid getting bitten.

Slam!

My eyesight went black. The next thing I knew, Annabeth
and I were on the ground. The monster had its forelegs on
our chests, holding us down. Hundreds of snakes slithered
right above me, hissing like laughter. Kampê raised her green-
tinged swords, and I knew Annabeth and I were out of
options.

Then, behind me, something howled. A wall of darkness
slammed into Kampê, sending the monster sideways. And
Mrs O'Leary was standing over us, snarling and snapping
at Kampê.

'Good girl!' said a familiar voice. Daedalus was fighting
his way out of the Labyrinth, slashing down enemies left
and right as he made his way towards us. Next to him was

someone else — a familiar giant, much taller than the Laistrygonians, with a hundred rippling arms, each holding a huge chunk of rock.

'Briares!' Tyson cried in wonder.

'Hail, little brother!' Briares bellowed. 'Stand firm!'

And as Mrs O'Leary leaped out of the way, the Hundred-handed One launched a volley of boulders at Kampê. The rocks seemed to enlarge as they left Briares's hands. There were so many, it looked like half the earth had learned to fly.

BOOOOOM!

Where Kampê had stood a moment before was a mountain of boulders, almost as tall as Zeus's Fist. The only sign that the monster had ever existed were two green sword points sticking through the cracks.

A cheer went up from the campers, but our enemies weren't done yet. One of the *dracaenae* yelled, 'Sssslay them! Kill them all or Kronossss will flay you alive!'

Apparently, that threat was more terrifying than we were. The giants surged forward in a last desperate attempt. One surprised Chiron with a glancing blow to the back legs, and he stumbled and fell. Six giants cried in glee and rushed forward.

'No!' I screamed, but I was too far away to help.

Then it happened.

Grover opened his mouth, and the most horrible sound I'd ever heard came out. It was like a brass trumpet magnified a thousand times — the sound of pure fear.

As one, the forces of Kronos dropped their weapons and ran for their lives. The giants trampled the *dracaenae*, trying to get into the Labyrinth first. Telekhines and hellhounds and enemy half-bloods scrambled after them. The tunnel rumbled shut, and the battle was over. The clearing was quiet except for fires burning in the woods, and the cries of the wounded.

I helped Annabeth to her feet. We ran to Chiron.

'Are you all right?' I asked.

He was lying on his side, trying in vain to get up. 'How embarrassing,' he muttered. 'I think I will be fine. Fortunately, we do not shoot centaurs with broken . . . Ow! . . . broken legs.'

'You need help,' Annabeth said. 'I'll get a medic from Apollo's cabin.'

'No,' Chiron insisted. 'There are more serious injuries to attend to. Go! I am fine. But, Grover . . . later we must talk about how you did that.'

'That was amazing,' I agreed.

Grover blushed. 'I don't know where it came from.'

Juniper hugged him fiercely. 'I do!'

Before she could say more, Tyson called, 'Percy, come quick! It is Nico!'

There was smoke curling off his black clothes. His fingers were clenched, and the grass all around his body had turned yellow and died.

I rolled him over as gently as I could and put my hand against his chest. His heart was beating faintly. 'Get some nectar!' I yelled.

One of the Ares campers hobbled over and handed me a canteen. I trickled some of the magic drink into Nico's mouth. He coughed and spluttered, but his eyelids fluttered open.

'Nico, what happened?' I asked. 'Can you talk?'

He nodded weakly. 'Never tried to summon so many before. I – I'll be fine.'

We helped him sit up and gave him some more nectar. He blinked at all of us, like he was trying to remember who we were, and then he focused on someone behind me.

'Daedalus,' he croaked.

'Yes, my boy,' the inventor said. 'I made a very bad mistake. I came to correct it.'

Daedalus had a few scratches that were bleeding golden oil, but he looked better than most of us. Apparently his automaton body healed itself quickly. Mrs O'Leary loomed behind him, licking the wounds on her master's head so Daedalus's hair stood up funny. Briares stood next to him, surrounded by a group of awed campers and satyrs. He looked kind of bashful, but he was signing autographs on armour, shields and T-shirts.

'I found the Hundred-handed One as I came through the maze,' Daedalus explained. 'It seems he had the same idea, to come and help, but he was lost. And so we fell in together. We both came to make amends.'

'Yay!' Tyson jumped up and down. 'Briares! I knew you would come!'

'I did not know,' the Hundred-handed One said. 'But you reminded me who I am, Cyclops. You are the hero.'

Tyson blushed, but I patted him on the back. 'I knew that a long time ago,' I said. 'But, Daedalus . . . the Titan army is still down there. Even without the string, they'll be back. They'll find a way sooner or later, with Kronos leading them.'

Daedalus sheathed his sword. 'You are right. As long as the Labyrinth is here, your enemies can use it. Which is why the Labyrinth cannot continue.'

Annabeth stared at him. 'But you said the Labyrinth is tied to your life force! As long as you're alive –'

'Yes, my young architect,' Daedalus agreed. 'When I die, the Labyrinth will die as well. And so I have a present for you.'

He slung a leather satchel off his back, unzipped it and produced a sleek silver laptop computer – one of the ones I'd seen in the workshop. On the lid was the blue symbol Δ.

'My work is here,' he said. 'It's all I managed to save from the fire. Notes on projects I never started. Some of my favourite designs. I couldn't develop these over the last few millennia. I did not dare reveal my work to the mortal world. But perhaps you will find them interesting.'

He handed the computer to Annabeth, who stared at it like it was solid gold. 'You're giving me this? But this is priceless! This is worth . . . I don't even know how much!'

'Small compensation for the way I have acted,' Daedalus said. 'You were right, Annabeth, about children of Athena. We should be wise, and I was not. Someday you will be a greater architect than I ever was. Take my ideas and improve them. It is the least I can do before I pass on.'

'Whoa,' I said. 'Pass on? But you can't just kill yourself. That's wrong!'

He shook his head. 'Not as wrong as hiding from my crimes for two thousand years. Genius does not excuse evil, Percy. My time has come. I must face my punishment.'

'You won't get a fair trial,' Annabeth said. 'The spirit of Minos sits in judgement –'

'I will take what comes,' he said. 'And trust in the justice of the Underworld, such as it is. That is all we can do, isn't it?'

He looked straight at Nico, and Nico's face darkened. 'Yes,' he said.

'Will you take my soul for ransom, then?' Daedalus asked. 'You could use it to reclaim your sister.'

'No,' Nico said. 'I will help you release your spirit. But Bianca has passed. She must stay where she is.'

Daedalus nodded. 'Well said, son of Hades. You are becoming wise.' Then he turned towards me. 'One last favour, Percy Jackson. I cannot leave Mrs O'Leary alone. And she has no desire to return to the Underworld. Will you care for her?'

I looked at the massive black hound, who whimpered pitifully, still licking Daedalus's hair. I was thinking that my mom's apartment wouldn't allow dogs, especially dogs bigger than the apartment, but I said, 'Yeah. Of course I will.'

'Then I am ready to see my son . . . and Perdix,' he said. 'I must tell them how sorry I am.'

Annabeth had tears in her eyes.

Daedalus turned towards Nico, who drew his sword. At first I was afraid Nico would kill the old inventor, but he simply said, 'Your time is long since come. Be released and rest.'

A smile of relief spread across Daedalus's face. He froze like a statue. His skin turned transparent, revealing the bronze gears and machinery whirring inside his body. Then the statue turned to grey ash and disintegrated.

Mrs O'Leary howled. I patted her head, trying to comfort her as best I could. The earth rumbled – an earthquake that could probably be felt in every major city across the country – as the ancient Labyrinth collapsed. Somewhere, I hoped, the remains of the Titans' strike force had been buried.

I looked around at the carnage in the clearing, and the weary faces of my friends.

'Come on,' I told them. 'We have work to do.'

19 THE COUNCIL GETS CLOVEN

There were too many goodbyes.

That night was the first time I actually saw camp burial shrouds used on bodies, and it was not something I wanted to see again.

Among the dead, Lee Fletcher from the Apollo cabin had been downed by a giant's club. He was wrapped in a golden shroud without any decoration. The son of Dionysus who'd gone down fighting an enemy half-blood was wrapped in a deep purple shroud, embroidered with grapevines. His name was Castor. I was ashamed that I'd seen him around camp for three years and never even bothered to learn his name. He'd been seventeen years old. His twin brother, Pollux, tried to say a few words, but he choked up and just took the torch. He lit the funeral pyre in the middle of the amphitheatre, and within seconds the row of shrouds was engulfed in fire, sending smoke and sparks up to the stars.

We spent the next day treating the wounded, which was almost everybody. The satyrs and dryads worked to repair the damage to the woods.

At noon, the Council of Cloven Elders held an emergency meeting in their sacred grove. The three senior satyrs were there, along with Chiron, who was in wheelchair form. His broken horse leg was still mending, so he would be confined to the chair for a few months, until the leg was strong enough to take his weight. The grove was filled with satyrs and dryads and naiads up from the water — hundreds of them, anxious to hear what would happen. Juniper, Annabeth and I stood by Grover's side.

Silenus wanted to exile Grover immediately, but Chiron persuaded him to at least hear evidence first, so we told everyone what had happened in the crystal cavern, and what Pan had said. Then several eyewitnesses from the battle described the weird sound Grover had made, which drove the Titans' army back underground.

'It was panic,' insisted Juniper. 'Grover summoned the power of the wild god.'

'Panic?' I asked.

'Percy,' Chiron explained, 'during the first war of the gods and the Titans, Lord Pan let forth a horrible cry that scared away the enemy armies. It is — it *was* his greatest power — a massive wave of fear that helped the gods win the day. The word *panic* is named after Pan, you see. And Grover used that power, calling it forth from within himself.'

'Preposterous!' Silenus bellowed. 'Sacrilege! Perhaps the wild god favoured us with a blessing. Or perhaps Grover's music was so awful it scared the enemy away!'

'That wasn't it, sir,' Grover said. He sounded a lot calmer than I would have if I'd been insulted like that. 'He let his spirit pass into all of us. We must act. Each of us must work to renew the wild, to protect what's left of it. We must spread the word. Pan is dead. There is no one but us.'

'After two thousand years of searching, this is what you

would have us believe?' Silenus cried. 'Never! We must continue the search. Exile the traitor!'

Some of the older satyrs muttered assent.

'A vote!' Silenus demanded. 'Who would believe this ridiculous young satyr, anyway?'

'I would,' said a familiar voice.

Everyone turned. Striding into the grove was Dionysus. He wore a formal black suit, so I almost didn't recognize him, a deep purple tie and violet dress shirt, his curly dark hair carefully combed. His eyes were bloodshot as usual, and his pudgy face was flushed, but he looked like he was suffering from grief more than wine-withdrawal.

The satyrs all stood respectfully and bowed as he approached. Dionysus waved his hand, and a new chair grew out of the ground next to Silenus's – a throne made of grapevines.

Dionysus sat down and crossed his legs. He snapped his fingers and a satyr hurried forward with a plate of cheese and crackers and a Diet Coke.

The god of wine looked around at the assembled crowd. 'Miss me?'

The satyrs fell over themselves nodding and bowing. 'Oh, yes, very much, sire!'

'Well, I did not miss this place!' Dionysus snapped. 'I bear bad news, my friends. Evil news. The minor gods are changing sides. Morpheus has gone over to the enemy. Hecate, Janus and Nemesis, as well. Zeus knows how many more.'

Thunder rumbled in the distance.

'Strike that,' Dionysus said. 'Even *Zeus* doesn't know. Now, I want to hear Grover's story. Again, from the top.'

'But, my lord,' Silenus protested. 'It's just nonsense!'

Dionysus's eyes flared with purple fire. 'I have just learned that my son Castor is dead, Silenus. I am not in a good mood. You would do well to humour me.'

Silenus gulped, and waved at Grover to start again.

When Grover was done, Mr D nodded. 'It sounds like just the sort of thing Pan would do. Grover is right. The search is tiresome. You must start thinking for yourselves.' He turned to a satyr. 'Bring me some peeled grapes, right away!'

'Yes, sire!' The satyr scampered off.

'We must exile the traitor!' Silenus insisted.

'I say no,' Dionysus countered. 'That is my vote.'

'I vote no as well,' Chiron put in.

Silenus set his jaw stubbornly. 'All in favour of the exile?'

He and the other two old satyrs raised their hands.

'Three to two,' Silenus said.

'Ah, yes,' Dionysus said. 'But, unfortunately for you, a god's vote counts twice. And as I voted against, we are tied.'

Silenus stood, indignant. 'This is an outrage! The council cannot stand at an impasse.'

'Then let it be dissolved!' Mr D said. 'I don't care.'

Silenus bowed stiffly, along with his two friends, and they left the grove. About twenty satyrs went with them. The rest stood around, murmuring uncomfortably.

'Don't worry,' Grover told them. 'We don't need a council to tell us what to do. We can figure it out ourselves.'

He told them again the words of Pan – how they must save the wild a little at a time. He started dividing the satyrs into groups – which ones would go to the national parks, which ones would search out the last wild places, which ones would defend the parks in big cities.

'Well,' Annabeth said to me, 'Grover seems to be growing up.'

Later that afternoon I found Tyson at the beach, talking to Briares. Briares was building a sandcastle with about fifty of his hands. He wasn't really paying attention to it, but his hands had constructed a three-storey compound with fortified walls, a moat and a drawbridge.

Tyson was drawing a map in the sand.

'Go left at the reef,' he told Briares. 'Straight down when you see the sunken ship. Then about one mile east, past the mermaid graveyard, you will start to see fires burning.'

'You're giving him directions to the forges?' I asked.

Tyson nodded. 'Briares wants to help. He will teach Cyclopes ways we have forgotten, how to make better weapons and armour.'

'I want to see Cyclopes,' Briares agreed. 'I don't want to be lonely any more.'

'I doubt you'll be lonely down there,' I said, a little wistfully, because I'd never even been in Poseidon's kingdom. 'They're going to keep you really busy.'

Briares's face morphed to a happy expression. 'Busy sounds good! I only wish Tyson could go, too.'

Tyson blushed. 'I need to stay here with my brother. You will do fine, Briares. Thank you.'

The Hundred-handed One shook my hand about one hundred times. 'We will meet again, Percy. I know it!'

Then he gave Tyson a big octopus hug and waded out

into the ocean. We watched until his enormous head disappeared under the waves.

I clapped Tyson on the back. 'You helped him a lot.'

'I only talked to him.'

'You believed in him. Without Briares, we never would've taken down Kampê.'

Tyson grinned. 'He throws good rocks!'

I laughed. 'Yeah. He throws really good rocks. Come on, big guy. Let's have dinner.'

It felt good to have a regular dinner at camp. Tyson sat with me at the Poseidon table. The sunset over Long Island Sound was beautiful. Things weren't back to normal by a long shot, but when I went up to the brazier and scraped part of my meal into the flames as an offering to Poseidon, I felt like I really did have a lot to be grateful for. My friends and I were alive. The camp was safe. Kronos had suffered a setback, at least for a while.

The only thing that bothered me was Nico, hanging out in the shadows at the edge of the pavilion. He'd been offered a place at the Hermes table, and even at the head table with Chiron, but he had refused.

After dinner, the campers headed towards the amphitheatre, where Apollo's cabin promised an awesome sing-along to pick up our spirits, but Nico turned and disappeared into the woods. I decided I'd better follow him.

As I passed under the shadows of the trees, I realized how dark it was getting. I'd never been scared in the forest before, though I knew there were plenty of monsters. Still, I thought about yesterday's battle, and I wondered if I'd ever be able to walk in these woods again without remembering the horror of so much fighting.

I couldn't see Nico, but after a few minutes of walking I saw a glow up ahead. At first I thought Nico had lit a torch. As I got closer, I realized the glow was a ghost. The shimmering form of Bianca di Angelo stood in the clearing, smiling at her brother. She said something to him and touched his face – or tried to. Then her image faded.

Nico turned and saw me, but he didn't look mad.

'Saying goodbye,' he said hoarsely.

'We missed you at dinner,' I said. 'You could've sat with me.'

'No.'

'Nico, you can't miss every meal. If you don't want to stay with Hermes, maybe they can make an exception and put you in the Big House. They've got plenty of rooms.'

'I'm not staying, Percy.'

'But . . . you can't just leave. It's too dangerous out there for a lone half-blood. You need to train.'

'I train with the dead,' he said flatly. 'This camp isn't for me. There's a reason they didn't put a cabin to Hades here, Percy. He's not welcome, any more than he is on Olympus. I don't belong. I have to go.'

I wanted to argue, but part of me knew he was right. I didn't like it, but Nico would have to find his own dark way. I remembered in Pan's cave, how the wild god had addressed each one of us individually . . . except Nico.

'When will you go?' I asked.

'Right away. I've got tons of questions. Like who was my mother? Who paid for Bianca and me to go to school? Who was that lawyer guy who got us out of the Lotus

Hotel? I know *nothing* about my past. I need to find out.'

'Makes sense,' I admitted. 'But I hope we don't have to be enemies.'

He lowered his gaze. 'I'm sorry I was a brat. I should've listened to you about Bianca.'

'By the way . . .' I fished something out of my pocket. 'Tyson found this while we were cleaning the cabin. Thought you might want it.' I held out a lead figurine of Hades – the little Mythomagic statue Nico had abandoned when he fled camp last winter.

Nico hesitated. 'I don't play that game any more. It's for kids.'

'It's got four thousand attack power,' I coaxed.

'Five thousand,' Nico corrected me. 'But only if your opponent attacks first.'

I smiled. 'Maybe it's okay to still be a kid once in a while.' I tossed him the statuette.

Nico studied it in his palm for a few seconds, then slipped it into his pocket. 'Thanks.'

I put out my hand. He shook it reluctantly. His hand was as cold as ice.

'I've got a lot of things to investigate,' he said. 'Some of them . . . Well, if I learn anything useful, I'll let you know.'

I wasn't sure what he meant, but I nodded. 'Keep in touch, Nico.'

He turned and trudged off into the woods. The shadows seemed to bend towards him as he walked, like they were reaching out for his attention.

A voice right behind me said, 'There goes a very troubled young man.'

I turned and found Dionysus standing there, still in his black suit.

'Walk with me,' he said.

'Where to?' I asked suspiciously.

'Just to the campfire,' he said. 'I was beginning to feel better, so I thought I would talk with you a bit. You always manage to annoy me.'

'Uh, thanks.'

We walked through the woods in silence. I noticed that Dionysus was treading on air, his polished black shoes hovering an inch off the ground. I guess he didn't want to get them dirty.

'We have had many betrayals,' he said. 'Things are not looking good for Olympus. Yet you and Annabeth saved this camp. I'm not sure I should thank you for that.'

'It was a group effort.'

He shrugged. 'Regardless, I suppose it was mildly competent, what you two did. I thought you should know – it wasn't a total loss.'

We reached the amphitheatre, and Dionysus pointed towards the campfire. Clarisse was sitting shoulder to shoulder with a big Hispanic kid who was telling her a joke. It was Chris Rodriguez, the half-blood who'd gone insane in the Labyrinth.

I turned to Dionysus. 'You cured him?'

'Madness is my speciality. It was quite simple.'

'But . . . you did something nice. Why?'

He raised an eyebrow. 'I am nice! I simply ooze niceness, Perry Johansson. Haven't you noticed?'

'Uh –'

'Perhaps I felt grieved by my son's death. Perhaps I

thought this Chris boy deserved a second chance. At any rate, it seems to have improved Clarisse's mood.'

'Why are you telling me this?'

The wine god sighed. 'Oh, Hades if I know. But remember, boy, that a kind act can sometimes be as powerful as a sword. As a mortal, I was never a great fighter or athlete or poet. I only made wine. The people in my village laughed at me. They said I would never amount to anything. Look at me now. Sometimes small things can become very large indeed.'

He left me alone to think about that. And as I watched Clarisse and Chris singing a stupid campfire song together, holding hands in the darkness, where they thought nobody could see them, I had to smile.

MY BIRTHDAY PARTY TAKES A DARK TURN

The rest of the summer seemed strange because it was so normal. The daily activities continued: archery, rock climbing, pegasus riding. We played capture the flag (though we all avoided Zeus's Fist). We sang at the campfire and raced chariots and played practical jokes on the other cabins. I spent a lot of time with Tyson, playing with Mrs O'Leary, but she would still howl at night when she got lonely for her old master. Annabeth and I pretty much skirted around each other. I was glad to be with her, but it also kind of hurt, and it hurt when I wasn't with her, too.

I wanted to talk to her about Kronos, but I couldn't do that any more without bringing up Luke. And that was one subject I couldn't raise. She would shut me out every time I tried.

July passed, with fireworks on the beach at the Fourth of July. August turned so hot the strawberries started baking in the fields. Finally, the last day of camp arrived. The standard form letter appeared on my bed after breakfast, warning me that the cleaning harpies would devour me if I stayed past noon.

At ten o'clock I stood on the top of Half-Blood Hill, waiting for the camp van that would take me into the city. I'd made arrangements to leave Mrs O'Leary at camp, where

Chiron promised she'd be looked after. Tyson and I would take turns visiting her during the year.

I hoped Annabeth would be riding into Manhattan with me, but she only came to see me off. She said she'd arranged to stay at camp a little longer. She would tend to Chiron until his leg was fully recovered, and keep studying Daedalus's laptop, which had engrossed her for the last two months. Then she would head back to her father's place in San Francisco.

'There's a private school out there that I'll be going to,' she said. 'I'll probably hate it, but . . .' She shrugged.

'Yeah, well, call me, okay?'

'Sure,' she said halfheartedly. 'I'll keep my eyes open for . . .'

There it was again. *Luke.* She couldn't even say his name without opening up a huge box of hurt and worry and anger.

'Annabeth,' I said. 'What was the rest of the prophecy?'

She fixed her eyes on the woods in the distance, but she didn't say anything.

'*You shall delve in the darkness of the endless maze,*' I remembered. '*The dead, the traitor and the lost one raise.* We raised a lot of the dead. We saved Ethan Nakamura, who turned out to be a traitor. We raised the spirit of Pan, the lost one.'

Annabeth shook her head like she wanted me to stop.

'*You shall rise or fall by the ghost king's hand,*' I pressed on. 'That wasn't Minos like I'd thought. It was Nico. By choosing to be on our side, he saved us. And *the child of Athena's final stand* — that was Daedalus.'

'Percy —'

'*Destroy with a hero's final breath.* That makes sense now. Daedalus died to destroy the Labyrinth. But what was the last —'

'*And lose a love to worse than death.*' Annabeth had tears in her eyes. 'That was the last line, Percy. Are you happy now?'

The sun seemed colder than it had a moment ago. 'Oh,' I said. 'So Luke —'

'Percy, I didn't know who the prophecy was talking about. I — I didn't know if . . .' She faltered helplessly. 'Luke and I — for years, he was the only one who really cared about me. I thought . . .'

Before she could continue, a sparkle of light appeared next to us, like someone had opened a gold curtain in the air.

'You have nothing to apologize for, my dear.' Standing on the hill was a tall woman in a white dress, her dark hair braided over her shoulder.

'Hera,' Annabeth said.

The goddess smiled. 'You found the answers, as I knew you would. Your quest was a success.'

'*A success?*' Annabeth said. 'Luke is gone. Daedalus is dead. Pan is dead. How is that —'

'Our family is safe,' Hera insisted. 'Those others are better gone, my dear. I am proud of you.'

I balled my fists. I couldn't believe she was saying this. 'You're the one who paid Geryon to let us through the ranch, weren't you?'

Hera shrugged. Her dress shimmered in rainbow colours. 'I wanted to speed you on your way.'

'But you didn't care about Nico. You were happy to see him turned over to the Titans.'

'Oh, please.' Hera waved her hand dismissively. 'The son of Hades said it himself. No one wants him around. He does not belong.'

'Hephaestus was right,' I growled. 'You only care about your *perfect* family, not real people.'

Her eyes turned dangerously bright. 'Watch yourself, son of Poseidon. I guided you more than you know in the maze. I was at your side when you faced Geryon. *I* let your arrow fly straight. I sent you to Calypso's island. I opened the way to the Titans' mountain. Annabeth, my dear, surely you see how I've helped. I would welcome a sacrifice for my efforts.'

Annabeth stood still as a statue. She could've said thank you. She could've promised to throw some barbecue on the brazier for Hera and forget the whole thing. But she clenched her jaw stubbornly. She looked just the way she had when she'd faced the Sphinx – like she wasn't going to accept an easy answer, even if it got her in serious trouble. I realized that was one of the things I liked best about Annabeth.

'Percy is right.' She turned her back on the goddess. '*You're* the one who doesn't belong, Queen Hera. So next time, thanks . . . but no thanks.'

Hera's sneer was worse than an *empousa's*. Her form began to glow. 'You will regret this insult, Annabeth. You will regret this very much.'

I averted my eyes as the goddess turned into her true divine form and disappeared in a blaze of light.

The hilltop was peaceful again. Over at the pine tree, Peleus the dragon dozed under the Golden Fleece as if nothing had happened.

'I'm sorry,' Annabeth told me. 'I – I should get back. I'll keep in touch.'

'Listen, Annabeth –' I thought about Mount St Helens, Calypso's island, Luke and Rachel Elizabeth Dare, and how suddenly everything had got so complicated. I wanted to tell Annabeth that I didn't really want to be so distant from her.

Then Argus honked his horn down at the road, and I lost my chance.

'You'd better get going,' Annabeth said. 'Take care, Seaweed Brain.'

She jogged down the hill. I watched her until she reached the cabins. She didn't look back once.

Two days later it was my birthday. I never advertised the date, because it always fell right after camp, so none of my camp friends could usually come, and I didn't have that many mortal friends. Besides, getting older didn't seem like anything to celebrate since I'd had the big prophecy about me destroying or saving the world when I turned sixteen. Now I was turning fifteen. I was running out of time.

My mom threw me a small party at our apartment. Paul Blofis came over, but that was okay because Chiron had manipulated the Mist to convince everyone at Goode High School that I had nothing to do with the band-room explosion. Now Paul and the other witnesses were convinced that Kelli had been a crazy, firebomb-throwing cheerleader, while I had simply been an innocent bystander who'd panicked and ran from the scene. I would still be allowed to start as a freshman at Goode next month. If I wanted to keep my record of getting kicked out of school every year, I'd have to try harder.

Tyson came to my party, too, and my mother baked two extra blue cakes just for him. While Tyson helped my mom blow up party balloons, Paul Blofis asked me to help him in the kitchen.

As we were pouring punch, he said, 'I hear your mom signed you up for driver's ed this fall.'

'Yeah. It's cool. I can't wait.'

Seriously, I'd been excited about getting my licence forever, but I guess my heart wasn't in it any more, and Paul could tell. In a weird way he reminded me of Chiron sometimes, how he could look at you and actually *see* your thoughts. I guess it was that teacher aura.

'You've had a rough summer,' he said. 'I'm guessing you lost someone important. And . . . girl trouble?'

I stared at him. 'How do you know that? Did my mom —'

He held up his hands. 'Your mom hasn't said a thing. And I won't pry. I just know there's something unusual about you, Percy. You've got a lot going on that I can't figure out. But I was also fifteen once, and I'm just guessing from your expression . . . Well, you've had a rough time.'

I nodded. I'd promised my mom I would tell Paul the truth about me, but now didn't seem the time. Not yet. 'I lost a couple of friends at this camp I go to,' I said. 'I mean, not close friends, but still —'

'I'm sorry.'

'Yeah. And, uh, I guess the girl stuff . . .'

'Here.' Paul handed me some punch. 'To your fifteenth birthday. And to a better year to come.'

We tapped our paper cups together and drank.

'Percy, I kind of feel bad, giving you one more thing to think about,' Paul said. 'But I wanted to ask you something.'

'Yeah?'

'Girl stuff.'

I frowned. 'What do you mean?'

'Your mom,' Paul said. 'I'm thinking about proposing to her.'

I almost dropped my cup. 'You mean . . . marrying her? You and her?'

'Well, that was the general idea. Would that be okay with you?'

'You're asking my permission?'

Paul scratched his beard. 'I don't know if it's permission, so much, but she's your mother. And I know you're going through a lot. I wouldn't feel right if I didn't talk to you about it first, man to man.'

'Man to man,' I repeated. It sounded strange, saying that. I thought about Paul and my mom, how she smiled and laughed more whenever he was around, and how Paul had gone out of his way to get me into high school. I found myself saying, 'I think that's a great idea, Paul. Go for it.'

He smiled really wide then. 'Cheers, Percy. Let's join the party.'

I was just getting ready to blow out the candles when the doorbell rang.

My mom frowned. 'Who could that could be?'

It was weird, because our new building had a doorman,

but he hadn't called up or anything. My mom opened the door and gasped.

It was my dad. He was wearing Bermuda shorts and a Hawaiian shirt and Birkenstocks, like he usually does. His black beard was neatly trimmed and his sea-green eyes twinkled. He wore a battered cap decorated with fishing lures. It said, *Neptune's Lucky Fishing Hat.*

'Pos—' My mother stopped herself. She was blushing right to the roots of her hair. 'Um, hello.'

'Hello, Sally,' Poseidon said. 'You look as beautiful as ever. May I come in?'

My mother made a squeaking sound that might've been either 'yes' or 'help'. Poseidon took it as a yes and came in.

Paul was looking back and forth between us, trying to read our expressions. Finally he stepped forward. 'Hi, I'm Paul Blofis.'

Poseidon raised his eyebrows as they shook hands. 'Blowfish, did you say?'

'Ah, no. Blofis, actually.'

'Oh, I see,' Poseidon said. 'A shame. I quite like blowfish. I am Poseidon.'

'Poseidon? That's an interesting name.'

'Yes, I like it. I've gone by other names, but I do prefer Poseidon.'

'Like the god of the sea.'

'Very much like that, yes.'

'Well!' my mom interrupted. 'Um, we're so glad you could drop by. Paul, this is Percy's father.'

'Ah.' Paul nodded, though he didn't look very pleased. 'I see.'

Poseidon smiled at me. 'There you are, my boy. And Tyson, hello, son!'

'Daddy!' Tyson bounded across the room and gave Poseidon a big hug, which almost knocked off his fishing hat.

Paul's jaw dropped. He stared at my mom. 'Tyson is . . .'

'Not mine,' she promised. 'It's a long story.'

'I couldn't miss Percy's fifteenth birthday,' Poseidon said. 'Why, if this were Sparta, Percy would be a man today!'

'That's true,' Paul said. 'I used to teach ancient history.'

Poseidon's eyes twinkled. 'That's me. Ancient history. Sally, Paul, Tyson . . . would you mind if I borrowed Percy for just a moment?'

He put his arm around me and steered me into the kitchen.

Once we were alone, his smile faded.

'Are you all right, my boy?'

'Yeah. I'm fine. I guess.'

'I heard stories,' Poseidon said. 'But I wanted to hear it directly from you. Tell me everything.'

So I did. It was kind of disconcerting, because Poseidon listened so intently. His eyes never left my face. His expression didn't change the whole time I talked. When I was done, he nodded slowly.

'So Kronos is indeed back. It will not be long before full war is upon us.'

'What about Luke?' I asked. 'Is he really gone?'

'I don't know, Percy. It is most disturbing.'

'But his body is mortal. Couldn't you just destroy him?'

Poseidon looked troubled. 'Mortal, perhaps. But there is something different about Luke, my boy. I don't know how he was prepared to host the Titan's soul, but he will not be easily killed. And yet, I fear he must be killed if we are to send Kronos back to the pit. I will have to think on this. Unfortunately, I have other problems of my own.'

I remembered what Tyson had told me at the beginning of the summer. 'The old sea gods?'

'Indeed. The battle came first to me, Percy. In fact, I cannot stay long. Even now the ocean is at war with itself. It is all I can do to keep hurricanes and typhoons from destroying your surface world, the fighting is so intense.'

'Let me come down there,' I said. 'Let me help.'

Poseidon's eyes crinkled as he smiled. 'Not yet, my boy. I sense you will be needed here. Which reminds me . . .' He brought out a sand dollar and pressed it into my hand. 'Your birthday present. Spend it wisely.'

'Uh, spend a sand dollar?'

'Oh, yes. In my day, you could buy quite a lot with a sand dollar. I think you will find it still buys a lot, if used in the right situation.'

'What situation?'

'When the time comes,' Poseidon said, 'I think you'll know.'

I closed my hand around the sand dollar, but something was really bothering me.

'Dad,' I said. 'When I was in the maze, I met Antaeus.

He said . . . well, he said he was your favourite son. He decorated his arena with skulls and –'

'He dedicated them to me,' Poseidon supplied. 'And you are wondering how someone could do something so horrible in my name.'

I nodded uncomfortably.

Poseidon put his weathered hand on my shoulder. 'Percy, lesser beings do many horrible things in the name of the gods. That does not mean we gods approve. The way our sons and daughters act in our names . . . well, it usually says more about *them* than it does about us. And *you*, Percy, are my favourite son.'

He smiled, and at that moment, just being in the kitchen with him was the best birthday present I ever got. Then my mom called from the living room, 'Percy? The candles are melting!'

'You'd better go,' Poseidon said. 'But, Percy, one last thing you should know. That incident at Mount St Helens . . .'

For a second I thought he was talking about Annabeth kissing me, and I blushed, but then I realized he was talking about something a lot bigger.

'The eruptions are continuing,' he said. 'Typhon is stirring. It is very likely that soon, in a few months, perhaps a year at best, he will escape his bonds.'

'I'm sorry,' I said. 'I didn't mean –'

Poseidon raised his hand. 'It is not your fault, Percy. It would've happened sooner or later, with Kronos awakening the ancient monsters. But be aware, if Typhon stirs . . . it will be unlike anything you have faced before. The first time he appeared, all the forces of Olympus were barely enough to battle him. And when he stirs again, he will come here, to New York. He will make straight for Olympus.'

That was just the kind of wonderful news I wanted to get on my birthday, but Poseidon patted me on the back like everything was fine. 'I should go. Enjoy your cake.'

And just like that he turned to mist and was swept out of the window on a warm ocean breeze.

It took a little work to convince Paul that Poseidon had left via the fire escape, but since people can't vanish into thin air, he had no choice but to believe it.

We ate blue cake and ice cream until we couldn't eat any more. Then we played a bunch of cheesy party games like charades and Monopoly. Tyson didn't get charades. He kept shouting out the answer he was trying to mime, but it turned out he was really good at Monopoly. He knocked me out of the game in the first five rounds and started bankrupting my mom and Paul. I left them playing and went into my bedroom.

I set an uneaten slice of blue cake on my dresser. Then I took off my Camp Half-Blood necklace and laid it on the windowsill. There were three beads now, representing my three summers at camp – a trident, the Golden Fleece and the latest: an intricate maze, symbolizing the Battle of the Labyrinth, as the campers had started to call it. I wondered what next year's bead would be, if I was still around to get it. If the camp survived until next summer.

I looked at the telephone by my bedside. I thought about calling Rachel Elizabeth Dare. My mom had asked me if there was anyone else I wanted to have over tonight, and I'd thought about Rachel. But I didn't call. I don't know why. The idea made me almost as nervous as a door into the Labyrinth.

I patted my pockets and emptied out my stuff – Riptide, a Kleenex, my apartment key. Then I patted my shirt pocket and felt a small lump. I hadn't even realized it, but I was wearing the white cotton shirt Calypso had given me on Ogygia. I brought out a little piece of cloth, unwrapped it, and found the clipping of moonlace. It was a tiny sprig, shrivelled up after two months, but I could still smell the faint scent of the enchanted garden. It made me sad.

I remembered Calypso's last request of me: *Plant a garden in Manhattan for me, will you?* I opened the window and stepped onto the fire escape.

My mom kept a planter box out there. In the spring she usually filled it with flowers, but now it was all earth, waiting for something new. It was a clear night. The moon was full over Eighty-second Street. I planted the dried sprig of moonlace carefully in the dirt and sprinkled a little nectar on it from my camp canteen.

Nothing happened at first.

Then, as I watched, a tiny silver plant sprang out of the soil – a baby moonlace, glowing in the warm summer night.

'Nice plant,' a voice said.

I jumped. Nico di Angelo was standing on the fire escape right next to me. He'd just appeared there.

'Sorry,' he said. 'Didn't mean to startle you.'

'That's – that's okay. I mean . . . what are you doing here?'

He'd grown about an inch taller over the last couple of months. His hair was a shaggy black mess. He wore a black T-shirt, black jeans and a new silver ring shaped like a skull. His Stygian iron sword hung at his side.

'I've done some exploring,' he said. 'Thought you'd like to know that Daedalus got his punishment.'

'You saw him?'

Nico nodded. 'Minos wanted to boil him in cheese fondue for eternity, but my father had other ideas. Daedalus will be building overpasses and exit ramps in Asphodel for all time. It'll help ease the traffic congestion. Truthfully, I think the old guy is pretty happy with that. He's still building. Still creating. And he gets to see his son and Perdix on the weekends.'

'That's good.'

Nico tapped at his silver ring. 'But that's not the real reason I've come. I've found out some things. I want to make you an offer.'

'What?'

'The way to beat Luke,' he said. 'If I'm right, it's the *only* way you'll stand a chance.'

I took a deep breath. 'Okay. I'm listening.'

Nico glanced inside my room. His eyebrows furrowed. 'Is that . . . is that blue birthday cake?'

He sounded hungry, maybe a little wistful. I wondered if the poor kid had ever had a birthday party, or if he'd ever even been invited to one.

'Come inside for cake and ice cream,' I said. 'It sounds like we've got a lot to talk about.'

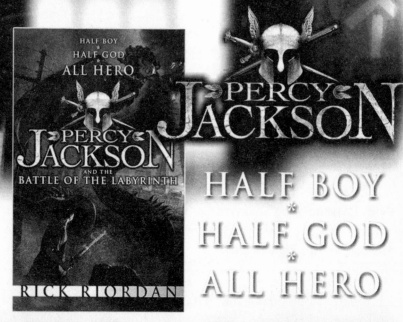

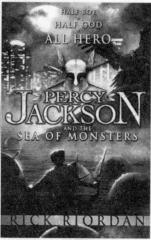

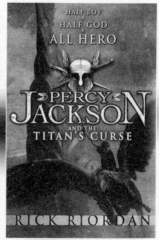

Puffin by Post

Percy Jackson and the Battle of the Labyrinth – Rick Riorda

If you have enjoyed this book and want to read more,
then check out these other great Puffin titles.
You can order any of the following books direct with Puffin by Post:

Percy Jackson and the Lightning Thief • 9780141319131	£5.99
'One of the books of the year . . . Vastly entertaining' *– Independent*	

Percy Jackson and the Sea of Monsters • 9780141319148	£5.99
'A fast-paced, entertaining read' *– Guardian*	

Percy Jackson and the Titan's Curse • 9780141321264	£5.99
'Funny and fast-paced . . . Percy is a hero that every kid will want to emulate' *– Sunday Express*	

Lee Raven, Boy Thief • Zizou Corder • 9780141322902	£6.99
The stunning new adventure from Zizou Corder, author of the highly acclaimed Lionboy trilogy	

Dangerzone: The Devil's Breath • David Gilman • 9780141323022	£6.99
'*The Devil's Breath* takes no hostages in an exciting fast-paced story that never lets up' *– Independent*	

Just contact:

Puffin Books, C/o Bookpost, PO Box 29,
Douglas, Isle of Man, IM99 1BQ
Credit cards accepted. For further details:
Telephone: 01624 677237
Fax: 01624 670923

You can email your orders to: bookshop@enterprise.net
Or order online at: www.bookpost.co.uk

Free delivery in the UK.
Overseas customers must add £2 per book.

Prices and availability are subject to change.

Visit puffin.co.uk to find out about the latest titles, read extracts and
exclusive author interviews, and enter exciting competitions.
You can also browse thousands of Puffin books online.